WISHING UNDER A
STARLIT SKYE

LISA HOBMAN

Boldwood

First published in Great Britain in 2022 by Boldwood Books Ltd.

Copyright © Lisa Hobman, 2022

Cover Design by Alice Moore Design

Cover Photography: Shutterstock

A CIP catalogue record for this book is available from the British Library.

Paperback ISBN 978-1-80048-896-0

Large Print ISBN 978-1-80048-895-3

Hardback ISBN 978-1-80415-486-1

Ebook ISBN 978-1-80048-897-7

Kindle ISBN 978-1-80048-898-4

Audio CD ISBN 978-1-80048-890-8

MP3 CD ISBN 978-1-80048-891-5

Digital audio download ISBN 978-1-80048-894-6

Boldwood Books Ltd
23 Bowerdean Street
London SW6 3TN
www.boldwoodbooks.com

For my two Claires.
The best friends a girl could wish for. You keep me sane and I'm eternally grateful to have you both in my life.

PROLOGUE

Caitlin Fraser sat, spine straight, shoulders back. Defiant. She would not back down. This was her wish, and no one would stop her from making it come true. She could only hope that her mother would accept her decision and still love her.

She glanced around the living room of the beautiful double-fronted house on Viewfield Road, Portree, on the picturesque Isle of Skye. She had grown up in the house and stayed there right up until she'd gone to catering college and got a flat on the mainland and nothing much had changed. The familiar scent of vanilla pot pourri made her overly sensitive stomach roil. She'd hoped she was out of the stage of pregnancy where smells affected her so negatively, but the sweet sickliness of the fragrance was just too much. She made a conscious effort to breathe through her mouth.

Her high-school portrait still took pride of place on the sideboard that stood in front of the pink and cream striped wallpaper. *So eighties*, she thought with a small smile. Her mother, Maggie, was stuck in the past with her fashion sense too. She'd never got the memo about shoulder pads and bouffant hairdos being out, judging by the two-piece outfit and string of pearls she was wearing and the amount of hairspray keeping her hair in place. But then again, the past was where all Maggie's happy memories lived, although not quite so far back as the eighties.

Caitlin's father, Malcolm, who had helped his wife to run their home as a successful guest house, had passed away when she was sixteen and had left his only child a chunk of money in trust for when she turned twenty-one. It was supposed to set her up for her adult life and she was about to put it to good use at the sensible age of twenty-eight, which is why she was here now and waiting for her mum to say something.

Her mother shook her head. 'I just think you should reconsider, Caitlin. It's not the way things are done. It's like... forgive me, but it's like playing God. And for goodness' sake, what will people say?' Her voice was strained and filled with anguish. Caitlin knew she had her best interests at heart, but there was also some major consideration for her own interests in there too.

Caitlin replied, 'And *this* is why I didn't tell you before. I knew you'd react this way.' More than anything, she wished she'd been wrong in her presumptions and that her mother would be happy for her, accept the decision she'd made. She was an adult after all.

Her mother scoffed. 'So, you waited until you were four months pregnant with some unknown man's child before you told me? Is that how much you think of me? Is that what I mean to you?'

Caitlin sighed, the weight of the situation pushing heavy on her shoulders. 'You know I love you, Mum. I've always been there for you. Especially since Dad passed away...'

Her mother stood and paced. 'And yet you decided to take this route to parenthood without even consulting me, your own mother. I can't tell you how disappointed I am, Caitlin; and how disappointed your dad would be.'

Ouch, Caitlin thought, even though she knew it wasn't true.

She'd always been a daddy's girl. She could do no wrong in his eyes, but it still hurt that her mother used those words.

Maggie sighed deeply. 'I mean, this man, this *donor* could be a psychopath. A lunatic. He could have all manner of diseases that will be passed to you and your... your *foetus*.'

Caitlin clenched her jaw until it ached and closed her eyes, her hand rested defensively over her as yet non-existent bump. 'They do all sorts of tests and health screening, Mum. And they ask lots of questions. So, me and my baby will be fine.'

Her mother dabbed at her eyes with a pristine white handkerchief. 'But you're so young. Why couldn't you wait until you'd met someone? A real man. What on earth are you going to tell it about its father? That you went to a sperm bank?' The expression on her face told of the bitter taste the words left in her mouth, and she shivered. 'A sterile, loveless room where some... some poor excuse for a man did who knows what to... you know what into a cup? Oh my god, Caitlin, what have you done?' The woman flopped dramatically into the chintzy, floral armchair beside the Adam style fireplace and bit her knuckle.

Caitlin fought an inappropriate giggle. Her mother's histrionics were something she had dealt with for years; she seemed to thrive on drama. But this was something Caitlin wanted for herself. She was ready and the time was right, meaning she wasn't prepared to wait around for the perfect man to procreate with.

'Mum, you know I've had boyfriends before, but not a single one has been someone I would settle down with and I certainly wasn't about to have a one-night stand with someone for the sole purpose of getting pregnant. I'm not that kind of person. And yes, I realise I'm young, but It's not like I am going to be a teenage mother. I don't want to put my life on hold hoping that the right man will come along. I want this now. It's important to me and anyway, it's done now, okay? You're going to be a grandma. Don't you think that's wonderful, regardless of how it came about? Can't you just be happy?'

Her mother gasped. 'It's wonderful, is it? My twenty-eight-year-old daughter is pregnant with a stranger's child. A perverted stranger who looked at rude magazines and deposited his...' she made bizarre hand gestures, 'into a plastic cup.'

'Mum! That's a horrible thing to say!' Caitlin scowled at her choice of words. 'These men aren't perverts. They're simply men who want to help other people to have children.'

'And I'm supposed to be happy about that, am I? Well, I'm not. And that won't change. I can't just be happy,' she snapped.

Caitlin's lungs deflated as exasperation and sadness set in. 'You could choose to be happy, Mum.'

Her mother ignored her and patted her perfectly set, dyed blonde hair. 'What on earth am I going to tell the ladies at my bridge club?' She gasped and closed her eyes. 'And Cynthia Goulding? Oh, my word, what on earth will Reverend Goulding think? Hmm? Answer me that, Caitlin!' Her voice rose in both volume and pitch. 'I'll be excommunicated!'

Caitlin's eyes stung and her lower lip trembled. She'd known her mother would react badly, but this was beyond the pale. 'It shouldn't matter to you what your bridge friends, or the vicar and his wife think. I'm your daughter.' It was true her mother was seen as a pillar of the community, regularly involved in everything, from church fetes to coffee mornings and all manner of things in between, as well as being a close friend of the vicar's wife, but that didn't justify such a reaction.

Her mother scoffed. 'Well act like it then. Be a normal person and get married before you have children. Or at least have the wherewithal to have children with someone you've actually met!'

Caitlin wiped at the moisture around her eyes. 'So, should I not set a place for you at the baby shower then?' She smiled without feeling the humour.

Her mother sneered. 'What do you think?'

Caitlin nodded and rose from her seat. 'That's a real shame, Mum. I hoped you'd be happy for me. And that you'd want to be a part of my baby's life. Your grandchild's life.' Her voice wavered as she spoke.

Her mother smiled almost pleadingly. 'Well, perhaps if you used some of your inheritance to... sort the matter out, sweetheart, you could wait and have a proper baby when you meet a real man to have a relationship with.'

Caitlin gasped and clamped her jaw shut at the thought of the unmentioned procedure her mother was hinting at. The hypocrisy wasn't lost on Caitlin. She wanted to scream at her, '*So your bridge club and the vicar are okay about abortion but not having a child by a sperm donor? Is that it? Or would you just brush it under the carpet and pretend it never happened?*' But of course, she didn't. She and her mother had never really been close, and this was just another way she was disappointing the woman who had wanted a son but couldn't have any further children after Caitlin was born.

Once again horrified at her mother's words, Caitlin spoke through clenched teeth as her eyes blurred with tears. 'This is a proper baby, Mum. How dare you suggest otherwise! And Dad wanted me to use that money to make myself happy. So that's what I'm going to do. I'm going to buy a little bakery that I've had my eye on down in Glentorrin and look after my child.' She turned to face the door. 'Maybe someday you'll realise you've made a mistake. I hope so because I want nothing more than to have you in our lives.'

Her mother stood and straightened her skirt. 'I'm sorry, Caitlin. But you have to make a choice here.' She pointed in the general direction of Caitlin's belly. 'That abomination... or me.'

Caitlin's heart lurched and her stomach roiled on hearing her mother's vile choice of words. She inhaled a deep breath, smoothed her hand over her tummy, shook her head and closed her eyes for a moment. Her heart ached at the posed ultimatum, but she knew, in reality, there was no choice to be made.

Her chin trembled and sadness washed over her like a tsunami. 'Mum, honestly, that's a decision I really don't want to make. But I'm sorry, if you're forcing my hand, I'm afraid I have another life to protect now.' Her voice broke and she paused, hoping that her mother would see sense and open her arms out to her.

The prospect of being a single parent was daunting, starting a new business at the same time was terrifying, but she knew in her heart she could and would do it. If nothing else, she had determination. But she could've really done with a hug from her mum. When none came, she swiped hot tears from her cheeks and cleared her throat.

'I really do love you, please remember that.'

Her mother looked on in shock, so she waited a split second more, but when her mother didn't move, Caitlin nodded in defeat.

'Bye, Mum.'

And with those final words, she turned and left her family home with the melancholic feeling inside that she may be leaving it for the very last time.

1

The early-evening June sun was still high in the sky over the pretty coastal village of Glentorrin, and it warmed the garden at the back of the bakery, as Caitlin Fraser handed out the filled wine glasses to her friends: Lifeboat House Museum guardian Jules Fairhurst, village shop owner Morag McDougal, and the newest resident, ex-Hollywood actress, Ruby Locke.

It was Friday evening and wonderful to be outside enjoying the clement weather, Caitlin thought, and the planting and weeding she had done in her little cottage garden was paying dividends. Birds were still chirping overhead and feasting on the feeding station she had made with her twelve – soon-to-be thirteen –year-old daughter Grace, and the buzz of bees could be heard as the little insects worked hard around the newly dug flowerbeds. The variety of colours were so cheerful and uplifting and she was happy that Grace's plan to plant a rainbow had come to fruition.

'So, I have news,' Caitlin told her friends with a sly smile.

The women shared an intrigued glance.

'Sounds ominous. What's going on?' Jules asked.

Caitlin took a large swig of the crisp, fruity wine for Dutch courage and placed her glass down again. 'Well, ladies, at the ripe old age of forty, I've decided I'm going to start dating.'

Morag chuckled. 'It's about bloody time if you ask me, hen. I thought we were waiting for hell to freeze over or something.'

'Thanks, Morag,' Caitlin replied with a roll of her eyes and a good-humoured smile. 'I've spent so many years putting Grace and the bakery first, but I think maybe the time's right. And I figure that now my parents' bed and breakfast up at Portree is sold, I have the space to include a man in my life.'

'I'm surprised it took so long to sell. It's been quite stressful for you, hasn't it?' Jules said with a sad smile as she tucked her blonde waves behind her ears.

Caitlin nodded. 'Aye, it has. Two and a half years since Mum passed away, and two years since I put the place on the market. Thank goodness it's done now though.'

'You did such a lot of work to the place. It was stunning when you put it up for sale,' Ruby said wistfully.

'Well, someone needed to drag it kicking and screaming out of the nineteen eighties. I've never seen so much chintz.' Caitlin laughed as she remembered the task of stripping the flowery, pink and blue, lounge wallpaper from the top of the walls, and the pink candy-striped paper from the bottom. Of course, the intricately decorated, oh-so-eighties border covering the join of the two had gone too. Thankfully, she had managed to find a team of painters and decorators to take over when she found the task too much on top of her day job.

Caitlin's Cakes and Bakes had gone from strength to strength and Caitlin was proud of all she had achieved as a single parent and businesswoman. And although it hadn't always been a piece of cake, Grace was a lovely, well-adjusted girl, despite her less than ordinary origins. Grace was fully aware of where she came from and although neither were ashamed about it, it wasn't something they talked about with others. Caitlin had discovered that, whilst not everyone was of the same opinion as her own mother, not many people understood her choices.

'Didn't you ever fancy moving up there to run the place yourself after all that hard work?' Morag asked. The woman, who was in her sixties, not only ran the village shop with her husband but a successful bed and breakfast too. Caitlin often wondered where she got her energy from.

Caitlin smiled and shook her head. 'No. Too many memories.' She shrugged. 'Mostly good but... Well, some that I'd rather not be reminded of.' She took a sip of her drink as she remembered the beautiful old house she had grown up in with its sweeping driveway and pretty, private garden. 'And I love my little bakery here in Glentorrin, so it wasn't a difficult decision to make.'

She was grateful she had made peace with her mother several years prior to her death, and that Grace had met her Granny Maggie. Once, when delivering a birthday cake to a customer, she had bumped into her mum in Portree when Grace was around seven. The woman had sobbed and apologised over and over when she had laid eyes on the beautiful, sweet-natured young girl for the first time. She had taken them back to her home and served tea and scones whilst showing her granddaughter old photos of her mum as a child. It was how things should have been all along, but at least Maggie had acknowledged that fact, even if it had been a little too late.

As if sensing a slump in the jovial atmosphere, Ruby chimed in, 'So, how are you going to go about this *finding a man* lark? Because let me tell you, it's not blooming easy.'

Caitlin laughed. 'Says the beautiful, red-haired ex-movie actress who bagged a sexy property tycoon.' *Good grief, if Ruby, a thirty-year-old stunner, thinks it's difficult, there's no hope for me!*

Ruby held up a finger and giggled. 'Ah, we're not allowed to call

Mitch a tycoon any more. He says it sounds too braggy. And you know what he's like about being the centre of attention.'

'Oh, we certainly do,' Caitlin replied with a knowing smile. Caitlin remembered the first time Hollywood actress Ruby Locke had walked into her bakery, and she had tried her best not to be too starstruck. Glentorrin resident Mitch Adair had been roped into helping the star, by a mutual acquaintance, to stay out of the public eye by staying at a couple of his properties. This all followed a horrible incident where Ruby's social media accounts had been hacked, and some horrid imposter had put out vile posts pretending to be her. Mitch was just the kind of healing Ruby had needed and now the pair were head over heels in love.

Caitlin's thoughts returned to the poster she'd seen on the noticeboard at the village hall. 'So, for starters, there's a singles night up in Broadford, at the Crown Hotel, tomorrow night. I thought I'd give that a go.'

'Oooh, a singles night. That could work,' Jules said, giving her a nudge. 'But... won't you be lonely going by yourself?'

Caitlin laughed. 'Probably, I'll see if I can get a date to go with me.' They all laughed.

'Seriously though, I'll worry about you,' Jules said once the laughter had died down. 'You never know who might be at these things. And being a woman on your own...'

Caitlin rolled her eyes. 'Well, it's not like I can ask any of you to go, is it? You're all blissfully, sickeningly happy with your perfect men.'

Ruby reached and squeezed her hand. 'Aww, hon, it'll happen for you too. I just know it.'

Morag scoffed as she patted her neat grey bob. 'And who was it saying that Kenneth was perfect? I'd like to talk to them and tell them a few home truths.' The girls laughed again.

Caitlin said, 'Aye, well, maybe not perfect then, but I want what you lot have got. I want someone to shout at for leaving his clothes on the bedroom floor. And someone who can reach me stuff from high shelves in the bakery,' she joked.

'And someone to warm your feet on at night, eh?' Morag said with a wink.

'Aye, that too.'

'I get into trouble every night from Reid for that very thing,' Jules laughed. 'Even in the summer.' She took a sip of her wine and pursed her lips as if racking her brains. 'I wish I had someone to set you up with,' she said thoughtfully with a tap to her chin. 'But the only single man I know is my brother.'

Caitlin smiled. 'And as much as I adore Dex, he's just such a good friend; I couldn't see him any other way. He's a drinking buddy and a good laugh, but—'

Jules laughed. 'Hey, you don't need to explain to me. I grew up in the same house as him, remember?'

Thinking of her friend, Caitlin asked, 'Have you heard from him this week? He messaged me last week to say he was enjoying his tour of the North Coast 500.'

'He texted yesterday to say he was camping somewhere where there was a battle re-enactment going on, so he somehow got roped in. Typical Dexter.'

Caitlin could imagine the huge hulk of a man dressed in a kilt with mud on his face, brandishing a Sgian Dubh. The image brought a smile to her face.

'It's a shame there are no single men in the village who you're attracted to, right enough,' Morag said with a shake of her head. 'And there's no point trying to fix you up with one of Kenneth's friends from golf. They wouldnae be able to keep up with you.'

Caitlin giggled along with Morag and her friends. 'Thanks, ladies, you're all a fat lot of use.' She huffed. 'Singles night it is, then. I think it said on the poster that it was for over thirty-fives. But I hope it's not full of over seventy-fives.'

Ruby almost choked on her wine. 'Ooh, you could get yourself a sugar daddy!'

'Erm... no thanks. I'd like someone more my own age. Does Mitch have any single friends?' Caitlin asked with a wink.

Ruby gave her a look of incredulity. 'His friends are Reid, Dex and Kenneth.'

Caitlin rolled her eyes and giggled. 'Like I said... fat lot of use.' Caitlin topped up their glasses and handed around the snacks she had prepared. 'Seriously though, I've wanted to get back out there for a while, but I've been too chicken. I mean, whoever I date has to accept Grace and me as a package deal. She's always been my priority. But I'd just like someone to cosy up to when Grace is in bed. Someone who's not a Yorkie Poo. Don't get me wrong, Cleo gives great cuddles, but her breath leaves a lot to be desired.' Laughter rang out around the garden again.

'What does Grace think about you looking for a boyfriend?' Jules asked with a tilt of her head.

Caitlin cringed. 'Well... I haven't *exactly* mentioned it to her yet. But she's always saying I should go out more and have fun.' She shrugged. 'I'm taking that as an encouraging sign.'

'I reckon she'd be great about it. Evin was wonderful with you, Jules, wasn't he?' Morag asked.

Jules beamed as she always did when talking about her soon-to-be stepson. 'Oh, he's just brilliant. Such a kind-hearted and thoughtful boy.' Jules had visited Glentorrin after the death of her husband. She had wanted to escape the piteous gazes and well-meaning friends who had wrapped her in cotton wool for fear she would break. After nursing her terminally ill husband, her visit to Glentorrin had been a way of finding her real self once more. She had ended up running the Lifeboat House Museum and falling in love with local artist, Reid MacKinnon, who had his own emotional baggage following the breakdown of his marriage. Along with Reid's son Evin and dog Chewie, the two had helped to mend each other's broken heart, and were now planning their Christmas wedding.

'I can definitely see Grace being like that. She just wants her mum to be happy,' Ruby said.

Caitlin raised her eyebrows. 'Let's hope you're all right, eh?' She stood from the table and went to the kitchen to collect a plate of shortbread from the worktop.

Grace walked into the kitchen, her red hair in a messy topknot that made her look older than her almost thirteen years. She was closely followed by Cleo, the little black Yorkie Poo, and she pinched a biscuit from the plate, breaking a chunk off for her canine companion. 'Mum, Cora wants to know if I can go for a sleepover tomorrow night with it being Saturday. I said I'd check with you and call her back.'

Perfect timing, Caitlin thought. 'Aye, love. That's fine with me. Shall I make you some tray bake to take with you? I know how much Cora likes my Mars crispy cakes.'

Grace grinned. 'Ooh yes, please. Although, there's no wonder she keeps inviting me over. I think I'm the only friend whose mum sends baking every time I go.'

Caitlin smiled. 'Ah you're so lucky to have me,' she said with a peck to Grace's cheek.

Grace flung her arms around her neck and hugged her. 'I already know that. Now go get back to your friends.'

Caitlin rolled her eyes. 'Yes, Mum.'

Grace giggled and skipped back towards the stairs, once again followed by her little black ball of fluff, the little dog's nails tip-tapping on the wooden floor.

* * *

As the sun ducked behind the houses, the friends moved inside to Caitlin's living room, and she made teas and coffees to take the chill away.

'So, Caitlin, what would your ideal man be like?' Morag asked as she sipped her steaming brew.

Caitlin thought for a moment. 'Well, for starters, he'll have to have a sense of humour.' She paused a while. 'And he'll need to be kind and thoughtful.'

'What about looks?' Ruby asked.

Jules nudged her best friend. 'Go on, Caitlin, describe that hunky caber tosser from the Highland Games last year.'

Caitlin felt her cheeks warming. 'Ooh yes, he was lovely. Although I'm looking for more caber and less tosser if you know what I mean.' She winked and her friends howled with laughter. When they had all calmed down, she continued, 'But... to be honest, I've no real preference. Dark hair, fair hair, no hair. It doesn't matter. I think when you get to my age, your priorities change. I'm not really looking for the thunderbolt to hit. I just want someone who's a decent person. Someone I can trust, you know?'

Morag nodded and smiled. 'Aye, lassie, that's the important stuff. Looks fade. Although my Kenneth just gets sexier and sexier.'

'Morag!' Jules whacked her arm playfully. 'Down girl.'

Morag laughed heartily. 'Hey, I'm just telling it like it is, ladies.'

Jules turned her attention to Caitlin. 'Don't go settling though, eh? It worries me when you say you're not looking for the thunderbolt. You deserve the bloomin' thunderbolt. I want to see you swept off your feet, head over heels in love. Not just settling for someone because they're nice.'

Caitlin shrugged. 'I'm just trying to be realistic.'

'Hey, have you thought about online dating?' Ruby asked. 'It's quite common these days for people to find the love of their lives online, or on an app.'

Caitlin scrunched her nose. 'Nah, I've read too many horror stories. Catfishing, I think it's called. So, I think I'd prefer to meet someone face to face right off. No point messing around chatting online to someone whose profile picture looks like Gerard Butler, only to find out that in real life, he looks more like Gerard Depardieu!'

Jules' cheeks turned pink. 'I actually think he was quite sexy in *Green Card*.'

Ruby rolled her eyes. 'I've met them both.'

All eyes suddenly focused on Ruby. 'And?' the three women asked in unison.

Ruby drew her fingers across her lips in a zipping motion. 'I couldn't possibly comment.'

They all sighed in exasperation.

'For a former A-list celeb, you're no good at spreading gossip!' Morag laughed.

* * *

Once her friends had gone home, it was close to midnight, so Caitlin blew out the scented candles and switched off the lamps in the living room before heading upstairs to her bedroom.

She stood for a moment looking out over the inlet, where the moonlight was dancing on the surface of the water. From her vantage point, she could see the Coxswain pub where she had spent many a raucous night dancing to ceilidh music, Morag's shop that she frequented regularly, and the whitewashed houses that joined onto it, and then, right at the end of the old slipway, the Lifeboat House Museum with its historical items and stories of the old lifeboat that brought the village's past to life. All the buildings had colourful summer bunting draped across them in true Glentorrin style. *No*, she thought, *I couldn't leave this place. Glentorrin is my home.*

'Mum?' Grace said with a yawn as she stepped into Caitlin's room.

'Hi, sweetheart. Did I wake you?'

Grace shook her head. 'No, it's okay. I just wanted to talk to you.'

Caitlin walked over and sat on her bed and Grace sat beside her. 'What's wrong, hen?' she asked, tucking her daughter's natural waves behind her ear.

Grace smiled. 'Nothing. I just wanted you to know that... I mean... I heard you talking earlier... I wasn't mooching. I just overheard when I came to get a drink.'

Caitlin narrowed her eyes, thinking back on some of the racy topics of conversation that had taken place. 'Heard what, exactly?'

Grace chewed her lip for a moment. 'What you said about getting a boyfriend.'

Caitlin quailed. 'Ah. Right.'

Grace took her mum's hand. 'I just wanted you to know that it's fine with me. I know you've not really dated since I was born, and that's a long time, Mum. I'm almost thirteen. I think you deserve someone who will bring you flowers and take you to the cinema. Or someone who will go dancing with you or cook nice meals for you. And I don't mean because you need someone. Because I know you don't. You're very... erm... independent. But I think it would be good if you had a nice man to go out with. So, I just wanted to tell you that, because I know you'll be wondering if I'm okay with it. And now you know I am.' She shrugged.

Caitlin's eyes stung a little and she put her arms around her daughter and pulled her close. 'Thank you, sweetheart. That means such a lot.'

Grace kissed her on the cheek. 'So long as they're a dog person. That's my only rule. Oh, and... maybe someone who doesn't smoke.'

Caitlin giggled. 'Is that all?'

Grace pondered for a moment, her lips pursed, and her eyes scrunched. 'I'll get back to you if I think of anything else.' She stood up and headed back to her own room.

Caitlin smiled and shook her head. 'Okay, love. Sweet dreams.'

2

Caitlin awoke early on Saturday morning, as she always did. There were things to prepare for the bakery, bread to put into the industrial oven that had already proved, shortbread to bake fresh and a delivery at 8 a.m. to accept. She showered, dressed and opened her curtains, smiling as she looked onto the waking village below. One of the village's elderly residents, Hamish Gair, was just walking back from the shop with his newspaper, whistling and smiling at passers-by. He was such a sweet old man. Evin was out with his huge, Hungarian Vizsla Chewie, followed by his dad, a half-asleep-looking Reid.

At around seven-thirty, Caitlin jogged upstairs and popped her head around Grace's door to find her fast asleep with Cleo curled up beside her. Caitlin patted her leg and Cleo jumped off the bed to follow her downstairs and into the back garden. Once she was finished with her morning ritual, Cleo ran back through the house and up the stairs, no doubt to get comfy for another hour or so with Grace. It was clear Caitlin wasn't going to be getting any help this morning.

* * *

The world was almost fully awake when her delivery of supplies arrived at eight and she waved over to Jules, who was leaving Morag's shop with a bottle of milk. She approached the bakery with a wide smile.

'I don't suppose you've any bread yet, have you? Evin used the last of ours for toast at suppertime and forgot to mention it.' She rolled her eyes. 'I could've bought a shop loaf, but yours is so much better.'

'Sure! Come on in. It's still warm.'

The delivery driver handed her a clipboard for her to sign the delivery note and she gave him a couple of pieces of shortbread in a paper bag.

He tucked straight in. 'And they wonder why I won't change my route,' he told her with a wink.

'He seems nice,' Jules said with a knowing smile when he'd left.

Caitlin shook her head. 'Don't even think about it. He's married with three kids.'

Jules curled her lip. 'Dammit.'

'Here you go, one white bloomer.'

Jules lifted the wrapped loaf to her nose and inhaled. 'Mm... yum.' She handed over the money and Caitlin rang the first sale of the day through the cash register. 'Thanks, honey. See you later!' Jules said as she turned to walk to the door but stopped. 'Ooh, are you all ready for your big night?' she asked.

Caitlin huffed. 'Hmm. Not really sure I should bother now. The more I think about it, the more I think I'm probably wasting my time. I mean, how many single men can there be on Skye who are my age and looking for romance, that I'll actually want to spend time with?'

Jules scowled. 'Don't back out now! You never know who you'll meet.'

Caitlin nodded. 'Aye, maybe that's the issue. Maybe you were right about weirdos and such.'

Jules narrowed her eyes. 'Erm... I don't remember saying anything about weirdos. I remember saying I was worried about you going alone.'

Caitlin rolled her eyes. 'Okay, okay, I'll go. I just don't feel as excited about it today. I think it was the wine talking last night.'

Jules tilted her head. 'Did you talk to Grace or was it too late when we'd all gone?'

Caitlin smiled as she reflected upon Grace's kind words the night before. 'She came to see me before I went to bed to say she'd heard us talking and that it was fine with her if I got a man in my life.'

Jules grinned. 'There you go then! No excuses now!'

Caitlin widened her eyes. 'It doesn't appear so, does it?'

'Look, let me know if you need any help getting ready or picking out an outfit. You've helped me out plenty of times.'

'Thanks, Jules. I'll probably just stick my jeans on to be honest. I don't want to look too desperate.'

Jules smiled and shook her head. 'Well, you'll look lovely no matter what. I must get going or the men in my life will be moaning at me. Speak later.'

Caitlin raised a hand. 'Bye, Jules.'

* * *

When the bakery was closed for the day, Caitlin returned through to the house to find Grace in the garden playing fetch with Cleo. The two-year-old Yorkie Poo had been Grace's shadow ever since they took her in as a pup.

'Hey, love. I've made you the tray bake to take to Cora's. It's here all wrapped up for you.'

'Thanks, Mum. You're a star,' Grace said with a wide smile. 'Are you going to the pub tonight with Jules?'

Caitlin began riffling through the cupboards to find something for dinner. 'No, not tonight... I have other plans,' she said, feeling heat rising in her cheeks.

Grace appeared beside her. 'Don't bother making anything for me. Cora's dad is ordering pizza. What plans have you got then?'

Caitlin gave up the search and straightened up to face her daughter. 'Well... there's a singles night up in Broadford. I thought I might give that a go.'

Grace scrunched her brow. 'Singles night? That's so last year, Mum. You need to get find-a-mate. It's an app. You get to see a wee video message from people who fit your criteria and if you like them, you can arrange a date.'

Caitlin flinched and pursed her lips. 'Oh, I don't know about that, love. I think maybe that's for young folk. I think I'm more of a find-a-mate-in-the-old-fashioned-way type of gal.'

Grace shook her head. 'No, lots of old people use it, too.'

Caitlin grinned and rolled her eyes. 'Thanks for that, hen.'

Grace covered her eyes with her free hand for a second and groaned. 'I didn't mean it to come out like that. It's just that Mhairi at school said so. Her aunty uses it and she's like forty-two or something.'

'Wow, that old?'

Grace gritted her teeth and narrowed her eyes. 'Yes, and Mhairi has a mobile phone. That's how she knows this stuff.'

Caitlin held in a sigh. 'I've said you can have one when you're fourteen.'

Grace huffed. 'I'll be practically an old maid by then. Anyway, go to your singles night, but make sure you don't let anyone buy you a drink unless the barman hands it right to you. There's people that try to drug you these days, you know.'

Caitlin widened her eyes, surprised and a little horrified at how much her daughter seemed to know. 'I'll bear that in mind. But... how—?'

'Autumn, in my class, watched a true crime programme with her older sister about a woman that was drugged and abducted. It really scared me. I don't think I'm ever going to go to pubs or drink alcohol. I think I'll probably just marry Evin. That way I don't have to do dating.' She shrugged like it was the most natural conclusion to come to.

Caitlin stifled a giggle. 'Aye, that sounds like a grand plan. So long as Evin's up for that.'

Grace smiled. 'He is. We've already talked about it. I mean, he's not my boyfriend now, but I might let him be when we're seventeen.'

Impressed with her daughter's decision to hold off on boys for five years, Caitlin planted a kiss on her cheek, even though she knew once the hormones kicked in, it would no doubt change. 'You'd better go get your stuff together if I'm to drop you off at six.'

Grace skipped through towards the lounge and stopped when she reached the hallway door. 'Cora's dad is single, you know.' She shrugged. 'I could say something to—'

Caitlin gasped. 'Don't you dare!' She laughed, shaking her head. 'I think I'll manage sorting my own love life out thanks.' His relationship status was an intriguing surprise, although come to think of it, she hadn't seen his wife Fenella on her travels, out jogging, for a while.

'Suit yourself. But if you change your mind...' Grace sang as she jogged up the stairs.

* * *

After Caitlin had showered and changed out of her flour-covered work clothes, they arrived at 6 p.m. sharp on the doorstep of Cora Budge's one-storey, whitewashed house in Breakish and knocked.

Cora's dad, Lyle, came to the door, drying his hands on a grey and white striped towel, and Caitlin found herself blushing bright pink at the sight of him, thanks to what Grace had said earlier.

'Oh, hi, Caitlin. You're looking very nice. Are you going out?' Lyle asked with a smile.

Caitlin touched her hair. 'Oh, thank you. I—'

'She's going to a singles night,' Grace blurted.

Caitlin's face turned from a slight blush to the point of near spontaneous human combustion, and she glared at her daughter.

Lyle nodded. 'Oh, the one at Broadford? Aye, I thought about going to that mysel', but then Cora invited Grace, so it's a pizza night instead.'

Caitlin widened her eyes. 'Oh gosh, I hope we haven't inconvenienced you. I can always take the girls—'

'Och, no, don't be daft. There'll be others. You'll have to let me know if it's good craic, eh?' Lyle grinned. 'Anyway, come away in, Grace. Cora is just on the phone to her mum.'

Grace kissed Caitlin's cheek. 'Bye, Mum. See you tomorrow. And remember what I said about drinks,' she said with a stern gaze and a pointed finger.

Too shocked to chastise her daughter, Caitlin simply nodded and said, 'Bye, love.'

Once Grace had disappeared inside the house with her overnight bag and platter of tray bakes, Lyle turned to her. 'Dinnae worry about that, lass. Kids will be kids, eh? No filter. Cora is just the same.' He shook his head and smiled warmly. 'And I don't know about you, but I'm not into the dating app things. My guess is someone on there will look like Cindy Crawford on their profile, but end up looking like Michael Crawford from *Phantom of the Opera* in real life.'

Caitlin burst out laughing, probably down to the nerves. 'Aye! I said the same.'

'Great minds, eh?'

She nodded. 'Indeed. Well, have a lovely evening with the pre-teen monsters. I hope they don't completely beat you into submission.'

Lyle rolled his eyes. 'Already done, I'm afraid. They're going to watch some soppy movie on the big screen, and I'm demoted to the little TV in ma room to watch the footy.'

'Well, make sure you at least get a piece of tray bake,' she told him.

'Oh, don't you worry. I always make sure I get some of your amazing baking. Anyway, have a nice evening. And... erm... good luck.'

Caitlin smiled. 'Thanks. You too.' She grinned.

He laughed lightly. 'Aye, I might need it more than you.' And with that he closed the door.

Caitlin couldn't help the smile that stayed on her face as she climbed back into the car.

Despite Grace's obvious excitement about the singles event, it didn't start until seven. She'd had every intention of calling in to see Jules for another pep talk, seeing as she had talked herself into knots over the idea of going. Instead, she headed home and was greeted by Cleo, skipping around at her feet, her whole body wagging in excitement.

She crouched to fuss the dog. 'What should I do, Cleo? Should I risk it and go? Or should I stay here with you and watch *Outlander* instead?'

Cleo gave a yip that sounded distinctly like 'Go!'

Caitlin stood again and flopped onto a kitchen chair. 'You're trying to get rid of me too, are you?'

Cleo tilted her head and continued to wag.

'A fat lot of use you are, eh? Come on then, come and help me decide what to wear. I'll go for an hour, but that's all. I wish I'd never bloomin' mentioned it to be honest. It was definitely the wine. I'm sure of it.'

3

Caitlin stood at the doorway of the Crown Hotel, a white-painted, old coaching inn in the pretty village of Broadford that faced the blue waters of Broadford Bay. She had been there for a few minutes, trying to pluck up the courage to enter.

A few women arrived as a group, all heavily made up, and as they pushed through the door ahead of her, she fought the cough that almost erupted when a fog of myriad different perfumes assaulted her nasal passages. She momentarily wished she had convinced her friends to come along for moral support. Although if she had, who would have paid any attention to her, when one of her best friends, Ruby Locke, was a former Hollywood movie star?

At almost ten past seven, Caitlin smoothed down her pale blue, layered, Lagenlook top, that she had paired with summery, white linen trousers and sandals and took a deep breath. With her fingers wrapped around the handle, she was just about to push through the door, when it was yanked open from the inside. Unable to let go in time, she lurched forwards and landed, on all fours, in the middle of the well-trodden welcome mat. A collective gasp travelled the bar, and she closed her eyes, willing the floor to open up and suck her in. Alas, it didn't happen, and she slowly raised her chin to find many piteous gazes fixed on her.

'Oh my god! I'm so sorry! Here let me help you up!' A hand reached out and grabbed her wrist, tugging her to a standing position. 'Oh, Caitlin! It's you. Are you all right? God, I'm so bloody sorry.'

Caitlin knew her face could have replaced the lighthouse at Neist Point, seeing as it was no doubt glowing with the embarrassment she felt. She glared up into the guilt-filled, brown eyes of the outdoor-wear shop owner – a friend of hers, from Glentorrin. 'Bloody hell, Archie Sutherland! You should be more careful!' she snapped.

He swallowed hard and frowned. 'Aye, I'm really sorry. I was just heading to my car to get a pen.' Caitlin realised he too was here for the singles event. He was quite a shy man really, kind of sweet though, around the same age as her, tall and broad-shouldered, a head full of shaggy, dark brown curls with a wee smattering of grey, and a constant five o'clock shadow. He was the type of rugged man that *other* women fawned over. He'd had a few girlfriends over the years, so seeing him here was indeed a surprise.

'Well, don't let me stop you.' Caitlin immediately felt guilty for her terse response. It had been an accident after all. 'Look, I'm sorry. My pride's bruised that's all.'

'Aye and your lovely outfit is all dirty now,' he said, pointing to her knees with a wince. 'I really am sorry.'

She glanced down at the mucky patches of grey on her otherwise pristine trousers and gave a deep sigh. 'I think I'll just go home,' she said as she made to turn around.

'No! Don't do that. Let me get you a drink, eh? It's the least I can do.' Archie's gaze was filled with apology, and she crumbled.

'Okay, thanks. Just a J2O though. I'm driving,' she told him.

'Okay, go grab a table and I'll bring it over. Do you need ice for your knees?'

She gave a light laugh. 'No, thank you, I'm good.' *Although a cold compress for my ego wouldn't hurt.*

'Aye, right. Back in a sec.' Archie turned and narrowly avoided a collision with a huge, rugby player type who could've launched him like a hammer, and Caitlin held her breath, hoping that a fight didn't break out. When it didn't, she heaved a relieved sigh and watched Archie hold up his hands in another apology, then make a quick detour to chat to a woman at a table across the room. The blonde was waving a pen around and he took it and scribbled something – probably his phone number – on a scrap of paper before he headed to the bar. He's a fast worker, she mused.

Caitlin glanced down and groaned. She rubbed at the dirt on her knees, but it was an exercise in futility. There was nothing else for it, she would simply need to remain seated for the rest of the night – and when she thought about the rest of the night, she intended that it would end, for her at least, at around seven-forty-five. This was a huge mistake.

Archie returned and placed a glass of orange-coloured juice before her. 'Passion fruit and mango, is that okay?'

She nodded and took a sip. 'Perfect, thanks.'

He frowned at her. 'You do know it's singles night tonight, don't you?'

She refrained from making a snide comment, even though one was biting at the tip of her tongue. 'Yes, of course.' She laughed and shook her head. Why else would she have walked into a pub she didn't really know, all alone? In spite of her outward show of confidence, she wasn't the type to do that. Popping into the Coxswain in Glentorrin was an entirely different thing of course. She virtually knew everyone who frequented the place.

Archie nodded. 'Oh, right, right. That's good then. I just wasn't sure this night would be... you know... specific enough for you.'

Confused as to his meaning, she pursed her lips for a moment and frowned. 'Specific?'

Archie nodded. 'Aye, with you having... how do I put it? Singular tastes.'

Caitlin laughed. 'Singular tastes? Is that what they're calling *overly picky* these days?'

Archie glanced around and then leaned in to whisper, 'No, I mean with you being into... you know... women.'

Caitlin raised her eyebrows and gasped. 'Sorry?'

Archie whispered again, conspiratorially this time. 'With you being a lesbian.' He almost mouthed the word, rather than saying it out loud.

Caitlin scowled. 'You think I'm gay?' she said rather too loudly, causing many eyes to turn in her direction for the second time that evening.

A look of confusion washed over Archie's face and his cheeks flushed. 'Wait... Are you not gay then?'

Caitlin rolled her eyes. 'No! I'm not!' she hissed. 'Why did you think I was gay? Not that there's anything wrong with being gay. Not in the slightest. But again, what made you think that about me?'

Archie cleared his throat and shrugged. 'I suppose I just... I assumed.'

Caitlin shook her head. 'Why on earth would assume that I'm gay? I have a daughter.'

He rolled his eyes. 'Gay people do have kids, you know; these are the twenty twenties not the eighteen twenties.' He seemed quite perturbed. 'And... it's just that... I've known you for years, but you've never had a man in your life that I've seen. You're not married, or divorced, that I know of. And so... I just guessed...'

Caitlin folded her arms across her chest. 'Well, you guessed wrong.'

'Aye. I know that now. I'm sorry.'

She glanced around, but everyone was back to their own conversations. 'Don't apologise. I'm not offended. Just a wee bit shocked, that's all.'

He shrugged. 'I've got lots of gay friends, you know. I don't judge,' Archie informed her.

She gritted her teeth. 'Again, Archie, I'm not a lesbian. I'm a heterosexual woman. I like men. With men's bodies and beards and... men.'

He held up his hands. 'Aye, I know now, I was just saying.'

'Well, don't!'

Archie gave a sad smile. 'Look, I'll go. I get the feeling I might be cramping your style. I didn't exactly help get your evening off to the best start, did I?'

Feeling a little deflated, Caitlin told him, 'It's fine. I think I'm going to go home anyway. I... I shouldn't have come.'

'No! Don't do that. Not because of me. I'll feel crappy if you go. Mingle a bit. You never know, your dream man might be in this very room.' He gestured around dramatically before leaving her alone.

Caitlin glanced over his shoulder at the other attendees who were all deep in conversation and sighed. 'I sincerely doubt it.'

Perhaps her dream man was currently serving pizza to her daughter instead. She thought back to Lyle's smile and compliment when she dropped Grace off. He was quite attractive, she'd always thought so, but had pushed that thought to the back of her mind, seeing as he was a married man... although now he was single. He was around forty-five, tall, stocky and had grey hair and a neatly trimmed beard. In fact, there was a look of that TV chef, Paul Hollywood, about him. Not that he had shown any interest in her, but after Archie's revelation, she wondered if he thought she was gay too. Then again Grace had just announced to all and sundry that she was desperate. Not that she had used those exact words, but she may as well have. *How to put a man off in one easy step.*

She finished her drink and gazed around the room. Lots of people had already paired off and were chatting merrily, some were even getting quite cosy. Archie had moved on from the first woman he'd been talking to and was now heavily ensconced in conversation with another. She had seen him with several women over the years, no one had ever really stuck around. It wasn't that he was repulsive, he certainly wasn't, but he had always seemed quite set in his ways. Although she didn't exactly know him well – they were more acquaintances than friends really – but his businesses, the outdoor shop, the campsite and his IT work, all seemed to take precedence over his love life, something she was all too familiar with, but evidently, he was trying to change that, just like she was.

'All right? Can I get you another?' a rather handsome man asked, nodding towards her glass. He was a fair bit younger than her and had an attractive face and smiling eyes. His T-shirt was tight and showed the outline of his muscular chest and arms. *Down, girl!*

She sat up a little straighter. 'Oh, that would be lovely, thank you.' She smiled warmly and was on the verge of deciding that perhaps the evening was about to improve. 'Just a J—'

'Aye, it's okay, I served your friend with the first round, I remember.' He winked, collected her empty glass, and walked across the room and behind the bar.

'Ugh... seriously. Talk about too good to be true,' she chuntered to herself, feeling a little foolish for thinking he had been flirting with her. *Sod it, I'm definitely going home now.*

She stood and began to walk towards the door.

'Hey, you're not heading home, are you?' Archie asked, appearing with the stealth of a ninja and making her jump.

She huffed. 'Yes, Archie. I don't think this is the type of event for me. You seem to be doing okay though.'

Archie crumpled his brow. 'I do?'

She laughed and whacked his arm playfully. 'Come on, Mr Smooth. I've seen you handing your number to a couple of women this evening.'

Archie grinned and his cheeks coloured. 'Oh, that. Nah, it was all work stuff. One was asking about camping in the area for her friends from down south in England, and the other was needing a virus clearing from her computer.' He shrugged. 'I think I must project a kind of oracle-cum-handyman aura, rather than a come-hither one.' He laughed. 'No nibbles at the worm for me tonight.'

'Archie! That's so rude!' Caitlin was shocked by his turn of phrase, and what man would refer to his todger as a worm? Eeuw!

Archie's eyes widened and he appeared horrified. 'Oh no, you misunderstood! I meant... you know, like fishing?' He mimicked casting an invisible rod. 'Plenty of fish in the sea and all that? That I'm here fishing, not trying to get a woman to nibble my—'

Caitlin held up a hand to stop him. 'Right, I get you. My apologies.'

He rubbed his chin and hesitantly said, 'Look, there's a singles event across on the mainland next weekend. A kind of speed dating thing. It's at a hotel in Kyle of Lochalsh. Do you fancy car sharing? Maybe there's strength in numbers, eh?'

Caitlin wasn't convinced. 'Speed dating? That sounds like a comedy sketch waiting to happen.' She remembered the episode of *Vicar of Dibley* where Geraldine was subjected to date after date with people from her own congregation, with hilarious consequences.

'Aye, it does, but you never know. Might be some good craic. What do you say? We can be each other's moral support.'

She thought about it for a moment and then decided she had

nothing to lose. And that surely the next event had to start off better than this one? If she actually attended with Archie, she could keep an eye on him and make sure he didn't leg her up, or slam a door in her face, or something equally as bad as this evening. 'Oh aye. Why not, eh?'

Archie smiled. 'Grand. I'll pop in to the bakery in the week and let you know the details.'

'Great. Thanks. Right, I'm heading home. See you later. Thanks for the drink.' She exited the door just as the handsome bartender deposited another J20 on the table with a look of confusion.

4

The following morning, Jules rang to invite Caitlin for tea and cake as the boys, and Chewie, were apparently heading off to the beach to go rock pooling. Caitlin accepted and grabbed a few pieces of shortbread to take with her and wondered if the other ladies would be there too. She clipped on Cleo's lead and the two of them headed across the village.

The sun was high in the sky over Glentorrin, and a gentle breeze played on the surface of the water in the inlet. Gus, the fisherman, was scrubbing the deck of his boat and raised his hand in a wave as she passed.

Summer Sundays in Glentorrin were usually a lazy affair; people walked their dogs or visited friends. There was the church service every other week now that Father McAllen was incumbent of two churches within the parish, and today was his day to be away. The new team of bell-ringers were making the most of the empty church and practising; the chimes rang out across the village, bringing a smile to Caitlin's face. At this time of year, there were plenty of tourists taking in the scenery of the village, too, and that fact made Caitlin proud to call the picturesque and friendly place her home.

Caitlin spotted Morag through the propped-open door of the shop. She was behind the counter chatting to Hamish, who had called in for his Sunday newspaper.

When Caitlin arrived at Jules' house, it was just the three of them: herself, Jules, and Ruby – four if you counted her canine companion, Cleo. Once they were all seated around the table with their plates of sweet treats and mugs of tea, all eyes settled on Caitlin, expectantly. She knew very well what they were after and she took great joy in ignoring their questioning gazes, choosing instead to tickle Cleo behind her ears as the dog waited for crumbs to fall from the table.

'What?' she asked her friends, eventually, with a smirk.

'Oh, come on, woman! You know exactly what!' Jules insisted with a huff.

'Yes, spill it, madam! How did it go last night?' Ruby asked eagerly. 'Did you meet your Prince Charming?'

Caitlin rolled her eyes. 'Nope. It was disastrous from start to finish. Hence my reason for staying schtum.'

Both her friends eyed her with pity and disappointment. 'Really? How come?'

'Surely it wasn't that bad?'

'Oh, believe me, I couldn't have made it up!'

She informed them about the debacle at the start of the night and how Archie, of all people, had caused it. How she thought some handsome, younger man was flirting with her and offering to buy her a drink, only to discover he was the bartender and simply doing his job; and to top it all off, how it had come to light that Archie thought she was gay.

'Good grief. I see what you mean,' Jules laughed. 'I know it's too early for wine, but that story made me feel like I should open a bottle. It's a shame you have to drive to collect Grace this afternoon.' She pondered a moment. 'Archie is such a wally.' She shook her head. 'I wonder why he was there anyway. He doesn't seem to be short on female companionship. Although none of the women he dates seem to stick around, so maybe he's looking for something more meaningful...'

Precisely what Caitlin had thought.

Ruby leaned across and squeezed her arm. 'Don't let it put you off though, will you? They won't all be like that.'

Caitlin shook her head. 'I don't know that I want to risk another night like that, to be honest. I mean, how many things can go wrong in one evening?'

Ruby shook her head, second-hand embarrassment causing her cheeks to flush. 'I can't believe you fell on the floor in front of everyone. You poor love.'

Caitlin huffed. 'Yes, to say I felt ridiculous would be an understatement. But Archie did his best to help, bless him.'

'After he caused the fiasco!' Jules replied with a laugh. 'It was the least he could do.'

'I think Archie's quite good-looking really,' Ruby said, completely out of the blue.

Caitlin tilted her head. 'Really?' She had never really thought of him in that way. He was a nice guy, admittedly, and he didn't repulse her. She simply had never really considered Archie romantically.

Jules sat up straight as if she'd had a light-bulb moment. 'Don't you think he looks a bit like... ooh, what's his name?' She clicked her fingers as if doing so would conjure up the answer. 'Erm... ugh!' She sighed in frustration. 'What's his name? You know... the Incredible Hulk?'

Caitlin scrunched her brow and chuckled. 'Eh? What are you on about? Archie's not green.'

Ruby gasped and waved an excited hand. 'Yes! That's who he

reminds me of! You're absolutely right! Do you know I've been trying to figure it out for ages!'

Caitlin glanced at her other friend. 'Again... he's not green?'

Ruby blurted, 'Mark Ruffalo, that's his name! The actor who plays the Hulk. Such a nice guy. I met him and his wife, Sunrise, at the Golden Globes. She's so sweet and he's quite ruggedly hand-some, in that just-got-out-of-bed way, don't you think?'

Jules nodded dreamily. 'Oh yes, and his eyes...'

Caitlin glanced with incredulity between her two closest friends. 'I think I've slipped into a parallel universe.'

Ruby smiled and nodded at Jules. 'Yes, such kind eyes...'

Catlin snorted. 'Oh yes, lovely eyes for a mutated humanoid who tears off his clothes and breaks stuff when he's pissed off.'

Jules whacked her arm and laughed. 'Mark Ruffalo, you muppet!'

Caitlin scrunched her brow. 'I know the name, but all I can think of now is a shirtless, green man with a thickset brow and fluffy green hair, wearing ragged shorts, like that man from the seventies TV show. You know? The one with Bill Bixby and Lou Ferrigno.' A memory returned and she smiled. 'My dad used to love that show. I used to watch reruns of it with him.' She shook her head. 'You do realise, it's unlikely I'll ever look at Archie the same again, don't you?'

Ruby picked up her phone. 'You've got the wrong bloke. We don't mean the guy from the seventies.' She tapped at the screen. 'Look, here, this guy.' She thrust the phone in front of Caitlin's confused gaze.

Caitlin pursed her lips and took the phone to get a closer look. She recognised the man on the screen from an early 2000s film she had watched recently with Grace called *13 Going on 30*. 'I suppose he is good-looking, yes.' She played down her response, remembering thinking how gorgeous he was when they had watched the movie.

Ruby rolled her eyes. 'Yes, but don't you think he looks like Archie?'

Caitlin tilted her head and narrowed her eyes as she scrutinised the image. They were right, the two men could've been brothers. 'Actually... I think I can see what you mean. He does have a look of him, doesn't he?' She shrugged and handed Ruby's phone back. 'Makes no difference though because I'm not interested in Archie. I've known him for years and there's never been a spark there. And I'm not being funny, but just because he's pretty much the only single man in Glentorrin, apart from Dex and lovely old Hamish Gair, doesn't mean I'm going to fall for him. And that's even if he was in the slightest bit interested in me. Which he's not. He's spent all these years presuming I like women, for goodness' sake.' She laughed.

'How does that saying go? There's plenty more fish in the sea?' Jules said with an encouraging smile.

Caitlin was suddenly reminded of the misunderstanding with Archie about fishing and worms and couldn't help snickering.

'What's so funny?' Ruby asked with an intrigued grin.

Caitlin shook her head. 'Oh, nothing. Just remembering something that Archie said last night.'

Ruby and Jules exchanged a strange look and Caitlin shook her head.

'Oh, seriously, you two, just stop!'

* * *

Around four that afternoon, Caitlin pulled up outside Grace's friend's house. She'd made a special effort to look nice, just in case there was the slightest chance that Lyle might be interested in asking her out.

She knocked on the door and it was tugged open.

'Oh, hi, Caitlin, come on in. The girls are just getting ready.'

Caitlin stepped through the door into the modern family kitchen, which was in juxtaposition to the very traditional exterior of the old cottage. It wasn't necessarily a design she would have chosen, with its sleek, shiny black surfaces and stainless-steel appliances, but it was spotlessly clean and that impressed her.

'Can I get you a cup of tea or coffee?' Lyle asked with a warm smile.

'Tea would be lovely, but only if you're making one. I don't want to impose.'

'I'm always up for a cuppa. It's no imposition, really.' He clicked on the kettle. 'Have a seat.' He gestured to the breakfast bar. 'So, how did last night go? Any dream men in attendance?'

Caitlin felt her cheeks heating and tucked her hair behind her ear. 'Sadly no. It was a bit of a damp squib of an evening.'

He widened his eyes. 'Really? That does surprise me. I felt sure you'd be full of the joys today after meeting some buff Sam Heughan lookalike.'

She laughed lightly at his reference to the extremely attractive *Outlander* actor. 'Oh, I wish. No, it turns out that singles nights may not be for me after all.'

Lyle placed a steaming mug of tea before her on the granite worktop. 'Oh no, you mustn't give up so easily. I haven't been to many, but they're not all bad, I promise you. Unless you've decided to give the apps a go?'

Caitlin scrunched her face. 'Oh god, no. I'm of the school of thought that actually meeting the person in real life beats being catfished any day. Like you said about Cindy Crawford and Michael Crawford.'

He laughed. 'Aye, I agree totally. Give me a real person rather than a touched-up, airbrushed photo any day. I don't get why people do that. If any of them ever went missing, they'd never be found from their photos!'

Caitlin laughed. 'Oh, I know! And what's with the pouting trout faces?'

'Och, don't get me started!' He took a sip of his tea, then paused before speaking again. 'Look, I was wondering...'

Caitlin held her breath. Was this it? Was he going to ask her out?

He cleared his throat. 'There's a singles night over in Kyle of Lochalsh at the weekend. I'm thinking of heading there myself. Do you think... I mean... Will you... erm, give it a go, do you think?'

Dammit. Feeling a little deflated, she nodded and tried to hide her disappointment. 'Oh yes, my friend, Archie, mentioned that one. He's offered to lift share.'

She thought she saw a hint of disappointment flash in Lyle's eyes. 'Oh, right. Well, there you go then. I might see you there.'

'You possibly will,' Caitlin replied. She took a sip of her tea and glanced around the room. Desperate to change the subject, she said, 'You have a really lovely home.'

Lyle asked, 'Is this the first time you've been inside?'

Caitlin nodded. 'Yes, it is. It's very modern, not what I expected.'

He shook his head. 'Cora was right. She said I'd never invited you in and that I was rude. I can't believe that in all the time our girls have been friends this is the first time you've stepped foot inside. I'm really sorry. It hasn't been intentional.'

Caitlin waved a dismissive hand. 'Oh, don't worry. I don't think I've ever invited you into my home either. In fact, you've only ever come into the bakery to collect Cora.'

He chewed his lip and smiled. 'I might have had an ulterior motive there. Notice how I always sneak a wee bit of shortbread to eat in the car?'

Caitlin laughed. 'Ah, it was all about the baking.'

'Aye. You see when Fenella and I were together she was always complaining about my weight. She was a health nut and I'm not; probably why we split up really. So, your shortbread was my treat. My saving grace from all the salad. No pun intended.' He said with a wink and Caitlin felt herself blush again.

'Did I hear my name mentioned?' Grace asked as she appeared in the doorway with Cora.

Lyle grinned. 'Aye, I was just telling your mum how badly behaved you've both been.'

Cora gasped and whacked her dad's arm playfully. 'Don't listen to him, Miss Fraser. It's not true.'

He held up his hands. 'Okay, okay, you got me. They've been good as gold, Caitlin,' Lyle said with mock reluctance.

Grace eyed the mug that Caitlin was clutching. 'Ooh, Mum, if you're having a cuppa, can me and Cora go practise our dance really quickly, pleeeease?' she asked, tugging her mum's sleeve, and sticking out her bottom lip.

Caitlin glanced at Lyle, who nodded, so she told her daughter, 'Okay, but we're going as soon as I've drunk my tea. I need to get home to sort tomorrow's baking out.'

Grace and Cora squealed and disappeared back in the direction they had arrived from.

'You've made their day,' Lyle said with a smile.

'Aye, so it seems.' She sipped at her tea again. 'So, who's the interior designer then? You or Fenella?' It was a slightly strange question and one, with all the questions in her mind, she was baffled to find herself asking.

'That would be me, I'm afraid. I had the kitchen ripped out as soon as Fen left. We still lived together for a year after we separated, which was an absolute nightmare. Her in our bedroom and me in one of the spare rooms. She hogged the bloody kitchen and it drove me mad, so having it redone was kind of a poke in her eye, if you get me? It was always her domain, even though I'm a bloody good cook, if I say so myself. But my recipes were "too carb-loaded and high in bad fats",' he said in a mock whine.

Caitlin was shocked to hear how negative his ex-wife had been towards him. 'Pfft! Give me a pie and chips over salad any day.'

He nodded. 'Right? Life's too bloody short to worry about how you look in spandex.'

She grinned. 'Exactly. Well, I think you have very good taste. In décor, I mean. This kitchen is great. Very sleek.'

He grinned. 'Coming from someone who works in a kitchen for a living, I'll take that as a huge compliment. Cora says it reminds her of something off an American sitcom. She thinks it's too black and grey and blokey. But then again, her favourite colour is purple, and I refuse to live with a purple kitchen.'

Caitlin laughed. 'Spoilsport.' She glanced at her watch. 'Right, I should get going. Thanks for the tea.'

'My pleasure. I'll go shout for the girls.' He left the room and she heard him call up the stairs. When he returned, he said, 'Maybe I could cook you a meal in my sleek kitchen some time. Although don't expect lettuce and quinoa.'

Caitlin's stomach fluttered a little and she nodded. 'That would be lovely, thank you.'

He grinned. 'Great. I'll be in touch. Maybe we could make arrangements when I see you at the singles night?'

'Absolutely.' It felt bizarre, to say the least, to be discussing organising a potential date at a singles night they were both attending, but she pushed the thought away.

Grace walked back into the room with her bag. 'I'm ready. Wait 'til you see our routine, Mum. It'll blow your mind. We're thinking of performing it in the talent show at the Glentorrin Highland Games.'

Caitlin hugged Grace to her side. 'Can't wait. What do you say to Mr Budge?'

'Thanks, Mr Budge. I've had a lovely time. And your pizzas were really good.'

Lyle smiled widely and bowed. 'Why thank you, kind miss. And come back soon, won't you?'

'I will, thank you.'

Once back in the car, confusion clouded Caitlin's mind and she wondered if the semi-invite for a meal had been a simple, friendly gesture. Or perhaps he had thought she was hankering after an invite by talking about his kitchen.

Shit! I hope that's not it, Caitlin thought.

'I think Mr Budge likes you,' Grace announced, pulling Caitlin from her thoughts.

Her stomach flipped. 'Why? Has he said something?'

Grace smiled. 'Maybe.'

Caitlin laughed. 'Come on, out with it, you minx.'

'He said you're very pretty.'

Caitlin's heart skipped. 'Really? When did he say that?'

Grace shrugged. 'When I asked him if he thought you were pretty.'

She sighed. 'Oh, Grace, you didn't?'

'I did. I said, "Mr Budge don't you think my mum is really pretty?" And he said "Yes Grace. She really is."'

Caitlin couldn't really say she counted that compliment as being 100 per cent genuine. What was he going to say? 'Actually no, Grace, she's a total minger!' But she decided that things were certainly looking up.

And it was quite a nice feeling.

5

The following week was a busy one seeing as the fine weather had brought a rather large influx of tourists to Glentorrin. After leaving the shop looking and feeling frazzled at the end of each day, Caitlin resolved she would need to find another assistant now that her former one was on a gap year in America. Grace was still at school for another couple of weeks until she broke for summer at the end of June, and despite her volunteering to help when school was finished, she wasn't at an age where she could legally work yet. And in any case, Caitlin wanted her to simply enjoy her break from school.

Thursday came around far too quickly for Caitlin to handle. She had lost track of the days, which had all blurred into one.

After another busy day, she spotted the school bus pulling into the village as she served a lady with the last of the rocky road, and as the bus pulled away, Grace walked into the shop with a huge smile on her face.

'Muuum! Guess what?' she said giddily.

Caitlin waited until the customer had left the shop and shook her head. 'What's up, chick?'

'I was right! Mr Budge does like you!'

Caitlin's cheeks flushed and she couldn't help the smile that spread across her face. 'Oh? How do you know? Oh heck, you didn't ask him again, did you?' She sincerely hoped this wasn't the case.

'No, silly, I haven't seen him. But Cora said so!'

Caitlin's interest was piqued, but she tried not to sound too excited. 'Really? How come? I mean... what was said? How did she bring it up? Have they been talking about me?' *Ugh, well done Caitlin, sounding really chilled you are.*

Grace pointed a finger. 'Mum, you've gone all pink! You like him too, don't you? I knew it! I told Cora you did!'

Caitlin covered her eyes with one hand. 'Grace, you really are going to have to learn that some things should be kept to yourself.'

'But why? If you both like each other, then you can get married, and Cora can be my sister!'

Caitlin held up her hands and gave a nervous laugh. 'Whoa! Hold your horses there, girlie. He hasn't even asked me out yet.'

Grace pondered this for a moment. 'Why don't you ask him out? I mean, it is the twenty-first century, you know, not the olden days. You are a strong, independent woman, I heard you telling Jules and Ruby that once when you were drinking wine... or it might have been Ruby who said it... But anyway, maybe you should put your pants on and go ask him out.'

Caitlin glanced down at her jeans. 'Put my pants on? My pants are on, I can assure you.'

Grace sighed. 'It's a saying, Mum. Haven't you heard it? You put your pants on and get on with it.'

'Oh! You mean put on my big-girl pants.'

Grace scrunched her face. 'That's what I said, durr! Anyway, I've got history homework. I can't believe they're bothering to give us homework when it's nearly the holidays. Those teachers insist on ruining our lives.' She huffed.

Ignoring her dramatic comment, Caitlin said, 'Okay, sweetheart, I won't be too much longer. I think I'll have to close early today. Hardly anything left. Oh, and Cleo is in the garden. She was asleep under the table last I checked, bless her wee heart. Is spag bol okay for dinner?'

Grace's eyes lit up. 'Can we have gelato for afters? It is Italian, so it goes.'

'Aye, go on. I think there's still some in the freezer.'

Grace had become obsessed with gelato after Ruby told them all about it when she was first in Glentorrin after spending some time in Sicily. And now they had to buy some, every time they did their weekly shop.

Grace disappeared through into the house and Caitlin began to check what stock she had left.

'Hi, Caitlin,' Archie said as he walked into the shop.

'Oh, hi, Archie. How are you?'

'I'm grand, aye, thanks. I'm needing some rolls if you've any left. I'm barbecuing tonight, seeing as the weather's so good.'

'That sounds like a good plan.' She checked the bread baskets. 'I've only a couple of wholemeal left, if that's any good?'

Archie smiled and nodded. 'Oh aye, that's fine.'

Caitlin eyed him for a moment, thinking back to the conversation with Ruby and Jules. When she looked at him now, she did so through fresh eyes. He was an attractive man, if you liked that rough-and-ready type, which, of course, she didn't, at all.

Realising she was staring, and that Archie was looking somewhat confused, she packed up the bread rolls into a paper bag and rang them through the till.

Archie handed over the correct change and turned to leave but stopped. 'Oh, erm, if you're still interested in the speed dating thing, it's starting at eight on Saturday night. I can pick you up if you fancy it.'

Caitlin was about to answer with a thanks-but-no-thanks when Grace chimed in, 'Ooh yes, Mum, you need to go to that. Mr Budge is going, and he told Cora that he's going to see you there.'

Caitlin swung around and scowled at her daughter. 'I thought you were doing homework, madam?'

Grace blushed and chewed her lip. 'I am. I just... erm... I heard Archie and...'

'Go and get your history done,' Caitlin pointed to the doorway before turning back to face Archie. 'Thanks, Archie, that would be great.'

Archie nodded. 'Grand. I'll pick you up at twenty to. We don't want to be too early, eh? Although it sounds like you've no need to be going really.' He winked.

Caitlin waved her hand. 'Oh, take no notice. Kids gossiping at school, that's all.'

'Aye, right enough.' His wry smile told her he wasn't convinced. 'Well, I'll get back to my burgers. See you later.' He raised a hand and waved as he left.

Caitlin watched him leave and sighed. 'What have I got myself into this time?' she asked aloud. 'I just hope it's not as bad as the last one.'

* * *

After dinner, Caitlin and Grace were watching reruns of *Friends* on TV and eating their gelato as Cleo stared hopefully at them each in turn.

'So... What exactly did Cora say that made you think Mr Budge likes me?' It had been preying on her mind all evening and she had eventually given in to curiosity.

Grace turned in her seat to face her mum. 'Oh... right, so Cora said that when we had gone the other day, he said that you made him laugh and that you were common.'

Caitlin gasped. 'Excuse me?'

'You know, you like the same kinds of things. You're both common.'

Caitlin stifled a laugh. 'I think you mean we have things in common.'

Grace pursed her lips. 'Oh yeah, that might have been it.'

'I certainly hope it was,' Caitlin mumbled.

'Her mum was a right crabbit wee woman you know,' Grace informed her.

'You probably shouldn't say things like that about your best friend's mum, Gracie.'

'No, it's okay. Cora says it too. That's why she lives with her dad. Her mum was always talking about people getting fat, and she wouldn't let Cora, or her dad, have cakes and stuff. They were banned from the house! Can you believe it? She was obsessed, I think.'

Caitlin agreed but didn't want to voice that opinion. 'Everyone's different though, love. Each has their own priorities.'

'Yeah, and Mrs Budge's was to make her family miserable. Do you know what she used to buy Cora for Easter?'

'Go on?'

'You'll not believe it,' Grace said dramatically.

'Is it that bad?'

'Nuts and seeds! Like she's a bird or something. I mean, if you bought me nuts and seeds for Easter, I'd be ringing Childline.'

Caitlin laughed. 'That's not really a reason to ring Childline.'

'Well, the newspaper then! Who wants nuts and seeds for Easter?'

Caitlin smirked. 'Fair point.'

'So do you think you might get married?' Grace's question was, as always, out of left field.

'I'd have to find someone to marry first, love.'

'I meant to Mr Budge.'

Caitlin sighed. 'I think you need to slow down, missy. He hasn't... I mean, neither of us have asked the other out yet. And that might not even happen. And even if it did, marriage isn't something you decide on after a few dates, you know? It takes a long time to get to know someone.'

Grace rolled her eyes. 'Boring! Shall I make a cuppa?'

Caitlin was relieved that the conversation appeared to be over. 'That'd be fab, thanks, sweetheart.'

* * *

Once Grace was tucked up in bed with her book, Caitlin took a glass of well-earned wine into the garden. The sun was setting, rendering the sky a golden, orangey pink and she sat at the table with Cleo on her lap. From the kitchen, the local radio station's weather forecaster predicted a sunny weekend ahead, which pleased Caitlin. She had Sunday off and thought it might be nice to take Grace somewhere for a picnic. Perhaps she'd pack some nuts and seeds as a joke.

Her mind drifted to Lyle Budge and his eyes that crinkled when he smiled. She guessed he was probably around five years her senior but had no clue what he did for a living. She'd have to do a little digging. Although she was still unsure if what Grace and Cora had decided between them was actual fact or just wishful thinking on their parts. She'd always thought he was an attractive man, but now that he was single...

'What do you think about marriage, Cleo? Can you imagine me in a white frock at a church?'

Cleo sneezed.

'Aye, I thought as much.'

Caitlin's phone pinged with a text message, and she picked it up, expecting to see a message from Jules. Instead, it was from Archie. She'd completely forgotten he had her number from the time he repaired her laptop. She tapped on the screen.

Hi Caitlin. I just wanted to say your rolls are huge and totally amazing, Archie.

She thought it was nice of him to say so. As she took another sip of her wine another text followed.

I meant your bread rolls. I wasn't insinuating you're fat!

Caitlin stared at the screen and snort-laughed, almost choking on her drink. She hit reply.

That's a relief. Although I actually understood your first message!

She placed her phone down when another text pinged through.

Good! You probably think that I do think you have rolls now that I mentioned fat! I always put my foot in it! Sorry! Anyway, just to clarify, I think you have a very nice figure.

Caitlin widened her eyes, surprised at his response and wasn't quite sure how to reply. 'I think someone's had a few beers, Cleo.' Luckily, or unluckily, depending on which way you look at it, he beat her to it.

Shit! I hit send and then read what I'd said. I wasn't meaning to be flirty or forward or anything by talking about your figure. I've had a few beers. My apologies.

Caitlin giggled and said aloud, 'That figures.' She imagined him in his garden, phone in one hand, bottle of beer in the other, cursing himself for his messages, smacking his forehead with his palm, and the reason he was single became very obvious. *If he's this awkward around women, there's no wonder.*

She hit reply.

Honestly, it's fine! I'm glad you enjoyed the rolls.

6

Friday started off much the same as the rest of the week, and by lunchtime, Caitlin was ready for a nap. Jules' brother and Caitlin's drinking buddy, Dexter, had texted again, this time to tell her he'd visited a distillery. By her count, this was probably the third of his trip. He was in his element all right. He deserved the holiday after he'd worked nonstop for Archie since relocating to the village, following in his sister's footsteps, a year before. Dexter and Jules had always been close, so when she settled in Glentorrin permanently he followed soon after.

Ruby appeared in the doorway just as Caitlin had stuffed a piece of lemon cake, aka lunch, in her mouth. 'Yikes, someone looks frazzled.'

Caitlin gulped down the sticky, citrus-drizzled confection and wiped her forehead with the back of her hand, then blew upwards towards her fringe. 'That's not surprising, seeing as it's exactly how I feel.'

'I just popped in for a loaf, but can I help at all? I've been watching the queues. It's been manic in the village today.'

She was right. Between the bakery and the café – Tea for Two –

next door, run by the village co-op, they must have sold a hundred-weight in food.

'Thanks, Roo, but I can't ask you to give up your day. And, to be honest, I think I'll have to close early again. I made extra of everything, but I'm still running low. And because the café has been so busy, I've had a mad run on takeaway sandwiches, so I've not much salad left.'

Ruby stepped closer to the counter. 'Look, all I'm doing is working on my dance teaching portfolio for college, so the break from that will do me good. Honestly, I'm happy to help, tomorrow too. Just say the word.'

'Actually… there is something you could do for me this weekend. Unless you have Saturday evening plans? Please feel free to say no.'

Ruby shook her head. 'Nothing at all planned. Mitch is up in Edinburgh from tonight. He has a business dinner for one of his housing charities and I asked if he minded me staying home. I'm not quite ready to do public functions like that. I don't want to take the focus off Mitch's charity, and if I'm there, the press will focus too much on me and why I'm not in Hollywood or New York.'

Caitlin nodded. 'Aye, it's not so long since you were the guest of honour at such events, eh? Although I reckon Hollywood has to be more glamorous than Edinburgh.'

'I'll admit, glamour's nice sometimes. It's exciting to dress up all fancy every so often, but when it's as regular as it was for me at one point, it loses its shine. Give me a night in and a chick flick any day, as long as it's not one I starred in.' Ruby laughed. 'So, how can I help?'

Caitlin felt heat rising in her cheeks. 'There's this speed dating event in Kyle of Lochalsh and I wondered—'

'If I could stay with Grace for the evening until you get back? Absolutely. She mentioned she had a dance routine to show me anyway when I saw her yesterday after school so this would be a perfect opportunity.'

Caitlin smiled. 'You're a star... literally! But in this case figuratively too and I'm incredibly grateful. Jules and Reid are taking Evin to the cinema to see the new Avengers movie, and Grace isn't into them so...'

'No problem at all. What time should I be here?'

'Archie is picking me up at twenty to eight, so any time just before that will be fine. I'll leave you something nice to have with a cuppa. And I'll make some pizza bases so you can put whatever toppings on that you fancy.'

'Yum! Can't wait. Now, are you sure you don't need any help this afternoon?'

Caitlin glanced over Ruby's shoulder and watched as a coach pulled into the village. 'How are you with making sandwiches?'

Ruby grinned. 'I'm a flipping expert. I was a penniless student once, you know. Lived on them!' she said as she removed a hair tie from her wrist and proceeded to swirl her hair into a neat bun atop her head.

'Fantastic, come on through and I'll show you where everything is.'

* * *

By the time Grace arrived home, Ruby was taking off her apron and washing her hands, and Caitlin had turned the sign to its closed side. She opened the door for her daughter.

'Wow, Mum, another sell-out day?'

Caitlin nodded. 'Yup. I managed to save you a gingerbread man though.'

'Yay! Oh, hi, Ruby! Have you been helping Mum today?'

Ruby walked into the shop from the preparation room in the back. 'I sure have. It's been hectic but great fun.'

Grace pursed her lips. 'I bet she's not bossy when you're helping, is she?'

Caitlin laughed. 'Oy, cheeky wee mare, I'm not bossy when you help me, either.'

Ruby grinned. 'I think the key is to keep her stocked up on cups of tea, Grace.' She winked. 'Oh, hey, I'm coming to stay with you for a bit tomorrow night while your mum goes out. You can show me your dance routine if you like.'

Grace jumped up and down and clapped her hands. 'Great! I can't wait to show you, it's awesome. But you might be able to add some cool moves to it. We're going for a street dance and tap mash-up.'

'Wow, that sounds different. I'm looking forward to seeing it. Do you want to look for a film for us to watch too? I'll bring some nuts and seeds for us to snack on.'

Grace's eyes widened in horror. 'But...'

Ruby burst out laughing and Caitlin joined in.

Grace realised what was going on. 'Mum told you about Cora's mum, didn't she?'

Ruby shrugged and played innocent. 'I couldn't possibly comment.'

Grace huffed in mock indignance. 'If you do bring nuts and seeds, I'll lock you out!'

Ruby laughed heartily. 'Ah, okay, noted, chocolate and popcorn it is then.'

'That's more like it. Right, I'm off to see Cleo, bye Ruby. See you tomorrow.'

'Bye, Grace.' Once Grace had disappeared through to the house, Ruby walked towards the door. 'The back's all cleaned up, so I'll be off if there's nothing else you need.'

Caitlin walked over and hugged her friend. 'Thanks so much for this afternoon. That influx of people would've floored me if you hadn't been here.'

'My pleasure. And I know you've said you're looking for an assistant, but if you need help in the meantime, just let me know.'

Caitlin laughed. 'I'd be careful if I were you. I might just take you up on that.'

* * *

Saturday was a little quieter and Caitlin presumed it was mainly down to it being a changeover day for holidaymakers, but nevertheless, it was a welcome relief. As the day wore on, she became increasingly anxious and a little excited about the singles night. After the last one, she was wondering if perhaps this app that Grace had mentioned might be a good idea after all. But there was the chance that Lyle would be there. Although she still wondered why he hadn't just asked her out. Perhaps, she decided, Grace was right in this matter, too, and that she should do the modern thing and ask him out. She figured she would see what happened tonight and if she felt their attraction was mutual, she would take the brave step and go for it. She had nothing to lose... except maybe a little pride...

Ruby arrived early, which was a relief. Caitlin was standing in her bedroom surrounded by at least four discarded tops, three skirts and five pairs of trousers.

'Ugh! I have nothing to wear, Roo!'

Ruby laughed as she glanced down at the piles of potential outfits. 'I think maybe you have. Look at all this stuff. You've some gorgeous things here.' She walked to the wardrobe and slipped the hangers along the metal rail until she came across a pretty, green, flowery sundress. 'What about this? It'll look amazing with your hair, and I've never seen you wear it. Stick your denim jacket on with it and some flats, jobs a good 'un.' She said in her Yorkshire accent and shrugged. 'Casual, summery, perfect.'

Caitlin tilted her head and pursed her lips. 'You think so? Is it dressed-up enough?'

Ruby eyed her with suspicion. 'Are you trying to impress someone, Caitlin Fraser?'

Caitlin's cheeks heated and she made an awkward noise. 'Pfft, nah, what do you mean? Who could I be trying to impress?'

Ruby grinned. 'A certain local outdoor-gear shop owner-cum-IT whizz?'

Caitlin burst out laughing. 'Archie? Seriously you and Jules are really intent on flogging that dead horse, aren't you?'

'Well, who then?'

Caitlin shrugged. 'I don't know... Cora's dad, Lyle, might be there...' She grabbed the dress from Ruby and turned her back, knowing full well that her eagerness would be plastered all over her cerise face.

'Oooh, I see now! Well, I think this dress would look fab on you. And he can't fail to fancy you in it. Trust me. Go on, get it tried on.'

Caitlin took the dress to the bathroom and stepped into it. Her fellow redhead, Ruby, was right. The green really did look great with her hair, and it was perfect for the warm evening. She walked back into the bedroom.

'Wow! You really do look gorgeous. Now go get your hair sorted and I'll see what Grace is up to.'

Caitlin curled the ends of her long hair and applied a little lip gloss and blusher. She assessed herself in the full-length mirror in her room and huffed. 'Ah, you'll do.'

When she got down to the kitchen, Ruby and Grace were adding toppings to the pre-prepared pizza bases and chatting comfortably.

'Mum, you look lovely! I think Mr Budge's jaw will hit the floor when he sees you.'

Caitlin made that awkward scoffing noise again. 'Pfft! Come on, you two are having a laugh, aren't you?'

Ruby raised her eyebrows and fixed her with a stern stare. 'Learn to take a compliment, will you? You look gorgeous.'

Taking compliments was something Caitlin wasn't that used to, so it felt awkward, and accepting them made her feel somewhat conceited. 'Aye... well thank you,' she replied begrudgingly.

There was a knock at the door and Caitlin went to open it.

Before her stood a ruffle-haired Archie, complete with a few days' old stubble and wearing dark jeans and a pale blue shirt with the sleeves rolled up to the elbows.

'Hi, Archie.'

He smiled warmly. 'W-wow... you look... you look really nice.' His cheeks flushed a little and he cleared his throat. 'Shall I wait in the car?'

Caitlin caught sight of Ruby and Grace watching their interaction and stuck out her tongue at them, causing them both to giggle. 'No, it's fine. I'm all ready.' She walked over and grabbed her handbag from the countertop and kissed Grace's head. 'Be good. And don't wear Ruby out.'

'I won't. I'm going to show her my dance routine while the pizzas cook. Have fun. And say "hi" to Mr Budge for me.' She giggled again.

'Aye, I will. Bye, Ruby, thanks again.' She waved and closed the door behind her.

Once she was settled in Archie's four-wheel-drive Land Rover, he set off towards Kyle of Lochalsh. He turned briefly to glance at her. 'You have such a great relationship with Grace,' he said out of the blue.

'Aw, do you think so? Thank you.'

'Aye. It's clear that you adore each other.'

She smiled. 'Well, that's one thing I'm certain of. She made my life complete.'

'Can I... Can I ask you something personal?'

Caitlin frowned and for some reason her tummy flipped as she wondered what on earth he was going to ask. 'Erm... Sure, I suppose so.'

'What happened to Grace's dad?'

'Oof... go for the jugular, eh?'

He winced and scrunched his nose. 'Sorry. You don't have to answer. It's none of my business. I'm just curious why you're not still together, that's all.'

Caitlin inhaled a long, deep breath as she readied herself to tell the story that very few people knew. She was in no way ashamed of her decision, but there were not many that could understand the route she took to parenthood. 'I never actually met him.'

In her periphery, she saw Archie's brow crumple. 'But... how...?'

'I was twenty-eight, I wanted a baby but wasn't with anyone. In fact, there hadn't been anyone for a while and certainly not anyone who was parent material in my opinion. I decided I didn't need a man in my life anyway. So... I went to a sperm-donation clinic.'

His eyes widened, but he kept his gaze fixed on the road. 'Really? Wow. I had no idea.'

'It's not really the type of thing I tell people.' She shrugged and turned her gaze to the scenery outside the window, awaiting the string of questions that would no doubt follow: *Why didn't you just wait? What about the poor girl not knowing her father? Don't you think it was selfish? Does she know how she came about? What about her future health, illnesses, and such? What if she needs a kidney and you're not compatible?*

When none of them came, she turned her attention back to Archie again. 'Go on, ask me.'

He shook his head. 'Ask you what?'

She narrowed her eyes. 'People always have questions when they find out.'

Archie glanced at her again. 'I don't. In fact, I think what you did was incredibly brave.'

She was shocked by his reaction. 'Some say I played God. I was selfish. That Grace deserves a father or at least to know who hers is.'

Archie unexpectedly pulled the car to a halt in a lay-by just after the Skye Bridge and turned to face her. 'Those people, the ones who ask those types of questions, clearly don't understand. But I think what you did was right for you, so it's no one else's business. You're a fantastic mum, it's completely evident, and Grace is clearly lacking nothing. What would that information do for her?' He shrugged.

In spite of his reaction, Caitlin felt herself knotting up inside. She folded her arms across her chest, a defensive action, she knew, but she couldn't help it. 'I don't know... that knowing her father would give her a sense of who she really is, I suppose. Well, that's what people say anyway.'

He shook his head. 'I disagree. I know who my father is. A right waste of space, as far as parenting is concerned, let me tell you. He was hardly around when I was growing up and when he was there, he was a little too eager with the old fists and belt. So, what good did knowing him do for me? Apart from it confirming how I didn't want to turn out. But Grace...' He smiled. 'Grace is surrounded by love. She's cared for. She's looked after. She knows very well who she is, Caitlin. She's your daughter and she's her own person. I say good on you. There are so many folks in this world who don't deserve the kids they've been blessed with. So, you tell me which child is happier? The child of a single-parent family who knows they're secure, they're a priority, that no harm will come to them, or the one who lives their life with two parents knowing that, really, they weren't wanted at all by one of them in the first place?'

Caitlin felt a lump forming in her throat. After all the years of knowing Archie, this was the most in-depth conversation they'd ever had. The most honest too.

She cleared her throat to try to dislodge the emotion restricting it. 'I'm... I'm so sorry you went through that, Archie. I had no idea.'

'Aye, well like you, I suppose, it's not the type of thing I usually tell people. But in this case, it felt quite pertinent.' He sighed. 'Look, I'm sorry for being nosey. But this has really made me understand you. I know we've been more like acquaintances over the years, so we don't really know one another properly. I made assumptions about you, and I was wrong. So far off the mark, in fact. But now I feel I really know more about who you are. And that's kind of nice. It's like the foundation of a real friendship is forming.' When she didn't speak, he pulled a face. 'God, that was all a bit deep, wasn't it? I'm not usually like that, all profound and such. But... I don't know... I think it's good to have friends. Real friends who we can be totally ourselves with.'

Caitlin wasn't sure how to respond. All she knew was that her respect for the man had grown in a matter of minutes. 'You're right. It is. Thank you for sharing that with me, Archie.'

'Thank you too. And hey, I really didn't mean to put a downer on things.' He grimaced, then smiled. 'I think I'm an expert at crappy timing.'

'No, it's fine. You haven't.' She assured him.

He turned back to face the front and started the engine. 'Right, let's go, eh?'

After a few minutes of silence, curiosity got the better of Caitlin. 'So... do you think you'll ever have kids?'

Archie smiled, but there was a hint of something in his expression that she couldn't quite decipher. 'I don't know. I think I'm getting a bit old and set in my ways to be honest.'

Caitlin laughed lightly. 'Don't be daft. And you're a man. You can father children into your old age.'

He scrunched his brow and laughed too. 'Aye, but who wants a wrinkly old dobber for a dad?'

'Archie, you're still bloody young. You've got plenty of time.'

He shook his head. 'Got to meet someone to have a child with first. I'm not as brave as you.'

That was fair enough, although she didn't see herself as brave. She saw herself as more of a coward. At twenty-eight, she'd feared that meeting the right man wasn't going to happen and wasn't willing to wait just in case she was right.

He went quiet again for a few moments and then said, 'I'd love to think that in a few years, I'll be settled down with a nice woman who wants to have kids with me, but... I don't know. I don't seem to attract the type of women who want that kind of thing. And I'm at an age where I'm not really interested in flings. That's why I'm still single. Who knows, tonight could be the night we both meet our true love. Fingers crossed, eh?'

7

At a couple of minutes past eight o'clock, Archie pushed open the door to the bar of the Kyle Hotel and they walked inside. The room was lively with people chatting and Caitlin glanced around, scanning the room for Lyle. There was no sign of him, which was disappointing.

At ten past eight, a woman spoke over the sound system in a very nasal voice. 'Good evening, ladies and gentlemen. My name is Monica and I'm the MD of Two's Company Events and I'd like to welcome you to this event at the Kyle Hotel, and to say thank you to our gracious hosts.'

Caitlin turned to face the woman who was heavily made up and wearing a dress that only just appeared to be containing her huge breasts.

'For those of you who are not familiar with us, my company runs singles nights all over Scotland and we have been very successful in pairing off many a happy couple. I've been to plenty of weddings.' She laughed humourlessly. 'I'm usually dedicated to my local area of Edinburgh, but we have a host off on sick leave at the moment, so here I am, you're welcome.' She held her hand out and did a little curtsey as if expecting applause. When none came, she continued. 'Ahem... You should all have a sticker to pop your name on, or your nickname if that's how you prefer to be addressed, so please do that before the event begins. Please refrain from fake names such as Lance Lyde, Ben Dover and Ivana Tinkle though. No one finds that funny.'

I do, thought Caitlin as she stifled a nervous giggle.

'Tonight, is a little different to our usual singles events, ladies and gentlemen, as this is speed... dating.' She emphasised her words with a wag of her fingers as she nodded and glanced around the crowd in quite a condescending manner. It was as if she thought they were not aware of what they had walked into and perhaps needed a moment to acclimatise or, indeed, leave. 'So, how this will work... We have lined up rows of tables where the women will sit. Each man will come and take a seat for four minutes and you'll chat and get to know each other...'

Archie leaned to Caitlin and whispered, 'Before tonight I'd have said it's not possible to get to know someone in four minutes, but now...' He grinned.

Caitlin looked up at him and smiled. He was right. They had found out the most fundamental things about each other in a matter of a few minutes on their short journey. 'I don't suppose there's any point you coming to my table now, eh?' she replied and giggled, but as soon as the words had left her mouth, she realised how bad they had, unintentionally, sounded. 'Ooh, I didn't mean—'

'Sorry, love, you with the ginger hair, I need your full attention, or you won't know what to do,' Monica, the host, said, pointing a long, red-painted nail directly at Caitlin and giving a snide smile.

Caitlin wanted the tartan carpet to open up and swallow her yet again as she felt her face turning furnace-hot as all heads spun towards her. 'Sorry,' she said just above a whisper. *Bloody hell, is it*

possible for me to not make a spectacle of myself at one of these things?
she thought.

'As I was saying, when the buzzer sounds, gents, you must move
on to the next waiting date, and so on, and so on. In a moment, I'll
ask all you lovely ladies to take a seat and your first gentleman
caller will join you. And remember, this is very important, when
you hear the buzzer, your time with that person is up, and you must
move on to the next table.' *Or else you will grow a second head and
possibly horns too...* Caitlin's mind mocked the orange-hued woman.
'At the end of the event, there will be a sixty-minute window where
you can approach anyone you're particularly interested in and see if
the feeling is mutual. All we ask is that you behave with respect,
and if a certain person takes your fancy, please feel free to swap
mobile numbers or email addresses. Please enjoy the event and
remember, two really is company. Thank you.' Again, she did a little
curtsey and again no applause followed.

A few moments later, Monica announced, 'Ladies, please take
your seats. Gentlemen, line up ready. When the buzzer sounds,
gentlemen, take your seat at the tables, making sure to leave no
gaps. We ask that you don't head directly for someone who has
caught your eye. Every one of our lovely ladies deserves a fair
chance.'

Caitlin was beginning to think she had signed up for a string of
job interviews instead of the chance to meet a potential life partner.
'Good luck,' she said to Archie as she turned to take the closest seat.

'Aye, you too,' he replied just as the first buzzer sounded.

* * *

'So, I'm ready to move out of my mother's and find a good woman to
look after me,' Reginald, Caitlin's third disastrous date, told her. He
had badly dyed black hair that held so much styling product it was

a wonder he could lift his head. And whatever aftershave he was wearing could've been used to fell lions ready for surgery. And that's before she considered his outfit, which was clearly straight out of a men's fashion magazine for twenty-somethings. *What was wrong with growing old gracefully? And why on earth had he told her he was forty-eight when he was clearly in his late fifties?* He was just ending a very long monologue where she had discovered all his mother's ailments and how she loved to potter in their small, but pretty garden. She'd learned that the woman's favourite singer was Engelbert Humperdinck but that she loved a male voice choir too. To be fair, she sounded like a pleasant enough woman but not the kind of person who needed a date, even though Caitlin felt like Reginald was trying to set *her* up rather than himself.

Buzzz! 'Ah, time's up, I'm afraid,' Caitlin said with no small amount of relief.

'I feel like we made a real connection. I'll find you afterwards,' Reginald informed her before he stood to leave her table.

Great, she thought.

'Now then, madam, how are you this fine evening? I'm Archie Sutherland, pleased to make your acquaintance,' Archie grinned as he held out his hand.

Caitlin rolled her eyes. 'Thank goodness it's you. I don't think I can take any more of this.'

Archie blanched. 'That bad, eh?'

She glanced around to make sure no one was listening in. 'It's worse. I've had the divorcee who couldn't stop talking about how his wife had ruined his libido, the funeral-parlour-owning career man who thinks it's about time he found someone to have kids with because "apparently that's what you do at fifty-eight". Fifty-eight, Archie. I'm forty, for goodness' sake. I know I'm no spring chicken, but bloody hell.' Archie smirked and shook his head. 'Oh, you think that's funny? Well, then there was Mr I-still-live-with-my-mother who wants someone to replace her and look after him.'

'Jeez, you really have had a disastrous evening, eh?'

'You could say that. How about you?'

Archie nodded. 'Not as bad as you, thankfully. I met a lovely lady from Balmacara. Divorced, no kids, thirty-five. Quite pretty. I think I might ask for her number at the end.'

'Wow, that's brilliant.' Buzzz!

'Och, that's me. See you later.'

Caitlin huffed. 'If I haven't run out and dived off a cliff.'

Archie laughed. 'Don't do that. This next one's it, I can feel it in my bones.' He winked as he headed off under the stern gaze of Monica, who was patrolling like some kind of prison guard at visiting time.

'Hi, I'm Lyle, what's your name?'

Caitlin gazed up into the clear, blue, smiling eyes of the person who could possibly be her dream man. 'Lyle! How lovely to see you. And how grateful I am.' He looked delectable in black jeans and a light grey shirt. His beard was neatly trimmed, and he smelled amazing – all fresh linen and spicy shower gel.

He smiled as he took the seat opposite her. 'Don't tell me, you've had as bad a night as I have?'

Caitlin gasped. 'Not you too?'

'Oh yes. I've been likened to Paul Hollywood by every woman I've met. Have you heard anything so ridiculous? I look nothing like him.'

Caitlin scrunched her brow. 'Pfft! Utter craziness! I can't see it myself at all,' she lied.

'I know. Bizarre, eh? I wish I had his money though.' He chuckled. 'I thought there'd have been a specific age range on this event seeing as I don't fancy dating my grandma. I don't know about you, but I think some of these attendees have been a little economical with the truth.'

She giggled. 'I totally agree. I don't fancy being a womb to rent for the guy who told me, "I'm a good catch. I own my own chain of funeral parlours, but I'm ready to have children now I'm fifty-eight. I'm looking for a woman with childbearing hips,"' she said in a mock deep, monotone voice.

Lyle's eyes widened. 'Shit! He really said that?'

Caitlin nodded; her lips pursed. 'Oh, he certainly did.'

'I bet that app is looking more appealing now, eh?'

Caitlin laughed out loud. 'You read my mind! I was just thinking that very thing earlier.'

He paused for a moment and leaned closer. 'Look… I don't know why I didn't do this before but—'

Buzzz!

'Dammit. Look, I'll find you at the end, okay? Better go before the Oompa Loompa in heels comes for me.'

Caitlin almost choked on her drink at his comment. 'See you later,' she sputtered as butterflies took flight in her stomach. She knew he was going to ask her out now. Maybe Archie had been right. She hoped his evening was going as well as hers was now.

'So? Did you get her number?' Caitlin asked as Archie arrived beside her at the end of the event. She'd been waiting for Lyle, who had started across the room towards her five minutes earlier but had been stopped by at least four women already.

'Aye, that I did. Her name is Rosabeth. Quite nice really. I think I'll ask her on a date.'

Caitlin smiled. 'That's brilliant, Archie.'

'How about you?' he asked.

'Well... I think I may have clicked with someone too.'

Archie chuckled. 'Let me guess, Mr Death? No... no... Mammy's boy?'

She whacked his arm playfully. 'Neither, thank you! No, I think Grace's friend's dad might be about to ask me out.'

Archie glanced over in the direction her attention was focused. 'Ooh, the Paul Hollywood lookalike? Good work.'

Caitlin leaned closer. 'If he comes over, please, whatever you do, don't mention the Paul Hollywood thing. He seems to be quite insulted by it.'

Archie scrunched his brow and nodded. 'Aye, all right. Wouldnae mind being a pound behind the bloke though, eh?'

As Archie finished speaking, Lyle finally made it across the room. 'Evening folks. How are you doing?' He eyed Archie suspiciously.

'Lyle, this is Archie, my friend from Glentorrin. He gave me a lift tonight.'

A look of relief crossed Lyle's features as he held out his hand. 'Ah, good to meet you, Archie. Any luck this evening?'

Archie nodded. 'Aye, I got the number of a very sweet lassie. In fact, I can see her over there, so I might go over and say goodnight.' He winked at Caitlin and left the two of them alone.

Caitlin smiled up at Lyle. 'So... how's it gone?'

Lyle sucked air in through his teeth and shook his head. 'There's only one woman that I'm in the slightest bit interested in. But I'm worried she may have found a date already.' He looked despondent and her heart sank. Too late again.

'That's a shame,' she said, trying to hide her disappointment.

He nodded. 'Aye, she had a very tempting offer of a life as a funeral director's wife. I think it was the childbearing hips comment that snagged her.' His eyes glinted and Caitlin realised what he was saying.

She burst out laughing. 'Well, that does sound like a tempting offer. You can hardly blame her, can you?'

He shook his head. 'Not really. I mean... who am I but a mere doppelganger for Paul Hollywood?'

Caitlin couldn't help the huge smile that spread across her face. 'I quite like him on *Bake Off*.'

'So... what do you say, Miss Fraser? Do you fancy a night out with an ageing financial director?'

She narrowed her eyes. 'I did wonder what your occupation was.'

He leaned closer and whispered conspiratorially, 'Aye, well my daughter assures me that no one wants to date a plain old, boring accountant so...' He shrugged.

Her heart skipped a little and she chewed her lip, trying to stop herself from grinning like an idiot. 'Oh, I don't know. I think I'd be happy to go on a date with an accountant... or a financial director for that matter.'

His eyes lit up. 'You would? That's grand. Shall we say next Saturday, and I'll cook?'

'That would be lovely, thank you.'

'Great. Although, don't expect Paul Hollywood standards, eh?'

She nodded. 'Noted.'

'I've got your mobile number. Cora got it from Grace.' He laughed. 'Kids, eh? Well, I'd better get going. My neighbour's staying with Cora just now and I don't want to be too late.'

'Yes, I'm the same. My friend is with Grace.'

'I'll be in touch.' He leaned forward and kissed her cheek, his fresh-scented aftershave once again clouding her senses, and she closed her eyes for a brief second to revel in it. He paused for a moment. 'Actually, I don't think I can wait until Saturday. Can I call you before that and we could go for a drink at the Coxswain in Glentorrin, maybe?'

Caitlin's heart skipped again. 'I'd like that very much.'

He smiled and his eyes crinkled at the corners. 'I'll look forward to that.'

'Me too. Bye, Lyle.'

When Lyle had left, Archie wandered back over and smiled warmly at Caitlin. 'Am I to presume that your evening didn't end up so bad after all?'

Caitlin chewed her bottom lip again, trying to stop the giveaway smile, but it was a futile action. 'You could say that.'

'All's well that ends well, eh?'

'Absolutely. Now can we get out of here please? I'm dying for a cup of tea.'

Archie laughed. 'Sounds like a good plan to me.'

* * *

'She's been as good as gold,' Ruby said when Caitlin arrived home. 'She's just gone to bed to read. So, how did your night go? Any fishes biting?'

Caitlin beamed. 'I think I may have finally met the perfect man. He's quite handsome, he's a dad, so he understands pre-teens, he has a good, stable job and he doesn't live a million miles away.'

'Ah, so Cora and Grace may get to be sisters?' Ruby asked with a knowing smile.

Caitlin rolled her eyes. 'Ugh, has Grace been filling you in on the details?'

Ruby made a zipping motion across her mouth.

Caitlin laughed. 'It's like being in that movie *Parent Trap* with those two girls. They keep trying to push us together, and they've been discussing the kind of wedding we should have. Talk about jumping the gun. We haven't even been on a date yet.' Her insides flipped with giddy excitement at the thought of an actual date with Lyle.

'It's sweet though and at least you don't have to worry about getting along with Cora or about the girls liking each other.'

'Very true, I suppose. Got time for a cuppa before you go?'

Ruby grinned. 'It would be rude not to. And I want to hear more about this dream man.'

'Right, I'd better put the kettle on then.'

8

Caitlin was in the garden singing along to the radio the following morning when Grace came out, closely followed by Cleo.

'You're in a good mood, Mum.'

Caitlin turned to her daughter. 'I am, lovey. What do you fancy doing today?'

'Aren't you going to tell me how things went last night?'

Caitlin knew for a fact that the girls would have already been talking nonstop about it. 'Nothing to tell.'

Grace folded her arms across her chest. 'I don't believe that at all. Cora says her dad asked you out.'

Caitlin laughed out loud. 'So, you don't need me to tell you then!'

Grace grinned. 'I wanted to hear your side.'

Caitlin ruffled her hair. 'Well, just as Cora said, Lyle, Mr Budge, asked me out. He's cooking for me next Saturday, but he mentioned he might contact me about going for a drink at the Coxswain in the week too.'

Grace clapped her hands together giddily. 'Oooh, Mum, I think he really, really likes you.'

'Well, let's not run before we can walk, okay? I don't want to get your hopes up. Just because two people like each other, it doesn't mean they're going to get married and live happily ever after.'

Grace pondered this for a moment. 'Well, duh! Obvs. But... if you do get married, can me and Cora be bridesmaids? And can we wear violet dresses? Pink is too babyish and we're almost thirteen now.'

Caitlin burst out laughing. 'Aye, you're doing a grand job of holding back your eagerness, Gracie, well done.'

After an impromptu afternoon shopping trip to Inverness, Caitlin and Grace arrived home at half past six. Cleo skipped and yipped as soon as they walked through the door with their shopping bags and Grace crouched to greet her canine best friend.

'Have you missed us? Have you? We bought you an ickle treat. Yesh we did.' She riffled through the bags until she found a box of dog biscuits. Opening them, she took one and held it out. 'See! We didn't forget you.'

Cleo took the biscuit and proceeded to crunch it loudly, creating a pile of crumbs on the floor.

Grace turned her attention to her mum. 'Which outfit are you going to wear for the pub and which for the dinner at Cora's?' she asked as they took their purchases upstairs.

Caitlin pursed her lips. 'I think the black lace top might be nice for dinner with my black pencil skirt. So, then I can wear the pale blue kimono and vest top with my jeans for the pub. What do you think?'

'I think you'll look gorgeous, and he'll propose to you straight away with a giant diamond ring and some doves.'

Caitlin shook her head. 'Doves? And what did I say about jumping the gun, missy?'

Grace scoffed. 'Ugh… boring.'

'Come on, let's take Cleo out for a nice walk. I'm stuffed from all that pasta we had earlier.'

'Me too!'

With their new clothes put away neatly, they went downstairs and Caitlin clipped Cleo's lead on. The little black dog jumped around in excitement as they headed out into the village. It was a balmy late June evening, and they were greeted by the sound of birdsong and children playing on the church field.

As they walked, they met with Jules, Evin and Chewie. Cleo and Chewie greeted each other like old friends and proceeded to jump around and play as the women and children talked.

'We were just on our way to see you as we missed you earlier,' Jules said. 'What have you been up to on your day off then?'

'We had a wee run out to Inverness to get some new clothes. Grace has had a growth spurt, so she needed a few bits, and I treated myself too.'

'Sounds lovely. I hear you're going on a date soon?' Jules grinned and nudged her.

'Aye, I can't believe it after all these years of being single.'

'Me and Cora are hoping that they'll get married so we can be sisters,' Grace interjected.

Jules widened her eyes and laughed. 'Oh! You've got it all planned then?'

Caitlin huffed. 'Aye, I keep trying to rein her in, but it's not working.'

'Aw, it's nice to dream though.' Jules gave a half-wink.

Evin eagerly blurted, 'Hey, Grace, do you want to come to our house for burgers tomorrow night after school? My dad's doing a barbecue. And I'm camping in the back garden on Saturday night if you want to come to that too! It'll be great fun. I've got torches and snacks and everything.'

Grace looked up at Caitlin with a hope-filled expression. 'Can I, Mum?'

Caitlin shrugged. 'If it's okay with Jules and Reid.'

Jules smiled. 'That's actually what we were coming to ask you. We thought we'd pop round rather than ringing, seeing as we were going out with Chewie.'

'That's fine then. Sounds like a great plan.'

'Can me and Evin go over to the field? Just while you two are talking about boring grown-up stuff?' Grace chipped in.

'Aye, go on.'

The two children and their dogs headed off in the direction of the expanse of green that lay between the new village hall at one end and the pretty, stone-built Victorian church at the other, surrounded by trees.

'Thanks for inviting Grace. The timing couldn't have been better as it means I'm sorted for my date with Lyle at the weekend.'

'Happy to help. So, is he as nice as Ruby told me?' Jules asked as they headed for the bench that face the water.

'He's lovely, Jules. But at this point I'm waiting for him to be awful in some way.'

Jules frowned. 'How do you mean?'

Caitlin sighed. 'I don't know... He just seems too good to be true. He's attractive, a single parent like me, employed with a stable job... Things like this don't happen to me, Jules.'

Jules nudged her shoulder. 'No, but they should. That's all this is – you getting what you deserve at last.'

Caitlin narrowed her eyes. 'Hmm. I'm not so sure about that. But I guess I'll just go and see how it pans out.'

'Just enjoy it. It's about time you had someone to share your life with. Kids grow up so fast and head off to uni or college and then us parents are left with empty nests, so I think it's nice to have someone to look forward to things with. I wish you all the happiness in the world, lovely.'

Caitlin's throat tightened with emotion at her best friend's words. 'Thank you. That means a lot.'

* * *

Once back home, Grace disappeared to her room to read, and Caitlin settled down with a cup of tea in front of the TV. She flicked through the channels and was almost tempted by the rerun of a series of *Bake Off*, but a text pinged through to her mobile to distract her.

Hi Caitlin, it's Lyle. I was wondering if you're free for that drink tomorrow at all? Cora is going to her aunty's house for dinner. I understand if you have plans but I'm hoping you don't. Lyle xx

He typed kisses at the end of the message, Caitlin mused with a flutter of excitement. She hit reply.

Hi Lyle. Great timing! Grace has just been invited over to her friend Evin's for a BBQ. Shall I meet you at the Coxswain? What time suits? Cait xx

She paused before adding the kisses, but eventually decided, seeing as he added some, she would do the same.

A few moments later, another message arrived.

Wow! That is good timing. Fantastic. Shall I meet you outside at 7 p.m.? L x

A wide smiled tugged at her lips and she hit reply.

Sounds good! See you then. Cait x

She placed her phone down and sighed contentedly. Maybe this single life was about to be not so single? It was all a very exciting prospect, and she couldn't wait to see what the future held. Although, she still couldn't help the niggle of doubt playing around in the back of her mind. When things seem too good to be true, they usually are... aren't they?

* * *

The following evening, after an excited text conversation with Ruby with instructions to report back on everything, Caitlin walked Grace over to Jules and Reid's house for the barbecue. Grace talked nonstop about how cool it would be if she and Cora ended up living in the same house. Caitlin wanted to tell her to stop getting her hopes up, but she couldn't get a word in. The last thing she needed was to end up with both herself and Grace broken-hearted. But she batted the negativity away. *Let's just see how it goes... no pressure...* she told herself.

'You look really pretty, Cait. That top is gorgeous! And I'm so excited for you,' Jules said, beaming, when Grace and Evin had run through to the back garden.

'Thanks. I'm so bloody nervous. I feel like a teenager. My palms are sweating, and my stomach keeps doing flip-flops.'

'That's a good sign, though. You clearly like him a lot if he has your stomach in knots.'

Caitlin smiled and nodded. 'I really do. I'm just scared to get my hopes up, you know?'

Jules reached out and squeezed her arm. 'Just take things at your own pace. Don't put pressure on yourself. Relax and have a lovely evening. It'll be a good prelude to your dinner date.'

Caitlin pursed her lips and scrunched her brow. 'I just hope we still have things to talk about on Saturday too. I don't want things to fizzle out before they start.'

Jules narrowed her eyes. 'What did I say about putting pressure on yourself?'

Caitlin rolled her eyes. 'Yes, you're right. Take things as they come. I need to make that my mantra, don't I? Anyway... I'd best be going. It's nearly seven and I don't want to keep him waiting.'

'Have a great evening. I want to hear all about it later.'

'You will, bye.'

Caitlin turned and made her way back up the tree-lined lane that led from Jules and Reid's pretty cottage back towards the village. The dappled evening sunlight cast dancing shadows on the ground, and a smell of wild garlic and pine was carried on the warm air. She absolutely adored Glentorrin. It was a place she had known all her life but had only lived in since just before Grace was born, but it was home. The kind of home people didn't ever leave because it was a part of them. It took hold and wove its spell on people, like it had for Jules, and Ruby too. Although she had been here longer, it was no different for Caitlin. She couldn't imagine fitting in anywhere else in the world like she did here. And it was a wonderful place for children. The pressures of social media, fashion labels and such were not quite so important here. Children could be children without the eager rush to become adults before their time and that had been one of the factors that had helped Caitlin make the decision to buy the bakery all those years ago. Looking around her now she was so glad she had taken the plunge.

As she rounded the corner to the pub and saw Lyle standing there, hands in his jean's pockets, and wearing a crisp white shirt, looking just as nervous as she was, she realised that there was nowhere else she'd rather be.

A smile lit up his face when they made eye contact. 'Wow, look at you. You look beautiful,' he said.

In that moment, it dawned on her that she had never been called beautiful by a man before and it gave her a boost in ways she couldn't have imagined. Butterflies began to dance around her insides once again.

She touched her hair. 'Thank you so much. You look lovely too.'

He held out his arms. 'What, this old thing?' He laughed. 'I've been looking forward to tonight since our texts yesterday.'

'Me too,' she admitted as her heart skipped a little in her chest.

9

Lyle held the door of the Coxswain open for Caitlin. The place was just beginning to welcome its early-evening crowd and she was relieved it wouldn't be just the two of them in there. There would be nothing worse than a first date with the inevitable awkward silences in an empty pub.

A familiar, booming voice called out, 'Caitlin, how are you doing? It feels like ages since we saw you in here.' It was Joren, the pub's owner, greeting her in his inimitable way.

'I'm good thanks, Joren. This is my friend Lyle.'

Joren reached his large hand across the bar and Lyle shook it. 'Good to meet you, Lyle. Now, what can I get you both?'

'I'm driving, so just a lime and soda for me. And for Caitlin...?' He turned to her.

'I'll have a Sauvignon Blanc please.'

'Coming right up!' Joren replied before turning to prepare their drinks and whistling along to 'Black Eyed Boy' by Texas as it played in the background on the sound system.

Lyle glanced around the cosy surroundings. 'I can't believe I've never been in here before. It's a great wee place.'

Caitlin smiled, briefly remembering some of the fun times she'd had in the village pub. 'It's grand. It has the best atmosphere when there's live music on. We have ceilidhs too.'

Lyle's eyes widened. 'In here? But... where do you all dance?' He laughed.

'You'd be surprised how big the place is when the tables are pushed back.'

He shook his head and grinned. 'Oh, I think I'll need to come to the next one. Impress you with some of my moves.' He waved his hands, and she couldn't help laughing along.

'That is something I definitely want to see,' she told him.

Joren handed over their drinks and Lyle paid. They walked over to a table by the fireplace and sat down. The grate was filled with fairy lights on this occasion; a relief considering the outside temperature.

'So, have you been hounded by Grace as much as I have by Cora?' Lyle asked with a smirk.

Caitlin rolled her eyes. 'And then some! It sounds like our girls have practically married us off and have us all living under the same roof. Grace has even picked out bridesmaid dress colours.' She laughed but hoped her words hadn't terrified him. 'Not that I've been encouraging that in any way, I'd like to add.'

He shook his head. 'Oh, don't worry. Apparently, the dresses are to be violet from what I've been informed?'

Relief washed over her when she realised he was taking things in his stride. 'Yes! Grace said so too.'

Lyle grinned. 'Aye, I've given up trying to calm Cora down now to be honest. I'm just letting her plan everything in her head.'

'Good idea. I can rarely get a word in edgewise, so I let Grace talk and I kind of switch off.'

Lyle laughed. 'Same here.' He sipped at his drink and things fell silent for a moment.

Caitlin knew she tended to waffle about rubbish when she was nervous, so she chose to remain quiet. But then panic began to set in as she feared that the conversation was already done.

Luckily, Lyle spoke again. 'So, when was your last date then?'

Caitlin racked her brains trying to remember the last date she had been on. 'Oof... It was a few years ago now. A guy I met at the supermarket on the mainland of all places.'

'Really? What happened?'

She scoffed. 'He didn't want kids and my ready-made family put him off.'

Lyle gasped. 'Bloody hell. How can someone be put off by Grace? She's a lovely wee girl.'

'Hmm. She was around eight at the time and hadn't quite learned how to apply her filter before speaking.'

Lyle laughed. 'Oh dear, what did she say to him?'

'Basically, that she didn't want a daddy and even if she did, she would rather have Mouldy Warts from *Harry Potter* than him.'

'Harsh!'

'Funnily enough he thought so too. I didn't see him again. In fact, I think he even changed supermarkets.' She laughed. 'How about you?'

He fixed his gaze on her. 'You're my first actual date since the divorce.'

'Wow, I'm honoured.'

He grinned. 'I'm very selective.'

She fanned herself. 'Well, now I'm flattered too.'

'To be honest, I've wanted to ask you out for ages, but I was wee bit fragile after the divorce. She really did a number on me. I had no confidence.'

Caitlin was delighted to hear he had wanted to ask her out for a while but was shocked to hear how awful his ex-wife sounded. 'You always seem so sure of yourself.'

'It was all bravado; I can assure you. I suppose there's something about having a failed marriage behind you that just makes you feel a wee bit... I don't know... crap.' He laughed lightly.

'Well, you have no reason to feel bad. It takes two to make a relationship work, so it stands to reason that it takes two to make that relationship stop working.'

'Ah, the wise words of Caitlin Fraser,' he said with a wry smile. 'So... what's your story? Do you see much of Grace's dad?'

Oh heck, thought Caitlin, *I was hoping we could avoid this for a while longer. Here we go.*

Caitlin recoiled involuntarily and Lyle widened his eyes. 'Shit, I didn't mean to pry. I just blurted that out without thinking, didn't I?'

She laughed lightly. 'It's okay. And no, I don't see him.'

He nodded. 'Right... right... This divorce lark can be tricky, eh?'

Caitlin closed her eyes briefly. 'Actually, I'm not divorced.'

Lyle had lifted his glass halfway to his lips, but at her words he stopped dead. 'Oh.'

Realising how bad that had sounded, she clarified. 'That is... I was never married to him.'

'Ah! Right, I see. I thought you were going to tell me you were still married. I mean... it wouldn't be a deal-breaker as such, if you know what I mean.'

The usual nerves that accompanied this conversation began to plague her. 'Never married and... never actually met.' She took a large gulp of her wine. 'I had Grace by artificial insemination using sperm from a donor, so I only know the man who fathered her as a set of statistics, with a reference number, in a file,' she waffled, the words falling rapidly from her mouth like a runaway train on a downhill track.

Lyle sat silently for a moment. At first, his wide eyes were fixed on her. Then they were fixed on his glass, but his mouth remained a perfect O.

That's done it, she thought, *game over*. 'Maybe it would've been best on this occasion if the girls had talked about the matter first, eh?' She laughed as her stomach knotted.

His eyes widened further. 'Oh, you're serious? That's actually how it happened? Sorry I was waiting for the punchline.' He closed his eyes and shook his head. 'God, I'm sorry... I didn't mean... It was just a shock. It's just not something you hear every day, is it? I mean, you do for infertile people and such, but... That's not to say... I mean, I don't—'

She rested her hand on his arm. 'Lyle, if you'd rather call time on the evening I understand. Some people feel less than happy about the choice I made. Especially people who've had children the "normal" way.' She hated that she had just made air quotes and wanted to slap herself.

He frowned and shook his head again. 'No... no, I don't want to do that. Who am I to judge? I just... I don't really know what to say.'

She shrugged. 'You don't have to say anything. It's not really a discussion topic, seeing as it happened over twelve years ago. I'm happy with what I did, and I wouldn't change it for the world.'

His brow lifted. 'Oh god, absolutely. No, you did what was right for you and that's... that's good. Does she know?'

Caitlin smiled. 'Of course, she knows. She's always known. She doesn't go around broadcasting it because it's no one else's business. She chooses to keep it to just us. You know how cruel kids can be, and although she is absolutely fine with it, she understands that not everyone else will be.'

'Oh... right. I see. Cora has never said anything.'

Caitlin shrugged. 'No, as I said, it's not something that Grace feels the need to tell people. It'd be like Cora discussing the very personal details of your divorce, I suppose. It doesn't have an impact on their friendship, so...'

'But...' He scowled again. 'Don't you ever worry about her

getting ill and needing something that perhaps only her father could give? I mean... things like bone marrow and organs are hard to match for and it's not necessarily a case that both parents are...' He shook his head and held up a hand. 'Forgive me. I've blurted again. It's not like me, honestly. This is none of my business.'

Caitlin had hoped Lyle wouldn't be someone to ask those questions. She'd hoped he would accept the truth of it and move on. She'd had to explain herself and her choices twice in the space of a week now and had received two distinctly different reactions. She only wished they had been swapped around so that Lyle was the one who had been non-judgemental. Because even though he said he wasn't, she could see something had shifted in his eyes. The fact that he was avoiding eye contact disappointed her.

She inhaled a calming breath. 'It's something I have thought about. But I try not to worry about what might happen and I focus on the bright, funny, loving girl I have in my life thanks to someone's generosity. I'm grateful to the man, whoever he is. But Grace and I do just fine.'

He nodded emphatically. 'Yes... of course. I'm sure you do. I just... I suppose the whole family unit thing has always been my norm.'

A little perturbed by his words, Caitlin felt defensive. 'Grace and I are a family unit,' she replied flatly.

This time, he held up both of his hands. 'Yes, of course you are. I didn't mean to suggest otherwise.'

A heavy cloud had descended on them, and Caitlin was almost ready to give up and go home.

Lyle eventually spoke again. 'Look, I'm sorry about the way I reacted. I really do like you, and I don't have to agree with all your life choices, just like you don't have to agree with all of mine. Can we maybe just... I don't know... start over?'

The fact that he admitted that he didn't agree with her choice to have Grace in a non-standard way hurt rather a lot more than she'd hoped. She'd never been one to be affected by people's opinions of her decision and she certainly didn't want to start now. But, in truth, this was partly why she had avoided dating for so long; the inherent fear of rejection over something she did for herself that made her the happiest woman alive. She had lost her own mother for a time over it, but she had held fast and stood her ground. She reminded herself again that she wasn't in the slightest bit ashamed or regretful of what she had done. She only wished others were as understanding. Especially the man she'd had a glimpse of a future with.

She sighed. 'Do you really want to start over? Or has this just put a spanner in the works?'

He paused as if choosing his words carefully and lifted his chin to look directly into her eyes. 'I want to start over. I was just taken aback, that's all. I expected the whole we're divorced or I'm a widow kind of conversation. But I have no right to judge you. I'm sorry if my reaction made you think that I feel negatively about what you did. I mean, it's in the past.' He paused, but she sensed he hadn't finished. 'I mean, I once cheated on a girlfriend when I was twenty, but I wouldn't expect you to hold that against me.' He laughed, but Caitlin was rather confused and irked by the comparison. And unlike his cheating, she would happily make her decision all over again. Lyle continued, 'Anyway, let's just move on, eh? Let's talk about something else.'

Caitlin couldn't help feeling that the relationship was already a non-starter and it angered her that this was the reason. She gritted her teeth, however, as she was aware she could be overly sensitive and defensive sometimes when she talked about this topic. She decided that perhaps she had made things more awkward than they should have been. 'Yes, let's talk about something else,' she replied before taking another huge gulp of her drink.

10

Caitlin wasn't really sure what to talk about now. Her mind was swamped with the idea that Lyle had turned out to potentially be one of those people who disagreed with her decision to have Grace by a donor. And as much as she couldn't expect everyone to agree, or accept the facts as they stood, she had sincerely hoped he would.

But she liked him and wanted to give them a chance. Perhaps it wouldn't matter in the great scheme of things? After all, he clearly liked Grace.

'So, how is the world of accounting these days?' she asked.

'Oh, you know, as exciting as it sounds.' He gave an awkward laugh. 'Although I've the big honcho coming over the week after next from Canada. He has friends in Clachan, so he's staying there, but I'm meeting him in Fort William on the Monday.'

'Wow, I didn't realise you worked for a Canadian company.'

'Aye, they set up over here a few years ago. I was working on the mainland, but this job meant I could work from home and that became invaluable when I got divorced.'

'There's a lot to be said for working from home,' Caitlin agreed.

'So, have you always been into baking?'

She smiled, finally happy to have a subject that couldn't possibly offend him. 'I have. When I was a kid, I used to bake with my dad. He had such a sweet tooth,' she said, remembering her dad fondly, in the kitchen at their family home with flour on his cheeks and his hands covered in whatever dough they were creating. 'He taught me well and it was always something that I had a knack for. My friends were all into fashion or music and I just wanted to perfect my clootie dumpling.' She laughed.

'And now you run your own bakery.'

'I do. Best job I've ever had.'

'Not great for the waistline though. Although I have to say, it's evident you don't partake in too much sweet stuff. At least not if your figure is anything to go by.'

His compliment jarred a little. *Is he trying to butter me up now?* she wondered.

'Hardly!' She was about to say, *you haven't seen me naked*, but stopped herself in the nick of time. 'To be honest, I think when you work with confectionary and cake, you smell the sweetness so much that you become kind of immune to it. Don't get me wrong though, if I try out a new recipe, I'm always the first to taste-test.'

'I should think so. Perks of the job and all that.'

The pub doors opened, and Caitlin turned to see Archie walking in with a laptop tucked under his arm. He glanced in her direction and waved before heading to the kitchen to see Joren. A few minutes later, he returned and made his way over to their table.

'Evening, lovebirds,' he said. 'Good to see you.'

Caitlin chose to ignore his comment. 'Hi, Archie. Been fixing Joren's computer?'

'Aye, bloody trojan horses. Bane of my life.' She guessed it must be a technical term and that she shouldn't expect to see a giant wooden structure outside that was leaking armed men. 'I'm heading to Reid's now to deliver a new tent. Apparently, they got the old one out to camp in the garden next weekend and the moths had got to it. Between you and me, it must have been ancient if that's happened.' He laughed. 'So, I ordered him a good one in for the coming weekend. Moth-proof.' He tapped his nose.

Caitlin smiled. 'That's good. Ooh, have you been in touch with Rosabeth from the singles night?'

Archie's cheeks tinted pink. 'Aye, I have. I'm taking her out on Saturday. Should be good craic.'

Caitlin was happy for him. He was such a lovely guy, and he deserved to be happy. 'That's great. I hope it all goes well.'

'Aye, cheers. Anyway, I'll be off. Good to see you, Lyle. Nice to see you too, Caitlin. Looking lovely as always.' Archie raised his hand in a wave and left.

'He seems like a top bloke,' Lyle said.

'He is. Would give you the shirt off his back if you needed it,' she replied with a smile.

'Have you known him long?'

Caitlin nodded. 'Known him since I moved to Glentorrin just before Grace was born. Although not that well. We're more acquaintances than friends really.'

'He clearly thinks a lot of you.'

Caitlin hadn't really thought about that, but now that she did, she realised he had always been sweet to her. Always willing to help her out. He had helped with deliveries when the bad snow had struck the year before and the village was almost cut off. Her bakery had been a lifeline for the villagers and with Archie's help, and his four-wheel drive, she had managed to deliver fresh bread to everyone who needed it. He'd asked for nothing in return.

He'd also helped her dear friend and actress, Ruby, when she had arrived in Glentorrin, hiding from the press after her social media accounts had been hacked, and her fans had turned against her. Again, he'd asked for nothing in return.

He'd helped when Chewie had fallen into the water, too, and couldn't get out.

He was like an unsung hero. *Why have I not noticed this before?*

'He's very well thought of by everyone here,' she replied after a few moments.

Lyle eyed her silently for a while. 'Has there ever been anything between you?'

Snapped from her reverie, Caitlin's attention returned to Lyle and his serious expression. *Was he jealous?* 'Me and Archie? No. He actually thought I was a lesbian until recently.' She laughed as she remembered the conversation they'd had about that.

Lyle's expression didn't change. 'So, he only avoided asking you out because he thought you were into women?'

She scoffed. 'No! It's not like that. We're just friends. I've never really thought about him any other way.' *Not that it's any of your business*, she thought, feeling rather discomforted by the line of questioning.

'I think he has the hots for you,' Lyle said before taking a gulp of his drink. 'I could tell by how he looked at you.'

She fixed a stern gaze on him. 'He was just being friendly. Look, I think perhaps it's time for a change of subject again, don't you?'

Lyle closed his eyes and shook his head. 'Sorry, god, I really am sorry. My own insecurities shining through as always.' He clenched his jaw and seemed angry with himself. Then he let out a long sigh and seemed to relax. 'I'm not making the best impression, am I?' His smile returned, and it appeared genuine.

'You're a little intense,' she admitted, nervously, as her cheeks flamed.

'I know... I know. This is all just... I haven't dated in so long I think I've forgotten how to do it.' He laughed.

The ice seemed to be melting. 'Tell me about it. It's all so difficult, isn't it?'

He nodded. 'It really is. I seem to have lost the ability to talk to women who aren't colleagues. If I'm not talking about exchange rates and tax rebates, I have no clue what to say... how to behave. It's ridiculous.' He shook his head. 'I hope I haven't put you off. I really do like you, Caitlin, a lot. I'm just not used to this, and I think it's so ridiculously obvious. I'm going to be kicking myself when I get home if you've changed your mind about dinner.' He frowned and almost pleaded at her with his eyes.

Once again, she was sucked in by his smile. 'It's fine, honestly. I haven't changed my mind. But maybe we've dived in a bit too quick with the deep personal stuff? We're both new to this and we need to have a bit more fun before we get serious,' she replied, hoping he wouldn't be offended.

He nodded vehemently. 'I totally agree. Let's make it fun all the way from now on.' He held out his hand and she took it. They shook.

'Deal,' she replied with a spark of hope once again ignited inside her.

* * *

At the end of the date, Lyle kissed her cheek. 'I promise things will be better on Saturday.'

'Honestly, stop worrying. I've had a lovely time,' she replied.

'I know you haven't really, but I appreciate you giving me a second chance.'

'I'd better go and collect Grace from Evin's house. See you Saturday.' She smiled and turned to walk away.

'Aye, I'd better get Cora from my neighbour. Bye just now, Caitlin.'

As she walked, she replayed their conversations over in her mind. She hoped the start of the evening had just been a wee blip.

The rest of the evening had been much lighter. They'd mostly talked about their children – an easy topic on which they found common ground – and Caitlin told herself that everything would be fine.

When she arrived at Jules' house, she made her way straight to the back garden where the sound of laughter rang out. The garden was large and edged with trees that gave excellent shade during the summer months. The sky was still a pale, dusky blue overhead; it never quite got completely dark at this time of year, meaning evenings in the garden were made the most of. Fairy lights and coloured lanterns were strewn around the fencing and across the front of Reid's art studio at the bottom of the garden. It looked utterly magical. Caitlin often dreamed of having such a large space to sit out in, but she couldn't complain, her small, cottage garden was sufficient for the three of them.

'Mum! You're back! How did it go?' Grace asked as she dashed to hug Caitlin.

Caitlin squeezed her daughter tightly. 'Oh, it was... lovely.' She hoped her reply didn't sound tinged with negativity.

'Yay! Me and Evin are playing swingball. Do you want a go?'

Caitlin laughed. 'No thanks, honey. And we really need to be getting home. You've school in the morning and it's really late.'

Jules walked over and hugged her. 'Hey, you. So... how was it?' Her expression was filled with hope.

Caitlin made sure Grace was out of earshot. 'It was...' She sighed, wondering how to explain. 'Intense in places.'

Jules' face dropped. 'Intense? In a good way?'

Caitlin shook her head. 'Not really. He was quite judgy about my choice to have Grace without a man being directly involved. He said he wasn't, but I've seen that expression so many times, Jules, I could read what he was thinking. He even asked the serious illness question.'

'The one about if Grace got ill and needed a kidney and you weren't a match?'

Caitlin nodded. 'That exact one.'

Jules curled her lip. 'Ugh.'

'And then Archie came in and we chatted, which seemed to make Lyle jealous.'

Jules' eyes widened. 'Really? Oh, heck, and that's all on a first date? What will you do about Saturday?'

Caitlin shrugged. 'I'll still go. We were both nervous and neither of us have dated in a very long time, so I've decided to give him the benefit of the doubt. I really liked him before, and I want to still feel that way. But... I think my feelings may have cooled a little. Probably not a bad thing though really. I was maybe setting myself up for heartache with the way I was gushing over him before.'

'I'm gutted for you. I had visions of you turning up here all floaty and in love.'

Caitlin smiled. 'There's time yet. I'm just overly cautious when it comes to Grace, and his reaction wasn't what I'd hoped. In fact, I had hoped that subject wouldn't even come up for a while. I'm not ashamed of my decision, nor do I regret it, but it's not really first-date conversation.' In truth, however, Caitlin was glad she knew where he stood on the matter.

Jules' expression told of her confusion. 'Why *did* you talk about it?'

'We hadn't been sitting down long and he asked me if I still had any contact with Grace's dad. And I didn't want to start things off by laying a foundation of untruths.'

Jules reached out and put her arm around Caitlin. 'No, that's fair enough. Crikey. No wonder things were intense, lovely.'

Caitlin was conscious of painting too negative a picture. She didn't want her friends to think badly of him in case things did work out. 'But things settled down after that. We did have a laugh. And he's such a good dad.'

Jules narrowed her eyes. 'I'm saying this as your best friend, so please don't hate me... but maybe you should stop looking for a father figure for Grace and start looking for someone you want for you.'

Caitlin was shocked at her words. 'Does that seem to be what I'm doing? Looking for a dad for Grace?'

Jules pursed her lips for a moment. 'You do seem to focus on his attributes as a father. But Grace doesn't need one. She has you and you've always been enough. Now is the time to find someone who you like. Of course, it's important that whoever the lucky man is adores Grace, treats her well, and they get on... but you need a man to make your heart flutter. Someone who you can't wait to see and who makes you laugh. Grace will grow up and leave home eventually, so it's important you think of your needs and desires too.'

Now that she thought about it, she realised Jules was right. She did tend to focus more on someone who would be a good influence for Grace. But she couldn't deny that she found Lyle incredibly attractive, at least physically. But was that enough when small cracks were already appearing in his handsome façade?

'I know. You're right. It's just been me and Grace for so long that I'm terrified of spoiling that. And I know she adores Lyle and Cora. It would be so easy to have a relationship based on those facts alone.'

Jules nodded. 'It would. But don't let your inner radar be over-ridden. Not even if it would break Grace's heart. You have to think about your heart, too, and if things don't go smoothly on Saturday maybe your gut feeling is right.'

Caitlin laughed, 'You've changed your tune. I thought you were ready to buy a wedding outfit.'

'Oh, don't get me wrong, I was!' Jules giggled. 'But you're my best friend and I want you to be happy with the right man. So, what do you want in your future?'

Caitlin paused for a moment. 'Someone who makes me laugh, has the same silly sense of humour as me. Someone who accepts me and all my foibles, my fierce independence especially. Someone who looks out for me and is there for me when I need him, even though I may not ask for help. Someone who can love Grace too. And someone who looks at me like I'm the best thing since sliced bread.' She giggled. 'Gosh, I'm a giant cliché, aren't I?'

'Not at all. They all sound like the best qualities. And I know there is someone out there who fits the bill. It's just a matter of finding him. Even though, admittedly, he might well be under your nose and not making the best impression right now.'

'Let's hope so,' Caitlin replied with a smile. The two women hugged again, and Caitlin shouted across to Grace, 'Come on, missy! Time to go home.'

Grace jogged over. 'Were you just talking about wedding dresses?'

'Not exactly. And not in the way you think, now what do you say to Jules, Reid and Evin?'

Reid arrived beside Jules and put his arm around her.

Grace beamed. 'Thank you for having me. I've had a great time.'

Jules cupped her cheek. 'You're always welcome, sweetheart.'

'You sure are. And we'll see you for camping on Saturday,' Reid added.

'It's going to be so cool! Archie has brought us a new tent and it's awesome!' Evin told them.

'I can't wait!' Grace replied with a wide smile.

'Goodnight, folks. Thanks again,' Caitlin said as she took Grace's hand and they headed for home.

11

The journey north to Portree from Glentorrin was always spectacular. The A87 followed the coastal route by the clear waters of Loch
na Cairidh and Loch Ainort, then eventually through the pretty
village of Sconser, and skirted around the edge of Loch Sligachan.
Caitlin was on her way to drop off a birthday cake for an elderly
customer, someone she knew through her mum who lived on the
outskirts of Portree, and the sun was shining overhead, bringing a
smile to her face. The Proclaimers were on the radio singing about
being on the way to happiness and she had put the conversation
with Lyle to the back of her mind.

As she reached the road that led directly into Portree, she was
greeted with a fabulous view of The Storr, a rocky hill facing east
off Skye, in the distance. The vista before her was of the gnarled
finger of the Old Man – a large, pointed peak of the rock formation
– aiming skywards as if counting the fluffy white strips of cloud at
its pinnacle. There was a wondrous sight to behold around every
corner on her home island and even though she sometimes took it
for granted, she knew that she would never want to live anywhere
else.

The elderly lady was thrilled with the ornate cake she had commissioned for her granddaughter's birthday and hugged Caitlin, telling her how grateful she was that she had made the trip all the way from Glentorrin. It was no problem really. As much as she loved her village, it was nice to travel further north on the island sometimes. Especially with her mother's house now being sold and there being no real reason for her to regularly go to the island's capital.

Before she made her journey home, Caitlin stopped at a florist and purchased a bunch of peonies, then she walked the few hundred yards to the cemetery, where a stone plaque marked her parents' resting place. She slotted the flowers into the empty plastic receptacle attached to the stone by a metal ring and poured water in from the bottle she had brought from home.

She placed her hand over the engraving of their names and whispered, 'I miss you both,' before turning and heading for her car once more. Even though Caitlin visited the cemetery as often as she could to refresh the flowers, she preferred to think of her parents alive and in happier times; they weren't in the cemetery but rather in her memory and her heart.

As she drove towards home, Caitlin admired the hedgerows filled with sunny yellow gorse and wildflowers against a backdrop of velvety-looking hills, and in the distance the Cuillin Hills rose out of the ground with dark and mysterious majesty. She was merrily singing along to KT Tunstall's 'Suddenly I See' when the car pinged and a light on the dashboard illuminated to inform her that the pressure in one of the tyres was too low.

Oh, great. Trust it to happen as soon as I arrive in the middle of nowhere.

She pulled over, climbed out of the car, and inspected the tyre. The dull, metal end of a nail was just visible on the surface of the rubber, and Caitlin sighed in deep exasperation before collecting the spare tyre from the boot. She suddenly regretted her decision to wear a bright white T-shirt on this sunny day.

Now, Caitlin was no damsel in distress, but after several attempts to free the wheel nuts, she gave up and let out her frustration. She kicked at the flat tyre with as much venom as she could muster that wouldn't result in broken toes. Then, after glancing at her watch, she called Jules and asked her to meet Grace off the school bus and take her to their house. This wasn't something that normally occurred. She always made sure to be home for Grace.

As she stood there contemplating who she could call for help, she fired off a text to Dexter.

Where are you when I need you? Probably in another distillery! Just think of me sitting here at the side of the road hoping someone drives by to rescue me from my seized-up wheel nuts!

A reply came quickly.

You need to keep your nuts greased, Cait!

It was followed by a laughing emoji, and even in her annoyed state, she couldn't help but chuckle.

Anyway, I hope the dating is going well. Jetty was telling me about Cora's dad. Go get 'em tiger!

She smiled at his lifelong nickname for Jules.

Ugh, why couldn't I have fancied Dexter? He's bloody perfect for me. If only one could control the heart's desires, Caitlin mused.

A car pulled up alongside her. 'Tyre trouble?'

Recognising the familiar, husky voice, she turned. 'Archie! Thank goodness. Can you give me a hand? I've got the blooming thing jacked up, but I can't loosen the nuts.'

'Ah, your nuts need greasing.' He chuckled at his own joke. You could tell he was friends with Dex. He climbed out of his car. 'Let me take a look.' He crouched down to pick up the tyre iron. Attaching one of the holes over a nut, he began to apply pressure. He was wearing a T-shirt with a mountainscape graphic on the front and Caitlin watched as his biceps bulged with the effort. She'd never noticed how muscular he was until now. His angular, stubbled jaw clenched as he forced the nuts loose. 'Bingo!' he said as the first one released.

Caitlin felt a little voyeuristic as she was mesmerised by the masculinity of him as he carried out the task and wondered why on earth her libido had chosen that particular moment to get hot and bothered.

Once all the nuts were off, Archie stood, lifted the hem of his shirt and wiped his brow. Caitlin gulped as his stomach was exposed, flat and lean with a fuzzy line of hair that branched out at his chest.

Bloody hell, Cait, put your tongue away!

He lifted the spare tyre, and as he did so, Caitlin was reminded of those male model photos from calendars in the nineties, of the oiled-up hunks holding the rubber-clad circles as if they weighed next to nothing. She averted her gaze as he slipped the tyre into place, then began to tighten the nuts again.

I'm like a bloody dog in heat!

She couldn't remember the last time she'd had sex and she decided that was the problem – after all, she'd never looked at Archie in that way before. She also decided that Ruby and Jules had a lot to answer for, comparing him to that attractive actor, because no matter how many times she tried to conjure an image of the green-skinned, monosyllabic Hulk, all she could see, in reality, was the ruggedly handsome man who played him.

'All done,' Archie said with a clap of his hands.

'Thank you so much. You're a lifesaver,' she told him. 'I owe you some complimentary cake the next time you're in the bakery.'

'Aw, it's nae bother. That's what friends are for, eh?' He smiled and her stomach flipped. *I really need to get a boyfriend... and soon*, she told herself. It was a hot day, and she blamed that fact for her warm cheeks and the beads of sweat on her upper lip. 'I've put your flat in the boot.'

'Thank you, Archie. I could've dealt with it myself usually.'

'I don't doubt that for a second. You're a tough woman.' His eyes widened. 'I don't mean that in a negative way though,' he insisted. 'I'm not trying to say you're butch or anything. Far from it.'

She gave a small laugh. His way of covering his tracks was quite endearing, if a little cringeworthy. 'No, I got you.'

'Right, well I'll be off. Any more problems, just give me a call.' He climbed into his car and before he drove away, he leaned out of the car window. 'How are things with you and Lyle?'

'Oh, really good!' she said a little too enthusiastically, considering the truth of the matter. There had been a few light-hearted text conversations between herself and Lyle since their first date, and although she was still a little wary, she was hoping that seeing him again would be good.

She thought she saw a hint of disappointment in Archie's eyes. 'Good, good. You deserve to be happy, Caitlin.'

'Thanks... how about you and Rosabeth?'

He frowned for a split second. 'Oh aye... grand... grand. Well, I'd best be off. Bye just now.' And with that, he pulled his car back into the road and set off towards Glentorrin.

A little perturbed by Archie's reaction to her question, and her almost lewd thoughts about him, she climbed into her car, started the engine, and headed home to drop it off before going to Jules' to collect Grace.

* * *

'I'm so excited about camping, Mum. I don't know why we've never done it,' Grace said as they walked across the village towards home.

Caitlin knew exactly why. She was more of a glamping type. She liked her luxuries too much. 'Oh, I think holiday cottages are more practical, don't you?'

Grace pondered this for a moment. 'I mean... I like cottages, but from what Evin and his dad have been saying, it's good fun to sit around a campfire and toast marshmallows and then sleep under the stars. And I love looking at the stars.'

Caitlin was reminded of the Christmas when Grace was ten and she had asked for a telescope. They had spent an hour on Christmas night in the back garden looking through the lens and consulting the book that came with it to figure out the constellations. Caitlin had been freezing, but Grace had loved it, so it was worth being so cold. 'I know you do, sweetheart. You'll have a lovely time.'

'Did you know that Archie knows all the constellations? And obviously he knows all about camping and tents. He's like some kind of outdoor genius! He came round to Evin's when I was there the other night and was telling me about how he's been to lots of different observatories all around the UK, including one called Jodrell Bank where they have the Lovell Telescope that looks *deeeeeep* into space. It's been there since the olden days, you know!'

'Really?' Caitlin grinned, loving her daughter's enthusiasm and making a mental note to thank Archie. Along with this, however, returned the impure thoughts that had entered her mind when he had rescued her from the roadside. She shook her head trying to dislodge them.

'Yes! Like the nineteen fifties or something!'

'Wow! That's a long time ago, eh?'

'It is. Archie was telling me about the constellation called Cassi... erm... Cassa... something... Anyway, she was a queen in Greek mythology, and she was totally in love with herself, I'm talking full on Kim K. So, she was cast into space by... the boss, I think. But he put her in her chair upside down in the sky to teach her to not be so vaunty! He's so funny, Archie. He makes me laugh.'

Caitlin glanced down to find Grace smiling as she recounted her conversation. 'Does he now?'

'Yeah. He knows all sorts of stuff. Like... did you know that it takes years for starlight to actually reach earth? So, if you see a star shining at night, there's a chance that star might not even exist any more!' Her eyes were wide and filled with wonder.

'Wow! I didn't know that.'

Grace beamed. 'Neither did I until Archie told me! Isn't he a genius?'

Caitlin cuddled her daughter to her side. 'Maybe he is, honey.'

* * *

Archie had definitely sparked Grace's love of the solar system all over again. On Saturday morning whilst Caitlin was working in the bakery, Grace sat in the back garden under a parasol with Cleo surrounded by the books about space that she had received the same Christmas as the telescope.

Around lunchtime, Archie called into the bakery. 'Hi, Caitlin. I'm after some more of your delicious rolls again please. Another barbecue I think, seeing as the weather is so nice.'

'Coming right up,' she replied as she packed the bread into a paper bag. 'Grace has been filling me in on your chat about the stars.'

Archie smiled. 'Aye, she's a bright wee lass. Keen to learn, that's for sure.'

'She's sitting in the garden with her books just now. Although I think maybe they're a bit young for her. I bought them for her when she was around ten, so I might need to get her some more advanced ones.'

Archie tapped his chin and narrowed his eyes. 'Now I think I might have just the thing. I've a few books at home that I got from the Royal Observatory in Edinburgh the last time I visited. I'll drop them around.'

Caitlin handed over the bread, floored yet again by the man's generosity and kindness. 'That would be great, Archie, thank you so much! She would love that.' She remembered her promise of cake after he'd rescued her from a fight with her wheel nuts. 'Actually, I have something for you.' She bent to pick up a chocolate cake from the display. 'Here you go.'

Archie's brow crumpled. 'They're only books, Caitlin. I'm not expecting payment.'

'This is a thank you for rescuing me yesterday.'

His cheeks coloured and he smiled shyly. 'Aww, it was nae bother, honestly. But thank you. I'll no refuse one of your cakes. It'll be lovely after my barbecue.'

'I hope you enjoy it. And Archie...'

'Aye?'

'Thank you for indulging Grace. She really enjoyed talking to you. She thinks you're really funny, oh, and a genius.'

His cheeks coloured brighter. 'Did she say that?'

Caitlin nodded. 'She did.'

'Aw, she's a grand wee lass. Tell her I said "hi" and that I'll drop her the books round soon.' He paused for a moment, seeming hesitant. 'I... erm... hear you're having dinner with Lyle tonight. He seems like a nice guy, and I hope it goes well. Enjoy yoursel'.' He raised a hand in a wave and left the shop.

Caitlin smiled to herself once he had gone. Who knew that she would form a real friendship with Archie Sutherland after all these years of being acquainted with him? All she needed to do now was stop remembering his biceps, toned stomach and overall masculinity...

* * *

Ruby texted from her romantic getaway with Mitch to wish her luck for her date. Caitlin sent a photo of herself dressed in the outfit she had chosen. She had foregone the original outfit that she had purchased for the occasion and had chosen a maxi dress and denim jacket instead. She decided the fitted black skirt and top were perhaps a little too sexy and she knew she had to give herself more time to suss Lyle out after their last date.

You look gorgeous! Have a fab night. We're going for a romantic meal in the hotel tonight and then onto the cocktail bar! Roo xx

The message was finished off with a drunken face emoji that made Caitlin laugh.

* * *

Grace was extra-giddy as they walked around to Jules' house for the campout. She had her turquoise sleeping bag tucked under her arm, and her pyjamas and Ugg boots in her bag, along with a fleece top, just in case the weather did its usual Scottish thing of changing on a ha'penny.

When they arrived, they walked around to the back garden to find Reid and Evin putting the finishing touches to their camp.

'Wow, fellas, this is looking rather fab,' Caitlin said as she appraised their set-up. Two tents sat on the level ground with glowing tent pegs to mark the corners, a table and chairs with enough snacks piled on top to feed an army, and a fire pit glowing and crackling already, the smell of a burning pine log floating through the air. 'What's Jules doing this evening?'

'I think she's looking forward to having the remote control all to herself!' Reid said with a laugh.

'I am! And there's a nice bottle of Pinot with my name on it! Actually, it's called Yellow Tail, but I'm willing to contact Deed Poll,' Jules said as she came from the direction of the house with a tray of marshmallows, skewers and pots of chocolate and caramel sauces. 'I may have secreted some marshmallows away for later, too, but don't tell this lot,' she whispered to Caitlin.

'What did you say, Sparks?' Evin asked, hands on hips and his eyes narrowed.

Caitlin couldn't help smiling at his nickname for Jules that had originated not long after they'd met, when he had misunderstood the spelling of her name and begun calling her *sparkly Jewels*.

'Nothing, buddy!' Jules replied with a wink in Caitlin's direction.

Caitlin whispered, 'I've sent shortbread and rocky road, so you might want to pinch a bit of that too.'

Jules giggled. 'Fantastic, thanks for the heads-up. So, how are you feeling about dinner tonight?'

Caitlin blew air through puffed cheeks. 'Okay, I think. I'm hoping the other night was just first-date nerves. After mulling things over, I think I may have overreacted. He's a nice guy, so I'm keeping an open mind.'

'Well, like I said before, if it's not right, don't force things because you think you should. There's someone out there for you, I just know it.'

'Well, I'm glad one of us does. Right, I'll be off. Thanks for having her. She's been so excited about camping and looking at the stars.'

'Oh yes! She was hanging on Archie's every word the other night. It was so sweet. He's even brought a telescope round for the kids to use in the garden tonight. Such a nice guy. I think he'd make a lovely dad. I hope he meets someone too.'

Caitlin felt her cheeks warming. 'Yes, same.' She didn't say anything further as she knew what Ruby and Jules were like for reading between the lines, and for adding two and two and making nonsense. 'Bye, Gracie! Have fun and don't make yourself sick on marshmallows and cake.'

Grace waved. 'Bye, Mum! I won't. Evin will probably eat more than me.'

Evin shrugged and nodded. 'Yeah, she's probably right.'

12

Caitlin knocked on Lyle's door and waited. Within a few seconds, he was there with a wide, handsome smile on his face as he stepped aside to let her in.

'You look as lovely as ever,' he said as he kissed her on the cheek.

'Thank you. I've brought a bottle of wine for you, and a bottle of alcohol-free for me,' she said as she handed over the gifts.

'Great! I hope you like lasagne. Cora says it's the thing I cook best so...'

'I do. One of my favourites,' she replied with a warm smile. 'So where is the lovely young lady this evening?'

'She's round at my neighbours. Aggie is like a grandma to her.'

Caitlin smiled but felt a twinge of sadness for her own daughter and her lack of living grandparents. 'Aw, that's so sweet.'

Once inside the modern kitchen, she began to relax. Lyle poured them each a drink, handed her a glass and kept one for himself.

He appeared nervous and a little fidgety. 'Look, before we sit down to eat, I want to apologise. Looking back on the things I said when we went for drinks, I realise I was an arse. Who am I to judge you for your desire to have a child?' He shook his head and sighed. 'I know how much I wanted Cora when she arrived, and to be without her now... Well, it just doesn't bear thinking about. Please accept my apologies. I don't judge you for your decisions.' Sincerity shone through in his eyes. 'How can I? In all honesty, I think you were incredibly brave for what you did. And Grace is lucky to have you. You really are a wonderful mum.'

Relieved, Caitlin felt heat flaring in her face. 'Thank you.'

'And as for the crap about me cheating when I was younger and comparing that to your situation...' He closed his eyes for a moment. 'God, I can't believe you agreed to come back. I really am a prize numpty. Please don't let that put you off. The cheating bit and the numpty bit.' He smiled shyly. 'I'm not like that any more. Well, not the cheating bit anyway.'

She nodded. 'Good to know. And... you're forgiven. I know it can be a hard thing for people to get their heads around, but... I really hoped you were okay with it.'

He stepped closer and bowed his head, so his lips were hovering dangerously close to hers. 'I really am okay with it. More than okay.' He gently touched his lips to hers and slipped his free hand around her waist to pull her close. The feel of his lips on hers was soft at first, but he placed his glass on the countertop and cupped the back of her head to deepen the kiss.

Caitlin felt a little light-headed and her heart skipped as parts of her body that had been sleeping were awakened in the most delightful way. She too placed her glass down and slipped her hands up and around the back of his neck. She could have easily got completely carried away, both literally and figuratively, but he pulled away.

'Shit, I'm so sorry. I don't know what came over me.' He huffed and paused for a moment. 'Actually, that's not necessarily true.' He gave a knowing grin.

She touched her lips as her legs weakened. 'Perhaps we should eat?'

'Perhaps we should.'

The lasagne was delicious. The bechamel sauce a creamy delight on her tongue and Caitlin found herself wondering if he'd made it from scratch. *Eat your heart out Paul Hollywood.*

'So, it's Grace's birthday next weekend. Are you ready to be the mother of a teenager?' Lyle asked once he had cleared the plates away.

'Nope. She's growing up way too fast.'

'I totally agree. Good that she has her birthday just after they break for summer though. Easy to make sure people attend. Unlike Cora's, which lands during the holidays. We never know who's coming until they turn up. What has Grace asked for? In the way of gifts, I mean.'

Grace was not the type of child who wrote lists and circled things in catalogues. She was always grateful for whatever gifts she received. During her early childhood, money had been fairly tight, and she had always understood this. But it saddened Caitlin to know it was something she had been aware of at such a young age. 'Nothing in particular. She just wants to have a party at the new village hall.'

Lyle frowned. 'That's it? No demands for a pony or a spending spree?'

Caitlin laughed. 'Oh, I'm sure she would enjoy a spree if I took her on one, but no, just a party. I've booked the hall, but now that Donny has moved away from the village, there's no one locally to ask about DJing. So, not sure what I will do about that.'

'Just stick an iPod in a docking station and turn up the volume. I reckon they'll be satisfied.'

Caitlin nodded. 'You're probably right.'

'Cora's is in the middle of July, and she already has a long list of things. How different they are in some ways. But so similar in others.'

'Grace is getting into astronomy again, so maybe I'll get her something related to that. She was into it a few years ago, but it seemed to fizzle out.'

Lyle's eyebrows rose. 'Astronomy? Wow, how come?'

'She went to Evin's for a barbecue and Archie was there. They got chatting and he told her all about the observatories he's been to. He was telling her about the stories behind the constellations too. She was fascinated. In fact, he's loaned the kids a telescope for them to have a look at the sky tonight during their campout.'

Lyle's smile disappeared. 'Archie... He seems to pop up everywhere that bloke.'

Caitlin thought she sensed that hint of jealousy again and it irked her. He had no right to be jealous. They had seen each other a couple of times and shared one, albeit passionate, kiss. Green was not a good colour on him.

Before she could put her feelings into words and explain that there was no need to be jealous of her friendship, Lyle changed the subject. 'Dessert! I've got tiramisu. It's not home-made, I'm afraid, but I've heard this is the best shop-bought one you can get, so...' He stood from the table and headed for the kitchen again, returning moments later with the pudding. He dished cocoa-powder-covered dollops into two bowls and placed one before her. 'I hope it's as good as I was told.'

* * *

The rest of the evening was lovely. No more signs of the green-eyed monster or his opinionated friend. Caitlin was relieved, to say the least, and she began to feel that perhaps the earlier blips had been just that – temporary bumps on the road to the couple's happiness. A road she very much hoped she was embarking upon.

When it was time to leave, Lyle walked her to the door. 'When can I see you again?'

'Well, you have your big meeting on Monday, and I have a busy week ahead too now the holiday season is kicking in, so why don't you come along to Grace's party on Saturday? Cora will be coming anyway.'

He nodded. 'Sounds good.' He stepped a little closer. 'Can I kiss you goodnight?'

She nodded and he lowered his face to hers again. This time, the kiss was a little more reserved. She could tell he was holding back, but it was still nice, and the physical attraction was definitely still there.

When he pulled away, he tucked her hair behind her ear. 'I've never had so much restraint,' he said with a chuckle. 'Anyway, drive safely and stay in touch this week. And I'll see you next Saturday.'

'I will. Thanks for a lovely evening. You really are a good cook.'

He feigned embarrassment. 'Oh, stop. I'll not fit my head through the door.'

She tiptoed up and kissed his cheek. 'Night, Lyle. I hope your meeting goes well.'

'Night, Caity.'

Hearing him use a shortened version of her name was strange, especially a version she wasn't used to, and she couldn't decide if she liked it or not. Her mother had always called her Cait, as did her friends, and she wasn't sure if Caity was a little too familiar. Surely they weren't at the 'pet names' stage yet?

She climbed back in her car and drove away, telling herself she really needed to stop overthinking things.

* * *

Sunday was filled with sunshine, cups of tea in the garden – in between rain showers – walks with Cleo and lots of talk of the night sky over Glentorrin, and how amazing it had been to see the moon so clearly. Grace was so enthralled about using Archie's telescope that she totally forgot to bombard her mum with questions about her date with Cora's dad, a fact that Caitlin was secretly grateful for.

Before Caitlin knew it, it was Monday again. Grace was excited because this was the last week of term before summer break and it was the lead-up to her birthday. She had got out of bed without cajoling, eaten her breakfast with a smile on her face and had hugged her mum so tight before she left, Caitlin thought she might pass out.

'Have a good day, hen!' she called as Grace left for the school bus.

'I will! I'm giving the remaining invites out today! Eeeek! I'm so excited. See you tonight!'

Cleo followed Caitlin around as she always did when Grace had gone to school.

She crouched to scratch the dog behind her ears. 'Don't worry, cutie-pie, at the end of this week, you'll be stuck with her for the whole summer.' As if she understood, Cleo yipped and gave her paw. 'High five!' Caitlin giggled as the dog's paw batted her hand. 'Now, I have work to do, and a star-themed birthday cake to design. Can you keep an eye on things through here for me?' Cleo tilted her head, hanging on her every word. 'Thanks, Cleo. Good girl.'

At around eleven o'clock, there was a brief lull in customers and Caitlin whipped out her sketch pad again. The design for Grace's cake was coming along well. It would be a base of dark blue that gradually faded lighter towards the bottom of the smooth icing on the tall, cylindrical structure. Then she would mark out constellations in edible jewels all around the sides, plus a made-up one that formed a letter G, and then, to give it a final flourish, there would be a starburst on the top with the number 13 in the centre. She couldn't wait to see Grace's reaction.

How on earth her baby was about to become a teenager she couldn't quite comprehend. The years had flown by, but she wouldn't have changed a single thing about being a mum. Even when there had been tough times when money had been tight and Grace's birthday gifts had been purchased second-hand from eBay and charity shops. She more than made up for it now the bakery was booming. And she couldn't be prouder of her daughter, who was growing up to be a sensitive, caring young lady. In spite of her less than conventional existence, she had a resilience that astounded Caitlin. Whenever guilt niggled at her as other children talked about their dads, Grace would shrug and say, 'Yes, but they don't have the best mum in the universe because she's mine.'

'Morning, Caitlin. What you sketching?' Archie asked as he walked into the shop.

'Oh, hi. It's a design for Grace's birthday cake.'

He leaned closer. 'Wow! That's really cool! She'll love it.'

'She's thirteen on Saturday, can you believe it?'

'Oh aye! She mentioned that when I saw her at Reid's. She's a smashing lass. You must be really proud of her.'

'Oh, I am. And thanks to you we have a theme for the party.'

He grinned. 'Thanks to me? How so?'

'She's decided she wants it to be star-themed. As in the ones in the night sky rather than the Ruby Lockes of the world.'

'Awesome! Need any help with preparations? I'm a dab hand at blowing up balloons.'

She appreciated his offer. 'All help is welcome, thanks. Ooh and you don't happen to know a DJ, do you? I'm struggling to find one, or an entertainer, and I'm not sure what to do.'

'I'll do it.' He shrugged as if it was the most obvious solution.

Caitlin gasped. 'I can't ask you to do that!'

He laughed, causing the corners of his eyes to crinkle and his face to light up. 'You didn't ask me. I offered. I'm a tech geek, remember? I have a laptop loaded with around a gazillion songs, a set of speakers big enough for the village hall and I even have some fancy lights I can bring along.'

Caitlin was gobsmacked. Was there nothing that this man couldn't, or wouldn't, turn his hand to? 'Wow, Archie you're a gem. That's incredible. Thank you so much.'

He shook his head and waved a dismissive hand. 'It's nae bother. I'd love to help. And, to be honest, I'm not sure that kids that age want entertainers these days. They're probably too cool for all that. Why not get Ruby to teach them some dance moves and have a boys versus girls dance-off instead?'

Caitlin widened her eyes and rushed around the counter towards Archie. She tiptoed and took his face in her hands. 'Archie, you're a genius!' she said as she planted a kiss on his cheek.

His face coloured the shade of cooked beetroot and he laughed. 'If I'd known I was going to get that reaction, I'd have offered sooner.'

13

During the rest of the week, Caitlin was bombarded daily with flower deliveries from Lyle. She was running out of vases and surfaces to put the vases on. He had messaged lots too and he told her how much he was looking forward to seeing her again. As much as she thought it was sweet of him, it was a little overwhelming and something niggled in the back of her mind. Each time the florist's van pulled up outside, there followed drop-ins and messages from her friends. Ruby, Jules and Morag all agreed that it was sweet but perhaps a little too much, considering how long they had been seeing each other. Caitlin didn't have the heart to say anything other than gushing thanks, however; she didn't want to hurt his feelings.

The party planning was coming along well. Ruby had jumped at the chance to be in charge of a dance-off. She was currently studying to officially become a dance teacher after her movie career turned out not to be what she really wanted in life. Dancing had always been her passion and she had studied it at university, so any chance to get stuck into creating routines and she was there!

The music was sorted, as was the lighting, thanks to Archie,

Jules was helping with the catering, and Morag was providing enough crisps and other nibbles from the wholesaler to sink a battleship. Caitlin was so incredibly grateful for the friends she had in Glentorrin. She didn't know what she would do without them under normal circumstances, but in the lead-up to the party she was astounded with how willing everyone was to help.

* * *

The day of the party arrived, and Grace had already been spoiled with gifts from Caitlin. A big box had arrived from Dexter too. Inside was a teddy that bore a striking resemblance to the mechanic and biker himself. The birthday card with it read:

> *Happy birthday Gracie! I saw this and immediately thought someone had made a furry version of me! So, meet Dextwo. Do you get it? Dexter and Dextwo! Happy birthday!*

Grace loved the bear with its faux leather jacket and shades, and Caitlin had laughed out loud when reading the card that accompanied it.

Later on, Grace was getting ready in her room as Caitlin was putting the finishing touches to the surprise birthday cake. Archie had texted to say he was over at the hall setting up and that he had 'sorted the cosmos theme'. She couldn't help the worry that niggled at her as she wondered what that would entail, and baulked a little, concerned it would be too childish for her now-teenage daughter. Jules and Morag had been to collect the food from Caitlin's fridges with the assurance that they would prepare everything so that Caitlin could enjoy her daughter's special day.

Around twenty-five children were expected to attend the party, along with some of the parents and her own friends too. Mitch arrived half an hour before the start time to collect the cake.

'Thanks so much for doing this, Mitch. I bet there are hundreds of things you could be doing on your weekend rather than fetching and carrying for us.'

Mitch waved her comment away. 'Not at all. It's absolutely no bother. Grace is a lovely wee lass. And Ruby's so excited about the dance-off. Honestly, her energy has rubbed off on me. I haven't looked forward to a party so much in ages.'

'Well, I appreciate your help. I expect Jules will tell you where the cake needs to go.' She pointed at the huge cardboard box that sat atop the counter.

'Aye. And don't worry, I promise I'll be careful with your creation. I can't wait to see it. See you over there,' Mitch said as he picked up the box.

'See you soon,' Caitlin called as he left the bakery.

Around fifteen minutes later, a text arrived from Archie.

We're all ready for the birthday girl! Archie x

She smiled at his use of a kiss and wondered if he was panicking over it now he had hit send. Sure enough, another text arrived seconds later.

Whoops! Don't go telling Lyle I'm sending kisses to his woman! A

This time a smiley face accompanied the message and Caitlin giggled to herself and shook her head. True Archie Sutherland style: act now, overthink later.

'Come on, Gracie darling, time to go!' she called up the stairs.

Moments later, Grace appeared in her navy-blue dress complete with sparkles. 'Does this look okay, Mum? It's not too babyish, is it?'

Caitlin gasped and her eyes welled with tears. 'You look absolutely stunning, sweetheart. Now come on, let's go and partaaay!' She did a silly dance on the spot.

Grace rolled her eyes. 'Yeah, maybe don't say, or do, *that* in front of people though, eh?'

Caitlin feigned hurt. 'Are you trying to say I'm not down with the kids?' Her rapper stance was the straw that broke the camel's back, apparently.

Grace burst out laughing. 'I'm not *trying to say* it, Mum. I'm being direct! And definitely don't do that either!'

'So, no backwards baseball cap then?'

'Nope.'

'I could get some—'

'Nope.' Grace giggled.

'Well, how about—'

'Absolutely not. Now come on, Mum, we're going to be late!' She tugged at her mum's hand and Caitlin locked the door of the bakery.

Moments later, when Caitlin pushed through the doors to the village hall and Grace stepped inside, she gasped and brought her hands up to her face.

'Mum! It's amazing!'

The blinds were closed and there were fairy lights strewn across the ceiling. There was a table stacked with gifts and a buffet laid out and covered to one side of the room. The balloons were no ordinary inflated latex, these balloons were filled with LED lights and were secured to the tables with star-shaped weights. Even the tablecloths were navy-blue and dotted with glitter. There were silver stars hanging from the ceiling in between the fairy lights and Archie had set up coloured searchlights on the stage that shone, twisted, and turned in time with the music that was playing over the speakers. When Archie had said he would sort things, this wasn't at all what Caitlin had expected. He must have spent a fortune.

Archie was perched on the stage, his laptop set up and ready. 'Afternoon, everyone! School's out!' A cheer rang out around the room. 'Now let's get the summer started by welcoming our birthday girl!' he announced into his microphone, and everyone turned to face Grace and Caitlin.

Applause rang out around the room, followed by a very loud rendition of 'Happy Birthday'.

It was magical and all down to Caitlin's wonderful friends; especially Archie, who had gone all out to make the event a special one. She would owe him a lifetime of free cake after this, but she didn't mind at all, seeing the joy and wonder on her daughter's face.

Grace was immediately swamped by a crowd of her friends, including Evin, but Cora was nowhere to be seen yet. *Maybe Lyle likes to leave things to the last minute*, Caitlin pondered.

Once the party was in full swing, Caitlin stood with Morag and Jules as Ruby explained the rules of the dance-off. Caitlin watched in awe as Ruby taught a few moves to the enthralled group of kids.

'She is going to make such a fantastic dance teacher,' Morag said.

'Isn't she just,' Jules agreed.

'I wish I could move like that without putting my back out.' Caitlin giggled.

'Same!' the other two women said in unison.

'I can't believe Archie is joining in. He's so funny,' Jules said as they watched him mirroring Ruby's actions.

'Aye, he's got rhythm that's for sure,' Morag said with a tilt of her head. 'And he can sing too. I remember his rendition of "Sweet Caroline" at the Highland Games.'

Yet more surprising things about the man, Caitlin surmised.

Cora and Lyle arrived around forty-five minutes into the party and Caitlin couldn't help the disappointment that niggled at her.

'I just couldn't get off the phone. There's so much going on and he wants my involvement. I couldn't just hang up. You're not angry, are you?' Lyle had said with a protruding bottom lip. Of course, she was, but she wasn't about to admit that in such a public place. Grace was just happy that Cora had finally arrived, so Caitlin chose a more positive stance.

'These things happen,' was all she said before turning her attention to the front, where Ruby had stepped aside to allow the festivities to continue.

The dance-off was suddenly in full swing and Archie was back in his spot dealing with the music and bobbing along as the kids were split into two groups. They had such energy and Caitlin was gobsmacked at how much they were all getting into the spirit of things. Evin was first up for the boys and the applause he received almost took the roof off. Grace was up first for the girls and once again the cheers and whoops rang out. By the time the winners were announced, the room was filled with laughter and music and Caitlin couldn't have been happier.

* * *

At the end of the evening, Caitlin and Grace stood by the doors to thank everyone for their gifts. The cake had been cut, but only after Grace had insisted on Caitlin snapping a gazillion photos of it first, and Morag had wrapped small slices in paper napkins for each guest to take a piece home. Grace had a beaming smile on her face that hadn't disappeared for the whole duration of the party and Caitlin was overjoyed to know that she had done her girl proud.

Ruby and Mitch came to say goodbye. 'Do you want any help

with the clearing up, Cait?' Ruby asked after she hugged the birthday girl.

'No, no, it's absolutely fine. Kenneth says we're okay to come over and sort it out tomorrow morning. I think I'm going home to put my feet up. Speaking of feet, you must be exhausted after that dance-off.'

Mitch laughed. 'Not a chance. She'll be buzzing for the rest of the night now. She was in her element, weren't you, Roo?'

Ruby giggled. 'He's right. It was such fun! Archie's idea was perfect.'

'He's great, isn't he?' Grace interjected.

'He certainly is, sweetie,' Ruby agreed.

'Aye, he's a top bloke.' Mitch glanced over his shoulder. 'Speaking of top blokes, why was your fella so late?'

'Oh, apparently he had a long chat with his boss who's been here from Canada. He couldn't get off the phone.'

Mitch scowled. 'It's Saturday. Does he ever stop working?'

Ruby nudged him. 'The phrase "people in glass houses..." comes to mind.'

Mitch blushed. 'Aye, right enough. Come on, Roo, let's get you home to decompress.' He chuckled. They said their goodbyes and left.

'Hey, Caity. Again, I'm so sorry we were late. But I hope the gift made up for it, eh, Gracie?' Lyle said as he and Cora came to say goodnight.

'It's lovely. I just need to pluck up the courage to get my ears pierced now.' The star-shaped earrings had been quite a shock and looked very expensive indeed. And while it was a thoughtful present, Grace hadn't mentioned having her ears pierced before and Caitlin didn't want this gift to force her into doing something she wasn't comfortable with.

'We'll have a chat about it, sweetheart,' Caitlin told her before turning back to Lyle. 'And don't worry. You made it and that's the main thing.'

'Should I come back to your house for coffee maybe?' he asked with an expression of hope.

Caitlin sighed. 'Would you mind if I took a rain check? I'm absolutely bushed. I think the dancing finished me off.'

The disappointment in his eyes wasn't lost on her. 'Aye, of course. No wonder. I'll have to enlist you in the party planning for Cora.'

Caitlin laughed. 'It's Archie you need, not me! He's sorted pretty much everything.' As soon as the words left her lips, she regretted them.

'Right. Aye. I see he's been involved in everything.' His tight-lipped response spoke volumes.

'He's a good friend,' Caitlin said with a raise of her eyebrows.

Lyle ignored her comment. 'Can I see you in the week? Maybe a drink at the pub or at yours?'

Caitlin nodded. 'Or we could meet up and go for a walk or something.' She was craving the stunning scenery of her island and the fresh air that surrounded them.

Lyle scrunched his face. 'Hmm... let me pop round to yours and we'll see how we feel. Is Wednesday good?'

'Wednesday's fine.'

He leaned and kissed her cheek, lingering a little before he stood again. 'See you Wednesday.'

Grace and Cora had been chatting through their whole exchange but hugged when Lyle got Cora's attention. 'Bye, Grace, I'm so sorry my dad made us late. See you the week after next. I'm at my mum's next week.' She didn't seem too happy about the fact.

'Bye, Cora, have fun at your mum's.'

Cora simply rolled her eyes and scrunched her nose.

Once the hall was clear of people, Caitlin made her way over to

Archie, who was picking up discarded paper cups, wrapping paper and napkins. 'Archie, you don't need to tidy up as well. You've done enough.'

Archie shrugged. 'It's nae bother. I've enjoyed today. Oh... am I okay to give Grace my gift now?'

Caitlin widened her eyes. 'You got her a gift too? After everything else you've done?'

'Of course. I didn't want to give it to her earlier because... well... looking at some of the fancy things she's been given, she might think this is... what do they say these days? Totes lame?' He laughed.

'I'm sure she won't think that at all. Grace! Archie has a gift for you.'

Grace came jogging over as Archie pulled an A4-sized parcel from behind the buffet tables.

His cheeks coloured as he handed it over. 'It's not much. I just thought it was kind of cool, but I'm old, so I could be wrong.' He winked at her.

Grace carefully removed the paper and gasped when she saw what was inside. 'Archie! This is so awesome! It's the best present ever!'

Caitlin smiled and said, 'Come on, show me! What is it?'

Grace turned the framed certificate around. 'He named a star after me! Mum, I have my very own star!' Her eyes glistened with emotion and she jumped up to hug Archie.

'You like it then?' he asked with a wide, handsome smile.

'Archie, I absolutely love it! It's the most perfect thing ever!'

He hugged her back. 'I'm so glad. I was worried you'd think it was boggin',' he said with a nervous laugh.

'Absolutely no way. Can I put this on my wall in my room, Mum?'

Caitlin was a little lost for words but managed to nod a yes.

Grace took the frame and the accompanying documents that came with it and went to put it safely with her other gifts.

Eventually Caitlin managed to speak, though her eyes were blurred with tears. 'Archie, that was such a thoughtful gift,' she whispered.

He smiled shyly. 'Och, it was nothing. I just saw a website when I was online, and I thought of her.'

Caitlin shook her head. 'You couldn't have got her anything more perfect. Thank you.' She stepped forward and hugged him tightly. He wrapped his arms around her, and she closed her eyes, enjoying the warmth of his strong body surrounding hers.

Suddenly guilt washed over her, so she stepped back. If Lyle had seen, he would be none too pleased. She didn't want to give him more reasons to think she felt more for Archie than friendship. Because she absolutely didn't. Not at all.

14

On Sunday morning, Caitlin met with Jules, Ruby and Morag to clear the room of the party detritus. Although considering the amount Archie had done the night before, it wasn't as bad as Caitlin was expecting.

'I meant to ask you, Cait, how is it going with Cora's dad?' Ruby asked as they collected the last of the black bin liners.

'He's lovely... for the most part.' She shrugged, knowing full well that her vague answer would spark more questions.

Jules straightened up and glanced over. 'For the most part?'

'Hmm... There was a conversation that led me to believe he wasn't keen on the choice I made to have Grace by a donor.'

'Well, it's none of his beeswax,' Morag interjected.

'I think we sorted that part out though, so it's okay,' Caitlin assured her friends.

'That part? You make it sound like there are other parts,' Ruby said with a frown. 'Is it the flowers? Because that was... well...' Ruby cringed as if unwilling to say anything negative.

Caitlin paused for a moment. 'Too much? Yes, I agree. But no, that's not it. I think... I think he has a jealous streak.'

Jules paused and tilted her head. 'What? Already? You've not been seeing each other that long. What can there to be jealous about?' There was a note of incredulity to her voice.

Caitlin pursed her lips. 'Archie. Well... my friendship with Archie anyway. It's just a couple of comments and facial expressions. I'm probably reading too much into it.'

Morag tied up one of the bags as she said, 'Hmm... Archie is a very attractive man though. I can see why he'd be concerned. And Archie obviously thinks a lot of you and Grace. I mean you've only to look at what he did yesterday,' she said. 'He was completely in charge of the decorations. Bought most of them himself.'

Caitlin nodded. 'Yes, I must offer to give him something for that. He must have spent a fortune.'

Morag shook her head. 'If you ask me, he was happy to do it. Wanted it to be perfect for wee Gracie.'

Caitlin smiled wistfully. 'And it was. He did an amazing job.'

Jules huffed. 'I think it's such a shame that he's single. He's so lovely. Can't do enough for others.'

'Oh, he met someone at one of the singles events. He was out with her last weekend. Heck, I forgot to ask how it went. He always asks after me and Lyle,' Caitlin said, mostly to herself.

'Maybe he asks because he's hoping you'll go off Lyle, so he has a chance,' Ruby said with a grin.

'I doubt it. Don't you remember he thought I was into women until recently?'

'Doesn't mean he doesn't think you're gorgeous though,' Jules said.

Caitlin rolled her eyes. 'Good grief. Not this again?'

'I'm just saying, Mrs Huffy Britches,' Jules replied with a nudge.

'Okay, I admit, Archie is an attractive, kind man who happens to think a lot of my daughter. There, I said it. Doesn't mean I want to jump into bed with him,' Caitlin insisted, but unexpectedly that damned image of him changing her tyre sprang to mind and an involuntary rush of blood travelled to her cheeks, warming them significantly.

'Do you want to jump into bed with Mr Hollywood though?' Morag asked with a cheeky wink.

'I'm not going to answer that, Morag. And his name is Lyle Budge.'

Morag giggled. 'Mr *budge over and make way for Archie* more like.'

The other women laughed along with her.

'For heaven's sake, I'm not in the slightest bit interested in dating Archie!' Caitlin shouted.

'That's good to know,' came a voice from the doorway. 'Although I wasn't going to ask, so you're fine.' Archie turned to leave, and Caitlin ran after him.

As she exited the village hall, her stomach roiled and her heart pounded. 'Archie! Come back!' Thankfully outside they were alone.

He stopped in his tracks and turned. 'It's fine, Caitlin. You don't have to apologise.'

'Yes, I do! I didn't mean that to sound so awful. The others have been ribbing me, that's all. I know they're just having a bit of fun, but I got in a strop. And anyway, you're with Rosabeth and I'm with Lyle.' She shrugged. 'I just didn't want you to think—'

'Didn't want me to think what?' She thought she saw hurt in his eyes.

'That I don't like you or... or appreciate you and what you did for Grace.'

He fixed her with a stern gaze. 'Like I said, it's fine. And you're right, I'm with Rosabeth, so I wasn't going to ask you out anyway.' He smiled, but Caitlin couldn't help thinking it wasn't genuine, seeing as his eyes didn't light up the way they usually did.

She hadn't intended for him to hear her, nor had she intended to sound so disgusted by the prospect of going out with him. 'Good. That's... that's good. So... how is it going with Rosabeth?'

He paused for a moment. 'Good. She's really nice. We had a nice time.'

Nice? Oh... 'That's good. I'm glad. So... what were you doing here?'

He glanced over her shoulder at the village hall. 'Oh, I just came to help tidy the place, but you seem to have it all under control, so...'

Caitlin sighed. Guilt niggled at her insides, knotting them uncomfortably. She reached out and took his hand. 'Archie, you're so lovely. Thank you for everything. You really made Grace's birthday extra-special and I'm so grateful to you. You must tell me what I owe you for all the balloons and lights and everything else.'

He snatched his hand away as if she had stung him. 'Pfft, you don't owe me anything at all. I was happy to do it.' As if realising his reaction was a little harsh, he added, 'She's a grand girl... just like her mum.' There was a hint of sadness to his gaze. 'Well, I'd best be off. I'm taking Rosabeth out again tonight. We're going for an Indian meal over on the mainland.'

Although a strange feeling twinged deep inside her, Caitlin smiled and nodded. 'That's lovely. Have a fab time, eh?'

'Aye, cheers. Bye just now.' He raised his hand in a wave and headed for his house.

Caitlin watched him leave and then closed her eyes for a brief moment, berating herself for her outburst before she returned to the hall.

'Was he okay? I feel so awful about that,' Jules said.

'Aye, he didnae deserve to hear that, poor lamb,' Morag added.

'He's fine. Like I told you, he has a girlfriend. He's happy,' Caitlin insisted although she couldn't help wondering if she had, in fact, cruelly bruised his feelings.

* * *

For the next couple of weeks, Caitlin busied herself with finding an assistant for the shop. She had been lucky to acquire the details of the daughter of one of Morag's friends, a young woman called Isla Kennedy, who was a graduate from the same catering college Caitlin had attended. She had also worked in retail during and after her studies so had plenty of experience. Now aged twenty-three, she was looking for something to do while she decided on a career path. Caitlin had initially taken her on for a trial period which had been a great success. She was a bubbly, smiley person and the customers seemed to like her. Things were going well, and the free time Caitlin had was being put to great use – mainly in enabling her to relax and spend time with Grace.

Caitlin couldn't help feeling as though Archie was avoiding her, however. He didn't come into the shop, and she didn't see him around Glentorrin. She couldn't help worrying that what he had overheard was the main reason. Perhaps he was busy with Rosabeth? And if he was, that was a good thing. After all, things were going well between her and Lyle. They had spent a few more evenings together, either at the pub or out with the girls. There had been a trip to the cinema where the girls had giggled on seeing their parents holding hands. There had been a shopping trip to the mainland where the girls had insisted on looking in all the jewellery shop windows and pointing out their favourite diamond rings. Luckily, Lyle had taken it all in his stride and had laughed along with Caitlin about them being desperate to be sisters.

Lyle had made himself at home more and more each time he visited and had taken to slipping his arms around Caitlin's waist and kissing her neck as she prepared the bread for the next day. Things were, to coin an Archie phrase, nice. There had been no other issues or blips, however, when she thought about it, they had tended to avoid any conversations involving anything too deep or controversial.

It was Thursday in the second week of July, and they sat around the table in Caitlin's dining room with the girls for a 'family' meal. Chat had been nonstop about Cora's thirteenth birthday and how she hoped her party was as good as Grace's.

'Ah, but you don't have an Archie to help, so maybe you need to get your dad to ask him,' Grace said, innocently.

Lyle put his fork down. 'I don't need Archie, Grace. I'm great at organising special occasions. Just you wait. Although it will be a party for the four of us. No need to invite everyone else. It will be extra-special because...'

Grace and Cora immediately turned to look at him.

'Because what?' Grace asked.

'Yeah, Dad, because what?'

'You'll see,' he said and tapped his nose. 'So, you're cordially invited to celebrate with us at our house on Saturday evening. Dress up posh. There will be lots to celebrate.' He winked and smiled at Caitlin who was a little surprised at the lack of plans for a big birthday party as she had expected.

'Oooh, this sounds good!' Cora said with a clap of her hands. 'Are you thinking what I'm thinking, Gracie?'

'Ah-ah, no speculating, young ladies. You'll have to wait for the surprise,' Lyle insisted.

'Will there be a birthday cake though?' Cora asked.

'I have to speak to Caity about the design, but... yes.'

This was all a bit last minute, in true Lyle style. And Caitlin hoped that he didn't want her to create something too elaborate when she only had a couple of days in which to produce it.

'Ooh, can we have Indian food?' Cora asked, her eyes wide with excitement.

'We can,' Lyle grinned.

'Yes! Archie likes Indian food. He's been to India, you know!' Grace said.

'Has he indeed?' Lyle asked with a hint of annoyance.

'So... Cora, what would you like for your birthday?' Caitlin cut in before Grace could talk about Archie further.

'Well... I've asked for...'

The list felt endless. And as she listened to Cora reeling off her wishes, Caitlin hoped that the jewellery box she had bought her would be okay, but considering the lengthy tome of requirements Caitlin feared Cora may, in fact, need a jewellery trailer.

'...And some diamond earrings to top it all off.'

Lyle huffed out a long breath. 'Well, I'm quite relieved. I thought you were going to be greedy!' He laughed.

* * *

At the end of the evening, Caitlin walked Lyle to the door as the girls dashed out and across to the inlet, where the lights were glinting on the calm water. It was a chilly July evening, but the glow from the lights strung around the inlet made it feel somehow warmer.

'So, we'll see you on Saturday. Lots to celebrate.'

'Well, yes, Cora will be thirteen.'

'Ah... but not just that.' He leaned to pull her into his arms. 'There are other exciting surprises afoot,' he whispered into her ear, making her shiver.

She hoped that, whatever it was, he wouldn't overshadow Cora's birthday.

'Can't wait,' she replied. Although deep inside something didn't feel quite right. She was unsettled. She could only hope that the feeling was unfounded.

* * *

Sitting in the garden at Jules' house as Evin and Grace played with Cleo and Chewie, Caitlin sipped at her glass of chilled white wine.

'I just want Cora to have a lovely birthday like Grace had. And I'm worried that whatever it is he wants to celebrate will pull the focus away from her,' Caitlin said to her friend.

'What do you think it is? You don't think he's going to ask you to move in with them or something, do you?' Jules asked with a wide-eyed look of shock.

After the barrage of flowers and his intensity, Caitlin couldn't be sure, but the thought vexed her. 'I honestly have no idea. Although I doubt it. We've only be seeing each other a matter of weeks. Surely he wouldn't.'

'But you said he's very affectionate and he gets jealous over Archie. Maybe this, along with buying out the florists, would be his way of marking his territory.' She shrugged and sipped her wine.

'I'm not a patch of grass he can just pee on though, Jules. I'm not comfortable with him thinking he needs to do that. And I'm not sure I want to be with someone who thinks that way.'

Jules held up a hand. 'Hey, I could be totally wrong. It might be a new car or something like that.'

Caitlin sighed and pondered this for a moment. 'I don't know. He made it sound like something big. Something important. Otherwise, why would he want to tell us on Cora's birthday?'

'Maybe he has bought Cora a pony or something?'

Caitlin shook her head. 'No, he's bought her some diamond studs. Personally, I think that's a bit over the top for a thirteen-year-old but...'

Jules widened her eyes. 'Hmm, it is really. I'm sure I was still playing with Barbie dolls at that age.'

'I think I was still into matchbox cars.' Caitlin giggled. 'I wasn't into dolls at all.'

'Changing the subject completely, have you seen Archie since the incident at the hall?' Jules asked.

Caitlin pulled her bottom lip between her teeth and shook her head. 'I think he may be avoiding me. I feel terrible. I didn't mean to sound so horrified by the prospect of dating him. He's a really great guy. Although, I think I may have blown our chances of being friends. We were getting on so well. I could kick myself every time I think about that day.'

'I don't think Archie is capable of holding a grudge. I'm sure he's just been busy.'

Caitlin sighed, feeling despondent. 'I hope you're right, Jules. The last thing I wanted to do was hurt him.'

'And I'm sure he knows that.'

15

'I'm back!' Dexter's voice boomed as he entered the bakery.

Caitlin immediately ran to the other side of the counter and hugged him.

'I've missed you, you hairy lout!' she told him as he picked her up and spun her in the air. Cleo skipped around at their feet making little yipping noises as Dexter dodged trying to avoid stepping on her.

'Aye, and I've missed you too,' he replied in that oh-so-familiar Durham accent. 'I'm not staying long, because I've heard on the grapevine, i.e. Jetty, that you've a hot date with Cora's dad.'

'Blimey, word travels fast,' she said as her feet hit the ground again.

He winked as he crouched to say hello to Cleo. 'Aye, well that's what you get for living in a small village, and for having a best friend with a nosey brother. So, is it serious?'

Caitlin sighed. 'I'm not really sure. He was a little odd about Grace's lack of dad situation, and he seems quite full on. I really fancy him but...'

Dexter gave a sad smile. 'You have to have the whole package, eh?'

She nodded. 'I'm afraid so.' She reached out and squeezed his arm.

Jules had told Caitlin that Dexter was attracted to her when he first met her, but sadly, although she adored him as a friend, she just wasn't attracted to him. He had since moved on, so it was all fine and their friendship had gone from strength to strength.

They went back through to the house and Grace, excited by the surprise visitor, hugged Dexter so tightly he pretended to pass out. Then Grace continued to watch a movie while Caitlin took her friend through to the kitchen and filled him in on her relationship so far with Lyle. He too had opinions about the celebratory dinner.

'I hate to say it, Cait, but I reckon there is something to what Jetty was saying. I reckon you need to be prepared for him to ask you to move in or something.'

Caitlin huffed. 'I'm just not ready for that yet. I don't want to hurt him, but it's too soon.'

'Nah, I think the speed of a relationship is entirely dictated by how quickly that spark ignites. If you know, you know. And I reckon he knows. But it's clear you're not on the same page. So, don't let him guilt you into something you're not ready for, eh?

Caitlin nodded. 'Don't worry, I won't.'

* * *

The invite for a family celebration dinner was exciting for Cora and Grace. For Caitlin, on the other hand, it was nerve-racking. What was there to celebrate other than Cora's birthday? And why did it all make her so nervous? All Lyle had said was there was something surprising and exciting afoot.

After trying to listen in on a whispered and secretive phone call between the two girls, Caitlin had finally confronted Grace to see if she knew anything more. Grace had told her that she had talked it over with Cora and they both thought Lyle was going to propose. Cora had said she was fine with that happening on her birthday because it would make her day even more special. But it had been mere weeks and although things were going well, for the most part, Caitlin couldn't help worrying that they may be right. He did seem enthusiastic about their relationship and had taken things in his stride when the girls insisted on talking about weddings in front of him.

What the heck would she say if he asked in front of the girls though? Surely it was a conversation they should have alone? And she wasn't going to rush down the aisle for a man she was still getting to know. Perhaps, she surmised, a long engagement would be okay. It would at least afford her time to get used to the idea.

Wait... what the hell am I thinking? It's been a couple of bloody weeks! Good grief, Cait, get a grip.

Truth be told, Caitlin wasn't even sure she actually wanted to get married at all... not yet... and not necessarily to Lyle. There were still so many things they didn't know about each other, and she couldn't let go of the fact that there were still concerns niggling at her about some of his opinions.

In the back of her mind, she was laughing at herself. Of course, he wasn't going to ask her to marry him. It would be far too fast and was quite frankly a little conceited on her part. Who was to say he felt so strongly after such a short amount of time? And who was to say he even liked her enough for that? No... it was more likely to be something like a new job or a new car, like Jules had suggested. Maybe even a house move. There were a million things it could be that didn't involve wedding bells and diamonds... At least she hoped so.

Grace came downstairs in a pretty, violet summer dress that she had been saving for a 'special occasion'. Of course, this confirmed Caitlin's thoughts about the evening ahead, considering it was the very colour she and Cora had suggested – more than once – for bridesmaids' dresses.

'You look lovely, sweetheart, but please don't get your hopes up. I honestly can't see him proposing to me. It's way too early in our relationship and we don't know each other that well. Now, I know how excited you are about the prospect of being a family with Cora but... I won't, rush into anything. We have to give it time to see if it's even heading in that direction. I know you might think me selfish but, believe me, it's better not rush these things because to do so could cause a lot of heartache down the line.'

Grace pondered her words for a moment with a crumpled brow and pursed lips. Then, as if a light bulb in her mind had illuminated, she gasped. 'Maybe he's going to ask us to move in together then? Would you prefer their house or ours?'

Oh god, thought Caitlin, *Jules said the same thing. How do I handle that particular scenario? What if she's right? It's slightly less of a big deal than engagement but...* 'Look, I think we'd better see what it's all about first. Let's not jump the gun, because it could be something really simple like a new dog or a new car.'

Grace huffed, clearly not happy with her mum's suggestions. She glanced at the clock. 'We'd better go, Mum! We don't want to be late.'

Oh, I think we do... 'Yes, I suppose we should go.'

Grace rolled her eyes. 'Don't sound so excited, Mum!'

As Grace put Cleo in her basket in the living room, Caitlin picked up the box containing the pink cushion cake complete with its high-heeled shoe and sparkles, just as Lyle had requested – a Cinderella theme for his princess – and they left the house.

For the duration of the short drive to Lyle's house, Caitlin's palms sweated. Her heart kept skipping and her mouth, unlike her hands, was dry as a bone. She pulled up outside the house and turned off the engine, inhaling a deep calming breath.

'Now, remember what I said about getting too excited. Just let Lyle tell us the news, whatever it may be, and whatever it is, be happy about it. If you're not actually happy, pretend!'

Grace grinned. 'I'm going to be ecstatic. I just know it,' Grace said dreamily.

Caitlin shook her head and climbed out of the car to retrieve the cake from the back seat. They approached the front door, but before they could knock, it was flung open.

'Yay! You're here!' Cora exclaimed before hugging Grace.

'Happy birthday, Cora,' Caitlin said as she fidgeted with the cumbersome box.

Grace added, 'Happy birthday! Are you excited? I'm so excited.'

'Oh, me too!' Cora said. 'I've been trying to get him to tell me all day, but he just won't.' She gave an overexaggerated, dramatic sigh. 'We've got balloons and I can see you've brought a cake! Yay!'

Lyle appeared behind his daughter. 'Cora! Let the ladies in for goodness' sake,' he said with a light-hearted grin.

'Thanks for the invite,' Caitlin said as Lyle kissed her cheek.

'My pleasure. It's nice to have something extra to celebrate alongside Cora's thirteenth.' He raised his eyebrows, but again gave nothing away.

Caitlin narrowed her eyes. 'Hmm, whatever it is we're celebrating.'

He cupped her cheek. 'All will be revealed soon. Now, come on, I've made curry and all the trimmings.' He took the box from her hands.

Caitlin followed Lyle through to the dining room, which was decorated with bunting, balloons and fairy lights.

He gestured to a chair. 'Have a seat, darling.' Then he took the box with him into the kitchen.

The girls were already sitting and chatting giddily at the lovingly set table. Lyle began to bring in dish after dish of aromatic food and place it on the mats in the centre, yet Caitlin's stomach insisted on turning over. Was she going to be able to eat?

As the last plate was placed down, Lyle said, 'Right, ladies, a veritable Indian feast at my gorgeous girl's request. Get stuck in.'

The girls began to take little spoonfuls of every dish and munched away on poppadoms dipped in mango chutney as Caitlin sat rigid, becoming more and more nervous as the moments ticked by.

'Come on, Caity, get some food,' Lyle said with a nudge.

She nodded and spooned some Bombay potatoes onto her plate, followed by what she thought smelled like chicken bhuna. 'It all looks so delicious. You must have been working all day to get this ready.'

'You're all worth it,' he told her with a kiss to her cheek.

Her stomach knotted again, and she wished he would just tell her what this was all about and put her out of her misery.

* * *

After the meal was done and the girls had cleared the table, Lyle appeared from the kitchen with the birthday cake. He began to sing, and Caitlin and Grace joined in the rendition of 'Happy Birthday'.

Cora blew out the number thirteen sparkler candle and clapped her hands. 'Miss Fraser, this cake is absolutely wonderful!'

'Please, Cora, just call me Caitlin, or Cait!'

'Well thank you, Cait. I absolutely love it! It's beautiful and you're so clever.'

Caitlin smiled and hugged the girl. 'I'm glad you like it.'

'Right, Caity, you can cut the cake and I'll be back in a second.'

Caitlin picked up the knife and cut four slices as Lyle dashed back to the kitchen and returned moments later with a bottle of Champagne and four glasses.

'Now, girls, as this is a very special occasion, I think it's okay for you both to have a tiny amount of alcohol.' Caitlin was a little disconcerted by the way in which he had given permission for *her* daughter to drink alcohol without consulting her but there was so much going on in her mind she couldn't form the words to protest, and he didn't pause long enough. 'And, Caity, I've ordered you a taxi for later on this evening so you can celebrate with us without worrying about getting home.' He leaned in to whisper, 'Or you could always stay the night.'

She tried to stifle the gasp that bubbled up from within her. They hadn't even remotely got to the point of sleeping together, there simply hadn't been an opportunity, and she wouldn't rush into it anyway, so his suggestion came as a bolt out of the blue. Unaware of how to answer, she gulped and forced a smile.

Lyle popped the cork to gasps and cheers from the girls and poured the bubbling liquid into the glasses. When he was finished, he remained standing.

'May I first of all say how wonderful it is to be surrounded by beautiful young women. I'm a very lucky man indeed.' The girls giggled, but Caitlin felt the colour draining from her cheeks. Lyle smiled at his daughter. 'Cora, you're growing up to be such a wonderful girl and I'm so proud of you. Happy birthday, sweetheart.' He raised his glass and took a sip before turning his attention on Caitlin. He sighed contentedly. 'Caitlin, you came into our lives just at the right time. And we couldn't be happier that you brought Grace too. Cora and I look on you already as family.' Caitlin's heart pounded at her chest, and she lifted her hand to rest it over the area in case her anxiety was visible to the others. Lyle raised his glass. 'So, the second toast is to Caitlin and Grace.'

The girls giggled again and said in unison, 'To Caitlin and Grace.'

Both girls slurped their drinks, and both coughed simultaneously.

'Euw! The bubbles went up my nose!' Cora exclaimed.

'Mine too!' Grace chimed in. 'I don't think I like it.'

Caitlin simply sipped once at the drink, the bubbles stinging her tongue. Then she waited for what was about to come. Her future could be resting on Lyle's next words, and she had no clue what she would say, or do, when the truth was revealed.

'Now, there are only so many times you can meet someone and know that you have something special. I had thought so with Cora's mum, but... well... we'll leave that there.' He smiled awkwardly. 'So, this is all a little fast, I'm aware, but I have some important news and a question to accompany it...'

The girls shared a wide-eyed glance and gripped each other's hands.

Caitlin felt her throat tighten and her eyes began to tingle. She'd have to say no. Watching Lyle standing there, her own truth dawned on her. She didn't love him. In fact, she didn't feel remotely close to loving him. She liked him a lot, she was definitely physically attracted to him, and could possibly love him at some point, but that point was so far off in the distant future, she couldn't even visualise it. And here she was, in front of their two girls, on his daughter's birthday no less, knowing full well that she was potentially about to break all of their hearts. Her stomach churned and she was riffling through her mind for the right words to stop him from saying anything further, but the words wouldn't come. She couldn't speak.

'So...' Lyle continued, 'as you know, I had a meeting with my boss who came over from Canada, and then several phone calls... and well, the upshot is... he wants me to relocate over there to take over as financial controller for the Canadian branch.' His words came out in an overexuberant rush, and his eyes were bright and filled with excitement. 'And... I want you to come with me.'

Caitlin scrunched her brow. 'I'm sorry, what?'

Still beaming, he said, 'I want you and Grace to come and live in Canada with me and Cora, as a family.' He held up a defensive hand. 'Now, before you say anything, I know it's ridiculously fast, and I know there's a whole lot to think about, but please say you will think about it.' The hope in his eyes made her heart ache.

Cora squealed. 'We're going to live in Canada!' And she hugged Grace, who sat statue still, watching everything unfolding with wide, terror-filled eyes, and a pale face. 'Grace! It will be amazing! We'll be sisters but in Canada! This is the best birthday ever! It's amazing! Don't you think it's amazing?'

Caitlin realised she hadn't replied, and she opened and closed her mouth like a fish out of water. 'I... erm... wow... you're right, that's such a lot to think about...'

16

———

Lyle sat beside Caitlin and took her hand in his. 'Like I said, I know it's fast. But I want to start the next chapter of my life with you and the girls. It all just feels right. Don't you agree? I... I love you, Caitlin, I'm already in love with you, and I'm pretty sure you feel the same. We don't have to get married right away, of course, but let's do this. Let's live dangerously and go on this massive adventure together. What do you say?'

Love? How could he talk so confidently about love? He hardly knew her, and she hardly knew him, yet here he was talking about starting a new life on the other side of the Atlantic. There was the bakery, Cleo, her friends, Grace's education...

She glanced over at Grace whose eyes were now filled with tears, her chin was trembling, too, and Caitlin could tell they weren't happy tears. 'I... I think perhaps Grace and I need to talk. This is huge, Lyle. I can't just make a decision like this at the drop of a hat. Please understand?'

Disappointment filled his eyes and Cora fell silent; her excitement suddenly quashed too.

Lyle nodded. 'I see.' He rubbed at his forehead and closed his eyes. 'Girls, why don't you go and get some ice cream to go with the birthday cake and take it out into the garden.'

Silently, the girls did as requested, but as they left the room, Grace paused and pleaded at her mother with her gaze, an unspoken but clear plea that made Caitlin's eyes well with tears. This was not something her daughter wanted. Certainly not the relocating part, that much was evident. Grace had always loved Glentorrin. Skye was her home and it had been all she had known since she was born. Leaving wasn't something either of them had ever anticipated.

Lyle huffed. 'Well, that was subtle,' he said, his face a blank mask.

Caitlin gave an incredulous laugh as anger began to bubble in the pit of her stomach. How selfish could one person be? 'You can't be surprised. I mean... it might have been better if you'd talked to me about this when we were alone, and then we could have discussed things rationally. Making such a huge announcement on Cora's birthday seems incredibly unfair. This day should be about her.' She sighed deeply.

He fiddled with his napkin. 'It is about her. And all of us. I wanted it to be extra-special and I knew she'd be happy. Shame I can't say the same about you.'

Caitlin fell silent for a moment, trying to figure out what to say to lighten the mood, but no appropriate words would come. 'Is your mind completely made up about leaving Skye? Or is this something you're in the process of considering?'

'I've already accepted,' Lyle replied in a monotone voice. 'We – Cora and I that is – move in a month.' He lifted his gaze and gripped her hand again. 'You could follow on at a later date, say the month after? That gives you a little more time to sort things out, put the bakery on the market and—'

That thought horrified her. 'Lyle, I... I don't want to sell my bakery. I've built that business up from virtually nothing.'

He waved a dismissive hand. 'Well, rent it out long term and then, when you've changed your mind, sell it at that point.' He shrugged as if it was the most obvious and simple decision. 'I want this for us, so much, Caitlin. I want you.'

'But Lyle, we haven't even...' She checked to make sure the girls were out of earshot. 'We haven't even slept together, and you're talking about us relocating to a whole other continent and living as a family? There are steps a relationship usually goes through, but I think we've skipped a few, don't you? You must see how crazy that is, surely?'

'The sleeping together part is easily remedied.' He gave a sort of lascivious grin, but when she didn't agree, he pulled his lips between his teeth and fell silent for a few moments. 'I'm never impulsive, Caity. I've spent my life doing whatever Fenella wanted. Taking no risks. Living a staid life. Eating what she wanted, living where she wanted. But this time, I want to be daring. I want excitement and I have that with you. You and I feel right together. You know we do. The girls are already like sisters, it would be such an easy transition.'

She scoffed. 'For whom? Certainly not for me. And not for Grace. Skye is all she has ever known. Her life is here.'

He huffed. 'Yeah, well maybe it's time to broaden her horizons. You can't keep her a prisoner on this island for her whole life, you know.'

'How dare you? I don't treat my daughter like a prisoner.' The anger that had begun to bubble now rose to a simmer. Her heart continued to hammer at her ribcage and her stomach roiled. How was this all happening?

Lyle sighed and stood to pace the room. 'That's not what I meant, and you know it. I just... I want this for all of us.' His gaze was pleading once again. 'I want us to be a family. We're pretty much one already. It's just a matter of relocating us.'

'Lyle, we've been dating for a matter of weeks. I can't move thousands of miles away and take Grace out of school on a whim. And there's Cleo to think of, too, I'd need to look into all of that.' In truth, however, she knew there would be no *looking into* anything. The fact remained that she didn't want to go and neither did Grace.

Lyle gave an evidently exasperated sigh. 'Cleo is a dog, for goodness' sake. We can get a new one over in Canada.'

Caitlin gasped, once again aghast at his attitude and his intimation that Cleo wasn't an important member of their family. 'I don't want another dog. We have Cleo and she's an integral part of our family, mine and Grace's. And what if we go through all of this and things don't work out? What then?'

Lyle stopped pacing and glared at her. 'Oh, it's great to see you thinking so positively about our future.'

Caitlin stood, too, knowing full well her face was no doubt beet-root-red. 'Lyle we may not even have a future. It's too early to tell. I can't rush into decisions this big so soon. I'm really sorry.'

Lyle clenched his jaw. 'I'm offering you a new beginning, Caitlin. A wonderful new life in a new country with new experiences.'

New, new, new. What's wrong with old? thought Caitlin. 'But that's just it, Lyle, I don't want a new beginning. Not such a drastic one, and not like this. And I don't want a new life either. I happen to like the one I have very much. I don't need to go on an adventure and move to Canada. I love Skye, I love Glentorrin. And what's more, I love Grace. I'm sorry, but she comes first, and I could see it in her eyes that she doesn't want to move to Canada. This just isn't right for us, I'm sorry.'

He rubbed his hands over his face. 'How can you say that? How do you know it's not right? You saw Cora's reaction, she's over the moon.' He pointed in the direction the girls had gone.

'For now, she is. But what about when she realises that she'll be thousands of miles away from her mum?'

'She'll get over it. And Fen can come and visit if she wants to. I've no problem with that.' He shrugged.

Caitlin couldn't believe how matter-of-fact he was being. 'Has Fenella even agreed to this?'

He folded his arms defensively across his chest. 'Actually, yes. She's all for it. I wouldn't be doing it otherwise, would I?'

Caitlin couldn't conceive of a mother agreeing for her child to be taken partway across the world and being – all for it. It just seemed wrong. It was wrong! 'Oh... well it's something I personally couldn't do. And I'm not prepared to take Grace away from every-thing she knows. Again, Lyle, I'm sorry, truly I am.'

He clenched his jaw and rubbed at his brow. 'Is this about Archie?'

She sighed and peered up at the ceiling. 'Oh, for goodness' sake. We're onto this now, are we?'

'Well, can you blame me? He's every-bloody-where we go. He clearly fancies you. He's obviously waiting around for you and me to not work out so he can swoop in.'

'Lyle, get your head out of the clouds! This is about me and my daughter, and only me and my daughter.'

'And your stupid dog,' he mumbled.

'And yes, our dog! And she's not stupid!'

In apparent exasperation, Lyle lifted his arms and let them flop to his sides. 'Okay, sorry for mentioning Archie. But you're going to let a thirteen-year-old girl and a bloody dog make decisions about the rest of your life, are you?'

It shocked her that he was so easily dismissing Grace in all of this. 'I have to consider Grace's feelings, of course, I do. She is my number one priority, and she always will be.'

As if a veil had dropped, his eyes filled with a bitterness she had never encountered before. 'That's it, is it? As soon as a man gets serious about you, you run away. Couldn't have a man in your life thirteen years ago, and can't do it now, either. You're just too scared to let someone else into your little party of two.' His tone was mocking. 'Using your child as an excuse is pretty pathetic. You're just being a coward.'

Her nostrils flared and the simmer of anger became a boil. 'Don't be ridiculous. Have you heard yourself and how childish you're being?'

He pointed to his chest. 'I'm being childish, am I? Yet here you are playing it safe because your daughter doesn't like the idea of a few changes.' His use of a namby-pamby voice angered Caitlin to the point where, if she'd been a violent woman, she would've slapped his face.

She inhaled and exhaled roughly, infuriated, her stomach knotting with a tumult of emotions, none of them positive. 'A few changes? You're calling moving thousands of miles away from home a few changes?' She gave a humourless laugh. 'I'm sorry, but you're being completely delusional.'

He scoffed. 'I'm delusional? You're the one telling me Grace is your number one priority when she doesn't even know who her father is! If ever she needs a transfusion or an organ transplant and you're not compatible, that poor kid will have to look elsewhere. How is that prioritising her? She's so much of a priority that she'll never be able to find out who her father is because of your selfishness! She needs a father, Caitlin. All children do!' he snapped.

Caitlin clenched her teeth. 'This,' she waved her finger back and forth in the space between them, 'us, it's over, Lyle, and I think it's time we left.' She walked to the door the girls had gone through. 'Grace!' she shouted. 'Come on, sweetheart, time to go!'

The atmosphere was thick with rage and bitterness when Grace appeared in the doorway. Her cheeks were wet with tears and her eyes rimmed with red. 'Mum? W-what's happening?'

With a deep inhale, Caitlin forced a smile and replied, 'Nothing, sweetie. We're just leaving, that's all.'

Cora arrived alongside Grace. 'Dad, if Grace doesn't want to go to Canada, can we just stay here instead? They could move into this house, or we could move to the bakery house,' she said with wide-eyed hope and a trembling chin. Caitlin's heart went out to the poor girl caught in the middle of everything.

Lyle sighed roughly through his nose. 'I'm afraid the wheels are already in motion, darling. We're going, with or without Caitlin and Grace.'

Cora's eyes spilled over with tears. 'But... I don't want to go if Grace isn't going, and she says she doesn't want to move all those miles away from Skye.'

Lyle spun to glare at his daughter. 'The decision is made, Cora. Unless you want to go and live with your mum and live off bloody spinach and turmeric smoothies!' he bellowed and Cora ran off, sobbing. Lyle turned his focus to Caitlin once again. 'See what you've done? I tried to do something special, and you've ruined it!'

Caitlin pulled Grace into her side and fought to calm the storm raging inside of her. 'I'm sorry you feel that way, Lyle. Right now, I think you should go and hug your daughter. You've just completely ruined her thirteenth birthday. I sincerely hope things work out for you. Good luck in Canada,' she said, in a clipped tone before turning and leaving the house, gripping on to her daughter's hand.

Once in the car and on their way back to Glentorrin, Grace sniffed and turned in her seat to face Caitlin. In the dim evening and the reflections of the dashboard lights, Caitlin could see tears leaving glistening trails down her daughter's cheeks as the young girl said, 'I'm so sorry, Mum. I don't want to ruin your life. I just don't want to move to a whole other country. Not even with Cora. Are you angry with me? If... if you want to go, then I understand. I'll go...' Her voice wobbled with emotion and Caitlin had to swallow down her own as she was driving.

She reached over and took her daughter's hand. 'I'm absolutely not angry with you, sweetheart. Just the opposite. I'm actually glad you don't want to go because I don't either.'

Grace's eyes brightened. 'Really? So, you're not upset?'

Caitlin smiled. 'Not at all. Well... not with you. I'm very upset with Lyle, to be honest. And I'm sorry, love, but there won't be a wedding or a moving in together day. In fact, after tonight, and some of the things that were said, I'm afraid there won't be a relationship between me and Lyle any more. I'm so sorry. I know how you and Cora hoped we'd all be a family. But it just won't work, sweetheart.' She gave a sad smile.

Grace shook her head. 'Don't be sorry. I don't like Mr Budge any more either. I heard what he said to you about me not knowing who my dad is and about you being selfish. That was really nasty of him. And he's wrong, you're not selfish at all. You've always put me first, so I don't need anyone else, just you, and no matter what he says, I don't need a dad because I think you're a brilliant mum. And I should know, shouldn't I?'

Caitlin's lip quivered and her eyes began to water. 'Oh, sweetheart. I love you so much.'

'I love you too.' Grace squeezed her hand. 'But I'm going to miss Cora. I might never see her again, Mum, and that hurts so much. He was *gallus* saying you were selfish when he's the one taking away my best friend.' Grace's eyes gave up more tears and she sobbed silently as she clung to her mum's hand.

17

Back at home, Caitlin had finally managed to calm Grace down. Once she was exhausted from sobbing, her daughter had eventually given in to sleep. It hurt desperately to see her only child so heartbroken at the prospect of her best friend moving thousands of miles away, and this was further compounded by the knowledge that there was nothing she could do to take the pain away. Lyle's mind was made up and neither she nor Grace wanted to move across the Atlantic. Their home was Skye, particularly Glentorrin. Their roots were here, Cleo was here, plus their friends who were more like family. And add to that the few glimpses Caitlin had seen of the *real* Lyle Budge and there was already a recipe for failure. She knew she had made the right decision, even if Grace was hurting. Time would heal... she hoped.

Cleo was a sensitive, wee soul. She curled up on the bed beside Grace as close as she could possibly get. Caitlin stroked the dog's fur, kissed Grace's forehead, and switched off the bedroom light, then made her way back to the kitchen, opened a bottle of Sauvignon Blanc and poured herself a large glass.

She was on her way back to the lounge to decompress from the day's events when there was a knock on the door. It was nine o'clock at night, so she hurriedly went to answer it, fearing the worst – that Lyle had followed her in his angry state. But instead, on her doorstep, stood a pale-faced, drawn and ashen-looking Archie.

She gasped. 'Whatever's the matter, Archie?' *Oh God,* thought Caitlin, *don't tell me Lyle has paid him a visit.* He appeared to be on the verge of passing out, so she reached out to grab his arm. 'Come in, please. Come on before you fall down.'

He frowned and shook his head. 'I'm sorry to bother you so late... I had no idea who else to go to... You seemed like the most logical person,' he informed her as he followed her inside.

She wasn't sure why he had come to that conclusion – unless it was something to do with her recently dumped ex – but she certainly didn't mind that he had. 'You look like you need a stiff drink. Can I get you one?' she asked as worry niggled at her. She'd never seen him like this before. Not even when his uncle had died and he discovered he had inherited the outdoor shop and campsite.

'Aye, whisky if you've got it.'

'I've got Drambuie, is that any good?'

He nodded.

'Right, go through to the lounge and I'll bring it in.' She dashed to the kitchen, grabbed a glass and the bottle of amber liquid from the cupboard, then made her way back to where Archie had slumped onto the sofa. She poured him a glass and handed it over.

'Thanks, Caitlin. I really appreciate this,' he told her in a quiet voice, his eyes staring as if in a zombified trance.

She regarded the usually jovial man who now looked broken. His unruly, naturally wavy hair was more dishevelled than normal, and his eyes were ringed with red. 'You don't need to thank me; I haven't done anything yet.' She smiled trying to lighten the mood. When it didn't work, she said, 'Come on, what's happened?' She sat beside him and fixed her gaze on his pale features.

He huffed out the air from his lungs and continued to stare ahead. 'I don't know where to start,' he said with a hint of incredulity in his voice.

'The beginning is a good place,' she suggested softly.

'Aye... aye... the beginning.' He lifted his chin, suddenly a little more lucid. 'Am I keeping you from anything? Are you meant to be with Lyle?' His mention of the man confirmed that whatever it was, Lyle couldn't be involved.

She smiled warmly. 'No, you're keeping me from nothing at all. Grace is in bed. Go ahead, how can I help?'

He cleared his throat and took a large gulp of his drink. 'Right... so the beginning. It starts way back when I met two friends at university in Glasgow. Kris and Jackie. Great people. We became really close. Did everything together, in fact. We were the Three Stooges, the Three Musketeers. Always together and always laughing. Towards the end of our degree courses, they fell in love and got married. I was their best man, and it was such an honour.' He smiled wistfully. 'But then life took over. I didn't know what to do with myself, couldn't find work in IT as it was quite competitive, so I came back home. Started working in the outdoor shop for my uncle and time ran away with me. Kris and Jackie went back to Edinburgh to live and start their married life together and we kind of lost touch, as you do when you leave uni, you know?'

Caitlin had chosen catering college over university, but she too had lost touch with most of the friends she had met there, so she could understand what he was saying. 'That's just life really. No one's fault.'

'Aye, you're right. But then... around six or so years ago they made contact with me again. It was completely out of the blue. I was surprised to hear from them, but don't get me wrong, it was a nice surprise. So, I went over to Inverness to meet with them for drinks. It was great to catch up and reminisce. But then... what they asked of me was huge...'

Caitlin was confused. 'What they asked of you?'

He took another gulp of his drink; his hand shook as he placed the glass on the coffee table. 'They wanted to have a baby, but... well, there was the obvious issue.'

Even more perturbed by his cryptic tale and where it was going, Caitlin shook her head. 'Obvious issue? What obvious issue? Have I missed something?'

He scowled then briefly closed his eyes. 'Shit... I forgot to mention they were both women. I should have made that clear, eh?' He gave a light laugh that tugged at his lips for only a split second. 'Kris is Kristine König, she was German, and Jackie is Jaqueline Fraser.'

'Ah, now it makes sense. Go on.'

'So, they wanted to know if I would... you know... donate my sperm. They needed someone they trusted. Someone they knew. They knew I'd always been clean. I've never smoked, never done drugs. I kept reasonably fit back then. But it was huge, you know? Emotionally, I mean. I'd always imagined if I was going to be a dad someday that I'd actually *be* a dad. Do you see what I mean?'

Caitlin nodded, intrigued. 'Of course.'

'So, I asked for some time. I couldn't just agree to it, not without giving it some serious thought, so I asked for a few months. I know it seems selfish of me but—'

'It certainly doesn't. It seems like a very reasonable request to me,' Caitlin insisted.

Archie smiled, this time it reached his eyes. 'Thank you, Caitlin.'

He had such a handsome smile, she realised. She shook her head; this was not the time to notice such things. 'Sorry, I keep interrupting. Go on.'

'So, I took around three months to think about it and I did some soul-searching. I went back and forth so much. Could I know there was a part of me in the world but not be involved? Could I stand by and watch two people I'm not related to bring up what would, to all intents and purposes, be my flesh and blood? I changed my mind so many times but didn't really have anyone to talk to who could advise me. Anyway, eventually I agreed.'

Caitlin huffed and widened her eyes. 'Wow. Now I understand why you came to me.'

His smile was tinged with sadness this time. 'I couldn't think of anyone who would understand like you,' he said, his voice breaking and his eyes glistening.

Caitlin remained silent and gave him the time he clearly needed. After a few quiet moments he continued.

'So anyway, I met with them again and told them the news. They were so happy that I knew I'd made the right choice. I could imagine them with a little one running around the place. I suppose the strange thing was that I knew they would possibly look like me, but they would never know who I was. Not in the real sense.'

He cleared his throat again, whatever he was about to impart was evidently affecting him deeply.

'Jackie got pregnant so quick that I didn't really have a chance to change my mind. Not that I would have. Not when I'd committed. That's not who I am. Sophie was born five years ago. I've never met her. I couldn't bring myself to when it came down to it. They understood, thankfully. And they sent photos of her as a baby. She was a cute wee thing. A mop of dark waves, just like Jackie... and just like me.' His chin trembled. 'Turns out the truth was, it was hard to know that there was a child out there with my DNA but that I wasn't directly involved. They named me on the birth certificate, with my permission. And I didn't say I'd never meet her. I just couldn't do it back then.'

There was a distinct note of regret to his voice and general demeanour, and a cold shiver travelled Caitlin's spine. Was the child deceased? Was that what he had just discovered? She couldn't imagine the pain that he would be in if that was the case. She had to fight the urge to rush upstairs and hug Grace. The thought of being without her daughter made panic set in, her chest ached, and her eyes began to sting. As she waited for him to continue, she watched the pain etched on his face and wanted to reach out to him, to hold him and help that pain to dissipate, but she needed to wait. He had come to her for a reason, and she had to respect him telling her at his own pace.

He huffed. 'Wow, I'm so sorry. I didn't expect to get emotional.' His voice wavered as he spoke.

Her own throat tightened, and she reached out and squeezed his arm. 'Don't apologise. It's absolutely fine. Take your time.'

He nodded and took a deep breath. 'After Sophie was born, she was given Jackie's surname. Kris had taken Fraser as her surname, too, so I suppose it was the natural thing to do. I received a couple of family Christmas cards. Photos of Sophie on the front dressed in wee Christmas outfits. It was lovely that they included me, but I found it hard. And to be honest, after the experience I'd had with my own dad, I figured she was probably better off without knowing me. I wasn't sure if I'd end up like him. An abusive, acerbic arsehole. Maybe these things are hereditary, I don't know.'

'Archie, you could never be like that. You're a lovely person. Kind, considerate... Don't put yourself down or compare yourself to that man. You're nothing like him.'

He shrugged. 'I sincerely hope not but... Apparently he wasn't an arsehole before I came along. Anyway... I didn't get a card for the third Christmas. I heard nothing. It was weird but also kind of a relief. That sounds so shitty but...' He sighed deeply. 'I received a letter from Jackie in the new year. Kris had left her and gone back to

Germany where she was from.' He clenched his jaw. 'She'd decided she didn't want a child after all. It was all too much for her. She wanted her old life back. Can you believe that?' Anger oozed from his very being as he spoke. 'That poor bairn didn't deserve that. I offered to step in, to help. Even if it was only financially, but Jackie refused. Said Sophie wasn't my responsibility and that it wouldn't be fair to expect that of me. But I didn't mind. I just didn't want Sophie to go through life feeling unwanted like I had.'

Caitlin wanted to reassure him. 'See, you're nothing like your dad, Archie. You do care.'

He went on, 'I started to send money, even though Jackie insisted I didn't. Eventually she accepted it and started a college fund for Sophie. She said that one day, when she was old enough to fully understand, she'd tell her who I was. I wasn't prepared for how excited that made me. But I was fair giddy at the prospect of meeting her someday.' His lip trembled again. 'I was waiting for that moment, but we lost touch again. I got the feeling Jackie felt like she'd made promises she couldn't keep. I know technically I had rights, with my name being on the birth certificate, but Sophie wasn't mine. Not really. And Jackie was dealing with a lot. She was quite poorly as it turns out. Then her mother had a stroke, and her dad wasn't in the picture. When I found out, I offered to help again, but Jackie assured me everything was okay. That Sophie was fine. But now—'

Caitlin's heart lurched in her chest, and she brought her hands up to her face. 'Oh, Archie, what's happened? Is Sophie okay? Please tell me she's okay,' she pleaded.

'Aye, she's fine. But Jackie...' He began to sob. His shoulders shuddered and he lowered his head, letting tears fall and hit the oak planks beneath his feet.

Caitlin scooted across the sofa and embraced him. 'I'm so sorry, I'm so, so, sorry.'

He rested his head on her shoulder and let all of his anguish pour out. 'I should have stayed in touch. I should have helped more. But Jackie had an undiagnosed heart defect. She died a couple of weeks ago.'

Caitlin's throat restricted and her eyes stung. 'Poor Sophie. How awful. That poor little girl.' She stroked Archie's hair as he clung to her. 'Will Kris come back to the UK for her?'

Archie straightened and wiped the tears from his face with his hand. 'No. That's the saddest part. Jackie's mum found a letter with the will. It contained my details and said I should be contacted in case of her death. I was shocked and I asked about Kris but... Kris doesn't want to take Sophie. She's moved on apparently, has another partner now, a whole new life that a child wouldn't really fit into. She travels a lot for work and says it wouldn't be fair. And Jackie's mum is too ill to take her in. But the thing is, Caitlin, Jackie named me as the one who should be legal guardian. Jackie's mum said if I don't take her, it's likely she will have to go into foster care.' Horror filled his wide-eyed expression. 'I can't let that happen. The poor kid doesn't deserve to lose everyone she's ever loved and to go into care. I have to do something. I have to... I have to take her.'

18

Caitlin gasped on hearing Archie's words. 'Archie, that's a huge responsibility. She's five years old and you've never had children. Are you sure you want to do that? I think perhaps you need time to process all this. Please don't let yourself be pressured into a situation you didn't—'

Archie stood and paced the room. 'What else can I do? She's my daughter when all's said and done. I can't see her go into care when I have a perfectly good, stable home here. I know absolutely nothing about kids, that's true. But I'll learn. I'll have to.' He stopped and turned to face Caitlin. 'And what's more... I want to.'

Caitlin's heart leapt. She could see in his eyes that his decision was already made and, in that moment, she had so many mixed emotions fighting for release that she just hugged him.

'Am I crazy?' he mumbled into her hair as he clung to her.

'Completely,' she replied with a laugh. 'But I can't tell you how much I admire you for the decision you've reached. I just want you to be sure you're not being pressured that's all. Parenthood is a life-long responsibility. And when you agreed to your part in this you didn't really sign up for that element of the journey. But having said that, I wouldn't be without Grace regardless of how difficult parenthood can be.'

He pulled away from her and locked his gaze on hers. 'Will you help me?'

She smiled and nodded. 'Of course. In any way I can.'

His eyes glistened with emotion once again. 'Thank you. Thank you so much.' The sincerity in his dark, chocolate-brown eyes made her heart squeeze and for a moment she couldn't look away.

He swallowed and opened his mouth as if to speak, but then stepped away and rubbed his hands over his face. 'Well, I wasn't expecting this when I woke up this morning.'

'No, it's certainly not an everyday occurrence. So, what's the next step?'

He dropped onto the sofa again and took another gulp from his glass. 'I think I need to speak to my solicitor. As I said, I'm named on the birth certificate, and Sophie was born in Scotland after 2006 so, according to the internet, I should have parental responsibility. Add to that the fact that Jackie named me in her will, I suppose it should be fairly straightforward, in theory. Although, these things are never as cut and dried as you expect.'

'No, I would imagine there will be hoops to jump through.' An awful thought popped into Caitlin's mind. 'Where is Sophie in the meantime?'

Archie's serious, crumpled expression spoke to his worry. 'She's staying with temporary foster parents up in Edinburgh, at the moment. The poor wee bairn. Jackie's mum is trying to visit, but it's not easy for her. That's why I need to get the ball rolling as soon as I can.' His nostrils flared. 'I don't want the girl to be with strangers for any longer than necessary.' He closed his mouth and grimaced as if an unwelcome realisation had just hit. He lifted his chin and Caitlin saw terror in his expression and crumpled brow. 'Shit, Caitlin... that's exactly what I am too. A stranger. The poor girl.' He lowered his head into his hands and ran his fingers through his hair. 'She won't know me from Adam.' There was such despondency in his voice. 'This is why I should have met her instead of being a selfish coward. This is why I should have done more. I don't even know if she's seen photos of me. What if she's terrified? What if she doesn't want to live with me? What do I do then?' The anguish he felt was evident in his eyes again.

Caitlin sat beside him once more. 'Hey, don't jump the gun, okay? And you weren't a selfish coward because she wasn't yours at the time. You had done such a noble thing for your friends, and you weren't to know what would happen years down the line. But you're named on the birth certificate, and you clearly have Jackie's backing. They are huge positive factors. And I'm afraid, at five years old, Sophie has no concept of what's good for her, not really, so she will have to learn to accept it. She's just lost the one constant in her life, so it may not be plain sailing, but you'll get there. I know you will.'

He reached out and took her hand. 'It's strange, isn't it? I never believed in fate until now.'

She narrowed her eyes. 'Fate?'

He nodded. 'Aye. You and I have known each other in passing for years. We've said "hi", shared the time of day, even danced at the ceilidhs together... all the while never really knowing each other. We were acquaintances but not really friends. Not in the true sense of the word. But I feel like something... someone... the universe maybe, made us friends just at the right time. And all because we were both looking for love.' He shook his head and smiled. His eyes were fixed on her, and she felt her face warming as her stomach flipped. Strange reactions, she mused.

Feeling a little unsettled, she scrunched her nose. 'You would have been just fine without me. You have other friends with kids in the village,' she insisted, trying to push her mixed-up feelings down and out of reach.

He shook his head slowly. 'None who would understand like you do.' His voice was a croaky whisper.

'Well, I'll help in any way I can. I remember what it's like to have a five-year-old.'

The movie screen in her mind was suddenly filled with images of Grace trying on her make-up and her shoes, of discovering her best lipstick mashed to a pulp thanks to being dragged around every inch of her daughter's chubby cheeks, and the look of sheer delight on the girl's face as she exclaimed, 'Mummy! I look like you!'; of Grace playing on the beach at the coast and building sand-castles with moats that they had to carefully carry buckets of sea water to fill; of Grace helping her to bake and getting dough in her hair and flour on her nose – evidently a skill she'd inherited from her grandad, a man she sadly never met – and the many, many laughs that had been created simply by the bond they shared. She hoped that Archie could experience this too. But she was very much aware he had a long, possibly difficult road ahead.

'Well, if Sophie does come to live with me, and she ends up anything like Grace, I'll be the happiest man alive.'

Caitlin smile as emotion bubbled up from somewhere deep inside her and she giggled. 'Stop or you'll have me in tears.'

Archie stood. 'Thank you, for everything and in advance too. I know I'm going to need your help. Look, I'd better go. It's late and I'm sure you have stuff to do. Grace will be wondering why I'm here.'

'It's absolutely fine. We've had quite an emotional day, so she's fast asleep.'

He turned and headed towards the door but stopped and came back to face her. 'Thank you. I know I keep saying it, but...' He sighed. 'I can't express how glad I am that we connected at those singles events. Who'd have thought it, eh? It's times like these when you realise who your friends are and how much you need them.

You're a wonderful mum to Grace and I know I can learn a lot from you about parenting. But...' He paused for a moment as if contemplating his next words carefully. 'I... I just wish that I'd...' He shook his head as if to shake away a thought. 'Ugh, listen to me still *havering* on when I said I was leaving.'

Caitlin wondered what he was about to say but didn't press him.

'Anyway, alls I want to say is I'm really glad we both met someone special, you know? We both deserve happiness. Rosabeth is lovely and it's clear that Lyle thinks the world of you, so... We did good, eh?' He huffed. 'I only hope Rosabeth has room in her life for an extra one.' His eyes widened. 'I can't believe I'm about to become a dad to a five-year-old girl... well, hopefully.' He reached out and squeezed her arm. His skin was warm yet rough against hers. 'Goodnight, Caitlin. And thank you again.' He bent and kissed her cheek before straightening and walking out the door.

She watched him leave and confusion clouded her mind. Her heart had skipped when he was close to her, and she had closed her eyes when he'd kissed her cheek, inhaling the scent of him and absorbing the feeling of his stubble gently scratching her skin. She reached up and ran her fingers over the place his lips had touched but huffed at herself and closed the door. *Stop being ridiculous, Cait, as if you need any more hassle.* She certainly didn't need any more complications in her life, not after Lyle. That was it. Dating was simply not for her and life as a single parent was the way to go. It was all she knew, after all, and it was absolutely fine with her if she stayed that way. Completely and utterly fine. The end.

* * *

After a fitful night lacking any real sleep, Caitlin made her way downstairs to the kitchen. The previous night had been filled with so much drama that her mind had been unable to completely shut down. Things had ended with Lyle, that much she was certain of, so she was surprised to see messages and missed calls from him on her mobile when she retrieved it from the place she had left it to charge.

Caity let's talk about this. We both said hurtful things. Lyle x

What hurtful things had she said? She couldn't think of a single one. All she'd offered was honesty and clarity.

Caity we can work through this, we love each other.

She rolled her eyes like an errant teenager and huffed. *Erm... nope. This is purely a one-way street and any chance there was of me loving you were shot out of the sky when you made comments about Grace's father, and Cleo being just a dog, actually.*

Look, you're being unfair. Just reply please. Cora is heartbroken here. Do you want that for her?

Oh, so now you're laying the guilt on thick in shovelfuls, are you? You're the one who chose to disrupt her whole life on her birthday! Well, as much as I feel for Cora with her dysfunctional parents, I won't be accepting blame there, thank you very much.

I know you're reading my messages so why won't you reply?

Actually, pal, I was trying to sleep after the trauma of the bloody evening!

I've left you a voicemail seeing as you won't pick up. This is your last chance, Caitlin. I won't beg.

Last chance rejected, thank you anyway. Have a nice life.

Come on, Caity, please just call me. Please! I want us to sort this out!
PLEASE!!

What happened to not begging?

Right. That's it. We're finished. Done. Happy now? I'm done.

Finally! You got the message! Phew!

Caitlin put her phone down and clicked on the kettle, but as it
heated, there was a knock at the door. Her heart began to pound
inside her chest and her stomach knotted.

Oh god, please don't let it be Lyle, she thought as she wrapped her
robe tightly around her and walked to the door. The last thing she
wanted was a face-to-face confrontation with the man after the tone
of his messages.

Hesitantly, she opened it a crack and smiled with relief.

'Archie, it's you. Is everything okay?' she asked as she opened
the door wider.

He held out a huge bouquet of flowers. 'These are for you. Just a
wee thank you for last night.'

'Where did you manage to get fresh flowers at nine o'clock on a
Sunday morning?' She laughed. 'They're beautiful.' The sweet
fragrance of the vibrant, sun-yellow roses filled her senses.

'I have my sources,' he said with a tap to the side of his nose.
'They symbolise friendship, yellow roses, just in case Lyle gets the
wrong impression.' He smiled shyly. 'Well, I'll be going. I just
wanted to thank you for your help. And for any future help you
may give me.'

'Thank you so much. Although you didn't have to. That's what
friends are for, eh?'

He nodded and his cheeks flushed a little. 'Aye, but you deserve them.' He turned to walk away.

'Hey, want to come in for a cuppa? The kettle's on just now.'

'But... what about Grace, and don't you have stuff to do?'

She shrugged. 'Grace is still fast asleep. Even Cleo has been out for a wee and gone back up to bed, so I have nothing going on that can't wait.'

He grinned. 'That'd be grand then. Thanks, Caitlin.'

He followed her into the kitchen and sat at the small, round table.

'I've been thinking,' he said as she arranged the roses in a glass vase and placed it in the centre of the table. 'I'll need to decorate a bedroom for Sophie, you know, if she comes to live with me. The actual application of paint and paper isn't much of an issue, I can handle that stuff with my eyes closed, but the choosing of colours and such might be a wee bit stressful. I was wondering if you and Grace might like to help me with that? You know, when the time comes...? If the time comes.'

After the previous night's events, Caitlin knew that Grace would need something to occupy her mind that didn't involve losing her best friend. 'That would be lovely. I know Grace would love to help.'

Archie chewed his lip and smiled with the other half of his mouth. 'Aw, great. That's really great.'

She poured tea from the spotty pot into two matching mugs. 'So, tomorrow will be a big day, I guess?'

'Aye. I've to contact my solicitor and set the wheels in motion. I'm nervous as hell. But I have a good advisor in Gordon Marr up in Portree, so I should be fine. And I've got as much paperwork together as I can locate. I even have a copy of the birth certificate.'

'Fantastic. Well, if there's anything I can do to help, just say the word.'

'I'll hold you to that,' he replied with a light laugh. 'Anyway, how's things with you and Lyle? I thought you'd have been out with him last night. I was kind of relieved when you weren't though.'

She smiled briefly. 'He and I are... well... let's just say we're not meant to be.'

Archie's eyebrows lifted. 'Oh, right. That surprises me. I thought things were going great. You seemed all loved-up the last time I saw yous together.'

'Hmm, looks can be deceiving.'

'Well, I suppose at least he doesn't live in Glentorrin, eh? You might not see much of him, which will make things less awkward.'

Caitlin sipped her tea. 'That won't be a problem actually. He's relocating... to Canada.'

Archie's eyes widened. 'Oh, right. Wow. That's huge. I bet you're gutted, eh? Just as things were going so well.'

Caitlin sighed. 'Things weren't going well, as it turned out. Not for me, anyway. He couldn't get past the fact that I had Grace without knowing her father. Said some quite hurtful things about it. Although that was after I'd just turned down his offer of moving to Canada with him. And he asked me in front of the girls, too, which was nice and awkward.'

'Bloody hell! He asked you to go with him? But you've only been dating a few weeks.'

'Exactly.'

'He must have thought a lot of you, I suppose, to ask you in the first place. So, I'm guessing he was upset.' It was clear that Archie was trying to put a positive spin on things for her.

'Hmm, I think it was the rejection that pushed him over the edge. But, suffice it to say, he wasn't pleasant after that. And I don't need that kind of negativity in my life. Plus, I don't want to leave Glentorrin. Neither does Grace. So, it was an easy decision in the end.'

Archie twiddled his mug on the table and watched as the liquid sloshed around it. 'Aye, well, purely for my own selfish reasons, I'm glad you don't want to go.'

She smiled. 'I'm sure you'd find plenty of volunteers to help you with Sophie.'

He shook his head. 'It's not just that though. Now that I feel like I know you properly, I'd... I'd miss you.' He fixed his gaze on her.

'Thanks. I'd miss you too.' Her voice came out in a whisper and there was a pause in the conversation where the air crackled with something Caitlin couldn't quite decipher. Perhaps it was the nervous energy coming off Archie in waves. His life had just been catapulted into the unknown after all. Realising the atmosphere had changed, Caitlin asked, 'So, when do you think you'll talk to Rosabeth about things?' She took a sip from her spotty mug.

'Probably when I know what's happening for certain. She's great, you know? No kids of her own, so we could kind of do this together. Once we've been together for a while longer of course. Things are still in the very early stages and I'm not going to expect her to dive right in after a couple of dates.'

Caitlin smirked. 'So, you won't be asking her to move to Canada then?'

'Shit, no, I won't. I can't believe he put you on the spot like that. And in front of the girls too.'

'Neither can I. Well, I wish you every happiness. And I hope things go smoothly. Let me know how you get on with your solicitor, won't you?'

'Of course. I can't imagine how much my life is going to change. But I hope she likes the outdoors. Camping, hiking, kayaking maybe.'

Caitlin laughed. 'I think maybe give her a chance to settle in first.'

He laughed along with her. 'Oh aye, I suppose I should.'

Caitlin smiled. 'You have so many fine qualities to offer Sophie, she's going to be so lucky to have you in her life and to grow up in Glentorrin.'

There was a loud, heavy knock on the door that made Caitlin jump. 'Oh god.'

Archie stood. 'Do you think that's Lyle?'

Caitlin cringed. 'It might be. He's been texting me and I haven't replied.'

'Right, you go answer the door and I'll go with you. If he starts anything, he'll have me to contend with.'

Grateful that Archie was there, she stood and walked to the door, held her hand on the handle for a moment as she inhaled a calming breath and opened it.

'Why the hell are you ignoring me? Is this what you do? One fight and you just give in?' He spotted Archie. 'Oh, now I get it. You came running home to your fancy man. Not satisfied with one bloke after all these years, eh? Is that it?'

She glanced over his shoulder and saw a wide-eyed Cora sitting in the front seat of the car. Poor girl. 'Not that it's any of your business, but Archie and I are just friends, like I've told you all along. The reason I haven't replied is because you're behaving like a teenager. Just go home, Lyle, we're over before we really began. I thought that much was clear.'

Lyle's nostrils flared and he glared at Archie, jabbing his index finger towards his apparent rival. 'You're the reason this has all gone tits up, Sutherland.'

Archie stepped forward, and evidently unwilling to stoop to Lyle's level, he kept his voice calm and even. 'You've got it wrong, mate. You need to calm down and go home.'

Grace appeared at the bottom of the stairs. 'Mum? Archie? What's going on?' Cleo was standing just in front of her at a diagonal as if creating a barrier between Grace and the brewing trouble.

'What's going on, Grace, is that your mother is sleeping with

Archie behind my back,' Lyle bellowed loud enough for the whole of Glentorrin to hear.

Archie stepped over the threshold; his hands held up as if Lyle was armed. 'Right, that's it. You need to leave, now! You're behaving inappropriately and irrationally. What's more, you're scaring Grace and no doubt, Cora too. Look at your poor wee bairn's face. She's terrified. That doesn't make you a great man in my book.'

'Mum?' Grace said, her voice wobbling.

Caitlin turned to face her bleary-eyed daughter. 'It's okay, sweetheart. Please go into the living room and wait there. Everything is fine, I promise.'

Grace nodded and backed away.

'I'll leave when I want to leave and not before,' Lyle replied with venom, through clenched teeth. Cleo stalked forward, snarling and growling and Lyle stared at the sensitive, protective dog. 'And you can sod off, you little rat.' Cleo began to bark, and Caitlin lifted her up to try to calm her down.

Archie lifted his phone from his pocket. 'Look, I'm trying to be reasonable here, which is more than you're doing, pal. You leave the village now, or I call the police. And we both know they won't let you into Canada with a criminal record, so I suggest you walk away.'

Lyle huffed, his face was red, and his brow scrunched. 'I don't know why you can't just give me a second chance, Caity. We were so good together. We had something special.'

'Lyle, we barely know each other. Just go and start your new life in Canada. You'll meet someone new. We're just not... we're never going to happen. And I think deep down you know that.'

He tugged at his hair and bent double. 'I'm such an idiot! Women are all the same! Users, manipulators, the lot of 'em.' He stood again and glared at Archie. 'Good luck to you, mate. You need it with her.' He sneered in Caitlin's direction and with his final words, he turned and stormed back to his car, got in and sped away, tyres screeching.

When Lyle's car was out of sight, Caitlin heaved a sigh of relief, placed Cleo on the floor and almost collapsed against the wall.

The little dog fussed around Archie's feet, so he bent quickly to stroke her. 'You're a brave wee mutt, eh? Yesh you are.' Cleo wagged her tail frantically, clearly proud of her role in proceedings.

Caitlin inhaled a shaking breath. 'Thanks, Archie. I don't know what I would've done if you hadn't been here.'

He stood and pulled her into a hug. 'Hey, it's nae bother. And I get the feeling the mention of him not getting into Canada with a criminal record may have put him off coming again. I don't think he'd thought this visit through. But if he does come back, you ring me right away, okay?'

She nodded, still a little shaken by what had happened. 'Thanks again.'

'Look, I'll be off. I think Grace might need you. But I'm on the end of the line if he comes back.' The next thing he did was strange but sweet. He kissed the top of her head before turning and leaving the house. It was an affectionate gesture that made her smile.

'Archie!' she called out to him, and he stopped and turned his head. 'You're going to make a wonderful dad,' she told him with a lump in her throat.

He didn't reply. Instead, a wide smile spread across his face, and he somehow stretched taller as if empowered by her words, and he lifted his hand in a salute.

19

Just as Caitlin was closing the bakery at the end of the day on Monday, Archie walked in. He looked so different in his suit and tie. Ridiculously handsome, in fact. His hair was still wild and shaggy, and his chin still graced with stubble, but it was clear he had attended the meeting with his solicitor with every intention of putting across the best of himself.

She closed the door and locked it behind him. 'So, how did it go?' she asked eagerly.

He loosened his tie and held out his arms. 'You're looking at the father of a five-year-old girl,' he replied with tears of joy in his eyes.

Caitlin flung her arms around him. 'Archie, that's wonderful! I'm so happy for you! How do you feel?' She pulled away and held him at arm's length.

'Bloody rung out to be honest. It was fairly straightforward, because of the birth certificate and the letter in the will that mentions me, so I now have full parental responsibility. I've been assigned a social worker just to make sure Sophie settles in okay, but – and this is the scary part – she will be with me at the weekend. I've to go up to Edinburgh and meet her at her foster carer's on Friday. And then I'll bring her home Saturday or Sunday.'

Caitlin was astounded at how calm he seemed at the prospect of being thrust into a whole new lifestyle. 'Wow. That's all so fast. What about getting her room ready? And what about your work?'

'The campsite isn't too bad. It's all tents, so they're fairly self-sufficient, and I have a cleaner for the shower blocks and toilets, and Dex to do check-ins and maintenance now he's back from his trip. The IT stuff, when it comes in, can be done from home. It's the shop that's the main issue, although Sophie will be enrolling in school, so I may just have to rethink my hours. If I need to get extra help in, I'll do that.' He shrugged.

Caitlin was impressed with the way he had just stepped up. He was putting the welfare of his child first, unlike Lyle, who put himself and his own desires before everyone. Archie was doing what any father should, but the fact that he didn't necessarily sign up for the full-time dad thing from the start meant that everything he was doing was because he wanted to.

'So, therein lies the reason for my visit...' he said rather sheepishly. 'I was wondering if you might come around to mine tonight and help me pick some things for her room?' He winced and narrowed his eyes. 'And Grace too?'

Caitlin laughed. 'We'd love to. I think Grace will have some nice ideas. What time shall we come round?'

'I've bought pizzas, so shall we say six? Bring Cleo too. I picked up some magazines when I was up in Portree, and I've got my laptop so we can order things online if necessary. Then, I'm going to close the shop from Wednesday and get the room done before I head up to Edinburgh on Friday. I've been put in touch with the foster carer and apparently Sophie's favourite colour is blue, like the sky.' He grinned. 'Her words. And she loves stars and rainbows too, which is wonderful. I was worried she'd be a really girlie wee thing and into pink and fairies but apparently not. Anyway, I've sent a couple of photos of me and a letter that they can read to her to make things a little easier.'

'That's so lovely. She's lucky to have you.' She hoped her sincerity shone through because she couldn't think of a better man to be the little girl's father.

'Aye, let's hope she feels that way too. Oh, and apparently she has a dog. A pug called Bowie. So, looks like I'm getting two for the price of one.'

'Bloody hell, Archie, you don't do things by half do you?' Caitlin laughed.

'Apparently not!' He turned and unlocked the shop door. 'See you in a wee while then.'

'You will. I'll bring something sweet to treat us all.'

He rubbed his hands together. 'Och, you're a star.'

* * *

Once back in the house, Caitlin found Grace cuddled on the sofa with Cleo. The little dog wagged her tail as she walked into the room. She reached down and scratched the dog's belly before bending to kiss her daughter on the head.

'Hey, sweetie. How are you doing?' Caitlin asked with concern. She knew that Grace had been melancholy all day and each time she had checked on her through the day, she had been cuddled up with Cleo.

Grace sighed and shrugged. 'I'm okay. I phoned Cora, but her dad said she wasn't in. I think she was, but I don't think she wanted to talk to me. Or her dad didn't want her to talk to me.' Her lip trembled.

Caitlin flopped down beside her on the sofa. 'Hey, come on, love. I hate to see you so sad.' She stroked her hair. 'I've got something that might cheer you up.' She proceeded to tell Grace about Archie's request for help and all about Sophie too.

'Wow. Isn't he scared? He's never been a dad before. He hasn't even looked after a dog, has he?'

'No, and I think he is a wee bit scared, but I think he's excited, too, and he needs our help. In fact, he specifically mentioned you. Anyway, go and get a good wash. We've to be there at six. He's making pizza.'

* * *

Just before six, Caitlin, Grace and Cleo set off on their short walk along the road to Archie's house. It had been a *dreich*, rainy day, but the gloom had finally cleared, and the sun was peeping through the clouds and forming a halo of light over the little coastal village. It was a tad chilly, and they had to dodge puddles as they walked. Although Cleo didn't avoid puddles, ever. Instead, she trotted through them with a wagging tail as if they were her very own personal foot spa.

The village, on the whole, was quiet, with the exception of Jules, her fiancé Reid and his son Evin out for a walk with Chewie. They waved and shouted their hellos and Caitlin made a mental note to get the girls around for drinks again soon. She had so much to tell them.

At six o'clock sharp, Caitlin knocked on the door of the stone cottage along the road from Archie's outdoor shop. He opened the door, and they were greeted by the smell of fresh herbs, baked cheese, and dough.

'Come on in, guys. The pizza is just about done.' He bent to fuss Cleo. 'Hey there, girl, I bet there'll be a sneaky bit of ham for you.' As if genuinely understanding the word ham, Cleo yipped and wagged her tail.

Caitlin and Grace stepped inside and removed their jackets. Caitlin had only ever been as far as the hallway at the front of the cottage and had only glimpsed the living room once before. Now she could see that it was neat and tidy. There was a grey and cream tartan carpet, plain cream walls, two two-seater black leather sofas and a huge inglenook fireplace complete with roaring fire to take away the chill outside. Caitlin spotted Reid's artwork on three walls, all depicting scenes from around the Isle of Skye, and the window on the fourth was adorned with a pale grey blind and sumptuous cream, jacquard curtains. It was fairly masculine, but she knew that would soon be about to change.

'We'll eat in the kitchen. Go on through,' Archie told them as he hung their coats in the small hallway.

Caitlin unclipped Cleo's lead and they made their way through to the back. The kitchen was a little more to Caitlin's taste, with grey, shaker-style units and grey and cream marble worktops. A modern twist on a country classic. A cream-painted wooden table at one end was surrounded by four mismatched chairs. Again, a painting by their mutual friend Reid featured on the wall by the table. This one was of the Quiraing, the mountain range in the north of Skye on the Trotternish Peninsula, a place Caitlin loved but hadn't been walking in for too long.

Caitlin and Grace sat, and Archie came in and removed three pizzas from the oven and placed them in the centre of the table. 'I wasn't sure what you'd like, so we have a veggie one, a chicken and mushroom, and a ham and pineapple. All home-made,' he added with a smile of pride.

'Fantastic. You didn't have to go to so much trouble though. We'll eat pretty much any pizza won't we, Grace?'

Grace was already munching on her first piece, and she nodded effusively whilst mumbling, 'Hmm, good!' Cleo watched her every mouthful, licking her lips in anticipation of any tasty morsel that might come her way.

'I forgot to show you this earlier,' Archie said as he handed a photo to Caitlin. A beautiful dark-haired little girl smiled from the print. 'It arrived in the post from Jackie's mum, bless her heart. It's a recent photo too. She's in the garden at the foster carer's.'

Grace leaned closer. 'Oh, she's so cute! Isn't she, Mum?'

Caitlin beamed. 'She's gorgeous. I can definitely see you in her features, Archie.'

Archie's cheeks coloured.

'So have you got lots of ideas for her room?' Caitlin asked as they ate.

'I'm thinking maybe a navy-blue ceiling and bedhead wall, then lots of stick-on glow-in-the-dark stars.'

'Yes! Oh, I'd love that!' Grace interjected before Caitlin had a chance to reply. 'Then a sky-blue on the other walls with rainbows. I've seen these rainbow wall stickers you can get online; I'll show you. And there's this really cool duvet set on one of the big shop websites that's got galaxies on. That glows in the dark, too, I think,' she added with enthusiasm, and it warmed Caitlin's heart to see her daughter's mood lifted. 'And we'll have to make sure we get things for Bowie the Pug too. He's Sophie's best friend, so we'll need to make sure he settles in.'

Archie nodded. 'That all sounds amazing, and you're right about Bowie, this will be his home too. The carpet in the back bedroom is fairly neutral and there's a single bed and wardrobe and bedside table, so that will all work. I'm so glad you guys are here to help me,' he told them with a wistful smile.

'We can't wait to meet little Sophie,' Grace told him. 'I can be like a big sister to her.' Her face paled a little and she glanced nervously as her mum. 'I mean... like a big cousin... or something like that.' Caitlin could see that Grace was still affected by the events that took place with Lyle. The hope she had been filled with at the start of the relationship had been dashed so harshly and it made her heart ache. All she wanted was for Grace to be happy and to help her get over it all.

'I'm sure Sophie will be very excited and happy to meet you, Grace,' Archie told her. 'Especially when I tell her you helped to design her new room.'

* * *

Once their pizzas were finished, Archie and Grace cleared the table and then they all sat on the living-room floor in front of the fire with the interior design magazines laid out before them and the laptop at the ready. Cleo dozed off after her treats and began snoring loudly, much to everyone's amusement.

After an hour, they had planned the whole room. They had also ordered toys and photo frames so Sophie could have pictures of her mum up in her room. Caitlin lost count of how much it was all going to cost, but Archie didn't seem bothered. Then a bookcase was purchased from a huge online store, along with books to go on the shelves.

After Sophie's needs had been addressed, they turned their focus onto Bowie, Sophie's pet pug. A navy-blue bed with a plush cream cushion for the floor of Sophie's room. Two bowls for food and water for the utility room, some chew toys and a huge sack of dog food that would no doubt last months.

'Jackie was always a David Bowie fan, so it's no surprise to hear that's what they named the dog. Her favourite song was "Star Man" which also explains a lot I suppose.' He gave a small, sad smile. 'It's amazing how many things I'd forgotten about Jackie and how many of them are coming back to me now.'

As they tidied the magazines into a neat pile, Grace asked, 'Will Sophie have your second name when she comes to live here?'

Archie paused and frowned. 'Oh... do you know, I hadn't even thought about that. I could maybe add my name to hers so she can keep her mum's name but also feel like she belongs here with me too. Sophie Fraser-Sutherland,' he suggested with a smile.

Grace beamed. 'I think she'll like that.'

Caitlin nodded. 'I think so too. It has a lovely ring to it. You're going to have a busy few days ahead of you. If we can help on an evening at all, just say.'

'Ooh, ooh, I can help through the day! School is finished and Cora is... Anyway, I'd like to help,' Grace said.

Archie reached out and patted her shoulder. 'I'd love you to help, Grace, if you don't mind. How are you with a paintbrush?'

'I'm an expert!' she said, but then glanced at Caitlin and burst out laughing. 'Okay... maybe not quite an expert, but I can paint!'

'I'll make sure to send her in old clothes,' Caitlin said with a chuckle. 'And I recommend covering the carpets. Last time she helped me paint her bedroom, she ended up wearing more than went on the walls.'

'That's it sorted then. I'll go first thing Wednesday and collect the paint, then when I get back, I'll call to your house for you. Deal?' Archie said, holding out his hand.

'Deal!' Grace replied with a smile.

* * *

At the end of the evening, Archie walked them to the front door. 'I bet the postman and the delivery drivers are going to be sick of visiting here by the end of the week,' he said with a grin.

'It's going to look amazing. I can't wait to see it all done. And I can't wait to meet your little girl,' Caitlin told him.

'My little girl. It sounds so strange. But I love hearing it already. Thanks for all your help, ladies.' He hugged them both and gave Cleo a good scratch behind the ears, then bid them all a goodnight.

As they walked the short route home, Grace stopped. 'Thanks for bringing me to help, Mum. I've had a fun evening. Archie is so lovely, and Sophie is lucky to have him to look out for her, isn't she?'

Caitlin hugged her daughter. 'She certainly is, sweetheart. She certainly is.'

20

Grace helped with Sophie's room for the rest of the week and when Caitlin was asked to pop round to see it, she was gobsmacked at how much they had achieved. It looked absolutely wonderful. Luckily, everything had arrived in time and the room now appeared like a bed on a space station. Sure enough, the wall behind the bed and the ceiling were navy-blue. Caitlin got the full effect of the glow-in-the-dark stars when Archie lowered the blind and closed the curtains. As if they weren't enough, there was the soft glow of a night light that cast stars onto the rest of the walls. When the lights were on again, she saw that the other walls were adorned with rainbows – applied by Grace no less, who seemed to have had a brilliant time helping, judging by how excited she'd been each night telling Caitlin about what they'd done – and the bookshelf was built and stacked with all manner of stories and picture books befitting a five-year-old.

'You've really done her proud, Archie,' Caitlin told him as they stood in the room, staring up at the stars.

'I think I'm going to take her camping so she can see the real night sky here. It'll be totally different to what she's experienced in the capital, and she's never used a telescope so that should be amazing for her.'

Caitlin's heart skipped as she watched her friend talking about his plans with his little girl. He really was a very special man. 'You really are going to be the best dad,' she told him.

He hugged her and she tried to ignore the way it felt to be in his arms.

* * *

On Saturday, Archie texted from Edinburgh to say his first meeting on Friday with Sophie had been a little rocky, and that he would be home on the Monday now instead of earlier as he'd originally anticipated. He said he'd had very little sleep, worrying if he was doing the right thing for her, so she immediately replied to reassure him that he was. She knew it wasn't going to be easy for either of them, but she couldn't think of a better father for the girl, and she was determined to help in any way she could.

It was now late July and Caitlin sat in her cottage garden with Morag, Jules and Ruby. Dexter was covering at the campsite for Archie, or she knew he would have tagged along too. When her friends had arrived, Caitlin had filled them in on the horror that was her brief relationship with Lyle. She was relieved not to have encountered him again after their last meeting, and it struck her, as she told her friends about the whole debacle, that she hadn't really given him much thought.

'I can't believe he went so psycho after only a couple of dates. That's just bizarre,' Ruby said once Caitlin had finished recounting her story. 'It's like something off a stalker movie.'

'You're not kidding. Talk about a bunny boiler,' Jules agreed with a wide-eyed expression.

'Bunny boiler?' Morag asked with a hint of disgust.

'It's a movie reference, Morag. *Fatal Attraction* with Glenn Close and Michael Douglas. And yes, that scene is about as disgusting as it sounds,' Ruby informed her.

'Ooh, might have to watch that. I love me a bit of Michael Douglas,' she said with a giggle. 'Just don't tell Kenneth.'

'So, what will you do now, Cait?' Jules asked.

Caitlin shrugged. 'Give up, I suppose. I think I'm destined to be single forever. I'm not prepared to go on an app, only to be catfished. And I certainly don't fancy singles nights again. I'm not open to a relationship with someone old enough to be my dad, or someone who still lives with his mother, and in my recent experience that's all I seem to attract.'

Morag reached out and squeezed her arm. 'Can I fix you up, hen?' she asked with a glint in her eye.

Ruby leaned forward. 'Ooh, Morag, who are you fixing her up with?' she asked eagerly.

'Yes, Morag, who?' Caitlin asked with narrowed eyes and a fair dollop of suspicion.

Morag told them, 'He's a delivery driver from the wholesalers. His name is Bram.'

'Like the Dracula bloke? Who names their child Bram?' Caitlin asked with a turned-up nose.

'Aye, but he's not a vampire, I can assure you of that,' Morag replied with a serious expression. 'He's a driver, remember?'

Caitlin frowned. 'Aye, Morag, and Bram Stoker wasn't... never mind, go on.'

With delight, Morag carried on, evidently needing no further encouragement. 'He's called Bram Wallace. He's from Glasgow originally, but I believe he lives in Kyle of Lochalsh. Handsome, no kids, steady job. Fair hair, what's left of it as it's shaved pretty close. But he's only in his early forties and so lovely. He's been delivering to me for a while now, but I always thought he was married, on account of his wedding ring, so I never mentioned him before. Anyway, he stopped wearing his ring, and me being me, a nosey old beggar, I asked after it. Turns out he's been widowed for five years but has only just started to try to move on, bless him. He's also on dating apps and such but hasn't had any luck yet, like you. Although he spotted you when you were out walking Cleo the last time he came, and he asked after you. Here, I took a sneaky pic of him on my phone.' She held out the screen towards Caitlin so she could see the image of the man. As Morag had said, he had a shaved head, a full, fair beard, a nice smile and was quite stockily built. 'What do you think? Can I put you in touch?'

All eyes were on Caitlin as she thought back to Lyle and his drama. Then she thought about Archie and how he had found someone he really liked, and the strange mix of emotions that fact evoked. She'd experienced weird sensations the last couple of times she'd seen Archie, but what did they mean? She wasn't feeling more than friendship for him, was she? She had to admit that he was an attractive man, something she'd never really noticed before, and he was fun to be around and was amazing with Grace... But, it was a moot point considering Rosabeth was in the picture. And if Morag knew this driver and considered him a decent human being, what did she have to lose? One thing was certain, he could be no worse than Lyle.

Realising she hadn't answered, Caitlin heaved a long sigh. 'Aye, why not. I had sworn off dating, but what the heck.'

The rest of the women cheered and toasted.

Caitlin, however, began to wonder what could possibly go wrong this time.

* * *

At the end of work on Monday, Caitlin headed into the house and was contemplating messaging Archie to see how things were going, when there was a knock on the door. She checked her reflection in the hall mirror. *Ugh, rough old hag*, she sneered at her reflection, before smoothing down her locks, and opening the door.

'Hey, Caitlin. There's someone I'd like you to meet,' Archie said softly from where he stood. His handsome smile was wide and his eyes bright, despite the lack of sleep he'd informed her about by text. 'Sophie, sweetheart, this is my good friend Caitlin Fraser. She has the same second name as you, how cool is that? Come and say hello,' he said to the little girl, who was standing out of sight.

Slowly a little mop of long dark hair appeared. Big brown eyes peered up at her from under long lashes. Sophie was wearing jeans with rainbows and stars embroidered on them and a pale blue T-shirt with a unicorn on the front. A toy pug was clutched in one hand and the fingers of her other were in her mouth. She was utterly adorable.

Caitlin crouched to her level. 'Hello, Sophie, it's lovely to meet you.'

Sophie huddled into Archie's thigh and seeing her do so melted Caitlin's heart.

'Would you like to come in and meet my little girl?'

Sophie glanced up at Archie and he nodded encouragingly. The little girl gave a couple of small, almost invisible nods and Caitlin stepped aside for Archie and Sophie to walk into the house.

'She's so painfully shy,' Archie whispered. 'There have been lots of tears, which is to be expected I suppose after what she's been through.' His worry and concern were evident in his eyes as he spoke.

Caitlin squeezed his arm. 'Well, at least the pug turned out to be a cuddly toy, I suppose. Small mercies.' She smiled, trying to lighten his mood.

He shook his head. 'No, no, the real thing, Bowie, is back at home having a wee nap. He doesn't travel well as I discovered to my chagrin.' He chuckled and rolled his eyes.

'Ah.'

They wandered through to the living room, where Grace was in her usual spot, cuddled up on the sofa with Cleo watching a movie. The dog's tail began to wag frantically when she spotted Sophie. Ooh, a small person! They give good cuddles, she must have thought.

Grace sat up immediately. 'Hi, you must be Sophie. I'm Grace. I think you and I are going to be good friends.'

Caitlin's heart was fit to burst as she watched Grace hold out her hand and Sophie take it.

Grace patted the sofa. 'Want to come and watch this movie with me? It's about a boy who lives in a train station in Paris.'

Sophie clambered onto the sofa beside Grace and immediately reached out to pet Cleo.

Grace told her, 'This is my doggie. She's called Cleo and she's a Yorkie Poo.'

Something magical happened then. Sophie giggled. 'Yorkie Poo, that's funny,' she said in a sweet little voice as Cleo licked her hand.

'It is funny, isn't it?' Grace replied with a quick glance at her mum, a huge smile on her face.

Caitlin's hand shot up to her mouth and when she turned to Archie, his eyes were glistening. He moved his attention from Sophie to Caitlin and mouthed the words, 'Thank you'. Caitlin reached out and squeezed his hand.

He placed his other hand on top of hers and whispered, 'I really mean it. Thank you from the bottom of my heart.' His gaze expressed his genuine gratitude, even though it was Grace who had made the miracle happen.

'Come on, let me make you a cuppa and we'll leave the girls to their film.' They walked through to the sunny kitchen and Archie sat while Caitlin made a pot of tea. 'I gather the first meeting was tricky then?'

Archie inhaled slowly and exhaled in a huff. 'You could say that. Bless the poor wee bairn. She's been through so much in the last few weeks that I don't even think it's all hit her yet. Then for a strange man to come into her life and claim to be her dad... well, it's enough to push anyone over the edge. She screamed when her foster mum introduced me. I panicked at that point and almost came home. I didn't want to put her through any more trauma. But... being with me is the best thing for her. The foster parents said so. And at least I'm not taking her out of her country. She's still in Scotland, like she was with her mum. I think I could be in for a long and hard time of it. But we'll get there.'

'I know you will. I've seen your determination. And the way you look at her already. She definitely looks like you too.'

Archie beamed at her words. 'You think so? I can only see Jackie.'

'She has your eyes and nose for sure,' Caitlin insisted.

He laughed. 'Poor kid.'

'What's next for you two then?'

'Tomorrow I contact the local council about registering her for school to start after summer. I need to register her with the doctors, contact the social worker so she can come out and check on her. And figure out what she likes to eat.'

Caitlin placed the pot of tea on the table and grabbed a couple of mugs from the mug tree. 'What did she think of her room?'

Archie frowned. 'I think she liked it, but she hasn't really spoken to me. I'm just getting nods at the moment. The first time I've heard her talking properly is when she spoke to Grace.'

'Give her time. She'll get there. I'm sure she will.'

'Aye, I was wondering about inviting a few folks round for a barbecue. Reid and his lad, you and Grace maybe. Just so she can get to know some of my friends and see some friendly faces. Do you think that would work?'

Caitlin was concerned about the girl being overcrowded. 'I'd maybe leave it a week or so. Just until she knows you better. Let her realise she can trust you first before you start thrusting her into being centre of attention. Maybe introduce her to Rosabeth?'

'Oh aye, Rosabeth. I'd almost forgotten about her. I should message her and let her know what's going on, eh?'

Caitlin was surprised he hadn't imparted news of his recent fatherhood yet. 'Might be a good idea. She will be one of the new constants in Sophie's life.' Hearing herself say the words made something twinge inside of her. She gulped her tea to push down whatever it was. 'Oh. Morag is setting me up with a delivery driver called Bram,' she announced out of the blue.

Archie's brows lifted. 'Really? Oh right. Great... great. Let me know how it goes.'

'Same with Rosabeth.'

'Aye, absolutely.'

* * *

Later on, when Archie and Sophie had gone home, and Grace had taken herself and Cleo off to bed, a message pinged on her phone. She opened WhatsApp to see a photo of Sophie, fast asleep in her newly decorated bedroom. Then a photo of Archie giving the thumbs up sign. Once again, her heart melted. For Sophie obviously. Not Archie. Absolutely not Archie.

She replied with a smiley face and placed her phone down, but it started ringing. A number she didn't recognise flashed on the screen. It was after ten at night and so the call unnerved her a little. She hit the screen to answer.

'Hello?' she asked hesitantly.

'Erm, Caitlin? Hi... This is Bram. Your friend Morag gave me your number and said I should call you about maybe going out some time.'

Caitlin straightened up in her seat. Bram had a very nice voice. Quite silky sounding and gruff. 'Oh, yes, hi Bram, lovely to hear from you.'

'I'm sorry it's so late, but I was on a run up north on the mainland and I've only just got in.'

'No, no, that's fine. I'm still up.' *Way to state the obvious, you dufus.*

A message pinged through, and she pulled the phone away from her ear to read the screen where there was a message from Archie.

I know you kind of advised against it but I'm throwing caution to the wind. BBQ at mine on Saturday, 6 p.m. Jules, Reid and Evin are up for it. Morag and Kenneth, Ruby and Mitch too. How about it? Archie

Bram cleared his throat. 'Anyway, I was wondering if you're free on Saturday at all? I thought we could maybe go grab a bite to eat.'

She hit reply to Archie.

So sorry Archie but I have a date. Grace would probably love to come if I can send her with Evin though.

She replied to Bram. 'That would be lovely. Where are you thinking of going?'

Another message pinged through from Archie.

Bring your date! PLEASE! I know Sophie would love you to be here.

Bram replied, 'I've heard the Coxswain is good for food. We could go there maybe?'

She hesitated for a moment before saying, 'Erm... I know this is a bit presumptuous, but my friend in the village is having a barbecue and I wondered if you would like to come with me?' She closed her eyes and chewed her lip as she waited for the reply.

'Erm... Yeah, that sounds grand. So long as they won't mind me tagging along.' He sounded quite taken aback.

Relief flooded her veins. 'They've invited you actually.'

'Oh, great. What time?'

She shot a quick reply back to Archie.

Okay. Bram and I will be there!

Then replied to Bram. 'Six? I think you know the bakery I own, so do you want to meet me there?'

'Okay, sounds good. Six it is. See you then. Oh... you don't even know what I look like,' he said, sounding unsure.

'Actually, please don't be cross, but Morag took a sneaky snap of you and showed me.'

'Oh! Great! And you still want me to come to the barbecue?' he laughed.

She grinned. 'Absolutely.'

21

Grace had been making a keepsake scrapbook for Cora in the hope that Lyle would let them say goodbye. She had included photos, messages and little trinkets collected from their many times together. But contact from Cora had been almost non-existent, just a couple of quick emails presumably when she was alone. Caitlin was grateful that at least she still had a good friend in Evin in the village because she would soon need him more than ever.

On Wednesday evening, Grace went to Jules' house to see Evin and Caitlin met Dexter at the Coxswain. It felt good to have her drinking buddy back after his extended holiday. Time spent with Dexter was easy and relaxed and meant she could simply be herself.

'So, have you heard anything more from Loony Lyle?' Dexter asked before taking a huge gulp of his pint.

Caitlin laughed. 'Loony Lyle? Thankfully no. I think he got the message when Archie saw him off and he is due to leave for Canada any time now.'

'Aye, he's a good bloke is Archie.' He gave her a knowing look.

She narrowed her eyes at him. 'What?'

'Nothin', mate. Do you think you'll see Lyle before he leaves?'

Caitlin sighed. 'I doubt it. I just hope he sees sense and allows the girls to say goodbye. As hard as that will be, I think they both need it.'

Dexter shook his head. 'Aye, poor Gracie. It's awful to lose such a close friend like that. Maybe someone needs to have a word in his ear.'

Caitlin glared at him. 'Dex, don't you dare go all guns blazing to Lyle's house. I'll be extremely pissed off if you do.'

Dexter shrugged. 'Well, you cannit go, can you? He's likely to kidnap you or something. Nah, I just want him to see sense.'

Caitlin shook her head. 'Still, you need to stay away, do you hear me? Hopefully he'll come to a sensible conclusion by himself.'

'Aye, we can but dream.' He took a drink of his beer and changed the subject. 'So, what do you think of Sophie? She's a little sweetheart, isn't she?'

Caitlin beamed. 'Oh, she's gorgeous. Archie was going to register her with the GP today. Have you seen him?'

Dexter nodded. 'Aye. He said she wouldn't speak to the receptionist, but he managed to get things done. Bless that poor lass and what she's been through. I couldn't think of a nicer dad for her to have.'

'No, me neither.' There was a long pause in the conversation where Dexter appeared deep in thought. 'Come on, Dex, I can sense you have something to say.'

He pursed his lips and rubbed his beard. 'I was just thinking... You and Archie would make such a cracking couple.'

Caitlin rolled her eyes. 'Ugh, not you as well?'

'Aye, I know our Jetty has hinted at it too. And so have Ruby and Morag but... I think they've got a point. He's dead fond of you, you know?'

'And I'm fond of him, but he has Rosabeth now, so it makes no difference how I feel. If I felt anything, which I don't,' she blustered. 'Anyway, I think Rosabeth's coming to the barbecue on Saturday, and it'll be the first time she meets Sophie, so I hope it goes well.'

'Hmm. Archie was telling me she was a little angry about the news that he had a daughter. She says she was never interested in having kids, but that she'll give things a go seeing as she likes him so much. So, that's good, I suppose.' Dexter's words didn't match the uncertainty in his eyes.

'You don't seem convinced.'

He sighed and scrunched his brow. 'I... I just don't get it... the not wanting kids thing. I'd love to have a family of my own. I see our Jetty with Evin and you with Grace, now Archie with Sophie... Yous are all so lucky. I can't understand anyone who thinks having kids is a bad idea.'

'I know what you mean,' Caitlin agreed. 'But I suppose not everyone feels that way. And it wouldn't do for us all to feel the same. I just hope she doesn't hurt him. He doesn't deserve that.'

'No, you're right, he doesn't.' Dexter eyed her in that suspicious way again. She could tell he was making more of her words than she had intended. As if reading her mind, he rapidly changed the subject. 'So, this Bram fella is coming on Saturday too?'

Caitlin felt her face heating substantially. 'He is, and you'd better be nice.'

Dexter held up his hands defensively. 'Hey, I'm a nice bloke, me! But I'm also a dickhead radar, so I'll tell you exactly what I make of him. I wouldn't be a good friend if I didn't. And it sounds like my radar might have come in handy with old Barmy Budge.'

Caitlin almost choked on her drink. 'Loony Lyle, Barmy Budge. Honestly you should be on a stage.'

He winked. 'Aye, I might just enter the talent show at the Glentorrin Highland Games this year.' He chuckled.

'Hmm and I'll be ready with my stock of rotten tomatoes.'

* * *

The sun was high in the sky on Saturday and Caitlin was relieved for Archie's barbecue plans. The one thing that was certain on Skye was the uncertainty of the weather.

She dressed in a floaty, long summer dress in a rich green that complemented her hair. Grace wore a T-shirt and shorts as there had been a mention of a water fight.

Caitlin had made a fancy tray bake with toppers that spelled out the words Welcome Sophie. She had decorated the chewy, chocolate squares with edible glitter and tiny stars made from white chocolate.

Caitlin's nerves had kicked in at the thought of her date. At five o'clock, there was a knock on the door and Caitlin glared at the clock. 'Shit! I hope that's not Bram! He's way too early.'

Grace giggled. 'Shall I answer the door, Mum? You look too scared.'

'No, no, love, it's okay. I'll go.' She took a deep, shaking breath and opened the door. 'Oh! Cora!' Grace's friend stood there on the doorstep with puffy red eyes. Caitlin immediately panicked and wondered if the girl had run away. 'Wh-where's your dad?'

Cora sniffed. 'He's staying in the car. We're on our way to the hotel by the airport. We fly out tomorrow, but I couldn't leave without saying goodbye.'

Grace appeared behind Caitlin. 'Cora?' She rushed past her mum and flung her arms around her best friend. 'You came!'

The two girls hugged tightly, both sobbing, and tears stung at Caitlin's eyes. She was partly angry that Lyle had left things so late, in his usual way, but partly relieved that he had seen sense. At least she hoped that's what had happened... she would need to speak to Dexter after their conversation earlier in the week.

Cora pulled away from Grace and handed her a wrapped gift. 'I got you a present.'

Grace took the small package and ripped off the paper to reveal a small box. Inside was a pendant in the shape of half a heart. Caitlin lost it at that point, tears streamed down her face as she watched Cora fasten the necklace on Grace.

'Look, Gracie, I have the other half,' Cora said with a wide smile as she held the pendant around her own neck.

Grace sniffed. 'I love it. I'll never take it off. Wait there though, I have something for you.' She dashed off up to her room and returned moments later with the scrapbook. 'I haven't had a chance to wrap it yet, but I made this for you.'

Cora wiped at the tears on her cheeks and took the book. She opened the first page to see a photo of the two of them when they first became friends. Her face lit up with a bright smile as she flipped the pages. 'Oh, wow! This is brilliant, Gracie, thank you so much.'

'Cora! C'mon, we need to go,' came Lyle's stern voice from the car with its engine still running.

Cora glanced back at the car and nodded. She turned her attention back to Grace. 'I'll email you all the time. And I'll phone when I can too. I'm going to miss you so much.' The two girls hugged again and then Cora pulled away. 'Don't forget about me, will you?'

Grace sobbed, 'Never, you'll always be my best friend. Forever, just like it says on the necklace.'

'Forever,' Cora repeated as she turned to jog back to the car.

Caitlin and Grace stepped outside and watched as Lyle turned the car around and drove away towards the bridge. Cora waved and Grace did so too until she was out of sight.

'I'm so glad he brought her,' Caitlin whispered as Grace flung her arms around her and sobbed into her shoulder. 'Shh, it's okay, sweetheart, it's okay.' She kissed the top of her daughter's head and led her back into the house.

* * *

Jules, Reid, Evin and Chewie called for Grace and Cleo at five forty-five in order that Caitlin could meet Bram by herself at six when he arrived.

'Dex is already at Archie's. I think he might be the one supplying the water pistols.' Jules laughed. 'He might live to regret that! Anyway, we'll see you up there. Good luck,' Jules said as she hugged Caitlin in the doorway.

'Thanks. After Lyle, all I can think of is things going wrong.'

Jules chewed her lip and glanced over her shoulder. Grace, Evin and the dogs were standing over by the inlet, but she lowered her voice, nonetheless. 'Speaking of the intense Mr Budge, I heard on the grapevine – and by that, I mean Evin – that they have packed up and gone. Cora and Lyle. They fly to Canada tomorrow, but they're staying a hotel tonight. All their stuff was put in storage and the house is up for sale.'

Caitlin nodded. 'He brought Cora by earlier to say goodbye to Grace before they headed off to the hotel. Thinking about it makes me want to cry again. They lost so much bloody time and I can't help blaming myself.'

'No! It's his fault, not yours! You weren't the one who went all stalkery. But I'm glad he saw sense after D— I mean after all,' Jules said and swallowed hard, her expression startled.

Caitlin's eyes widened. 'I knew it! I'll bloody throttle him!'

Jules cringed and shook her head. 'Please don't be mad with Dex. He just wanted to do the right thing. And it worked, didn't it?'

Caitlin huffed. 'I suppose so. But I want to know what he said.'

With a quick glance over her shoulder, Jules insisted, 'Don't worry, he was very calm and polite. Just told him that he was being selfish if he didn't let the girls say goodbye. Apparently, Lyle was quite decent about it. Apologised and even said the break-up was all his fault but he couldn't bring himself to visit you in case he made it worse. That's why he was keeping Cora away – so he said anyway.'

'Hmm, well I suppose he did the right thing eventually. Maybe I won't throttle Dex after all.'

Jules sighed in evident relief. 'Thank you. He only did what he thought was right.'

'Aye, well, I'll let him off. I'll see you up at Archie's.'

Jules hugged her. 'You will, honey. Good luck with Bram.'

Jules and her family left with Grace in the direction of Archie's house and Caitlin spotted a vintage, two-seater sports car, with the top down, pulling into the village from the direction of the pub. Her stomach knotted.

Bram parked up outside the bakery and climbed out of the car. He looked smart in dark blue denim jeans and a turquoise polo shirt with shades atop his head. He was carrying a bottle bag with what looked like a bottle of wine and a bottle of cola. He struck a great first impression and her nerves subsided a little.

'Hey. Caitlin, right?' He held out his free hand.

Caitlin smiled and took his hand to shake it. 'Yes, nice to meet you, Bram. I hope you're hungry because Archie loves to barbecue, and I'm told he pretty much cleared out the butcher's van when it came around earlier.'

Bram laughed lightly. 'I love a good burger. Are you ready to go? I'm sorry. I'm a little early, I think.' He glanced at his wristwatch.

'I'm ready, yes. We can have a wander up. I just need to get the tray bake I've made.' She nipped back to the kitchen and slipped her handbag over her shoulder before picking up the large, weighty, flat box.

Bram's eyes widened. 'When you said tray bake, I was expecting something a little smaller. Here, let me,' he said as he handed the bottle bag to Caitlin and swapped her for the cake. 'This smells incredible.'

'Thanks. I just hope wee Sophie loves it.'

As they walked towards Archie's house, Bram asked, 'So is this a barbecue for your friend's little girl's birthday?'

'In a way. He's just taken guardianship of her after her mum sadly passed away. She's been through a lot and he's trying to help her settle in.'

'Ah, that's sweet. And your daughter, she's thirteen, is that right?'

She laughed. 'I see Morag has been filling you in.'

'Just a wee bit, aye. I have to say I'm pretty rubbish with kids, but a teenager I think I can manage.'

Caitlin smiled. He seemed warm and not too intense which was a good sign. 'She's a great girl. My pride and joy.'

'I look forward to meeting her.'

When they arrived at the house, Archie greeted them with a wide smile. He shook Bram's hand and hugged Caitlin, then apologised to Bram for doing so. Typical Archie, Caitlin thought. Bram was evidently oblivious to the issue, another good sign.

He took the tray-bake box from Bram and told them, 'Go on through. Everyone's in the back garden. Dex is soaked already. The kids thought it would be fun to gang up on him with the water pistols. Sophie's having the best time.' The pride he felt was clear in his expression. Caitlin had never seen him looking so happy and it warmed her heart.

When they arrived in the back garden, they were greeted by the sound of laughter and the tantalising, smoky aroma of barbecued burgers. The garden was decked out with balloons and bunting and a home-made sign that said *Welcome Sophie!* Just like the tray bake she had made.

For a moment, they watched Grace, Evin and Sophie running

around firing streams of water at each other as they squealed, and Dexter went running after them, reciting the giant's line from *Jack and the Beanstalk*. In amongst all the chaos, Cleo, Chewie and Bowie raced around as if they were having the time of their lives.

Archie came from the house and made a beeline for Caitlin. 'That cake is incredible, and I can't thank you enough for making it. You need to let me know what I owe you though, it's huge and I wasn't expecting you to go to so much trouble.'

'Archie, you know me, I can't go anywhere without bringing sweet treats along. And after Grace's party, let's just call it quits.'

Archie grinned. 'You're a star. Oh, hey, let me get Rosabeth and I'll introduce you.' He jogged off to where a tall, slim brunette was standing chatting to Jules and Ruby. She wore a slinky mini dress and strappy sandals, and had that perfect, shiny hair that fell in natural waves down her back. Something about the look of her made Caitlin bristle. Archie whispered something and she turned to Caitlin's direction to wave. The couple walked over to where she stood with Bram.

'Guys, this is Rosabeth. Rosabeth, this is Bram and my good friend Caitlin.'

Rosabeth held out her hand. 'Lovely to meet you. This one can't stop talking about you. If I didn't know better, I'd be so jealous.'

Caitlin shook her hand. 'Great to meet you too. And you've no need to be jealous, Archie and I are just good friends.'

'Really good friends,' Archie added.

'So, how long have you two been a couple?' Rosabeth asked with her gaze firmly fixed on Bram.

'This is our first official date,' Caitlin replied.

Rosabeth's eyes were still narrowed on Bram. 'You look ever so familiar.'

He blushed. 'Aye, I was at the singles mixer, up in Broadford.'

Rosabeth's eyes widened. 'Oh yes! That was the night that poor woman fell flat on her face, wasn't it? I think I would've wanted the ground to open up and swallow me if that happened to me.' She threw her head back and laughed. 'She looked so utterly ridiculous there on her hands and knees. I know I shouldn't laugh, but it was hilarious!'

Bram scrunched his brow. 'Oh, I missed that. Poor lass. I bet she was mortified.'

As her face almost spontaneously combusted, Caitlin wanted Archie's garden to open up and swallow her. She lifted her chin and made eye contact with a panicked-looking Archie, pleading with her eyes for him to keep his mouth shut. The last thing she needed was to be outed as the 'poor woman' Rosabeth had just been ridiculing.

'Come and get food!' Archie blurted.

And Caitlin exhaled, grateful that he had understood her unspoken plea, but still a little hurt by the callousness of Rosabeth's amusement.

Rosabeth ran her red-painted nails down Archie's arm. 'Oh, he's so demanding,' she said in a sexy purr that made Caitlin feel physically sick – although it could still have been the ridicule.

'Aye, I'm starving,' Bram replied as he followed in the direction Rosabeth and Archie walked.

Before Caitlin could take a step, she was stopped by her friends Ruby and Jules.

'We *have* to get rid of her!' Ruby stated with determination.

Feeling incredibly sorry for Sophie, Caitlin gasped. 'You can't say that!'

'We bloody can. She's awful! And he just can't see it,' Jules said. Her face in a crumple of disgust. 'She's using him.'

'She's only just got here, give her a chance,' Caitlin pleaded.

Jules shook her head and pursed her lips. 'Look, you weren't here earlier for her display. I'm telling you; she is going to make Archie's life a misery.'

'But... But...'

Ruby folded her arms across her chest. 'Seriously, Cait, we're not joking. She has to go. I'm not prepared to give her a chance. Not after what she did earlier.'

Caitlin was perturbed. She thought her friends would be willing to accept Archie's new position as a dad. And although it was going to take Sophie a while to acclimatise, they were being unnecessarily harsh about the child in her opinion. 'Whatever she did earlier, I think you need to consider her age and what she's been through,' Caitlin replied with a scowl.

'I'm not ageist in the slightest and, to be honest, the fact she's four years younger than him means nothing. But she's already flirted with Reid, and she basically fawned all over Mitch,' Ruby said indignantly.

The penny dropped and Caitlin covered her eyes with her hand. 'You mean Rosabeth.'

Jules frowned and shared a confused glance with Ruby. 'Who else would we mean?'

'I thought you meant little Sophie.'

Jules' eyes widened. 'Oh god, no! She's adorable! Rosabeth, on the other hand, is a disaster waiting to happen. You'll have to say something, Cait. You're the closest to him and he'll listen to you.'

Caitlin scoffed. 'Not a chance. He's an adult and he'll make his own decisions and mistakes, thank you very much. I am his friend, but I have no intention of interfering. Imagine how that would look!'

The other two women shared another disgruntled look. 'He's going to get hurt, Cait.'

'Ruby's right,' Jules agreed. 'She's a massive flirt. Look!'

Caitlin glanced over to see that Rosabeth and Bram were

huddled in a corner chatting. Rosabeth was eating a hot dog rather too seductively for her liking and Bram appeared to be hanging on her every word. Luckily, Archie appeared and dragged Rosabeth away.

Her friends were right, Caitlin decided, Rosabeth looked too good to be true and evidently was. And what kind of influence would someone like that be on little, impressionable Sophie? She shivered at the thought but knew she couldn't really interfere... could she?

Caitlin made her way across to Bram. 'Sorry I got collared by my friends. I hope you're okay. It's not typical first-date stuff this, is it?'

Bram smiled. 'Don't worry. I'm having a great time. Although that huge beardy bloke tried to arm me with a water pistol, and I had to decline. Not my scene really.'

'Ah. Dex is all about fun and he's pretty much a big kid himself.'

'So I see. I hope you don't think I'm boring. I just... I'm an only child and I grew up on a farm, so I'm more at home with cows than kids.'

His comment niggled at her, but she tried to push it aside. 'It's fine. Although don't mention that to Dex, he's likely to go and hunt down a cow for you to befriend.'

'Your friends seem nice. Archie's a great guy. Very warm. How long have him and Rosa been a couple?'

Rosa, eh? Caitlin glanced over to see Rosabeth crouched down talking to Sophie. Sophie was wide-eyed with her hands scrunched under her chin, Bowie was glued to Sophie's side with his head tilted as if he was listening to whatever was being said, and something about the scene made Caitlin uncomfortable. 'Oh, not long. They met at a speed dating thing he and I attended.'

'Oh aye, the speed dating. I couldn't make that one. Shame really. I could have met you sooner.'

* * *

As the evening wore on, things calmed down and Archie put some music on in the background. The food was all but gone and the tray bake had been a huge success. Sophie seemed a little more subdued as night began to fall, but Caitlin put that down to the party being overwhelming and perhaps she was tired too. It was understandable, she was only five and it was getting late. But wherever she went, Bowie the pug was there, like her little protector.

The garden looked magical in the light of the moon. The fairy lights hung across the pergola illuminated automatically as it got darker, and everyone sat around chatting. Even the dogs were exhausted; Chewie and Cleo curled up on the grass, relaxing in the warm evening air, while Bowie nestled into Sophie's side, where she sat on the grass, propped up against one of the pergola posts.

Bram was chatting to Mitch across the garden. Evin and Grace were playing a card game as Sophie watched. Rosabeth unravelled herself from Archie and went into the house. Ruby and Jules were deep in conversation and Reid and Dex were having a beer together, no doubt plotting some crazy scheme.

Caitlin sat staring into the firepit as the flames danced and one of her favourite songs came on, causing her to smile. 'Rule The World' by Take That always gave her goosebumps and tonight was no different.

As she raised her chin, she made direct eye contact with Archie. His features were highlighted by the firelight, an angular jaw, high cheekbones and dark yet friendly eyes. He tilted his head and smiled serenely at her, making her stomach flip. In the background, Gary Barlow sang about the stars in the night sky, and it seemed so incredibly apt.

As if reading her mind, Archie glanced heavenwards and then back down to her again, his smile a little sad this time. She couldn't seem to remove her gaze from his and she suddenly felt a little overcome with emotion. *Why does this keep happening?* she wondered.

Bram appeared by her side and pulled her from her reverie. 'Hey, Caitlin, I think I'm going to make a move. But can I give you a call and maybe we could go out somewhere just the two of us?'

She stood. 'That would be lovely. I'll grab my bag and walk down with you.'

He held up a hand. 'No, don't do that. You stay with your friends. I'll give you a call in the week, eh?'

'Yes, please do. I'll walk you out at least.' They headed into the house, which was quiet apart from the end of Take That's song playing on the Bluetooth speakers that Archie had linked throughout the house. When they reached the front door, Caitlin opened it. 'Look, I'm sorry about tonight. I feel like we've hardly had a chance to speak.'

He smiled warmly. 'Honestly, I've had a great night. Your friends are lovely, and I was made to feel very welcome.'

'I'm really glad. They are a smashing bunch, but maybe next time a night out just the two of us like you suggested.'

'Aye, and I can't believe you're friends with Ruby Locke! I didn't expect to see her here tonight. I've seen all her films.'

'She's very sweet, not at all what you'd expect from a former Hollywood star.'

'Nah, she seems great. They all do.' He leaned forward and kissed her cheek. He smelled of fresh laundry and pinecones mixed with a bit of firepit smoke. 'Goodnight, Caitlin.'

'Goodnight, Bram.'

'Oh, are you leaving too? Maybe you could drop me off at home?' Rosabeth appeared, as if out of nowhere.

Cheeky wee mare.

Bram looked a little taken back. 'Oh... erm, sure. Where do you live?'

'Just at Balmacara.'

'Aye, okay.' He looked uncomfortable but clearly felt he couldn't turn her down. 'Right, goodnight again.'

Caitlin raised her hand. 'Bye, Bram. Bye, Rosabeth.'

Rosabeth linked arms with Bram, and they headed back towards where he had parked his snazzy little car.

'And another one bites the dust,' Caitlin said aloud as she watched them walk away. After all, they had hardly spoken, and she got the feeling he was just being kind when he offered to call her. He seemed like a nice enough man but there really had been no discernible spark between them.

She closed the front door and headed back through to the garden, where Archie was frantically looking under the bushes and trees. Everyone was on their feet and following suit and an air of panic hung around the place.

Caitlin made her way over to Archie and grabbed his wrist. 'Hey, what's going on?'

He ran his hands through his hair. His eyes were wide and even in the dim lighting, she could tell the colour had drained from his cheeks and his chest was heaving. 'She's... she's gone. Sophie's gone.'

22

'She must be here somewhere!' Caitlin said as they virtually ransacked the house, checking in every single room, cupboard, nook and cranny. Bowie was gone too, along with his lead, which meant Sophie had left on purpose. 'She can't have gone far.' Her heart was hammering at her ribcage and her stomach was knotted so tight she feared she may throw up.

Grace was sobbing uncontrollably, she felt entirely responsible, and Caitlin tried to explain to her that it wasn't her fault at all. Evin was sitting quietly staring at the floor in a state of shock, his skin pale and his eyes filled with tears. The poor kids. They couldn't take the blame for this. Not when they were surrounded by supposedly responsible adults.

Mitch had phoned the police and they were on their way, so he was standing guard at the front door awaiting their arrival.

'What time did you notice she'd gone?' Ruby asked in a wavering voice as she closed the cupboard under the stairs after checking it for a third time, just in case.

Archie checked his watch. 'I don't know... about eleven-thirty? I know I shouldn't have let her stay up so late, but I figured it was a special occasion. If I'd only made her go to bed...'

Caitlin placed a hand on each of his arms. 'Hey, stop it. If she was going to run away, my guess is she would do it regardless. Let's just focus on finding her. What was happening when you noticed?'

Archie rubbed his hands over his face and back through his hair. 'Rosabeth had just come to say goodbye and I tried to find Sophie so she could say goodnight to her, but there was no sign of her. Rosabeth said it didn't matter and that she had to go as Bram had offered her a lift.'

Well, that's a lie, Caitlin thought. *What other lies has she told?*

'I just let Rosabeth go as I needed to keep looking,' the pain Archie was feeling was evident in his strained voice.

Dexter returned from upstairs. 'Nothing up there, I'm afraid. I've checked the wardrobes and under the beds, as well as every cupboard big enough.'

Everyone was frantic, pale and filled with the dread no parent wants to experience.

'I can't sit here and wait for the police,' Archie said through gritted teeth as he paced around the room. 'I'll have to go out and look for her.'

Caitlin walked over and gently took hold of his arm. 'Hey, you stay here. We'll go. The police will want to talk to you, and Sophie will need to see you when she comes back.'

Archie knotted his hands in his hair. 'What if she doesn't come back? Oh god, this is all my fault. She must hate me. I've dragged a traumatised child away from her hometown and tried to squeeze her into my stupid life. What was I thinking?'

Trying to help him see reason, Caitlin said, 'Archie, she doesn't hate you at all. She's been through a lot, and something must've spooked her. Stay by the phone. We will keep in touch with you via your mobile, but keep the landline free, okay?'

Archie's jaw ticked and his nostrils flared. She thought he was going to argue but instead he nodded. 'I knew I'd be a shit dad. I should've listened to my gut. I'm just like him.'

'Stop it!' Caitlin snapped, hoping to shock some sense into him. 'You are nothing like your father. And you did listen to your gut. That's why Sophie is here. You absolutely did the right thing and deep down you know that. Now, you're the only family that girl has got, so you need to stay strong. Just sit tight here and we'll find her. I promise you that, Archie.' As soon as the words had left her mouth, she regretted them. *Why make promises that you may not be able to keep, you idiot?* Then, as if a devil and angel inside her were having a confrontation, another thought sprang forth. *No! You can't think like that. Stay positive.*

Archie closed his eyes for a moment as if trying to calm himself. 'I've some torches if they would help,' he told them, pointing to the cupboard under the stairs.

'Already grabbed one,' Ruby said, waving the shiny cylinder in her hand.

'I've got my phone torch,' Jules said.

'Aye, me too,' Reid added.

'And me,' said Dexter.

Mitch walked to the cupboard to grab a torch for himself. 'Come on, let's get out there. Evin and Grace, you stay here so we know you're safe, eh?' The two bewildered children nodded.

* * *

As they left the house in the dark of night, the only illumination was provided by the moon overhead and the pretty lights strung around the inlet. There was a little glow of lamplight in the windows of the village's night owls who were blissfully oblivious to what was going on outside.

'I'll go knock for Kenneth. His mountain rescue training might help,' Reid informed the small group.

'Good idea. Jules, you walk over towards the museum,' Caitlin said. 'Ruby, you check around the hall. Dex, can you check all around the campsite? And Mitch, you go up the road leading out of the village going north.' Her friends headed off in their separate directions.

Where would a tired-out, scared five-year-old girl go? She doesn't know the area. She has no friends here. Where on earth would she go? Caitlin headed for the Skye bridge. If Sophie was planning to go back to Edinburgh, she'd know they had accessed the island by that route.

As she walked, Caitlin saw the police car with its blue lights flashing, entering the village from the north. It slowed when it reached Mitch and she saw him gesturing towards Archie's.

Caitlin walked up onto the bridge, but there was no sign of Sophie. With her little legs, she surely wouldn't have gone much farther. After around fifteen minutes, she saw that the police had joined the road search. She could see their hi-vis jackets glinting in torch light and could hear the intermittent calling of the little girl's name.

She didn't want to think about the time she had lost Grace in a large supermarket, but the panic she'd felt on that day came back to haunt her. She had turned her back for a split second and was then plunged into the worst kind of distress a parent can experience. She remembered the way she had frantically rushed around the aisles calling Grace's name, her heart almost bursting from her chest, and her mind conjuring up the worst of scenarios. Some shoppers stared blankly at her as she manically asked them if they'd seen a little red-haired girl, while some joined in the search, assuring her that her daughter couldn't have gone far – the same thing she'd said to Archie.

Grace had eventually been found in the toy aisle, under a pile of teddy bears where she'd hidden 'to be safe'. After that, Caitlin had sat Grace down and they had formulated a plan for the future should they, god forbid, be separated like that again. The relief she'd felt on finding her child had rendered her an emotional, sobbing wreck for days as she played over in her mind the 'what ifs'.

* * *

The search for Sophie had been going for an hour now and the sinking feeling inside of Caitlin had worsened substantially. Archie had texted repeatedly asking if there was any news and she had stopped replying because telling him no was breaking her heart. She knew it must be upsetting for Reid too, seeing as Evin had run away when his mother had decided he was to live with her. Thankfully, the woman saw sense and he was returned to his dad, albeit with a broken ankle. Caitlin's stomach lurched at the thought of Sophie being injured and she had to stop to bend double for a moment until the feeling of nausea passed.

As she stood, she heard movement behind the nearby bus stop. A rustling and a snuffling sound. Warily, she tiptoed to the location of the noise, unwilling to spook whoever, or whatever, it was. *It's probably a fox*, she thought, but had to check.

Behind the bus stop was a large gorse bush and the branches at the bottom were moving even though the night air was still. She shone her phone torch at the bottom edge and a bark made her jump.

'Bowie!' she exclaimed. 'Sophie? Sophie, are you there?'

No reply came and Caitlin's breathing rate increased. What was she going to find? Her palms were sweating, and her head was pounding. *Please let her be okay. Please, please...*

A shuffling sound could be heard again, and Bowie was pulled back with a yelp. Oh god, had someone got Sophie under there? Were they trying to keep her quiet?

'Who's there?' Caitlin asked in a stern, assertive voice that she'd had to pull from nowhere. 'The police are here, so you'd better come out.'

Caitlin realised she was unarmed, so if there was indeed an assailant under the bush, she was putting herself in danger. However, undeterred and putting her own safety aside, she stepped closer.

'You're surrounded. Come out!' she hissed.

Another scuffling noise ensued, and Bowie pulled loose and ran from under the bush. Caitlin managed to step on his lead to stop him from going anywhere.

'Got you.' She gripped the lead in her hand and wrapped it around her wrist. 'Now who is under this bush?' she demanded, again sounding far braver than she was feeling with her weak knees and thumping heart.

Suddenly, from amongst the sharp spikes a mop of dark hair appeared. 'Ouch! Owww,' Sophie cried as she freed herself from the thorny branches.

'Sophie! Thank goodness!' Caitlin lurched forward and pulled the little girl into her arms. 'Are you okay, sweetheart? What were you thinking? Why did you run away?'

Sophie didn't answer.

Releasing Sophie, Caitlin fired off a text to Archie, not wanting to let go of the girl long enough to make a call.

Got her! All fine. Bringing her back now!

She called out into the night, 'I've found Sophie! She's safe! We're over by the bus stop!'

Sophie was sobbing now. Her arms were covered in scratches and her face was dirty from where she had been hiding.

'Sophie, sweetheart, can you tell me what happened?' Caitlin asked in a soft voice as she cradled the crying child.

'I want my mummy,' Sophie replied through sharply inhaled breaths.

Caitlin smoothed back the hair that was sticking to the dampness on her cheeks. 'Oh, sweetheart, I know you do. But... do you understand that she's gone?'

Sophie nodded. 'But that lady said I could go see her.'

Caitlin frowned. 'What lady, sweetheart?'

'Wozadeath.'

'Sorry, who?'

'Archie's friend, Wozadeath.'

Caitlin stopped the smile from forming on her lips. 'Ah, I think you mean Rosabeth?'

Sophie nodded. 'That's what I said. She told me I could go see my mummy in Devon, so I want to wait for a bus.'

Confused, Caitlin wiped at the tears that were still streaming down the little girl's face. 'I don't understand, lovey. Your mummy isn't in Dev—' She closed her eyes briefly. Heaven... Rosabeth told her that her mummy was in heaven. 'Oh, sweetheart.' She pulled Sophie into her arms and picked her up. 'Come on, let's get you home.' Bowie trotted along beside them, tongue lolling out and panting. Caitlin got the distinct impression he was happy the ordeal was over.

* * *

Back at Archie's, Caitlin watched as he scooped Sophie up into his arms and sobbed into her hair. The police officers looked on with concerned expressions and the rest of their friends hugged and shook hands.

Caitlin thanked Kenneth and he embraced her. 'Well done, lassie. You did a grand job,' he told her before saying goodbye to the others and leaving.

Dexter came over and put his arm around her shoulders. 'Are you okay, Cait?'

She nodded. 'I am now.' She whispered, 'Sophie said that Rosabeth told her she could go see her mum in Devon, bless her.'

Dexter smiled. 'Out of the mouths of babes, eh? Look, I'm going to shoot off. I think you and Archie might need some time to just calm down.'

She smiled. 'That'd be good. Thanks for all your help, Dex.'

He squeezed her arm. 'It's no bother. Come on, guys, let's leave these folks to it, eh?'

'Hey, honey, Grace can come and stay at ours tonight if you like?' Jules said with her arm around the girl and her soon-to-be stepson.

'What do you think, Grace?' Caitlin asked, secretly hoping her daughter didn't want to leave her side after the events of the evening, but also knowing it would be good for her to be with her friend after the whole awful ordeal.

Grace nodded. 'Yes, I'd like that. I'm so tired and I know you need to be here a bit longer.'

Caitlin hugged her daughter. 'Thank you for being so understanding, sweetie.'

The other friends hugged Caitlin and left along with Dexter, with promises to check in tomorrow.

Archie was on the sofa with Sophie nuzzled into him. 'You mustn't do that again, sweetheart. I was so worried about you. Why did you run away?'

'Wozadeath told me my mummy had gone to Devon and that I would see her again one day, so I wanted to wait for a bus.'

He smiled and stroked her hair. 'Oh, sweetheart. I think we need to talk about this when you've had a good sleep. I'm so glad you're home. I missed you so much.'

'But Wozadeath said you didn't really want to be a daddy, and that you were a last report because no one else wanted me. She said I had spoiled everything by coming to live here.' Her chin trembled. 'She said I'm tecklickly an awful.'

That bitch, Caitlin thought. *Sophie isn't technically an orphan, far from it, she has Archie, and Archie was not a bloody last resort, he's her biological father!*

Archie scowled and his nostrils flared; anger evident in his eyes even though his voice remained calm and soft. 'Rosabeth said that to you?'

Sophie nodded her head and chewed her finger. 'She... she told that mister with no hair who came with Cakelin. I heard her saying it. She said you were happier when you weren't a daddy.'

He pulled himself upright and placed a hand on either side of her face. 'Sophie, I can assure you with all my heart that I am happy to be a daddy. I'm happy to be *your* daddy. So don't you listen to what anyone else says. You and me, we're a team. And I promise you I want you to be here with me, so very, very much. Okay?'

She nodded and nuzzled back into him. In a matter of moments, she had fallen asleep.

He picked her up and whispered to Caitlin, 'Would you make sure the door is locked and the key is out of the lock, please? I'm going to take her up and clean up these scratches and put her to bed.' Poor Archie was terrified of her trying to run away again.

'Of course. Shall I make some tea?'

'I need something stronger. But actually... tea will be fine. Better keep my wits about me, eh?' He headed up the stairs and Caitlin went to the kitchen to flick the kettle on.

Ten minutes later, Archie returned, so Caitlin poured the water into the cups and they sat at the kitchen table.

'I can't believe what Rosabeth said to Bram. Why the hell would she make assumptions like that when I've said no such thing? Why would she call Sophie an orphan? She's not a bloody orphan, for goodness' sake.'

Caitlin knew it was a rhetorical question, but she had her own opinions. 'I'm sorry, Archie, but if you ask me, I think she maybe isn't as happy about Sophie as you'd hoped.'

'Aye, I think that much is clear. Well, I'll be calling her tomorrow and telling her it's over.'

Caitlin immediately felt guilty for expressing her opinion. She didn't want to influence him in any way. 'Aren't you going to give her a chance to explain?'

Archie shook his head with vehemence. 'Absolutely not. Sophie has no reason to lie. She's five and was clearly distressed by what she had heard.' He sighed deeply. 'The poor wee lass. I'm going to have to talk to her about her mum's death again. She obviously doesn't really understand.'

Caitlin knew instinctively that Archie was making the right decision. In his place, she would do exactly the same. And in any case, she had disliked the woman immensely. 'No. Bless her, I think you're right. It'll be a difficult conversation to have.'

'Aye, I think it will. Poor wee lamb.'

23

After an eventful and exhausting weekend, Caitlin was glad to be back to some semblance of normality, safe in the knowledge that everything was all right with the world... for now. It was Wednesday and Grace had gone with Evin to take Chewie and Cleo to play on the field. The bakery was bustling with tourists and Isla was in to help with the influx of the holiday crowd. The takeaway sandwiches, drinks and rocky road tray bake were going down a treat.

Caitlin was in the back room taking a five-minute break at around three o'clock when Isla appeared in the doorway. Her blonde hair was tied up in a neat bun and she wore her apron over shorts and a T-shirt, the perfect attire for the scorching day.

'There's a guy here to see you, Caitlin. Shall I send him through?'

'Oh? I'm not expecting anyone. But yes, that's fine, thanks.'

A few moments later, Bram appeared. 'Hi Caitlin. I was just chatting to Morag, and she was telling me about your friend's wee lassie. Is she okay?'

She hadn't heard from him since the barbecue and figured her assumption on the night about not seeing him again had been correct, so his visit was a surprise. 'Aww, thanks for checking in. She's fine thankfully. Upset at what she overheard, but fine.'

Bram tilted his head. 'What she overheard?'

Caitlin nodded and sighed. 'Yes, the poor lamb overheard Rosabeth telling you that she wasn't wanted. It hit her pretty hard after what she's been through.'

Bram rubbed his hands roughly over his face. 'Shit. I'm so sorry. I hope you know I wasn't commenting. Although I did tell her she was being a bit unfair because he seemed really happy. He didn't look like he was put out at all that she's living with him.'

'That's because he's not. What she said was quite bitter. But don't worry, Sophie was very adamant about who'd said what, so I knew you weren't involved. I'm just glad we found her safe and well.'

Bram's face had paled. 'God, I feel terrible. She's a right one that Rosabeth. Very flirty. That's my other reason for coming to see you. She had me walk her to her door and then tried to kiss me. I told her to back off. Said I wasn't interested but she got really pissy after that. I reckon she's a few tanks short of an army that one.'

Caitlin couldn't help laughing at the thought she'd be a good match for Lyle. 'You might be right. But it's fine. Don't worry.'

He cleared his throat. 'Can I... erm... sit down a minute? There's something I want to talk to you about.'

'Sure.' Caitlin gestured to the opposite chair. 'What's up?'

He sat and paused for a moment as if considering his words carefully. 'I hope you don't think me a bit... I don't know... nosey... but...'

Caitlin huffed, expecting him to have heard on the grapevine about Grace's father situation. 'Come on, out with it.' She crossed her arms over her chest, ready to defend her position even though she didn't have to.

'You and Archie... Has there ever been... you know... anything between yous?'

Relieved that this was his question, she couldn't help the laugh that escaped. 'What is it with the universe trying to put me and Archie together?'

He shrugged. 'Maybe if I'm not the only one who's asked, could it be something we're all seeing that you're not?'

Caitlin made a very unflattering noise. 'Pfft! Don't you all think I'd know if I was in love with him?'

Bram eyed her with pity. 'Honestly? No. I think you've somehow convinced yourself that you're not into him. But your eyes give you away. I saw it at the barbecue. The way you watch him with a little smile on your lips. The way your pupils dilate when he talks to you.'

She scoffed again. 'I'm sorry, but you've imagined that. And you don't really know me well enough to see my signs of attraction.'

He smiled sadly. 'I know when I don't see them, Caitlin. And I didn't see that spark when you looked at me like I did when you looked at him.'

She sighed in exasperation. 'But I've only just met you. Give me time.'

He shook his head. 'Caitlin, why force yourself to like someone else when your heart's already chosen for you?'

She had no idea what to say to that. She couldn't tell him he was wrong and that scared her.

'And if you're worried that he doesn't feel the same, don't be. He couldn't take his eyes off you either. I really don't understand why you're both fighting something that's so clear to everyone else.'

She opened her mouth to speak but closed it again. What could she say? She didn't want to try to convince him that he was the one she liked because, in all honesty, he was a lovely guy, handsome, sweet, kind, but there was no spark. He got that bit right. But then again, she wasn't expecting one. She was no longer hoping for that thunderbolt. She just wanted someone to spend time with, who made her feel important and special, who adored Grace, who made her laugh, who went the extra mile for her, who was a good father...

Shit...

She inhaled a sharp breath, and her hands covered her mouth.

Bram smiled. 'Ah, methinks the penny hath dropped.'

With wide eyes, she said, 'Oh, Bram, I'm so sorry. You must think I'm awful.'

He shook his head. 'Not at all. Now, do yourself a favour, eh? Tell him how you feel. Don't leave it until it's too late.' He stood from his seat. 'Good luck, Caitlin. See you around.'

And with that he left her sitting there, stunned into a stupor at her realisation.

* * *

'Mum! What's for dinner? Can we have spaghetti? And garlic bread if you've a baguette left over?' Grace entered the kitchen where Caitlin had been sitting since she'd arrived through from the bakery at five-thirty. It was now six o'clock. 'Mum? Are you okay?'

Caitlin was tugged from her thoughts. 'What's that, love?'

'Dinner? Spaghetti?'

Caitlin smiled. 'Oh, sure, honey, yes. I could make some garlic bread too if you like. I've a baguette left over.'

Grace giggled. 'I just asked that.'

Caitlin gave an embarrassed smile as her cheeks flushed. 'Oh... sorry, love.'

'It's okay. I saw Archie at the field. He was with Sophie and a woman I haven't seen here before. She was really pretty. Long blonde hair like Cinderella.'

Caitlin's interest piqued. 'Oh? Did he introduce you?'

'Nah. We were playing with the dogs. He waved though.'

'Right... right.' Who would that have been? The different possibilities played around her mind, social worker? New love interest? If it was the latter, he'd wasted no time. If it was the former, perhaps he would fall for her, and her Cinderella charm and they would bond over their care of Sophie. She realised that she was probably being irrational, and a tad crazy, but it didn't stop her imagining a myriad different scenarios.

Caitlin went through the motions of cooking dinner. Grace set the table and Caitlin served the food, then they sat to eat, but her mind wandered to Archie again. His smile, his awkward way of acting then apologising even when there was no need. The way he had arranged Grace's party. His biceps when he helped her change her tyre. The giddy feeling she experienced when he was around. The way she felt protective over him after the things Wozadeath said. When had it happened? How had it happened? But, more to the point, what the hell could she do about it? Should she even do anything about it? What if Bram was wrong and Archie didn't feel the same? How could she tell him how she felt and then live in the same village knowing that someday she would see him with someone else?

'Mum? Did you hear what I said?'

'About what, love?'

'I knew you were daydreaming again. Have you got the hots for that Dracula man?'

Caitlin almost choked on her drink. 'Dracula man?'

'Yeah, Evin said that Bram Stoker wrote *Dracula* and that he wondered if your Bram might be a vampire.'

'You and Evin have some bizarre conversations,' Caitlin observed.

'Aye, we do. That's why I'll probably marry him some day. He makes me laugh and we always have stuff to talk about. Even if it's weird. You should always have stuff to talk about with the person you marry.'

She definitely had a point. 'You certainly should.'

'You and Archie always seem to have lots to talk about. But you didn't seem to speak much to that vampire man. Are you going on another date with him?'

Caitlin shook her head. 'Oh... erm... probably not, to be honest, love, and maybe stop calling him vampire man, eh?'

'You should just marry Archie. I'd love him to be my dad,' Grace said wistfully.

Caitlin closed her eyes for a moment. 'It's not really that easy, Grace.'

Grace shrugged. 'It should be though. If you love someone and they love you, why not cut out all the middle bit and get married and start your lives together?'

Caitlin narrowed her eyes. 'Grace, Archie and I don't love each other,' she insisted. What was that phrase about protesting too much? 'Anyway, where on earth has all this come from?'

'Me and Evin were talking about Jules and Reid getting married. I'm hoping she asks me to be a bridesmaid. I'd love that. Maybe now I'm not wearing a violet dress for yours and Lyle's wedding and you and Archie aren't getting married either, I'll get to wear one at Jules and Reid's,' Grace said wistfully.

Caitlin rolled her eyes and shook her head, but in her mind, her brain had conjured up the image of Archie in a suit standing under an arch of flowers smiling affectionately as she walked towards him...

* * *

The following day was a little quieter and although it meant business wasn't quite so good, Caitlin was relieved for the reprieve, no matter how temporary in nature.

Archie and Sophie called in just before lunch and Caitlin found herself unnaturally flustered on seeing him. *Damn you, Bram, for making me notice things I was happy to ignore.*

'Good morning, folks, what can I get you today?' she asked with a wide smile and the hope that her embarrassment wasn't visible in her expression.

Sophie tugged on Archie's T-shirt, and he bent to see what she wanted to whisper. 'Aye, of course, sweetheart,' he replied to her with a smile. 'Sophie would like a chocolate cupcake please and I'll have an apple pie for after dinner and... make that three chocolate cupcakes, eh?'

Caitlin wondered who the third was for and guessed the blonde woman Grace mentioned would be the recipient. At first, she had presumed the woman was probably the social worker. *But surely, he wouldn't be buying cupcakes for her? Perhaps he'd been in touch with another of his adoring fans from the singles event? He had seemed quite popular, despite him laughing the interest off as work-related; from the looks on the women's faces, it wasn't work they were thinking of.*

'Coming right up. So, Sophie, are you having fun with your d— with Archie?'

Sophie nodded and Archie told her, 'You can talk to Caitlin. She's not a stranger, remember? Sorry, Cait, we've had a wee talk about stranger danger today.'

Sophie chewed on her finger and pulled her toy pug closer. 'Yes, thank you,' she whispered.

'Good lass,' Archie said with a wide, beaming smile.

'That's good. Maybe I can send Grace round to play sometime?' Caitlin suggested warmly.

Sophie's eyes lit up as she nodded and tugged at Archie's T-shirt again. Once more he bent for her to whisper to him. When he straightened, he said, 'Sophie would like to know if you and Grace would like to come camping with us at the weekend.'

Caitlin's heart skipped. 'Oh! Erm... No, that's okay, you two should go and have some quality time together. Thank you though.'

Grace appeared in the doorway. 'Did someone say camping?'

'Aye, I was just asking your mum if the two of you would like to join us on an expedition at the weekend, but—'

Grace gasped, her eyes wide with excitement as she clapped her hands. 'Can we, Mum? Can we? It would be awesome! I loved camping with Evin, and I'd love to go again. Please!'

Caitlin's cheeks flushed. As much as she loved the great outdoors, she also loved her luxuries, and she wasn't sure she was cut out for sleeping in something without a solid roof. But if the truth be told, she was reluctant to spend alone time with Archie, torturing herself over something that wasn't going to happen. 'But we don't have a tent, or any gear, love.'

Archie interjected, 'I've got all the gear you need, and a spare tent.'

Shit, how do I get out of this? 'But it depends if Isla can work in the shop, and it might be too short notice.'

Archie pondered her words for a moment. 'If it helps, I can take the girls and you could join us afterwards. We're only going up to Kinloch by Dunvegan. It's about an hour away from here. I want to show Sophie the night sky up there as there's very little uplight and the stars are spectacular. I'm going to take a telescope too.'

All eyes were on her. Archie looked hopeful, Sophie too as she flicked her gaze between Caitlin and Grace, and Grace was blatantly standing there, hands clasped in prayer, bottom lip thrust out and her eyelids fluttering.

'Oh, for goodness' sake, fine!' She laughed.

Grace cheered and hugged Sophie, and Archie simply grinned like a loony.

She huffed. 'I presume it's a dog-friendly trip?'

'Absolutely. Bowie and Cleo got on well at the barbecue so it should be fun. We're just staying the one night, Saturday. The forecast is good so it should be great weather for stargazing.'

Caitlin nodded as she handed over Archie's purchases and took his payment. 'Okay, text me the details of the campsite and I'll come right up after I close on Saturday. I'll bring midge repellent.' She rolled her eyes.

'Great! Right, we'd better be getting back, Sophie. Say "bye" to Caitlin and Grace.'

Sophie gave a sweet smile and waved. 'Bye, Cakelin. Bye, Gwace.'

Once they had left, Caitlin turned to her daughter. 'I'm not sure I'm up to sleeping outdoors.'

'Mum, you'll be absolutely fine, I promise. It'll be such fun, you'll see.' Caitlin forced a smile but couldn't be sure that her daughter's assertions were correct on account of the risk to her heart.

* * *

After the bakery had closed, Caitlin decided to take Cleo for a walk to get some fresh air. The heat had been stifling in spite of the overcast clouds. Perhaps there was a storm brewing. And if there was, it had better come and go before the camping trip.

As she walked, she spotted Archie and Sophie standing by a taxi that was parked outside his house. They were chatting to a blonde woman, no doubt the same one that Grace had mentioned. Caitlin tried not to watch, but her curiosity got the better of her, so she pretended to tie her shoelace. *Pathetic attempt at subterfuge, Caitlin. You'll be cutting holes in newspapers next.*

Archie reached out and touched the woman's cheek. Caitlin wished she could hear what they were saying. If only she'd listened to her heart and acted earlier when she realised her true feelings, he may not have hooked up with someone new so quickly. But then again, she had no real proof of Archie's feelings, so things may have been no different.

Her stomach knotted as she watched the scene before her. What happened next made her wish she hadn't been watching. Archie pulled the blonde woman into an embrace, and she wrapped her arms around him. *Definitely not the social worker then.* Next, the blonde crouched to Sophie's level and hugged her too. *Bloody hell, she's won Sophie over already.* A twinge of jealousy tugged at Caitlin's heart but was soon replaced by sadness.

It was too late.

Whatever she was feeling needed to be pushed way down and locked away. *What was the point in feeling something for someone who wasn't interested?* Perhaps she really was destined to remain single. And that was fine. She didn't need a man. Admittedly, a relationship would've been nice. A relationship with Archie – even though she never realised it was something she wanted until it was too late – would've been lovely. But Grace didn't need a dad, that was one thing she was absolutely certain about. And they were fine just the two of them.

Absolutely fine.

24

'Have you got everything you need?' Caitlin asked Grace as she stood in the doorway of the bakery with Archie, ready to head off for the camping trip.

'Yup. All sorted,' Grace said with a pat to her backpack.

'Thanks for taking her and Cleo, Archie. I'll be there as soon as I can.'

'Aye, no worries. Don't rush though. Just text when you're setting off and I'll light the barbecue.' He frowned and then laughed. 'Is it just me or do you think our relationship revolves around barbecues?'

She laughed and crinkled her nose. 'It kind of does, doesn't it?'

He raised his hand in a wave and gave a handsome smile. 'Bye, then.'

'Bye, Archie, be good, Grace.'

Grace rolled her eyes. 'I always am!'

When they had left, Caitlin stood at the door of the bakery looking out across the inlet. The sky overhead was a beautiful corn-flower-blue, and the air was still and warm. Seagulls were hovering over a couple who were sitting on the bench with the cakes they had purchased from her half an hour earlier. One landed and dared to hop closer, almost begging for a morsel to be dropped. A family were leaving Morag's shop complete with ice creams that were already melting and Caitlin smiled to herself. Next door, the tables outside Tea For Two were all full of people eating and drinking as they chatted and soaked up the sunshine. *Such a wonderful place to be*, she thought.

She returned to her spot behind the counter and replayed what Archie had said. Relationship. Didn't he mean friendship? Although she knew a friendship was also a relationship, she usually felt the R-word held more romantic connotations, although that was clearly not the case here.

How the hell was she going to survive a camping trip, surrounded by nature and the romance of the starlit sky, with the man who she now knew was perfect for her, when he had just found another woman? She had no clue. What was the point on wishing on stars anyway?

Friends was good. Being friends with Archie was lovely. But now she knew she wanted more; she would struggle to get past that. Especially if she saw him around Glentorrin with his new girl-friend. No doubt he would want his new love to meet his friends, too, how would she handle that? He deserved to be happy. He deserved to be with someone who gave him all her attention, unlike Wozadeath who seemed to flirt with anything that had a penis. Archie was a lovely guy, incredibly sexy in that unkempt, just-got-out-of-bed way that she never even realised she liked, but now she knew it, she couldn't unknow it. And he was such a good person. Such a kind, generous, caring person.

* * *

'Hey, lovely! Long time no see. How goes it?' Jules asked as she walked into the bakery and pulled Caitlin away from her thoughts. They were doing her no good anyway, so she was grateful for the distraction.

'All good thanks, you?'

Jules narrowed her eyes. 'Caitlin Fraser, I know you well and you don't seem right. What's up?'

Caitlin sighed. 'Oh, it's nothing. Well, nothing you can help with anyway.'

'Might it help to talk about it? Even if there's nothing I can do to actually improve things?'

Caitlin did want to talk. She wanted to cry and eat ice cream too. But she had work to do. 'Honestly, it's fine.'

Clearly not convinced, Jules asked, 'Have you had a lunch break?'

Caitlin glanced at her watch. It was already two o'clock. 'Not yet, it's only just quietened down so I haven't had a chance.'

She knew Jules wasn't going to give in. She was a good friend and would always drop everything to help if she could.

'Right, get the closed sign on and let's go have a cuppa. I've closed the museum for an hour, so we've got time.'

Caitlin did as instructed and they went through to the back room.

'Come on, out with it,' Jules said as Caitlin placed two steaming mugs of tea on the table.

Caitlin wondered where the hell to start. She huffed out through puffed cheeks and tried her best to gather her thoughts. 'You know how a while ago we were talking about Archie, and you were all saying how attractive he is?'

Jules tilted her head. 'I remember, yes.'

'I'd never really looked at him that way. Not in all the years I've known him. He's always just been Archie – decent, upstanding, fun Archie. But since that day... I've looked at him differently.'

Jules' face lit up. 'You have?'

She nodded. 'I've noticed him more. How lovely he is. How sweet. How he's always there for me and Grace... And annoyingly how bloody attractive he is. It's like a light bulb has flicked on and won't bloody go off again.'

Jules' smile widened. 'Eeek! This is so exciting.'

Caitlin frowned and shook her head. 'No... it's not.' Her throat restricted and she had to pause before clearing it. 'Even Bram pointed out that I like Archie and he said he could tell Archie likes me.'

Jules appeared confused; a crinkle appeared between her brows. 'Well, if you like each other where's the problem?'

Caitlin stared at her mug. 'Because I didn't act when I should have. I said absolutely nothing and now... he's met someone.'

'Ah. Are you sure? It seems rather fast.'

Caitlin nodded. 'I saw them together at his house. She's a very pretty blonde. Far classier than Wozadeath. She looked like just the kind of woman he should be with. And you should've seen the way he hugged her, Jules, there were definitely feelings there. He clearly thinks a lot of her even after only a few days. And now I feel... well... a bit lost, to be honest. And annoyed with myself for not realising or acknowledging how I felt sooner.'

Jules reached out and took her hand. 'Oh, honey, I'm so sorry. That's really rough.'

'Yeah. My timing is crappy.' She forced a laugh even though the emotion of her situation had sneaked up on her, making her heart ache and her eyes well with tears. 'I really like him, Jules. And now I've lost him.' Her heart squeezed as she heard her own words out loud. 'After all these years and those daft conversations we've had, I realise my feelings right at the time when he finds someone new.'

'I'm so very sorry,' Jules replied.

'And now I'm going camping with him and the girls tonight, all platonic, because that's what friends do, and I don't want to go. I think... I think he'll be able to tell how I feel when he looks at me. I don't think I'll be able to hide it.'

Jules held out her hands. 'Look, tell him you and Grace can't go, something's come up.'

Caitlin gave a sad smile. 'Too late. Grace is already up there. And Cleo. He took them earlier. I can't abandon Grace when she's so excited about me going.'

Jules pursed her lips. 'Ah. Maybe you could just go pick her up and come home?'

Caitlin shook her head. 'As tempting as that is, it would look strange. It would be even more clear that something was amiss, only I wouldn't be able to explain what.'

Jules nodded. 'Yes, true. Oh, heck, Cait, it looks like you can't really get out of it.'

'Nope. You're right, I'm afraid. I'm going whether I want to or not.'

* * *

As Caitlin drove along roads lined with gorse and dotted with pretty, whitewashed cottages, the sky overhead was still a vivid cornflower-blue with swathes of fluffy, candyfloss-type clouds, and she was relieved that the weather had behaved itself at least. She switched on the radio, hoping it would distract her from the stampede of butterflies marching around her insides.

'Next up, one for all you old romantics out there,' the radio announcer said. 'This is Take that with "Rule the World"...'

'Oh, for f—'

The intro to the song began and Caitlin was immediately taken back to Archie's garden when they were surrounded by their friends but had locked eyes on each other. She'd thought she had seen something in his expression. Had she imagined it? Had he felt something too but been too scared to say anything? Knowing Archie, he wouldn't have said anything when he was with Rosa-beth, even if he had felt it. He was such a loyal person. And now he would presume that she was still with Bram. She hadn't told him anything to the contrary and Archie had already moved on. Now, her favourite Take That song had been ruined for her, forever destined to remind her of Archie's eyes on that fateful night.

She pulled into the picturesque campsite on the edge of Loch Dunvegan at seven in the evening. The surface of the loch was glasslike, and the mountain known as MacLeod's Table could be seen across the water in the distance, silhouetted against the sky. It really was a stunning location, and she could see why Archie had chosen it.

Grace came jogging over to where she had parked, Sophie was holding her hand.

'Hi, Mum! Did you bring anything nice?' Grace asked.

'I like the biswits you make,' Sophie said, then hid behind Grace as if she had spoken out loud by mistake.

Caitlin's heart swelled at the interaction. 'Aww, that's really lovely, Sophie, I'm glad. And yes, Grace, I have all sorts of goodies. Give me a hand with the bags.' She handed Grace her overnight bag – something she knew made her appear a total townie – and Sophie took her sleeping bag, but it was almost as big as she was. She huffed and puffed, fighting to see over the top of it, but refused to hand it over when Caitlin offered to help. Admiring the little girl's determination and trying not to giggle at the stubborn streak that reminded her of Grace, Caitlin carried the bag of food she had brought.

'Archie has got some burgers on the go,' Grace informed her.

'Good thing I brought bread buns too then, eh?' she said with a grin. 'What have you been doing today then?' Caitlin asked as they walked across the campsite to the neatly mowed area that Archie had chosen for their camp.

'We've played badminton, been for a long walk, ate lunch down by the loch and looked at the flowers. It's been really fun, hasn't it, Sophie?'

'It's been fun, fun, fun!' Sophie said loudly with a skip that surprised Caitlin. She was definitely coming out of her shell.

In a little oasis, there were two decent-sized tents set up with their entrances opposite each other, and a camp table and chairs in the middle. A colourful windbreak shielded them from the other campers and, for a moment, Caitlin wished they were there for more than one night, it looked so cosy.

'Ah, you made it!' Archie said as he walked towards her. He pulled her into a hug, which took her by surprise. Being in his arms, even for a brief second, felt right somehow, comfortable even but she mentally slapped herself.

Get a grip, Caitlin.

'I brought bread and a few sweet treats,' she said, holding the bag aloft.

'Great! Come on and have a seat. Fancy a bottle of beer?'

If she had a beer, she was definitely staying the night. This was it, make or break…

She nodded. 'Beer sounds good. It's so warm.'

'Aye, it's lovely. I thought we'd go for a walk along the edge of the loch after we've eaten and then tonight, when it's dark, we'll get under the blankets and look at the stars.'

Oh gosh, it all sounded so perfect. So romantic. 'Sounds wonderful.'

They sat at the table that was perfect for the four of them, Grace and Caitlin on one side, Archie and Sophie on the other, and ate their burgers. To anyone looking in, they would seem like a normal, little, happy family and Caitlin couldn't help wishing that were true.

Breaking the silence that had fallen over them, Archie said, 'One of these days I'll have to cook you an actual meal that doesn't consist of junk food.'

So, this tyre-changing, party-organising, computer genius of a businessman could cook? Ugh, she didn't need more reasons to find him attractive. 'Don't tell me you're a whizz in the kitchen too?'

'I do a mean chicken salad. And I can cook a decent chilli.' He laughed. 'But I'm in no way a chef, don't get me wrong. I just don't want you to think I'm all about the barbecues and pizza.'

'Your new lady friend is one lucky woman,' Caitlin replied before she could stop herself, her cheeks flushing as red as the ketchup on Sophie's chin.

Archie frowned and opened his mouth to speak, but Grace interjected.

'Hey, Mum, we saw something in the water earlier. I reckon it's the Loch Ness Monster on his holidays, what do you think?' Grace winked as she nodded towards Sophie.

Sophie giggled. 'Monsters don't go on holiday.'

Archie grinned. 'Aye, they do! Don't you think they need it after spending all their time hiding? It must be exhausting scaring people and pretending not to be real.'

Sophie giggled again, her face lit up and her eyes were bright with adoration as she looked up at Archie. 'You're a bit bonkers, Daddy.'

Archie halted his burger's route to his mouth, and he stopped dead with his mouth still partly open, as if in shock.

Realising what had happened, Caitlin inhaled sharply, and her eyes widened and welled up. She had just witnessed Sophie calling Archie Daddy for the first time and it was magical. Her throat tightened and she had to chew on the inside of her cheek to fend off the tears.

Archie was clearly affected too. His eyes turned glassy, and he locked them on Caitlin as his mouth turned up into the most glorious smile. She had to fight the sudden urge to hug him, to tell him what an amazing thing he had done stepping into the breach like he had, and what a fantastic job he was doing... and that she thought she might love him.

He placed down his burger, rubbed at his eyes, cleared his throat, and pulled Sophie into his side. He kissed the top of her head and said, 'I think all daddies are a bit bonkers, don't you, Soph?'

Sophie chuckled again, her laughter like music. 'You're the mostest bonkers though, Daddy. I bet you are the mostest bonkers in the whole wide world!'

Archie beamed. She'd said it twice. It wasn't a fluke and she had evidently made his life complete with that one, simple little word.

25

The girls ran ahead with the dogs, their laughter could be heard ringing through the still evening air.

'I reckon the fresh air will knock them out,' Archie said with a grin.

'We can only hope,' Caitlin replied. 'This is such a lovely spot.'

They were walking along the water's edge as the sun had begun to make its descent behind the mountains. The sky was an array of pastel colours, from orange to pink to pale blue, and a buzzard was hovering overhead waiting to catch its supper. The ripple of the water as it reached the shore was a soothing background to their conversation.

'I love it here. So peaceful. But I'm guessing you're not much of a camper,' he said with a glint in his eye.

Caitlin giggled. 'Uh-oh, busted. What gave me away?'

'I think I can read you quite well, and there was a distinct look of horror in your eyes when camping was mentioned. I think you even tried to get out of it but were beaten by a five-year-old and a thirteen-year-old.' He chuckled lightly.

'Ah... definitely caught red-handed.' She gazed out across the water, watching the remains of the sunlight glinting on the surface. She thought about the places on Skye that she loved to visit, from the rugged beauty of the Storr rock formation to the peaceful serenity of Staffin Beach. 'Don't get me wrong, I love the outdoors. I love a nice long walk in the fresh air and taking in the scenery. Especially up at the Quiraing. The views from up there are spectacular. The fact that on a clear day you can see for miles... I think I'm maybe just getting a little set in my ways these days. I like my luxuries.'

He smiled and gestured back towards the site. 'There are toilets and a shower block here, what more do you need?'

She shrugged and tapped her chin. 'Hmm, I don't know, let me see... good lighting to put my make-up on, a hairdryer, a comfy mattress, a cover that I can't get trapped in if the zip catches, maybe a massage or a jacuzzi.'

He laughed now. 'Ah, I see. Those kinds of luxuries. Although as for the make-up, you really don't need it. You look lovely without. All fresh-faced and youthful.'

Caitlin felt heat rising from her chest to her cheeks. 'Oh, stop it. My head won't fit through the tent door.'

He held out his hands. 'I'm just being honest.'

They walked along in companionable silence for a while, watching the girls bending to examine the flora and fauna by the edge of the sea loch, then chasing each other and laughing uncontrollably. They seemed so comfortable together. Even the dogs were behaving like they'd know each other a lifetime, jumping and yipping before rolling around on the ground and starting over again.

'So how are you finding parenthood?' Caitlin asked eventually.

Archie inhaled a deep breath and let it out quickly. 'Exhausting. Exasperating sometimes. But always wonderful. Sophie is so smart. Seriously, she blows me away with the things she says.' Pride emanated from him in waves. 'I read to her every night, and she loves story time. When we're there, snuggled up with a book, I can almost believe she's forgotten all the painful stuff she's been through, and I can't think of anything I'd rather do more than read to her. Watching her little eyes light up when we read her favourites. She especially likes one about a mouse called Contrary Mary, she giggles like crazy every time, even though she's heard it before. She's been asking me about the stars, too, so we've been looking at a book about the night sky. She lived in quite a built-up part of Edinburgh so seeing the stars for real just mesmerises her. She's a bright, wee thing and can remember loads. I know it's early days, but I can't put into words how much I love her. Is that weird?'

Caitlin was suddenly hit with a wave of emotion on hearing his words. He was such a wonderful man. She shook her head. 'Not at all. You seem so natural with her. And it's clear she adores you. No one would believe you've only been together a matter of weeks.'

Archie's cheeks flushed a little. 'Really? That means such a lot coming from you. Thank you.'

There was a deep sincerity to his words that was also evident in his eyes. Caitlin's stomach flipped again, and she found her gaze drawn to his lips. What would it feel like to kiss him? Would there be passion? Would he be sweet and romantic... *Oh, good grief, I need to stop this right now.*

Archie stopped. 'You know earlier when we were at the table, and we were talking about my culinary skills... or lack thereof?' She nodded and he continued, 'You mentioned my new lady—'

'No! Bowie! You're all wet!' Grace squealed as the pug came out of the water and shook all over her. Sophie's belly laugh was contagious and soon they were all howling.

'Whoops! Better take them back to dry off,' Caitlin said, happy for the rapid change of topic. Whatever he was going to say about his girlfriend could wait until she felt stronger, whenever that might be.

Archie scowled. 'Aye, looks that way.'

Grace and Sophie came back to where they stood, and Bowie shook again. Causing the girls to shriek once more as droplets of water covered them. Who knew such a little dog could create such a downpour?

* * *

Once the dogs were dried and the girls, too, Archie set up the telescope in readiness for later. Then he handed out the blankets and the four of them huddled together on the ground to look up at the night sky. Bowie curled into Sophie's side, his favourite spot, and within moments, he was snoring loudly.

Even though it wasn't completely dark – that was due to something called astronomical twilight that occurred on Skye, between April and August, according to Archie – Caitlin's breath was stolen as her eyes acclimatised to the loss of daylight, and myriad twinkling stars became visible overhead. Some appeared to be solitary, whereas some seemed to be attached by an invisible thread keeping them together. 'Wow! That's incredible,' she whispered. 'I've never really looked so closely at the night sky before, but it's...'

'Magical, isn't it?' Archie replied. 'It's even better later in the year, but I think it might be a little too chilly for the weans.'

She turned her face towards him. 'And the biguns,' she said with a laugh, and he joined in.

Archie shuffled under his blanket and pointed to the distance. 'Grace, see there, that constellation that looks like a double u? That's Cassiopeia, where your star is.'

Grace gasped. 'Oh, wow! Yes! I can see it.' Grace had been overjoyed with Archie's thoughtful gift and the picture was hung on the wall where she could see it from her bed.

He continued, 'And just a little higher in the sky you can see Polaris, otherwise known as the North Star. People have used it for navigation for many, many years. And then a little higher still, you can see a constellation that looks like a saucepan, do you see?'

'I see it, Daddy! It's the Plough, isn't it?' Sophie said.

'That's right, well done, sweetheart, you remembered!' Pride filled his voice.

Sophie giggled. 'I did.'

Archie scuttled out from under his blanket and pointed the telescope up to the heavens. 'Who wants to see them up close?'

'Ooh, me!' Caitlin said, caught up in the moment, the romance of the setting, the adventure of being outside. She'd never seen the stars through a telescope before and the thought of it excited her. She scrambled from under her own blanket.

'Okay, put your eye here,' he told her, pointing at the eyepiece. 'And adjust this here to focus it. If you point it that way you should see Polaris quite clearly.'

Caitlin crouched and looked through the eyepiece. What she saw astounded her. 'Oh, wow! Look how bright it is!'

'Aye, cool, eh? It's used for navigation in the northern hemisphere because it pretty much stays in the same place all year round and the other stars move around it.'

'Fascinating.' Caitlin was once again amazed by the man's knowledge. He was some kind of unassuming genius with his computer skills and expertise in astronomy. Yet more reasons to admire him, sadly.

Sophie suddenly blurted, 'Daddy! I saw a shooting star! We have to make a wish!' Her excitement was evident in her high-pitched tone.

'I saw it, too, Sophie! Come on, everyone. Let's make our wishes, but don't say them out loud, say it in your minds or they won't come true,' Grace added.

The four of them closed their eyes and called out silently to the universe for their heart's desires. Caitlin couldn't help wondering what Archie had wished for.

'I made my wish,' Sophie said in a quiet voice. Caitlin guessed that she had wished to see her mum again and with that knowledge her eyes began to sting.

As if he'd had the same thought, Archie pulled the little girl into his lap, and she nuzzled into him.

After an hour of staring skyward in wonder with the girls, Sophie was yawning and dozing off in Archie's arms. The dogs were already snuggled up inside their respective tents and Archie helped Sophie inside to change into her pyjamas and climb into her sleeping bag.

The night air held a distinct chill now and Grace cuddled up to Caitlin. 'I think I'm going to go to bed, too, Mum. It's been a busy day,' she said. 'But I've had such a lovely time. And I know you didn't really like the idea of camping, but it's been fun, hasn't it?'

Caitlin nodded. 'It has. I've enjoyed it.' She was surprised at the fact, but it was true, thanks to Archie and Grace she had acquired a newfound love for the night sky and all it entailed.

Grace hugged her and kissed her cheek. 'I'm so glad. Thank you for coming, Mum. Love you. Goodnight.'

'Goodnight, sweetheart. Love you too. I'll be in soon.'

Archie returned and laid back on the ground, where Caitlin remained, still mesmerised by the stars.

'I can't get over how beautiful it is,' she told him.

'It takes my breath away.' After a small interlude of silence, he continued, 'I could spend hours just looking up. And the more you look, the more you notice.' Was he still talking about the stars? 'You know, I heard that Take That song the other day again on the radio while I was in the shop. The one that was on at the barbecue that's about the stars?'

Her heart skipped a beat. 'You mean "Rule the World", it's one of my absolute favourites,' she whispered.

He fell silent for a moment, but then said, 'It's strange, but it immediately makes me think of you. Such a beautiful song, don't you think? The lyrics are... kind of poetic.' He chuckled. 'Not something I ever expected to be saying about Take That.'

She felt his fingers entwine with hers. He rubbed his thumb gently over the skin of her hand, and she shivered. What was happening?

Suddenly he propped himself up on his elbow and gazed down at her. 'I've never been great at saying how I feel. About expressing things in a way that comes out coherently. I tend to bumble around and make an idiot of myself. And I often don't say things when my heart is telling me that I should, so I leave things too late.' That sounded familiar. 'So... here goes... I think... and I know this is a little out of the blue, but it's been on my mind such a lot lately... I think the lyrics of that song express perfectly how I feel about you...'

Caitlin gulped air into her lungs as his words rang around her mind. What did he say? Had she imagined it? Was this actually happening? She'd wished on that star only minutes before, but here they were, having this conversation already. Quick work, universe!

She gazed up at him there above her, silhouetted against the night sky, a halo of stars around his head, and the outline of his unruly curls moving in the gentle evening breeze. She wished she could see his eyes, read his mind. She lay frozen to the spot, afraid to move in case she woke up from a dream.

In a split second, his lips were touching hers and her hands found his hair. His arm slipped across her waist, and he pulled her closer until their bodies were touching, perfectly aligned, like the stars above them. The kiss began slowly, but passion built inside her as she relished the feeling of his mouth on hers, and as if he felt the same, his kiss deepened. She'd been longing for this moment, hoping and wishing it would happen, and now it had, guilt niggled at her.

He'd met someone else. She'd seen them together and the way they had hugged. This couldn't happen. Not now. Maybe not ever. She couldn't be the reason they broke up, not even if their relationship was new. She'd hate to be in that position herself so she certainly couldn't do that to someone else.

She pushed at his chest. 'I'm sorry, I can't... I just... It's not right.' She pulled herself up to standing, grabbed her blanket and let herself into the tent, where her daughter was sleeping soundly. Her heart hammered at her ribcage and her eyes stung with tears that were threatening to spill over at any second.

She'd almost had her wish come true, but how could she accept it when she knew he could be thinking about someone else and was with someone else, someone who Sophie clearly adored too?

26

The next morning, Caitlin woke Grace early. 'Come on, love, we have to get going. I have loads of stuff to prepare for the bakery. You know how busy Sundays are.'

Grace groaned. 'But, Muuum, it's only eight o'clock. Please let me sleep a bit longer.'

'Grace, I need you to get up now!' she snapped, immediately feeling rotten for taking out her mood on her daughter. 'Please, love. I have such a lot to do with not doing it last night.'

Grace's appearance took on that of a sad puppy. 'Okay. Give me a minute.'

'I'm going to nip over to the shower block. You can shower at home, so just get dressed. You can sleep for a bit longer when we get back too if you like,' Caitlin informed her as she grabbed her washbag.

Over at the shower block, Caitlin stood under the cascade of hot water and allowed it to relax her muscles. She was so tense after the events of the night before. Partly because she had let Archie kiss her when she knew he was seeing someone else. And partly because she hadn't just confronted him about the whole thing so she could find out the truth. But it was too late for that now. They couldn't talk in front of Grace, that wouldn't be fair on her. So, it would have to wait. Or maybe it just wouldn't happen at all. She was so damned confused. Why the hell would he kiss her if he had feelings for someone else? Did he even have feelings for someone else? Maybe she was just a friend? But if so, why hadn't he said something about her? Was he trying to hide his relationship?

Oh, for goodness' sake, Cait, just stop it! It doesn't matter now! You've blown it! Her inner voice hurt, and she once again felt her throat tightening. *Just go back to the tent and act like nothing happened, then maybe you can return to normal, to being friends?*

Yeah, right...

* * *

Back at the tent, Archie was sitting on one of the chairs with a mug of coffee in his hand. His eyes were puffy through apparent lack of sleep – she knew how that felt – and he was chatting to Grace about the stars they had observed the night before.

'Morning,' Caitlin said with a forced bright smile.

'Hi,' Archie replied. 'You know I can bring Grace home later. That way she can stay a wee bit longer. I think Sophie might be upset if she wakes and finds you both gone.'

Caitlin glanced at Grace whose eyes were now filled with hope. 'Erm... okay. So long as you don't mind? Sorry to be rushing off. It's just...'

Archie shrugged, but his face remained stoic. 'It's okay, I understand.'

I don't think you do and therein lies the problem. She nodded. 'Right... okay... good. Do you need help to take my tent down?'

He shook his head. 'I can manage.'

'I'll help,' Grace said brightly.

Archie smiled at her. 'Thanks, sweetheart.' His smile was tinged
with sadness and Caitlin wanted to smack herself in the head. *Idiot!
You could've just been straight with him.*

'Right, well my stuff is packed, so I'll be off. See you later,' she
said, awkwardly stepping from foot to foot.

Archie gave a single nod. 'Aye, see you later.' It was clear from
his expression and minimal replies that he was hurt, or perturbed...
or both.

Grace ran over to hug her. 'Bye, Mum, love you. And thanks for
letting me stay a while.'

Caitlin nodded, smiled, and turned to walk to the car. *Follow me,
Archie, follow me and we can talk. I want to explain, please...*

But he didn't. She wasn't really surprised.

For the rest of the day, Caitlin busied herself preparing stock for the
bakery and trying to blot Archie out of her mind. But the memory
of that kiss and of his fingers entwined with hers made her heart
ache. What had she done? She vowed to herself that she would go
and explain at some point because even if he had found someone
else, the last thing she wanted was to ruin their friendship.

The radio mocked her with every love song the DJ could find,
but when 'Rule the World' came on she figured that was enough
torture for one day and immediately switched it off. *Pfft, do they only
have five songs on this bloody station?*

She was surrounded by the smell of fresh baking bread, shortbread, and tray bake. The sweet and savoury aromas mixed and
sent her senses into overdrive, and she had to step out to gulp in the
crisp salty air coming in off the sea. The village was quiet, apart
from Morag and Kenneth's shop with its steady run of locals calling
in for essentials. Mitch waved as he turned the corner and drove out

of Glentorrin with Ruby in the passenger seat. Why couldn't she have a love like theirs? Uncomplicated – apart from Ruby's ex-Hollywood star status of course – and true.

By the time Grace and Cleo arrived home at around four, everything was ready for the start of the week. As they bustled into the kitchen, Caitlin glanced over Grace's shoulder, half expecting Archie, Sophie and Bowie to follow her, but they didn't, much to her disappointment.

'Hey, Mum. We went to Dunvegan Castle today! Have you ever been? It was built by the MacLeod clan, and it's been their family home for eight hundred years! Imagine that! And it's so fancy. The main staircase is beautiful and looks just like something you would see a princess coming down in a ball gown, or maybe Cinderella. It's amazing!' her words fell in a long run, enthusiastically from her smiling lips, and Caitlin wondered if she would stop for breath. 'The gardens are so pretty too! Bowie and Cleo loved it, but we had to keep them on their leads. We saw lots of bees too. I've always been scared of bees, but Archie says they keep the planet going, so I have a whole new respect for them. He also said that they will never sting you on purpose because they'll die if they do, which is so sad. But anyway, I'm not scared of them any more. They're tiny but have such an important job.'

Eventually Caitlin got a word in. 'It sounds lovely. I'm glad you had a fab time. Did Archie say anything? Any messages?'

Grace scrunched her brow. 'Erm... nope. Nothing. Sophie is so cute. When she laughs, you can't help laughing too. She's like the little sister I never had. But I do miss Cora...' Her mood dipped suddenly on mentioning her best friend. 'I can't believe she's gone to Canada, and I'll never see her again, Mum.' It was quite a dramatic change and her eyes welled with tears.

Caitlin pulled her daughter into her arms. 'I know, sweetheart. I'm so sorry about how things turned out.'

Grace clung to her mum. 'It's okay. I don't blame you. Even Cora said her dad was acting like a tube. I blame him completely. But at least he let us say goodbye. And I have her email address. She has only emailed a couple of times, but I know she's busy getting settled. I just miss her so much.'

Caitlin's heart ached for her daughter. 'Look, why don't you go get changed and we can take Cleo for a walk.'

'Okay. Come on, Cleo!' Grace picked up her bag and headed upstairs, followed by her furry canine companion whose tongue was lolling out and tail wagging at the mention of her favourite W-word.

When they headed out into the village for their walk, the sky was overcast. Caitlin couldn't help her eyes drifting towards Archie's house, but there was no movement. They wandered up to the Skye Bridge and admired the view looking out across the Inner Sound where the horizon of grey met the sea. On a clear day, you could see Raasay and beyond, but today it was a little hazy. It was days like this that Kyle Lighthouse, visible beneath them on Eilean Bàn, would've come into its own; these days it was more of a day mark, however, since being decommissioned in the nineties.

The wind had picked up now and was blowing Cleo's ears back. She looked so cute standing there with her head up, eyes closed and tongue out as if tasting the salt in the air. A chill ran through Caitlin as they turned around to make their way home again.

As they reached the inlet, a cursory glance towards Archie's gave her a view she didn't want to see. The blonde woman was back again. A taxi had just dropped her off and she was being greeted at the door by Archie. She handed him a bottle of wine and they hugged again. Caitlin's stomach knotted. *Okay, so I did the right thing in stopping the kiss*, she told herself. Still, Archie's behaviour seemed out of character. He didn't seem the type to have two women on the go at once, nor to attempt to do so. Good thing she'd held fast to her reserve even if she was still a little regretful of doing so. *You can't help what your heart wants*, she told herself.

Monday was quiet. The weather was overcast again and there was a chill to the air, the kind of which usually indicated summer was waning. It was, however, only the start of August and Kenneth and Father McAllen were reattaching the Highland Games banner to the posts outside the new village hall after the rope had snapped at one end in the wind. It appeared to be a fight on account of the breeze, and it was flapping around like a yacht sail in a squall. Luckily for them, Dexter turned up to help. The games were to take place a week later than normal due to an oversight with a village hall booking, but preparations were well under way.

The year had flown and so much had happened, but Caitlin couldn't help feeling a little sad. At the start of summer, she had been full of excited anticipation at what may come of her search for love. Now, however, she'd realised who she wanted but her wishes wouldn't be granted.

She had seen Archie that morning when she was putting out her A-frame by the Coxswain pub, but he had either seen her and avoided her or he had simply not seen her. She hoped it was the latter. He was walking Bowie, but Sophie was nowhere to be seen. Did this mean the blonde had stayed over? Her stomach lurched at the thought.

At lunchtime, Jules popped over from the Lifeboat House Museum for a piece of shortbread.

'Phew! It's a busy one today. There's been hardly any visitors, but that's meant I can get some proper cleaning done. I almost forgot to take a lunch break. Hamish Gair found some more old photos of his wedding day, bless him, so he brought them in to add to his display case. He still visits regularly, you know.'

Caitlin's heart squeezed. That was true love for you. Hamish had lost his wife many, many years ago but still adored her and had never really got over her passing. He had donated wedding photos of their special day, and his wife's pretty, lace veil and had continued to visit the museum regularly to reminisce. 'Such a sweet old guy.'

'He is. He was the only visitor I had today until around half-eleven. Where have all the tourists gone?' Jules asked with a laugh.

'I know. Quiet here too. Trouble is that gives me too much thinking time.' Caitlin was thinking out loud really.

'Ah, how was the camping?' she asked with intrigue.

'Disastrous,' Caitlin admitted with a furrow in her brow.

'Oh, honey. Was it that bad?'

Caitlin sighed deeply as she once again recalled that kiss. 'Yup. He hasn't spoken to me since.'

'Shit, what happened?'

With a glance around to make sure no one was about to come in, she said, 'We kissed.'

Jules gasped. 'Wow! But that's something you wanted, isn't it?'

Caitlin shrugged, feeling the weight of it all pressing her down. 'I did, but... I stopped him. After seeing him with that blonde woman, I couldn't let him kiss me. It felt wrong. I'd hate to be the woman on the receiving end of that kind of behaviour. And it turns out I was right to stop him because I've seen her there again. She turned up with a bottle of wine looking all perfect last night, and this morning he was out walking Bowie without Sophie.'

Jules tilted her head. 'And?'

'Well, think about it. It means the blonde must have stayed over. He would never go out and leave Sophie alone.'

Jules' eyes widened. 'Oh.'

'Hmm. I was feeling guilty about stopping things so abruptly and for rushing off yesterday morning, but then seeing her there again...'

'But what if she's just a friend? What if he really does want you?'

'I know what you're trying to do, Jules, and I'm grateful, honestly, but I saw how close they were. And I'm not going to play second fiddle. Nor am I going to be the other woman. It's just not who I am.'

Jules nodded. 'Yes, I totally understand, and I'm gutted for you.'

'I'm gutted for me too. Now I just have to work on getting past this so I can still have Archie in my life. The last thing I want is to lose his friendship.'

Jules paused for a moment as if deep in thought. 'For what it's worth, I still think you should just talk to him.'

'I can't, Jules. I wouldn't know what to say.'

'The truth is the best option,' Jules said with a sad smile.

'I wish I was brave enough.'

27

———

Caitlin didn't see Archie on Tuesday or Wednesday either. He was clearly avoiding her. There had been no funny text messages or memes like he usually sent. Just radio silence. She missed him terribly. On Tuesday evening, she had seen the blonde's taxi leaving again but didn't go out to watch Archie holding the woman. Twice was enough.

After dinner on Wednesday evening, Caitlin sat in silence in her living room. Grace had gone upstairs to watch a movie in her room, and of course, Cleo had followed close behind like her little shadow. When the room was silent, Caitlin had opened the novel she was reading but had read the same page at least three times before she gave up and placed it beside her on the sofa. She was dozing off when there was a knock at the door. Could it be Archie? She doubted it, but it didn't stop her hoping.

She opened the door to find Dexter standing there. 'Hiya, pet. I thought I'd bring a bottle and some boxing gloves.'

Confused as she glanced at his hands, she asked, 'Boxing gloves?' He didn't appear to be carrying any.

'Aye, don't worry, they're metaphorical ones. I was speaking to

Jetty, and she told me what had happened when you were camping, you know, Archie kissing you? And that you stopped it. I have no idea why you would do that when I know how you feel about him, so I've come to knock some sense into that head of yours.'

She folded her arms across her chest. 'I don't need any sense knocking into me, thank you. But you can bring the wine in.' She grinned.

He followed her to the kitchen, where she took two wine glasses from the cupboard, placed them on the table and they sat.

'You need to go talk to Archie, you know,' Dexter said as she poured the wine. 'He must be wondering what the heck's going on.'

She huffed. 'Not you as well? Look, I've already told Jules I can't do that. I don't know what to say.'

'Erm... that you've fallen for him and want a relationship, the same as him?'

She scoffed. 'Pfft. Not a chance. And there's no point now anyway.'

Dexter huffed and rubbed his hands over his face, then fixed her with a bemused expression. 'So, let me get this straight, you have a chance at happiness with someone you actually fancy, who more than fancies you back and you're going to pass? You're daft, do you know that, Caitlin Fraser? Completely batty!'

Feeling more than a little indignant, she huffed. 'Thanks for the support, friend. And for your information, he's already moved on.'

Dexter scrunched his brow. 'Eh? What are you talking about?'

Caitlin took a large gulp of wine to help muster up the courage to explain without bursting into tears. 'The blonde. I saw them together before we went camping and things looked quite cosy. Then we kissed at the camp, under the stars no less, and yes it was lovely, but I stopped him because I couldn't get her out of my head. I know how shitty I would feel if things were the other way around and I was in her place. Then I saw him with her again. He clearly isn't that upset by my rejection, is he?'

Dexter appeared completely flummoxed. He scratched his beard and then his eyes widened as if a light bulb had flicked on. 'Shit! You've totally got it wrong! I know who you mean!'

She shook her head. 'I'm sorry what?'

'I didn't meet her, but he said she was here for a few days. That was why he asked me to cover the shop. Ugh, why the hell didn't you just ask him about her? This needn't have happened at all, you daft wazzock.'

Caitlin was the confused one now. 'Hang on, backpedal a wee bit. Who? Who was here?'

'Kristine. Sophie's mum's ex.'

Caitlin's stomach dropped as if the ground had fallen away beneath her. 'Kristine? The blonde was Sophie's other mum?'

Dexter scrunched his brow. 'Well, technically not any more... in fact, not at all, seeing as she gave up that right when she buggered off back to Germany. But yes, it was her. She came over from Berlin when she'd heard through friends that Archie had taken Sophie in. She wanted to check that he was okay with everything since he didn't really sign up for parenthood when he... you know...' He made a weird hand gesture that she would've ordinarily laughed out loud at, but under the circumstances it was no laughing matter. 'And I guess she wanted to see if Sophie was okay.'

Caitlin placed her head in her hands. 'Oh god, I'm such an idiot. He must think I'm crazy.'

Dexter chuckled. 'Well, we've all known that for a while, pet.'

With a knot of panic in her gut, she ran her hands through her hair. 'What do I do? I think he's avoiding me and, let's be fair, he has good reason. For all he knows, I rejected him because I'm not interested.'

Dexter glanced at his watch. 'Well, there's no time like the present, eh? It's only eight o'clock.' He shrugged and nodded to the door.

'But, Grace?'

Dexter gave a derisive shake of the head and pointed at himself.

She lurched up from her seat and flung her arms around him. 'Thank you. Thank you so much. I owe you one.'

He laughed. 'I'll add it to your tab, shall I?'

Without answering, she yanked open the front door and let it slam behind her, then set off running up the road towards Archie's.

* * *

When she reached the door of Archie's cottage, Caitlin was out of breath but managed to hammer on it regardless whilst gulping in the fresh evening air.

Archie opened the door and widened his eyes with horror. 'Shit! Caitlin, whatever's happened?'

Without saying a word, she launched herself into his arms and planted her lips on his. It wasn't subtle, but she hoped it would get the message across.

He stumbled backwards and pushed her away, holding her at arm's length. 'What the hell, Caitlin? Have you been drinking?' The look of consternation on his face made her stomach lurch.

What had she done? She covered her mouth with her hands. 'Oh god, I'm so sorry, Archie. I was... just... out of breath and... words...' Her chest heaved.

He shook his head and touched his fingers to his lips. 'I don't understand what just happened.'

She swallowed hard and tried to catch her breath. 'I'm sorry. I'll go.' She pointed back towards the bakery and turned, but he grabbed her wrist.

He scowled. 'Wait a minute. No explanation? Just some random knock-my-socks-off kiss, and then you do a runner?'

Her heart pounded at her ribs and her head swam. *God, I'm so bloody unfit. I've only run five hundred yards!* She nodded. 'Sorry.'

His frown remained in place. 'Sorry for the kiss, or for attempting to run away?'

She managed a small smile. 'Both?'

He let go of her wrist and folded his arms across his chest. 'Right. I see. Well, if I was to give the kiss marks out of ten, I'd say it was a definite seven.'

She widened her eyes, suddenly a little indignant. 'Excuse me?'

'I think you'd better come in and see if you can improve on it.' He tried to stop a smile from forming. 'And while you're at it, you can explain what the Dickens is going on. Deal?'

She nodded. 'Deal.'

He stepped aside to let her in and the moment the front door was closed he pulled her into his arms and crushed his mouth to hers, one hand scrunched in her hair and the other held her in place at the small of her back. This time he was in control, and it was magnificent. Her legs jellified and her skin vibrated with desire. She slipped her arms up and around his neck and relished the feeling of his muscular body flush against hers. She inhaled the familiar scent of him and suddenly she knew what it felt like to see stars when being kissed. Kissing Archie was like nothing she had ever experienced before. It felt right, it felt wonderful, it felt like a Hollywood screen kiss, but it was real.

When he pulled away, she gazed up into his dark, chocolate eyes where so many questions lay. He smiled and softly said, 'Now that was definitely a fifteen out of ten. Come on. Let's go sit and talk, something I think we should've done a long time ago.' He took her hand and led her to the black leather sofa.

They sat and he kept her hand in his. She felt suddenly shy and couldn't pull her attention away from their entwined fingers. She had forgotten how amazing it felt to be touched in such a way.

After inhaling a calming breath, she managed to lift her chin and lock her gaze on his. 'I owe you a massive apology.'

With a look of confusion in his eyes, he tucked her hair behind her ear. 'How so?'

'I thought... I thought you'd met someone else. I'd seen the blonde woman at your house and the way you hugged her. I put two and two together and came up with a mess.'

He closed his eyes. 'Kristine.'

She nodded. 'Archie, I've had feelings for you for a while now, but the timing has always been rubbish. First Lyle, then Wozadeath—'

'Eh?'

'Erm. Rosabeth?' she replied, hoping he would think he had misheard her the first time. 'Then Bram... But even he noticed my feelings for you. Said he could see it in my eyes. But then, when you kissed me, I felt so bad. I'd seen you with Kristine and I wouldn't want to be on the receiving end of a cheater, no matter how new the relationship.'

His expression became serious. 'You should know I would never, ever cheat. It's just not something I'd do.'

Her heart leapt. 'I know that now. I feel like such an idiot. I know I should've just come to you and talked to you but... I was scared you weren't interested in me that way. Especially after thinking I was a lesbian to begin with!'

He laughed. 'For what it's worth, I've been attracted to you from the day we met. Your sexual orientation didn't stop that. And now, obviously, I realise I should've maybe not presumed either. We're a grand pair, aren't we?'

She smiled again. 'We are.'

He pulled her close. 'So, this... us... are we giving it a chance?'

She wanted to jump into his lap and tear off his clothes but managed to restrain herself, knowing Sophie was upstairs in bed. 'Do you want to?'

He moved his face closer until their lips were almost touching. 'I definitely do.'

His mouth met hers again and she closed her eyes, giving into the pent-up feelings she'd held on to ever since the day her friends had made her see him in a totally different light. His hand cupped her face and his tongue danced with hers. Her mind wandered to inappropriate things considering a child was upstairs asleep. But she couldn't help it. It was like a flame had ignited inside of her and she had no intention of extinguishing it. Her heart felt whole... but not the kind of whole that meant she had needed a man to complete her. Simply that being held and kissed and desired made her feel ten feet tall. Invincible. And it was a wonderful feeling indeed.

Archie pulled away. 'I'm going to have to take a breather. This is all a bit overwhelming. Sophie is—'

She placed a finger on his lips. 'I totally understand. We can't get carried away.'

'So long as you know there's nothing I'd like more than to carry you away,' he said with another kiss. 'So, what do we do now? Do we keep things quiet? Or do we tell people?'

She ran her fingers through his hair. 'We shout it from the rooftops. My friends already know how I feel about you.' She realised there was a chance he may wish to keep things on the down low due to his new position as a father and cleared her throat. 'Unless you'd rather keep it quiet of course. I mean, I—'

He crushed his lips to hers once more and she felt him smile against her skin. 'The rooftop is a good place to start.' His kisses had slowed now, and he rested his forehead on hers. 'Do you think Grace will be okay about this?'

'I think Grace will be over the moon. She adores you. How could she not? How about Sophie?'

'Same answer. She likes your biswits.' He chuckled.

'Bless her. She's so cute. Her name for Rosabeth has kind of stuck in my head.'

'Wozadeath,' he said with a laugh. Dammit, he had heard her after all. 'And Cakelin.'

'I love that she calls me Cakelin. It kind of fits.'

He grinned. 'It does. You've made me so happy, Cait. I can't tell you how good this feels,' he whispered.

'I agree. I feel like I've known you a lifetime, but it hasn't been that long really.'

'No... but when you know, you know. And boy do I know,' he said with a sexy smile and kissed her once more.

28

The Highland Games was in full swing. Glentorrin looked as picturesque as ever with the coloured bunting strung around every building, flowers blooming in every hanging basket, and the sun high in the sky overhead. It was a perfect day for the event.

Caitlin's cake stall ran out of food around lunchtime, so she had the afternoon to spend with Archie and the girls. With Ruby's help, Grace had taught Evin the moves to her dance routine, now that Cora was gone, and they were excited about the talent contest.

The week since she fell into Archie's arms had been amazing. Caitlin knew, regardless of how fast it was happening, that she had completely fallen for him. Of course, she hadn't told him yet. She didn't want to appear anything like Barmy Budge, but in a way, she felt guilty for not believing Lyle when he said he'd fallen fast. She'd now done the exact same thing, even though she'd had no clue it was actually possible.

Watching Archie's interactions with Sophie and Grace made her heart sing. Sophie was on his shoulders and Grace's arm was linked through his as they walked around the stalls. Jules had a fundraising stand for the museum's children's area and Reid had painted mini Glentorrin pictures to sell. Archie had bought three already.

Kenneth was on the plant stall this year and Grace was, of course, first in the queue for that one. She had saved her pocket money for the day and had bought a plant based solely on its name – Cosmos. The flowers were bright pink and had the appearance of daisies. Grace had said they made her think of Archie because of the name. It was lovely to see Archie's influence shining through. It was wonderful, too, how Sophie and Grace had taken to the new development. To see them you'd be forgiven for thinking things had always been this way.

As the sun shone down on them and Caitlin and Archie walked hand in hand, she remembered the previous year's games and how she'd been jokily lusting after one of the contenders. How time had changed. This year she only had eyes for Archie, even when the same caber tosser took to the field, all kilted and muscled. Every so often, Archie would glance down at her, lift her hand to his lips and kiss her skin softly. He made her insides turn to jelly and she couldn't help wondering when they were going to take the next step.

Later that evening, the talent contest in the new village hall wowed everyone as always, and when it was Grace and Evin's turn, they took to the stage in their baggy jogging bottoms, bright T-shirts and baseball caps, and struck a pose. The opening bars to Bell Biv DeVoe's 'Poison' began and Caitlin was immediately transported back to 1990. Where on earth had they found this song? She turned to see Ruby miming the lyrics and doing a more sedate version of the dance, and she laughed. *Ah, okay, that explains it.*

Ruby turned to face her and beamed. It was clear she was proud of her protégés. Evin would have looked right at home spinning on his head on a cardboard sheet in a street in the USA, complete with a boombox, and Grace added some quirky tap moves to the street dance piece. Caitlin too was almost bursting with pride.

Archie leaned down and whispered, 'Wowsers, Cait, Grace is a star! And who'd have thought Evin could dance like that?'

'I know! Brilliant, eh?'

Sophie stood between them waving her hands and trying to copy Grace. It was so blooming cute.

The whole audience clapped along as they watched the routine and at the end of the performance, Grace did the splits and Evin stood behind her in a hip-hop pose, arms folded across his chest. The applause was raucous, and everyone cheered and whistled. The smiles on Grace and Evin's faces spoke volumes and the ones on Ruby, Mitch, Reid and Jules were just as wide.

When it came time for the announcements, it was evident there was a clear winner. And when Grace and Evin had collected their trophy, they joined their parents and were immediately engulfed in a group hug.

'In your face, last-year me!' Evin shouted with a fist bump to the air as the group of adults cheered and applauded once again. He had missed out on winning the previous year by a hair's breadth when he performed tricks with Chewie, but he'd more than made up for it this time.

'We're so proud of you!' Archie told Grace as he picked her up and spun her around. Caitlin loved the way he was with her daughter. It was a special relationship indeed and Grace seemed to revel in his presence. The way she looked at him with such adoration made Caitlin's heart sing.

After the talent show came the ceilidh and by the end of the evening, Caitlin's face hurt from laughing and her arms were aching from being swung around by Archie, Mitch, Reid and Dexter.

The slow dance at the end of the event was a welcome relief for Caitlin's poor feet and as she slipped her arms around Archie's neck and gazed up into those dark eyes of his, she couldn't believe her luck. Not so long back, she was ready to give up on love, but not any more. Who'd have thought she'd end up falling for the boy next door but one?

'We've had an offer we can't refuse,' Archie whispered in her ear, sending shivers down her spine.

'Oh? What might that be?'

'Jules has invited the girls and the dogs for a sleepover. Evin says they're planning on making a den in the house, and they're going to eat junk food and play games. If you're okay with that.' Archie smiled and rubbed his nose down the length of hers.

'I'm definitely okay with that. What did Sophie say?'

'Let's see, how did it go? Oh yes, I was subjected to, "Please, Daddy, pleeeeeease can we? Pleeeease." So, I don't know, but I think she might want to go.' He laughed.

'That's it then. We get some alone time.' Her heart skipped with anticipation, and she suddenly became worried about being naked in front of him. She wasn't twenty any more.

As if sensing her concern, he said, 'Hey, we don't have to do anything you're not ready for. I'm just happy to spend time with you without either a dog or a child squeezing in between us.'

She felt warmth rising in her face. 'I'm just... I haven't... not for a very long time. So, I'm a wee bit out of practice.'

He pulled the side of his lip between his teeth and raised his eyebrows. 'Well, if that's your only fear, I say practice makes perfect.'

Her panties almost burst into flames at that sexy smile, and she replied, 'Is it time to go yet?'

* * *

Back at Archie's house, he pulled Caitlin inside the front door and slammed it behind him, leaving the last of the revellers behind and closing them into a world where only they existed. In a split second, she was in his arms, and he stole her breath with a kiss she was sure had propelled her into outer space. His hands were scrunched in her hair as he backed her against the wall, his desire evident as he pressed himself against her.

Suddenly he pulled away, his chest heaving. 'Do you think Sophie will be okay?' he breathed. 'I mean, I know she's safe with Reid and Jules but... Do you think I'm a bad parent for wanting to get you alone with no interruptions?'

She gazed up at him and smiled. 'If you're a bad parent, so am I, because all I've been able to think about today is when I can be alone with you. But she'll be absolutely fine. Jules won't let her out of her sight. And Grace is there too. They'll have a whale of a time.' She hoped she'd reassured him enough because she was about to spontaneously combust from need.

'You're right. You're right.' His mouth took hers again and he moaned as his hand slipped lower down her back. 'I want to take you to bed. Is that okay?' he whispered as he fixed his eyes on her.

'More than okay,' she replied breathlessly, and, needing no further encouragement, he picked her up and carried her up the stairs to his bedroom, managing to navigate their ascent while still kissing her.

Once inside his room, Caitlin's feet touched the floor and she watched as he stepped back slowly and removed his clothes. She chewed on her lip as each part of his sculpted body was revealed to her: those biceps she had admired before, his toned stomach, narrow hips and a smattering of dark hair across his chest. He really was gorgeous. And what made things even better, he was all hers.

Why had she not seen his beauty before? Not just his physical beauty – which she now realised she must have been in a haze not to see – but his soul, his heart, his mind. Everything about him was perfect for her. If only she'd realised years ago.

Once his clothing was relinquished to the floor, she cast off her own. She'd expected to feel self-conscious, embarrassed, but with the way he was devouring her with his gaze, she felt like the most beautiful woman in the world.

He stepped closer again and tenderly reached out to stroke her cheek. 'I love you, Caitlin Fraser.'

Her breath caught in her throat and her eyes welled with tears. He had been the first to utter the words she'd felt for a while now, so she had no qualms in saying it back. 'I love you, too, Archie Sutherland.'

* * *

Lying there in Archie's arms, breathing heavily with a hammering heart, Caitlin listened to the thud, thud, thud, coming from his chest as she rested her hand between his pecs.

'Wow,' he said. 'I have no words.' He kissed the top of her head as he traced his fingers down her side to her hip and back up to her arm.

This is what bliss truly feels like, she thought as she replayed over in her mind the way he had held her, and moved over her, the adoration in his eyes.

'Hmm,' was all she managed. She wanted to stay there, relishing the memories until she could live them for real all over again.

Archie manoeuvred and faced her. 'I don't think I've ever been this happy,' he whispered.

She smiled, feeling the exact same way. 'I'd have to agree. Why didn't we find each other sooner?' she asked.

'I think it's all about timing. This is the right time for us. I know it might sound stupid, but I feel I have something to offer you now that perhaps I was too insecure and awkward to offer before. I was quite self-centred, maybe stuck in my ways too.' Caitlin completely disagreed with that observation but allowed him to carry on without interruption. 'Having Sophie in my life has changed me so much already. I appreciate things now that I didn't before. It's like she's opened my eyes somehow and I'm so grateful. I've always found you so attractive. And I've always thought you were an amazing mum. But having the opportunity to get to know the real you has been...' He shook his head. 'I meant it when I said I love you. I hope that doesn't freak you out because I know it's fast. I mean, I know you said it too, but I don't want you to feel pressured into—'

She stopped his words with a passionate kiss and when she pulled away, she said, 'Archie, I meant it too. I feel like everything has fallen into place now. I think you're right. It's about the timing. I'll be completely honest, I always really liked you as a person, but lately I've seen you through fresh eyes. And I don't just mean the physical you... which I have to say I like very, very much,' she said with a rush of blood to her cheeks. 'I see you. And I love everything about you. Your kindness, your self-deprecation, the way you're so patient with Grace and Sophie, the way you make me laugh...' She sighed. 'I think we have a real chance of happiness here.'

He smiled and cleared his throat before huffing the air from his lungs. 'Wow... what did I do to deserve so much love in such a short space of time?'

She kissed him tenderly. 'You were just you.'

He laid her back in the bed and worshipped her once more.

* * *

Archie and Caitlin walked through Glentorrin, hand in hand, towards Jules and Reid's place to collect their kids and dogs, and this garnered smiles from the locals.

Morag waved from the doorway of the shop. 'Och, you two are a vision of happiness,' she called out. 'You make such a lovely couple.'

'Thanks, Morag,' Archie replied with a smile at Caitlin.

They arrived at Jules and Reid's and were greeted with hugs from Sophie and Grace.

'Have you been good?' Caitlin asked.

'They have!' Jules answered for them. 'They've been a pleasure to have around.'

'We've had fun haven't we, Sophie?' Grace said with her arm around the shoulder of the little girl.

Sophie jumped up and down on the spot. 'It's been fun! We played with the dogs, and we made cupcakes.'

'Wow, you have been busy! Could you both go and get your things together and the dogs' things too please? We're going to Portree for fish and chips,' Caitlin told them.

'Yay!' both girls cried in unison as they headed off with Evin to collect their belongings.

'Thanks for having them, both of you. It meant a lot to have some alone time,' Archie said with a glint in his eyes.

'It's no bother,' Reid replied. 'We know what it's like trying to steal moments.' He slipped his arm around Jules' shoulder. 'We'll happily take them again for you.'

Archie grinned. 'How about now?' He laughed out loud, and the others joined in. 'Seriously though, let us return the favour some time, okay?'

'Thanks, Archie. We'll take you up on that offer, I'm sure.'

29

After collecting their fish and chips, Caitlin, Archie, Grace, Sophie, and the dogs walked down the hill to Quay Street in Portree, with its pretty, multicoloured houses overlooking the water. The light breeze coming off the sea caused the boats in the bay to bob up and down and created a clinking sound as ropes and masts collided gently. It was a quiet, lilting, almost musical sound. They found a bench to sit on and eat their food. Bowie and Cleo had their own little wrappers of batter bits and little scraps of fish, so they all sat happily enjoying their feast in the evening sunlight.

As they enjoyed the view and munched on their evening meal, Sophie said, 'I really, really miss my mummy. And I know I can't go to Devon to see her but... I really, really like my new family.' It was a comment that came out of the blue, but Caitlin and Archie shared a glance, and she could see the glassiness of tears in his eyes.

Archie bent to kiss Sophie's head. 'I'm so happy to hear that, Sophie.' There was a slight waver to his voice and Caitlin reached over to squeeze his shoulder.

Sophie lifted her chin and squinted up at him in the evening sunlight. 'Daddy, your voice has gone all funny.' She giggled.

Archie laughed. 'I think it must be the fish,' he said with an even more pronounced, purposeful wobble and a funny face, which made Sophie giggle even more.

'You're so silly, Daddy,' she said with a shake of her head and Caitlin's heart melted.

Evidently, Archie's heart had melted too as he looked away towards the boats and Caitlin saw a sneaky raise of his hand to swipe at his eyes.

After they had finished their food, they went back to the car and Archie drove them home towards Glentorrin. The sun was setting behind the silhouetted mountains as they travelled and the hazy golden glow that was cast created a magical end to a wonderful Sunday.

* * *

Once back in Glentorrin, Archie carried a very sleepy Sophie up to bed and Grace followed too. She had promised Sophie that she would sleep over, so with Caitlin's permission, Archie had set up the spare bed in his third bedroom so she could be there first thing in the morning. It was the last chance she would get for a while as school was due to start again on Tuesday. She had borrowed a book on the constellations from Archie's massive book collection and had faked a yawn.

'I'm soooo tired,' Grace had said with a smile as she headed to her room for the night.

Once alone again, Archie and Caitlin snuggled up on the sofa. 'Thank you for a wonderful weekend,' he said with a kiss to her forehead.

She cuddled into his side. 'It's been so lovely, hasn't it?'

'It has. It doesn't have to end here though, you know... You could stay over too.'

She gazed up at him. 'Oh... I don't know... what about the girls?'

He shrugged. 'I get the feeling they're absolutely fine with everything. Don't you? And it seems silly you going home. I know you have stuff to do for the bakery, but you get up early anyway, so...' His expression was filled with hope. 'Do I have to do a Sophie?' He stuck out his bottom lip. 'I will you know. I'll do it.'

Caitlin started laughing as he pulled her down until she was flat on her back on the sofa.

'Pleeeeeeease, Cait, pleeeeeease stay over, pleeeeeease,' he said in between blowing raspberries on her neck. She tried her best not to squeal and wake the girls. 'Pleeeeeeease,' he repeated.

'Okay! Okay! I'll stay!' she replied as she tried to calm her breathing and hold back loud guffaws of laughter.

Archie sat upright. 'Bloody hell, it really does work.'

* * *

Caitlin couldn't help the smile that remained etched on her face every time she thought of Archie, which, of course, was frequently. She met up with Ruby, Jules, and Morag after work on Monday in the garden of Glentorrin House as it was Ruby's turn to host.

'Are we allowed to say we told you so yet?' Ruby asked as she poured the Prosecco.

'Nope,' Caitlin replied with a giggle.

'You two make the most adorable couple. Even Dex said so,' Jules told her.

'Well, that's very sweet of him,' Caitlin said, raising her glass to her absent friend. 'So, what are the kids doing tonight?' Grace was, once again, around at Evin's house. He seemed to be helping her to get over Cora's absence, along with Sophie, of course.

'Well, Archie and Mitch have gone around to look at the big tree at the bottom of the garden. There's talk about a tree house now.'

Jules rolled her eyes. 'So, my guess is the kids will be drawing up plans of what they want in it.' She laughed. 'Sophie apparently wants the roof to open up so they can look at the stars.'

'Oh, bless the wee bairn. She's a real character that one,' Morag said.

'So, is it love then?' Ruby asked with a smile and a tilt of her head.

Caitlin's cheeks flushed. 'Oh god, do I really have to answer that?'

'Now that you've turned cerise, I think we know the answer, but a confirmation would be good,' Jules said, nodding to the others, and of course, they agreed.

Caitlin sighed. 'Actually... it is.' Her friends clapped their hands and squealed in delight. 'I'm crazy about him. We've actually used the words too,' she said with a wide smile.

'Oh, I hear wedding bells on the horizon,' Morag said excitedly.

'Give them chance, Morag! It's been a matter of weeks and you know what happened when Lyle tried to pull that one.' Ruby laughed.

Caitlin didn't speak.

When the others fixed her with a questioning stare, she shrugged. 'I think I'd say yes this time.'

'Bloody hell, Cait! That's amazing! It's the real deal then,' Jules said, her eyes as wide as her smile.

Caitlin shook her head. 'I mean, it's early days and I won't ask him in case I make an arse of myself. But... we'll see what the future holds. But for the first time ever I'm not against the prospect.'

Ruby raised her glass. 'Well, ladies, I think we should drink to that!'

* * *

The following weekend hadn't come around fast enough for Caitlin. She'd had a crazy week in the bakery and Archie had been busy at the campsite and the outdoor gear shop too – that was holiday season on Skye for you. Scottish schools may have gone back to their studies, but English schools didn't go back until September. They had caught a few kisses here and there, but that was all they had managed. Now that it was Saturday, Caitlin had every intention of remedying that. Isla was working in the shop for the day and so the four of them and the dogs were going to Staffin Beach for a picnic. Sophie and Archie were staying over that night, too, and Caitlin couldn't wait to snuggle up to Archie in her bed.

The picnic was packed and when Archie and Sophie arrived at Caitlin's, she flung open the door ready to hug him. Instead, Sophie lurched at her and hugged her legs tightly.

'I've missed you, Cakelin. I haven't seed you for ages and ages!' the five-year-old said as she gripped her.

Cakelin, bless her heart. The name definitely was quite fitting. Caitlin hugged the child back and a lump of emotion lodged in her throat as she lifted her gaze to meet Archie's.

He shrugged. 'She's missed you as much as I have,' he said as if it was a simple matter of fact.

'Where's Gwacie?' Sophie asked.

'Go on in, sweetheart, she is just looking for her sunglasses.'

Sophie let go of Caitlin's legs and dashed into the house.

Archie stepped forward and pulled Caitlin into his arms. 'Do you mind if I don't just hug your legs?' He chuckled.

She grinned. 'Not at all.'

He lowered his face and kissed her tenderly. 'I really have missed you.'

'I've missed you too. We're like teenagers,' she giggled, but secretly relished the very fact.

'Hmm, but I can't wait to get you alone later and play at grown-ups,' he whispered, sending shivers of delight traversing her spine.

A loud throwing-up noise came from behind them, and they both turned to see the girls making pukey faces.

'Eeeeeuw! Kissing is gusting!' Sophie informed them.

'Yeah, totally gusting!' Grace agreed with a giggle.

'Come on you, wee monsters. Bowie is waiting in the car, so let's go have a picnic!' Archie announced as he took Cleo's lead, and they cheered and followed him while Caitlin grabbed the picnic basket and locked the door.

* * *

Staffin Beach was one of Grace's favourite spots. Mainly because of the dinosaur footprints etched into the rocks by the creatures thousands of years before. And partly because twice a year, in spring and autumn, the local crofter accompanied his swimming cattle across the shallow and short spit of water from the mainland to the island, and vice versa. These days, he didn't swim with them but used a boat instead, but Grace still loved to watch.

Another sunny day meant the place was fairly busy when they arrived, but they managed to find a spot by the cliffs that was plenty big enough for their blanket and parasol. The girls ran down to the water's edge with their buckets and Bowie and Cleo proceeded to dig holes as if in competition to see who could reach Australia first.

From their vantage point, they could see the little fishing bothy on Staffin Island in front of them and around to their left they could see the sun glinting off the rocks of the Quiraing.

Archie laid back on the blanket and closed his eyes as Caitlin watched the girls filling their buckets with wet sand. She kicked off her sandals and pulled her sundress up over her knees to allow the sun to warm her skin and she closed her eyes.

'Oh, what a lovely wee family,' an elderly lady's voice said.

Caitlin opened her eyes and shielded them from the sun to see the grey-haired woman smiling down at her.

'I'm just having a wee walk to see the dinosaur footprints. I bet your wee girls would like to see them if they haven't already. Sorry for interrupting, I just felt I had to say it's so nice to see you all together and having fun when so many families are broken apart these days.'

Caitlin smiled. 'Thank you.' She didn't bother to correct her and say that what she was actually witnessing was the blending of two single-parent families, and unusual ones at that.

Once the lady had walked further up the beach, Archie sat up. 'Did you know her?'

Caitlin shook her head. 'Never seen her before in my life.'

'Hmm. She had a point though, didn't she?' Archie said as he propped himself on his elbows. 'We do look like a family.'

Caitlin smiled. 'I suppose we do from the outside looking in.'

He sidled closer to her. 'I think we do from the inside too. Sophie clearly thinks of us that way. You heard what she said when we went for fish and chips. And the way she hugged your legs earlier.'

Caitlin fell silent for a moment letting his words sink in.

'Shit, I didn't mean... Don't worry, I'm not going to do a Lyle or anything like that.' She felt a little sad on hearing his comment. And as if he read her mind he frowned. 'Unless... you want me to do a Lyle?'

She snickered. 'Can we maybe not call it doing a Lyle and it may be easier to think about?'

He sat upright, his eyes wide. He ran his hands back, roughly, through his shaggy hair; hair that she loved to tangle her fingers in. 'Caitlin... are you... are you saying you'd think about it?'

She tilted her head. 'Think about what exactly?'

He swallowed hard. 'About... about us becoming a family... properly.'

Her heart leapt. Was he hinting at a proposal? Was it crazy that she was hoping he was? She shook her head, feeling a little light-headed suddenly. 'I don't... I mean... what would that entail... exactly?'

He fixed her with an intense gaze. 'You, me, Grace, Sophie, Cleo and Bowie... all living in one house... maybe there'd be a band on each of our ring fingers...' As if thinking he'd said too much again, he added, 'Some day of course... I mean, I don't want to rush you. I totally understand how crazy this must sound, and I'm not expecting you to be on the same page as me. But is there a possibility that you might be, some day?'

So, he was on that page? Caitlin's heart pounded at her ribs and butterflies took flight inside her. She gave a wry smile. 'You'd have to ask me to find out.'

A handsome grin spread across Archie's face, and she waited for the words to come. But, on that occasion, and much to her disappointment, they didn't.

30

The next two weeks seemed to fly by, and now they were heading towards the end of August, Caitlin wondered if Archie had changed his mind about their conversation at the beach. No proposal had materialised, but she couldn't really be disappointed, considering their relationship was still in the very early stages. It just felt like they had always been together. Perhaps he had been joking? Perhaps it had been a question he had hinted at to see how the land lay for future reference? Whatever it was, she had put things to the back shelves of her mind... well, she had tried to, at least.

Grace was back to school and Sophie had started her new school too. Archie confided in Caitlin that he was worried about her settling in, but after the first day, she'd asked if she could go back again. They took that as a good sign. Their time had been split between their two houses and they had settled into an easy routine. Not that it was boring, not in any way. Archie was such good fun and when it came to night-time... let's just say Caitlin was enjoying being a more nocturnal creature these days.

Friday night had been fun, and it started early with them

watching the first *Captain America* movie, with some parts skipped in case they terrified Sophie. But the little girl had been mesmerised when a short and skinny Steve Rogers had become Captain America and had asked if it was just the big machine that had caused it.

'No, no, Soph, he ate his veggies too. It was the veggies that made him big and strong!' It was a ploy, seeing as they had been struggling to get the child to eat anything green. It worked though.

On Saturday morning as Caitlin prepared a picnic to take on their trip, Sophie asked, 'Cakelin, could we have some cumber and letters on our samiches?' Of course, she meant cucumber and lettuce, but with a shared triumphant gaze, Archie and Caitlin agreed wholeheartedly.

Isla was working in the bakery, so they had made plans to take the girls and the dogs to the Fairy Pools. After *Captain America*, they had watched *Tinkerbell* and Archie had told Sophie a story about the vibrant blue waters of the little pools at Glen Brittle at the foot of the Black Cuillins, and how it would be the perfect location for Tink to live. He had promised he would take them someday soon, but of course Sophie and Grace had convinced him that Saturday would be a good day to go, although it hadn't taken much convincing. Once the picnic was ready – their favourite way to dine – they had set off nice and early to beat the rush of tourists, considering it was such a glorious day.

The view from the path that led down and away from the car park was truly spectacular. It was a bright day and visibility was incredibly clear. The sky was a vivid cornflower-blue and the mountains that provided the stunning backdrop to Glen Brittle were haloed by the golden glow of the sun. The light of which picked out each indentation and striation of the rock face, like lines on an elderly person, telling their life story. It was clear why so many cinematographers chose Skye for their movies, as the rugged peaks of Bruach na Frìthe and Am Basteir really were otherworldly. The path that wound its way from the car park went on for what felt like miles, but the views at the end were worth it.

The waters were a vibrant turquoise and, of course, the girls were mesmerised by the magical location. They took off their shoes and socks and dangled their feet in the freezing-cold pools and explored the many waterfalls, not really caring about getting soaked in the scorching temperatures of the day. Even Bowie and Cleo paddled to cool off. People of many nationalities were visiting, and each wore a smile inspired by the enchanting place.

It was well before lunch when they sat and ate sandwiches just off the path and admired the view of the Black Cuillins. But the girls were apparently starving after their early start and the one-hundred-mile walk – Sophie, it was decided, liked to exaggerate.

'This is one of my favourite places in the world,' Archie told Caitlin as the girls chatted happily, allowing their bare feet to dry in the sunshine. The two dogs were panting and lay on the soft, green mossy ground beside their humans. 'It's one of those places that takes your breath away regardless of the weather.'

He looked so ridiculously handsome when he was in his element. His face lit up, his cheeks flushed and the smile that stretched his lips did funny things to Caitlin's insides.

'Yes, I'm enjoying the view too,' she replied with a grin.

He turned his face towards her. 'But you're not looking at... Oh, I get it. Well played Fraser, well played.' He laughed. 'So, dinner and sleepover at mine tonight, eh?' he asked with a knowing glint in his eyes.

'Sounds like a great plan,' she said as she snuggled into his side, rested her head on his shoulder and gazed out towards the waterfall just before them.

'I think I'll live on Skye when I grow up,' Sophie announced as she squeezed herself in between them, sitting on Archie's lap but resting her head on Caitlin. 'I don't want to live in another place because it's pretty here and I can work on the campsite saying "hello" to people when they come to stay, or in the welly shop where I can tell them which wellies are the best colour.' She shrugged as if it was an obvious decision to make.

Caitlin loved the way Sophie had latched on to those particular elements of her dad's businesses.

'Sounds like a good idea to me, sweetheart,' Archie said with a kiss to her shoulder. 'Then you can visit your old dad all the time.'

'And Cakelin,' Sophie added.

'Well, that goes without saying,' he agreed.

Sophie pondered things for a moment, then said, 'But we could all stay in one house instead of more than one house because that would be easier.'

Archie glanced over at Caitlin and smiled. 'Aye, right again, Soph.'

* * *

Later that night, the girls were tucked up in bed and Archie lit the firepit in the back garden of his house. It was almost midnight, and they should probably have been tired considering their long day, but the sky was so mesmerising that they sat, drinking hot chocolate and gazing up at the stars, listening to a Spotify track list that Archie had made especially for them. Biffy Clyro's 'Space' played in the background and Caitlin smiled at the lyrics.

'Ooh, I have a wee gift for you,' Archie announced, jumping from his seat. 'I almost forgot!' He went dashing into the house and returned moments later with a box that was too large to be an engagement ring. Caitlin tried to push her disappointment down as she knew whatever gift he had bought her would be special no matter what it was.

He grinned. 'Now, there's a bit of a story attached to this, but I'll let you open it first.'

The box, which was the size appropriate for a tea mug, was wrapped in sparkly paper and had a tag that read:

To my love, from Archie.

'You don't have to buy me gifts,' Caitlin told him, although excitement bubbled in her stomach, because who was she kidding? She loved surprises.

Inside the wrapping was another box that simply said:

Your Custom Perfume from Scents.

'I made it,' he announced from where he knelt on the ground before her. 'Well... I helped make it. I went to this place near Portree that I'd heard about, where you can design your own fragrance and it was amazing. But do you want to know the funny part?'

Caitlin grinned at his enthusiasm. 'Of course.'

'The guy who helped me was called Frank.' He chuckled. 'The shop was called Scents. So, I was helped by Frank-in-Scents.' He snickered and she couldn't help but join in.

'I think Sophie was right. Her daddy is a bit bonkers.'

'Aye. I had to really force myself to not laugh when he introduced himself. It's almost as funny as the mate of mine called Frank that used to be a bartender at the Stein Inn up in the northwest of Skye... Frank in Stein...' He chuckled to himself again, then waved his hand. 'Anyway, I digress, so... I put all these fragrances together that made me think of you.' He gazed lovingly at her; his laughter gone but his smile still in place. 'This was the result. I hope you like it.'

Her heart squeezed. He never ceased to amaze her with how thoughtful he was. 'Archie, that's so wonderful. And so unique. How lovely.' She eagerly took out the next box, which was navy-blue and clearly handmade, with silver stars embossed on the outside.

Archie cringed. 'Erm... excuse the crappy craftsmanship. I made the box as I wanted it to be special. I might have failed a wee bit there.'

'Not at all. It's beautiful,' she insisted.

He had named the perfume 'Starlight' and she took the round, iridescent glass bottle out of the box to open it. She dabbed a little on her wrist, closed her eyes and inhaled with a tiny bit of trepidation. But she needn't have worried. The fragrance was incredible. Fresh, flowery and clean. Possibly how starlight would smell if you could bottle it.

'Now, I know it's completely mushy, and I'm a bit of an old romantic but...' He sidled closer on the ground before her. 'You're my starlight, Caitlin. That's what you've brought to my life. A glint of brightness in what was becoming a dark, lonely time. You and Sophie, and Grace too. I'm so grateful to have you all in my life. Things feel so... complete.'

Her eyes welled with tears, and she bent forward to kiss him. 'You really are the sweetest man.'

'Actually, there's something you missed.'

She frowned. 'Really? What?'

'There's something around the neck of the perfume bottle. Look again.'

She glanced down and gasped. Unsure of how she hadn't spotted it, she reached out. There, resting on the glass, was a silver-coloured band with the most stunning arrangement of stones she had ever seen. A larger clear stone was surrounded by eight smaller stones of the same clarity that were set into tiny, pointed arms forming a star shape. She removed the ring from bottle and lifted her chin to find Archie now repositioned, and on one knee.

'It's white gold, but they're not diamonds, I hope that's okay. I wanted something more unique, a little different. The stones are moissanite, which was originally discovered in a meteor crater. Can you believe that? It seemed perfect. Do you mind that they're not diamonds?' His loving gaze flickered uneasily, telling her he was nervous about her response and her heart melted further.

She shook her head, a little in shock as her eyes blurred with tears.

'So... Caitlin Fraser... my starlight... I know this is probably crazy seeing as we've only been together for what feels like a matter of weeks. But we've known each other for so much longer. And this just feels right. I think... no, I know I've found my soulmate in you. And I don't want to lose that... ever. Now, if this is too soon and you're not ready, this ring can be a symbol of where I hope we're going, but... if you decide you're as crazy as me – which I really hope you are – then... Will you marry me?'

She lurched into his arms and kissed him as tears streamed down her flushed cheeks. 'Yes! Of course, it's yes. Absolutely 200 per cent yes!'

A loud squeak came from the doorway and Archie and Caitlin both turned to see their girls running towards them. They were quickly enveloped in a group embrace.

'Am I to take it you're happy, Grace? Sophie?' Archie asked with hope in his eyes.

'Yes!' They both shouted simultaneously.

'One hundred, billion, squillion, badillion, flabillion, yeses!' Sophie added, just to be clear.

Archie pulled away and took the ring from Caitlin. She held out her left hand and beamed as he slipped the ring onto her finger. Then the group hug commenced once again.

* * *

The following morning, Caitlin snuggled up to Archie in his bed. She lifted her hand to watch the stones glint in the sliver of sunlight that crept in through a gap in the curtains.

Archie shuffled and took her hand in his. 'So, what do you think? Long engagement? Short engagement? Huge wedding, small wedding? It's entirely up to you,' he told her as he pulled her even closer.

She manoeuvred herself to look down at him. 'Are you one for big fancy weddings?' She sincerely hoped not.

He pursed his lips. 'Honestly? Not really, but if that's what you want, then I'll happily do that. I'd do anything to make you happy.'

Relief flooded her. 'I'm really not into that idea either. I think it's an awful lot of money and hassle to go through when you just want to start a new life with someone, you know? I'd rather just run away and get married, like the people who ran away in the eighteen hundreds and married in secret. I think that would be exciting. We could just take the girls and the dogs. It could be our special day.'

Archie sat upright and excitement glinted in his chocolate-brown eyes. 'Gretna Green. Let's do it! Just us. And as soon as possible, what do you think?'

'I think absolutely!' Since Archie's proposal Caitlin hadn't stopped smiling. She never imagined she could be so happy nor that the man she would fall for had been under her nose for years.

Archie leaned forward and kissed her passionately, her insides jellified as they always did and for a moment, she lost herself.

He pulled away. 'I'll phone them tomorrow and see what the procedure is.'

'Perfect. We can stay in a dog-friendly hotel.' Her internal butterflies loved the idea too as they set to performing a ceilidh.

Archie frowned. 'Where should we live? Both our houses are big enough but... yours is attached to the bakery. My shop is just up the road, and the campsite isn't attached to that, so...'

The butterfly ceilidh inside her kicked up a notch. Regardless of the speed at which this was all happening, the thought of moving in together and making a real family home excited her beyond words. 'You could definitely move into my house. I'd be happy with that.'

'Are you sure you wouldn't rather find something we could start over in?'

Caitlin pursed her lips. 'Perhaps a little further down the line maybe? If you'd rather we moved into your place...'

He slipped his hand into her hair. 'I just want to be where you are. And to be honest, waking up to the smell of fresh baking every day is something I could definitely get used to.'

She leaned forwards and nibbled on his bottom lip. 'My place it is.'

'Hey, you know what would be absolutely perfect?'

Caitlin tilted her head. 'Can it be more perfect?'

He nodded. 'Why don't we double-barrel our surname?'

Caitlin pondered for a moment. 'Double-barrel?'

Archie grinned. 'Think about it. It would mean the world to Sophie if she could keep her name to remind her of her mum. And the fact that your surname is Fraser, like Sophie's, means that both girls get to keep their own identities. But we still get to share our names and be a family. We can all become the Fraser-Sutherlands.'

A lump of emotion tightened her throat and she reached out to hug him. 'You're right. It's perfect. Thank you.'

'Right, let's go get the girls up, make a family cooked breakfast, and have a chat to them about it all, eh?' Caitlin couldn't help her contented sigh at his use of the word *family* and loved how easily it had tripped off his tongue.

* * *

'Can we have pretty dresses?' Sophie asked after Archie and Caitlin had explained the plan for the secret wedding.

Grace giggled with enthusiasm. 'And can Bowie and Cleo have outfits too? You can get tuxedos for dogs! And tutus!'

'Yes! Please can we, Daddy?' Sophie asked before leaning close to Grace and whispering, 'What's a tadeedo?'

Grace grinned. 'It's like a little suit and tie for a dog.'

Sophie's eyes widened. 'Oh yes! One of those!' she said with excitement.

Caitlin giggled, loving the way the girls had already become such firm friends and how they were excited to be involved in wedding plans, even if their ideas were a little unorthodox. 'I'm sure we can arrange all of that. Now, you girls must promise to keep this a secret, okay? Just for us. You can't tell anyone, not until afterwards.'

Grace scrunched her brow. 'But why not? Why is it a secret?'

Caitlin and Archie shared a glance. 'Well... Reid and Jules are getting married at Christmas and we're kind of jumping in first, so we don't want to spoil it for them... you know, steal their thunder. We don't want lots of fuss either. Plus, we just want it to be a special time for us as a family.'

Grace nodded. 'Oh, okay.'

'Erm... Daddy...'

'Yes, Sophie, what's up, darlin'?'

Sophie tucked her hands under her chin as she so often did when she was shy or nervous. She climbed down from her chair and walked around to where Archie sat. He lifted her onto his lap, and she whispered into his ear.

Archie smiled and nodded at her, and the child hugged him hard. Caitlin glanced at him questioningly and he said, 'She was just asking...' He cleared his throat, clearly emotional. 'If this means Grace can be her big sister forever, and for real, and... if you can be like a new mummy, but so she doesn't forget her real one could she call you Mummy Cakelin?'

Caitlin had no words. Just emotions that trickled down her face as she beamed at them.

31

Keeping the news of her impending nuptials from her best friends was trickier than Caitlin had anticipated. It came with a certain amount of guilt, too, but she didn't want to make a huge fuss, nor did she wish to take the shine away from Jules and Reid and their wedding later in the year.

Her marriage to Archie was due to take place in two weeks at Gretna Green, thanks to a cancellation, and Isla was booked to cover the bakery for the Friday and Saturday. They had agreed that Caitlin wouldn't wear her ring on her finger until they were married, so for now, it was on a chain around her neck, hidden under her T-shirt. Caitlin had told everyone she was going on a long weekend trip with Archie and the girls to Glencoe, but every time she talked about it, she blushed bright pink. Although no one seemed to suspect anything, so that was a relief, at least. She and Archie had discussed whether they were crazy to travel the five-plus hours to get married at Gretna, but they had decided it was definitely what they wanted. A private ceremony in a place synonymous with romance, no guests, just their own little family of six – because, of course, the dogs were included.

Grace had found a tuxedo for Bowie and a tutu for Cleo, both that were as inobtrusive as possible, seeing as none of them knew if either dog would comply with the silly outfits. Caitlin had ordered the most beautiful, fitted, ivory lace dress with long sleeves from an online bridal boutique, and it fit perfectly, hugging the curves she knew Archie adored, whilst remaining classy for a woman of forty. She had, so far, managed to keep it a secret from her fiancé and intended to do so until their wedding day, but she had shown the girls who insisted she looked like a fairy princess.

A Saturday shopping trip to Inverness had been successful in acquiring matching dresses for Sophie and Grace, in a dusky blue with lace and a tiny bit of sparkle. Blue velvet ballet pumps finished off their ensemble perfectly.

The two girls had done an amazing job of keeping the secret. Caitlin had periods of guilt around that as well, where she felt she had asked too much of them, but they were being so grown-up about it all and had turned it into a game.

Under cover of darkness, Archie had started moving small amounts of belongings into Caitlin's cottage and they were staying there more than they were staying at his place. They didn't announce anything, however, as doing so may trigger further questions, hence the manoeuvres being carried out at night, with plenty of giggles and a little swearing on account of stubbed toes.

An estate agent had been to value Archie's house, and they were now considering their options around renting it out or selling. Renting seemed a good way to create an income stream, so that was the clear favourite so far.

It was the Thursday before the wedding and Caitlin had met Jules, Ruby and Dexter at the Coxswain after work while Grace and Evin walked the dogs with Reid.

'Have you heard about the local lottery winner?' Jules asked in a theatrical whisper as they sat out the back of the pub in the newly renovated beer garden.

Ruby leaned closer with intrigue. 'Ooh no! Anyone we know?'

Jules curled her lip. 'Morag knows because the winner went into her shop to try to claim the couple of hundred quid they thought they had won. Apparently, she had to get a chair out for them because they thought they were going to collapse. But she won't say who it was. Keeps making that zip sign over her lips.'

Dexter laughed. 'Who took the real Morag? This one must be an imposter. Our Morag loves a bit of gossip.'

Jules shook her head. 'Not this time. She's being a pillar of discretion. We'll get it out of her eventually though, eh?' she said with a wink.

Dexter narrowed his eyes and turned to Caitlin. 'It isn't you, is it, Cait? You've been walking around all smiley and acting a bit suss.'

Caitlin felt her cheeks flush. 'Pfft, don't be daft! If I'd won the lottery, I'd be in here buying everyone drinks.'

Jules interjected, 'No, this is what being head over heels looks like, Dex.'

He rolled his eyes. 'Aye, Jetty, don't worry, I remember it when you were all doe-eyed over Reid.' He turned to Caitlin again. 'So, you and Archie are all loved up, eh, Cait? It's great to see and I'm glad you took our advice finally.'

Jules tilted her head. 'Yes, and while we're on that subject, what was going on last night? I was out with Chewie, and I spotted you and Archie carrying boxes down to yours.'

Oh, shit. Busted. 'Erm...' Caitlin winced; how much could she say without totally dropping herself in it?'

'Caitlin Fraser, are you not telling us something?' Ruby asked with a nudge to her arm.

Caitlin knew that at this point an egg would've fried nicely on her face. Sadly, she wasn't as good as Sophie and Grace at keeping secrets.

'Boxes, eh?' Dexter said. 'That can mean only two things... One, he's run out of space for all his gadgets and comic collections... Or two, he's moving into your place.'

All eyes were on Caitlin, this seemed to be a habit. She held up her hands. 'Okay! Okay, Archie, Sophie and Bowie are moving in. There, now you know.'

Her three friends cheered, and she was enveloped in a strange group hug across the wooden bench table.

She shushed them and waved her hands. 'Guys! Please, we just want to keep it quiet! We don't want a fuss.'

Jules squeezed her arm. 'I'm so bloody happy for you, Cait! Why didn't you just tell us?'

Guilt niggled at her once more. 'Like I said, neither of us is big on being the centre of attention and we just wanted it to be a kind of seamless transition rather than a big deal.'

'Of course, we understand that, honey, but we're your besties. You can tell us anything.' There was a pause as if they were waiting for something else, but Caitlin wasn't prepared to say anything further.

'Thanks, guys. I really appreciate that. But we're really good. We're happy.' She grinned because it was completely true. And she was head over heels in love for the first time in her life.

'Ooh, hey did you hear that the Co-op is selling the tearoom?' Jules announced and Caitlin was happy for the change of subject. 'They've decided to concentrate on the village hall now. Morag was happy to tell me that snippet of gossip.' She huffed.

Ruby's eyes widened. 'Really? Oh, wow! I wonder who'll buy it. Maybe we'll get someone new into the village.'

'Aye, and maybe they'll want to buy Archie's house, eh?' Dexter said with a wink at Caitlin.

Secretly she hoped they might.

* * *

The day of the wedding arrived, and Caitlin, Archie, Grace and Sophie all got ready in their pretty hotel room on the outskirts of Gretna. Even Bowie and Cleo seemed to be happy in their new outfits.

The journey down the day before had taken around six hours, including a toilet stop for everyone and a brief detour for snacks. They had travelled south through the bustling town of Fort William, by the glorious mountains at Glencoe and past the shores of Loch Lomond with its millpond-still surface, mirrorlike, reflecting the vivid blue sky. Both girls were fast asleep as they crossed the Erskine Bridge, but both awoke to watch the people of Glasgow rushing around on the outskirts of the city. It really was a totally different pace of life than Skye.

Now, looking at herself in the bathroom mirror, Caitlin's stomach was filled with butterflies. She wondered if her mum would be proud of her. Would she be happy she had finally met the man of her dreams? A lump lodged in her throat, and she paused for a moment to compose herself.

She had slipped on her dress and had pulled her hair into a neat chignon to one side and was now applying her make-up. Archie had strict instructions to stay out as she only wanted him to see her once she was totally ready.

As soon as she was happy with her appearance, she stepped back into their family-sized suite and Archie turned to face her. He looked so incredibly handsome in his pristine white shirt, waistcoat and kilt. She'd hoped he'd wear one but hadn't been sure what to expect. The Sutherland tartan was a dark green, red, white and navy fabric, rich in both colour and history. She'd always loved a man in a kilt, but her man in a kilt truly was a sight to behold.

He shook his head as he gazed at her with adoring eyes. 'Wow! You really are the most beautiful woman in the world. I'm so lucky.' His voice broke and he walked towards her and took her hand. 'Are you still sure about this?' he asked. 'I know it's fast and I don't want to rush you.'

She fixed him with a confident gaze. 'I've never been surer of anything. How about you? You're going to be surrounded by women.' She laughed lightly. 'You've still got time to change your mind.'

Archie smiled and raised his eyebrows. 'With you looking like that? Sorry, sweetheart, but you're stuck with me for life.'

She squeezed his hand. 'I could certainly think of worse things.'

He bent forward and kissed her gently as if scared to ruin her make-up, and the obligatory sicky noises came from the girls, followed by an outburst of laughter and giggles. Caitlin turned to see them standing there in their pretty, dusky blue dresses with their hair pinned up and curled by Grace.

'You girls look so beautiful,' Caitlin told them with a wobble to her voice and tears in her eyes.

'Mum, don't cry! You'll ruin your make-up and *you* look so beautiful,' Grace insisted as she hugged her.

Sophie hugged her legs. 'You look pretty, mummy Cakelin.'

Caitlin dabbed at her eyes. 'Thank you, my lovely, lovely girls.' She glanced down and laughed out loud. 'And wow! Bowie and Cleo... Don't you look the part?' She crouched to straighten Bowie's bowtie and to scratch Cleo behind her ears. The little blue ruffle of the tutu and sparkly hair clip just added to the Yorkie Poo's cuteness. She stood again. 'Well, we'd better get going, the ceremony is at eleven and it's twenty to.' She picked up her little posy of thistles, lavender and white roses, which were tied with a ribbon of Sutherland tartan – a surprise from Archie.

'Aye. Come on, lasses, before she changes her mind!'

* * *

On arrival at the old Blacksmith's Shop, they walked underneath the arch of horseshoes and into the room where the wedding would take place. The officiant waited at one end of the whitewashed room with a welcoming smile. Candles stood on the steps giving a cosy warm glow and flowers decorated the edges of the room and the windowsills. The famous anvil sat before the officiant and, much to Caitlin's delight, the sound of the Outlander theme song, 'The Skye Boat Song', played over the sound system.

'A little whisper of home,' Archie told her with a smile. She squeezed his hand.

Archie and Caitlin walked down the centre of the room, followed by Grace and Sophie, Bowie and Cleo. Then, after confirming their names, the ceremony began.

Archie and Caitlin faced each other and held hands and his gaze was fixed on her as he recited his vows, his eyes were glassy with emotion and his voice wavered as he repeated after the officiant. Once his vows were finished, he whispered, 'I love you.' And swiped at his eyes.

Caitlin's turn came and she recited her own vows with a smile. They exchanged the white gold Celtic wedding bands that Archie had purchased and the registrar hit the hammer against the anvil to mark the occasion before announcing them as husband and wife, which garnered a loud cheer and a dance from Sophie and Grace.

After the ceremony, their photographer arrived and took pictures of them at the anvil and then outside standing by the famous Gretna Green sign. After that, they were snapped under the weathered steel sculpture of the clasped hands. The photographer took a wonderful family photo of all of them together in their finery, and Caitlin immediately knew it would be framed.

Although the wedding was over so soon, Caitlin couldn't have been happier. They were going to eat lunch and then set straight off for Glentorrin. They sat around the table in the hotel and toasted each other with lemonade. The hotel provided them with a bottle of fizz for when they arrived home to Glentorrin and the girls had gone to bed, which was incredibly sweet. Over lunch, they relived the wedding and the photographs. Caitlin had taken selfies on her phone, too, and they had one of them all staring into the lens making funny faces. Caitlin and Archie presented the girls with white gold bracelets with a little Celtic family knot dangling from the clasp. The same knot appeared on their wedding rings and as Caitlin and Archie fastened the bracelet on each girl's wrist, Archie told them, 'This little knot ties us all together as a real family now.'

Grace beamed and Sophie hugged her big sister. Caitlin slipped on her engagement ring, alongside her wedding band and admired the way the two looked together, glinting in the sunlight.

'Mummy Cakelin, can we keep our nice dresses on until bedtime?' Sophie asked.

Still touched by her new title, Caitlin reached out and took the little girl's hand. 'You can as far as I'm concerned, sweetie.'

'I mean all of us. Can we all stay in our fancy clothes until bedtime?'

Caitlin glanced at Archie who shrugged. 'I'm up for it if you are. It's not often I get to wear a kilt.'

Caitlin glanced down at her beautiful lace dress. If she was honest, she didn't want to take it off anyway. 'Why not!'

Full of food and love, they climbed into the car for the long journey back to Glentorrin. Grace and Sophie were whispering in the back seat and the dogs curled up together in the footwell.

'Thank you for a lovely day, Mr Fraser-Sutherland.'

Archie glanced across at her. 'Thank you, Mrs Fraser-Sutherland.' He lifted her hand to his lips and kissed her knuckles. 'I love the sound of that.'

Caitlin leaned her head back on the headrest and smiled. 'Me too.'

'I think I'm going to whisk you away to Glencoe for real in the near future. It could be a delayed honeymoon,' he whispered with a brief glance over his shoulder, but the girls were still whispering.

'I think I could be easily whisked away, given the right amount of notice to cover the bakery.'

'It's a date. Whatever date it turns out to be. Let's see when Isla and Dex are free and if Jules and Reid will take the girls for a night or two.'

'If they'll even speak to us when they find out what we've done.'

A look of concern crumpled Archie's brow. 'Hey, you don't regret it, do you?'

'No, not at all. I just hope they're not too upset.'

Archie shook his head. 'Nah. They're good friends. They'll understand why we did it this way.'

Caitlin turned to look out of the window at the passing scenery and hoped Archie was right.

32

At six-thirty, a text came from Jules that worried Caitlin.

Hey Cait. What time will you be home from Glencoe? I need to speak to you urgently. Don't call though. Just tell me what time and I will meet you. J x

She had shot back a reply.

Probably half seven. Is all okay? Should I be worried? C x

It took a while for a reply to come back and when it did it was vague.

Will explain all when I see you. J xx

When she relayed this to Archie, he sucked in air through his teeth. 'Do you think they've sussed us out and she's upset?'

'Oh, don't say that. What happened to "they'll understand"?'

'You're right, sorry. Ignore me. I'm sure it'll all be fine.'

At seven-thirty, they crossed the Skye Bridge and took the turning for Glentorrin. Caitlin's knee bounced up and down as she wondered why Jules had sounded so serious in her text message. She loved Archie and wanted to be married to him but didn't want to lose friends over her decision to run away to get hitched.

'She's there!' Grace said as she pointed to Jules standing by the outlet.

Caitlin tentatively raised her hand to wave and Jules waved back, although there was no smile on her face.

They parked the car outside the bakery and Caitlin glanced down at her dress. 'Oh god, she's going to think I'm rubbing it in by wearing my dress. I should've got changed.'

Archie kissed her forehead. 'Hey, stop worrying. Just hear her out. It could be nothing at all to do with us.'

She opened the car door and reluctantly climbed out.

Jules walked towards her, a serious expression on her face. 'Thank goodness you're back. Can you come with me, please? We can't start the meeting without you.'

'Meeting? What meeting?'

'Just hurry up, Cait!' Jules said as she dashed towards the village hall, neither seeming to notice Caitlin's attire, nor wanting to comment on it.

'But what about Archie and the girls? And the dogs?'

'Bring them too! Come on! You're late!'

Caitlin had never seen Jules like this, and her stomach knotted. Something major must have happened for there to be a meeting on a Saturday night. What was it though? Was some big corporation going to build a supermarket on the village field? Was there going to be a ban on whisky on Skye? Was there a compulsory demolition order on the Coxswain? Whatever it was, it must be serious.

Jules pushed through the doors to the main hall and Caitlin

followed. It was all in darkness. Confusion clouded her mind. What the hell?

'Let the meeting commence!' Jules shouted, and suddenly the lights came on. A gathered crown cheered and applauded, and Caitlin stood there, stunned. The main hall was festooned with balloons, bunting and flowers and a painted sign hung above the stage that said:

CONGRATULATIONS
MR AND MRS FRASER-SUTHERLAND!

It had clearly been painted by Reid, and each member of the family could be seen in between the letters. It was no ordinary banner, that was certain. What wasn't certain was who had arranged the party, or how they had found out about the wedding.

Take That's 'Rule the World' began playing from the chorus, over the sound system as everyone continued to cheer and Caitlin looked around for Archie. Had he planned this whole thing without her knowledge? When she spotted him just inside the doorway to the hall, he too appeared stunned. His mouth and eyes were wide as he took in the surroundings.

Amidst the cacophony, he made his way over to her. 'Did you...?'

She shook her head. 'I thought you did.'

As the applause and cheers rang out around the room, they turned to where Grace and Sophie stood with Jules. They both wore huge, cheeky grins on their faces and Caitlin gasped. The girls ran towards their parents and hugged them tightly.

'Did you girls do this?' Caitlin asked with tears in her eyes.

Grace nodded. 'You're not upset, are you?'

Caitlin shook her head. 'Not at all, sweetheart, just so surprised, that's all.'

Grace giggled. 'Phew! That was the idea. We just wanted you to have a proper party and so we talked, Sophie and I, and we decided to get Evin involved, he told his dad and Jules where we were really going this weekend, and this all just happened from there.'

Caitlin pulled Grace and Sophie into her arms. 'Thank you so, so much, you sneaky wee munchkins. You're too good at keeping secrets! We had no clue.' She swiped escaped tears from her cheeks. 'But thank you so much, this is wonderful.'

'You girls are so clever! What did we do to get so lucky, eh?' Archie said as he picked up Sophie and hugged Grace into his side, his eyes filled with love and emotion.

It seemed the whole of Glentorrin had shown up to wish them well, and they were all dressed as if they were attending a royal wedding. There were suits, posh frocks and kilts galore from every tartan imaginable. Morag was wearing a Skye tartan dress, rather like the mother of the bride and a fascinator adorned her hair. Jules and Ruby both looked like movie stars and, of course, Dexter, Mitch and Reid looked handsome in their kilts, too, although in true Dexter style his waistcoat was leather.

Once their shock had worn off, Caitlin and Archie were surrounded by dear friends who congratulated and hugged them. They were handed glasses of sparkling fizz and congratulated yet again.

In the centre of the buffet table, which was covered in delicious-looking food that made Caitlin's stomach growl, there was a wedding cake.

'It'll no be as good as yours, Caitlin, but I did my best!' Morag told them. 'I even watched a FaceTube video on how to make little people out of icing. So, there you two are on the top.'

'Morag, it's stunning!' Archie told her with a wide smile.

Avoiding giggling at her mix-up of two social media platforms, Caitlin told her, 'It's beautiful, Morag, and I love the little Archie and Caitlin! Aren't you clever? I'll be hiring you if you're not careful!'

But Jules had another surprise in store. 'I can't tell you who organised it, so don't even ask, but someone has arranged for Greg McBradden to come over from Clachan and do a set for you later.'

Caitlin was a huge fan of the singer and guitarist and was thrilled that 'someone' had asked him to come and play for their party. 'Wow, you've all done so much and now I feel terrible.'

Jules frowned. 'Terrible, why?'

Caitlin's eyes welled with tears once again. 'Because we ran away to get married and didn't invite you all.'

Jules placed a hand on each of her arms. 'Hey, we're best friends, aren't we? So, you don't need to feel bad about anything. You did what was right for the two of you and your girls, and that's totally fine. But now we get to help you celebrate!' She pulled her into a bear hug. 'Grace is so happy you married Archie. She adores him.'

Caitlin wiped at her eyes as relief flooded her. 'He is rather adorable.'

'Aww, shucks.' Archie chuckled, feigning shyness.

Jules whispered, 'Oh, and to top it off, the girls and the dogs are staying with us tonight. There's champagne chilling in the fridge at your cottage.'

Caitlin squeezed her friend even tighter. 'You are so wonderful. Thank you!'

Jules pulled away. 'Well, we can't have you not celebrating properly, can we?' she replied with a knowing smile. Caitlin realised she'd had no need to worry about upsetting Jules and Reid ahead of their big day because they were true friends, and she was incredibly fortunate to have them in her life. She really did have everything she needed right here in Glentorrin.

'We owe you, big time,' Archie told her with a kiss to her cheek.

Kenneth's voice came, loud and clear, over the speakers. 'Ladies and gentlemen, I think you'll all agree that it's tradition for the groom to say a few words!'

The room erupted with chants of 'Speech!' and a blushing Archie took to the stage.

'Evening, everyone. And thank you so much for doing this for us. We didn't want to make a fuss and we certainly didn't want to steal the spotlight from Jules and Reid who are getting married at the end of the year.' Applause and a chorus of 'awwws' rang out. 'Anyway, I'm sure I can speak for my beautiful wife and I...' His eyes widened and he smacked his own cheek. 'Jeez-o, I have a wife! And she is beautiful!' Laughter erupted around the space. He shook his head. 'As I was saying, we're so grateful to have all of you in our lives and we love you all.' More applause. 'I was thrilled and shocked when I asked Cait to marry me, and she said yes. As you all know, our relationship has been somewhat of a whirlwind. A ridiculously fast whirlwind. But when you know,' He shrugged, his gaze fixed on Caitlin. 'You just know. And I knew a long time ago that I adored her. I just had to convince her that she felt the same.' Laughter travelled the room. 'And now that she does... I truly am the luckiest man on the planet. In the space of a few crazy, rollercoaster months, I've gained a wife and two beautiful daughters. What more could any man possibly want? Here's to my wife and girls.'

The whole gathered crowd held up their glasses and toasted them and Caitlin's throat tightened with emotion at his words.

When everyone was quiet again, Archie continued. 'Now, there's something I want to ask a certain young lady here tonight. I hope she doesn't mind me doing this in front of everyone. But it's an important question.' He cleared his throat and took a deep breath. 'I know you're a strong girl, Grace, and you and your mum have always been a team. I know you certainly don't need a dad...' His chin trembled. 'But I had a secret chat with your mum, and I have her permission. I'm kind of hoping you'd like a dad because I'd love to make things official and to be able to call you my daughter and really mean it. So... Grace Fraser... please would you let me adopt you?' His voice broke and the room fell silent.

Even though Caitlin and Archie had had a long discussion about the situation, and Caitlin had been more than touched when Archie had suggested making things official with Grace, she was now a little worried that being asked here, in front of everyone they knew, she may feel coerced.

Standing beside her mum, Grace gave an audible gasp, and her hands covered her face.

Unsure what to make of the reaction, Caitlin gulped and put her arm around her daughter. 'Grace, sweetheart, there's absolutely no pressure,' Caitlin whispered. But as she finished speaking, Grace lurched forward and ran to the stage.

Archie picked her up and the girl sobbed in his arms. Caitlin waited with bated breath, a lump of raw emotion trapped in her throat, until Grace pulled away and took the microphone from Archie.

She sniffed and wiped at her eyes and with a wavering voice she said, 'I was really hoping you'd say that. Does this mean I can call you dad?'

Tears streamed down Caitlin's face and when she glanced around, she realised she wasn't alone.

Archie laughed out loud and nodded. 'Absolutely, sweetheart, abso-flippin-lutely!' he replied and once again pulled her into his arms as the gathered guests cheered.

Caitlin and Sophie walked onto the stage to join the hug and the room erupted as the new little family embraced once more.

* * *

Greg McBradden was a popular performer based over on the mainland and had known Stella and Joren from the Coxswain for many years. He was a firm favourite with everyone and seemed to be roped into performing at every major village event, not that he seemed to mind.

He took to the stage when the party was in full swing. 'Evening, yous lot! You cannae seem to get enough o' me, eh?' Laughter travelled the room. 'I just want to say a massive congratulations to Caitlin, who, I have it on good authority, is my number one fan.' Caitlin blushed and buried her head in Archie's shoulder. 'Archie, you're a very lucky man, but I don't need to tell you that. This one is dedicated to the bride and groom! It's a favourite of mine by the inimitable Proclaimers and it's called "Let's Get Married"!' A loud raucous cheer rang out. 'And even though I'm wasting my bloody breath, what do I always, always say?'

The crowd yelled in unison, 'Don't sing along!' And as he started to sing, of course, his number one rule was immediately broken.

The whole crowd linked arms in a huge circle and swayed as Caitlin and Archie danced in the centre.

As the song came to a close, Archie whispered, 'That night, at the camp, when we saw the shooting star, this is exactly what I wished for.'

Caitlin gazed up into his chocolate-brown eyes and smiled tenderly. 'Me too, Archie. Me too.'

EPILOGUE

Caitlin and her friends were sitting around Morag's kitchen table when she made her announcement.

'Triplets?' Jules asked with raised eyebrows. 'That's amazing, but what on earth are you going to do?'

Caitlin sighed. 'I honestly don't know that there's anything we can do really. It was totally unexpected though. I'm just glad we asked for the extra scan, or it would've been a complete shock on delivery day. I had a feeling it was more than two. I think Archie is stunned, poor guy.'

'No flipping wonder,' Ruby said.

'I'd initially thought it was just weight gain,' Caitlin said with a sigh. 'But nope. More babies.'

'What have the girls said?' Jules asked.

'Of course, they are absolutely over the moon,' Caitlin replied. 'Although it's raised lots of awkward questions from Sophie that we were hoping to avoid for a little while longer.'

'Aw, I bet,' Ruby said with a crinkle of her nose. 'They're so inquisitive at that age.'

'Well, you're certainly going to have a house full, hen,' Morag said before taking a large gulp of wine.

'Yes. Three more mouths to feed too,' Jules added.

'Yeah, but they'll only be small mouths to begin with, at least,' Ruby said, clearly trying to make Caitlin feel better.

'That's true,' Morag said, then she leaned forward, and as if afraid to ask she whispered, 'Is there definitely only three?'

Panic set in for Caitlin. 'Oh god, don't say that, Morag! I know the first scan got it wrong, but the new scan said three, so I'm sticking with that unless I'm told otherwise. Good grief, it's scary enough as it is.'

Morag flinched. 'Whoops, sorry hen. I... I didn't mean to make things worse. Me and my muckle cake hole.'

Caitlin's mind whirred. 'It's okay. They seemed pretty sure it was just three.' She knew she was trying to convince herself. 'Please don't let it be more than three,' she mumbled to the universe.

The friends fell silent for a moment and Caitlin noticed a distinct drop in the atmosphere.

'Anyway, enough about my situation, what's happening with the tearoom? There have been all sorts of rumours flying around. The latest one is a doozy.' She laughed. 'Apparently, Ruby, you're buying it to host parties for all your old Hollywood friends.'

Ruby laughed. 'Erm... I don't think so. And I don't think Mitch would dare surprise me with something that big. The last thing Glentorrin needs is more famous folk landing on their doorstep.'

'Come on then, Morag. You're the one in the know. What's going on?' Jules asked as she leaned her chin on her hand and fixed Morag with an expectant stare.

Morag's eyes lit up. 'Well, there's an offer on it. A cash offer, no less.'

Ruby leaned forward now, with intrigue. 'Who is it from? Do we know them?'

Morag glanced around as if looking for spies in her own kitchen. 'Well... I'm not really supposed to say... but... You must keep it quiet,' she insisted. 'I'll be in such trouble if it gets back that I told you.'

Ruby nudged her. 'Come on, Morag, you know you can trust us.'

Morag paused and pursed her lips, clearly unsure about sharing her intel. With another quick glance around her kitchen, she whispered, 'You know my friend Aileen Kennedy?'

Caitlin frowned. 'Isn't that the mum of my assistant, Isla?'

'Aye, that's right. Well... you know that lottery win that I couldn't talk about? It was them – Aileen and her husband Malcolm. They won a fair bit, but I won't say how much. They asked the lottery company for privacy, so it won't be announced to the public. Anyway, after paying off their mortgage, splashing out on a new car and a brand spanking new kitchen, they've decided to buy the café. From what I can gather, I think the plan is that Isla will run it. The poor lass has been stuck for what to do with her life, as you know, Cait. So, I think this is her mum and dad's way of helping her out.'

'Oh, wow. That's so lovely of them. Does Isla know already then?' Caitlin asked, pleased for Isla but a little sad at the prospect of losing a good assistant.

Morag shook her head vehemently. 'She knows about the lottery win but not the café and you mustn't tell her. It's to be a surprise. They're going to let her do it all up and make it her own.'

'Blimey, she's a lucky young woman,' Ruby said with wide eyes.

Morag nodded. 'Aye, she is that, indeed. I think they're just worried she'll waste her life in dead-end jobs. No offence, Caitlin.'

Caitlin burst out laughing. 'Gee thanks, no offence taken, Morag.' Morag was right to a point, Isla was young and needed to spread her wings.

'So, when is the deal being finalised?' Jules asked.

'I think they're hoping she'll be in for the new year. Lots to do though. It is a bit dated after all.'

Ruby turned to Caitlin with a sad expression. 'So, not only do you lose your assistant, but you might have competition in Glentorrin if it's a fancy new coffee shop.'

Caitlin shook her head. 'To be honest, I'm hoping she takes my sandwich business away! It's the worst part of the job, and I'd be able to do more speciality cakes if I didn't have to deal with takeaways.'

Jules smiled. 'Brilliant! It could be just what the village needs.'

Caitlin's mobile rang and flashed up with Archie's number. 'Excuse me, loves. I'd better get this.' She stood to walk into the hallway. 'Hey, handsome, what's up?'

'Hey, my love. Two things. One, we've got a tenant for my house. They've actually asked if we'd be interested in selling it.'

'Oh, that's fantastic! Who is it?'

'A woman called Aileen Kennedy wants it for her daughter.'

Caitlin gasped. 'That's Isla, my assistant – the daughter, I mean.'

'Oh right. She doesn't live that far away now, does she?'

'No, but she lives with her parents, so this may be their way of helping her gain her independence.' She knew she couldn't really elaborate on the café story yet.

'So, what do you think about selling it? The money would be handy. We could maybe look at getting a bigger place somewhere.'

Caitlin pursed her lips at the thought. 'Hmm… I just love Glentorrin and I don't really want to leave the village. Are you not happy at the bakery cottage?'

'I'm happy wherever you are, you know that. And the girls love being in the village too.'

'So, we're staying?'

She could hear the smile in his voice as he replied, 'If that's what you want. So, we could sell my old place and update the kitchen.'

Caitlin's stomach flipped with excitement. 'Now you're talking!'

'Great. Okay, well, I'll give the agent a call back tomorrow and talk numbers.'

'Fab. And what was the other thing you needed me for?'

'Oh, shit, yeah! Cleo is acting a bit weird. I think you'd better come home.'

Caitlin gasped. 'Oh no. I'm on my way.' She hung up and went back through to Morag's kitchen. 'Ladies, I'm needed at home, I'm afraid.'

'Is everything okay?' Jules asked, her voice laced with concern.

'It's Cleo. I'm sure it's nothing, but I'd better go check.' She hugged each of her friends in turn, grabbed her jacket and dashed out of Morag's house.

It was a chilly November day, and the sky overhead was heavy with potential snow clouds. Caitlin walked across the pretty village as fast as her legs would carry her, wrapping her jacket tighter around herself as the wind whipped through her hair. Even on a dull and cold day like today she wouldn't want to be anywhere else.

She pushed through the front door and dashed to the kitchen to find Cleo panting and wide-eyed in her basket.

After a very long night Caitlin, Archie, Grace and Sophie sat staring at the new arrivals. The triplets – two boys and a girl – were finally here, and they were so tiny, their eyes still closed, as they snuggled up to mum. Cleo had done so well. Three little Puggie-Poo pups, all black and tan with the beginnings of tufty curls. Bowie was a little baffled to say the least. Not half as baffled as the Fraser-Sutherlands had been when they found out, however.

'Can we keep them all, Daddy? Cleo and Bowie will miss them if they go live somewhere else,' a teary-eyed Sophie asked as she stroked one of the pups on its back as he fed.

Archie glanced at Caitlin, a question in his eyes. 'Oh, I don't know, sweetheart. Five dogs are a heck of a lot of responsibility.'

'Can we at least name them?' Grace asked. 'That way they feel like they belong for now.'

Archie and Caitlin shared a smile. 'I think that would be okay. How about me and Dad name one and you girls name one each?'

'Yay!' Sophie said. 'Can I name a boy one? But I need to think for a minute...' She sat at tapped her finger on her chin.

'I'll name the girl puppy Twinkle, because it was night-time when she was born and the stars were out,' Grace said.

'That's lovely, Gracie. What do you think, Archie? We have a boy to name. Any ideas?'

'How about Cosmo. Because it sounds a bit like Cosmos and I'm totally stealing Grace's idea,' he said with a wink.

'I love that! Cosmo really suits this one,' Grace said, pointing at the puppy. 'And it sounds a bit posh too. So, he'll have lots of pride in himself.'

'Perfect. Cosmo and Twinkle it is. Who'd have thought we'd end up with an even bigger family?' Caitlin asked rhetorically.

'Hmm, Bowie is booked in for a wee operation next week, so this won't happen again,' Archie informed her with a knowing glance.

'So, Soph. What's it going to be? Have you thought of the perfect name for the third pup? He's the smallest one, so I think he needs a big name to live up to.'

Sophie's eyes lit up and she clapped her hands together. 'Ooh, ooh, I have a name! It's perfect! It's so perfect!' She stood up and turned to Archie. 'Daddy, do you remember when we saw that film about that little man called Mr Rogers who was tiny, and he wanted to be a soldier, but he was too small, then he ate all his veggies, and went in that big machine, and got some medicine from the science people, and he went really big, and they made him into a super-hero, and he caught baddies, and won the war?' Her words came out in an excited rush.

'Oh, you mean Captain America! Aye *The First Avenger*, great film,' Archie replied with a wide smile and a nod, and they all shared glances, clearly wondering what name she had chosen. Cap perhaps? Captain? Hero? Avenger? 'Lots of great name possibilities there, Soph... so... what have you chosen?'

'Yes!' She pointed at the remaining nameless ball of fluff where it lay sleeping. 'This puppy is tiny right now, but I know he'll grow up big and strong so... I'm going to call my puppy... Steve!'

ACKNOWLEDGMENTS

First and foremost, I want to thank every single person who has picked up and read one of my books. You're the reason I keep doing this and I'm so honoured and humbled that you continue to get lost in my stories.

Thank you, as always, Rich, Grace, Mum and Dad for your unending support and encouragement. For the cups of tea and the garden chats. And for the wonderful holidays we have spent together on Skye. It's such a magical place and I know you love it too. Let's get another trip booked soon!

Thanks to Caroline and the whole gang at Boldwood: editors, designers, marketers and the other fantastic authors, for your support, tenacity, attention to detail and for making it clear that I belong to something wonderful. Go #TeamBoldwood!

Lorella and the team at LBLA, you are such hard workers, going above and beyond for your writers and I know I won't be alone in saying I am incredibly grateful to have you backing me.

Massive hugs to the lovely people in my Facebook group *Hobman's Hub*. I love how I can be so preoccupied and a bit rubbish at posting but when I do, you interact and it's like I've never been away!

Thank you to Sue B and Fiona J for finding me and for arranging such brilliant online launch parties and for introducing me to even more fabulous friends in the book world! I love our chats and hearing your ideas!

Finally, I want to say thank you to every single author who I have met along this crazy writing journey, not only for your words of wisdom but for being a shoulder to cry on and for being the best sounding boards I could wish for. There are so many of you that I would need a whole new book just for all your names and I don't want to mention a few and offend anyone. So, if you're an author and you know me, consider yourself thanked!

MORE FROM LISA HOBMAN

We hope you enjoyed reading *Wishing Under A Starlit Skye*. If you did, please leave a review.

If you'd like to gift a copy, this book is also available as an ebook, digital audio download and audiobook CD.

Sign up to Lisa Hobman's mailing list for news, competitions and updates on future books.

https://bit.ly/LisaHobmanNewsletter

Dreaming Under An Island Skye, another uplifting and feel-good read from Lisa Hobman, is available to order now.

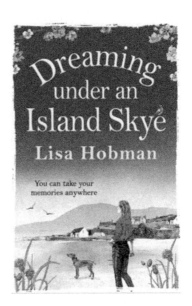

Dreaming
under an
Island Skye

Lisa Hobman

You can take your
memories anywhere

ABOUT THE AUTHOR

Lisa Hobman has written many brilliantly reviewed women's fiction titles - the first of which was shortlisted by the RNA for their debut novel award. In 2012 Lisa relocated her family from Yorkshire to a village in Scotland and this beautiful backdrop now inspires her uplifting and romantic stories.

Visit Lisa's website: http://www.lisajhobman.com

Follow Lisa on social media:

        facebook.com/LisaJHobmanAuthor
        twitter.com/@LisaJHobmanAuthor
        instagram.com/lisahobmanauthor

ABOUT BOLDWOOD BOOKS

Boldwood Books is a fiction publishing company seeking out the best stories from around the world.

Find out more at www.boldwoodbooks.com

Sign up to the Book and Tonic newsletter for news, offers and competitions from Boldwood Books!

http://www.bit.ly/bookandtonic

We'd love to hear from you, follow us on social media:

 facebook.com/BookandTonic

twitter.com/BoldwoodBooks

 instagram.com/BookandTonic

Printed in Great Britain
by Amazon